ONE NIGHT WITH DR NIKOLAIDES

ANNIE O'NEIL

TEMPTED BY DR PATERA

TINA BECKETT

MILLS & BOON

First Published in Great Britain 2018
by Mills & Boon, an imprint of HarperCollins*Publishers*
1 London Bridge Street, London, SE1 9GF

One Night with Dr Nikolaides © 2018 by Annie O'Neil

Tempted by Dr Patera © 2018 by Tina Beckett

ISBN: 978-0-263-93355-0

MIX
Paper from
responsible sources
FSC
www.fsc.org
FSC™ C007454

This book is produced from independently certified FSC™ paper
to ensure responsible forest management.
For more information visit www.harpercollins.co.uk/green.

Printed and bound in Spain
by CPI, Barcelona

Annie O'Neil spent most of her childhood with her leg draped over the family rocking chair and a book in her hand. Novels, baking, and writing too much teenage angst poetry... most of her youth. Now Annie splits her time between corralling her husband into helping her with their cows, baking, reading, barrel racing (not really!) and spending some very happy hours at her computer, writing.

Three-time Golden Heart® finalist **Tina Beckett** learned to pack her suitcases almost before she learned to read. Born to a military family, she has lived in the United States, Puerto Rico, Portugal and Brazil. In addition to travelling, Tina loves to cuddle with her pug, Alex, spend time with her family, and hit the trails on her horse. Learn more about Tina from her website, or 'friend' her on Facebook.

ONE NIGHT WITH DR NIKOLAIDES

ANNIE O'NEIL

MILLS & BOON

This book is dedicated,
for the rollercoaster ride of creativity,
to Amalie, Amy and Tina.
You're all amazing.
xx A

CHAPTER ONE

THEO'S EYES FOLLOWED the wheeled supplies trolley as it rolled past the exam bed. The moan and creak of concrete against steel shot his senses to high alert.

When his fingers were unable to gain purchase on the delicate needle he'd been reaching for he knew what was happening.

"Up you come!" He pulled the little boy he'd been treating from the exam table to his chest, careful to mind his freshly sutured knee. "You too." He beckoned for the boy's mother to stand in the doorframe, grateful for the modern reinforced framework they'd insisted on for the clinic.

She stood frozen with fear. Pragmatism demanded he pull her close to him, certain it was the safest place to be. Earthquakes weren't common in the Greek islands, but the archipelago had been subject to more than its fair share over the past few years.

"I know it's frightening, but you must stay here!" He held the terrified mother, a young woman he'd gone to school with, close to him. "Alida, please."

He tightened his grip, fighting the urge to cough as the shift and strain of drywall released chalky clouds of gypsum into the air.

"The clinic is the safest place to be."

His voice ended up sounding harsher than he'd intended. Harsh for the voice of a schoolfriend and a doctor. But the clinic had never borne the test of an actual earthquake, and as the seconds ground and rasped into minutes he knew the uncompromising deal he'd made with his father had been the right one. Pride for money.

An infinitesimal wince crossed his face as he remembered the handshake that had sealed his fate.

"What is happening?"

He held the pair of them tight, the toddler clinging to his shoulders, soft whimpers of fear vibrating along his small chest into Theo's.

Alida tried to take her son and run. A natural instinct, he presumed. To care. Protect. Put one's own life on the line to save that of your child.

His lips thinned. That wasn't a childhood *he'd* known. And what had followed in its wake wasn't worth thinking about. Not anymore.

Waves splashed up against the back of the clinic... the secure dock had been rendered invisible. The normal gentle hum and buzz of the clinic had been replaced by a cacophony of tightly issued instructions. Phones. Alarms.

Theo lifted his eyes to the invisible heavens in thanks for the emergency training they'd insisted upon for all the staff. He and his "brothers" had never wanted anyone to feel any unnecessary pain or fear when they entered the doors of the Mythelios Free Clinic. The Malakas of Mythelios. His best friends. The closest thing he had to a real family after his own had proved to be nothing more than a mirage.

He'd get on the phone to them as soon as possible. His gut told him that whatever was happening beyond these sheltered walls would demand all of them this time. If he could even track them down...

Ares was usually in the world's latest hellhole, doing his best to put a dent in its need for medical care. Deakin's specialist burn treatment skills were in demand worldwide. Heaven knew where *he* was now. And Chris, a neurosurgeon, could usually be found in New York City. If he wanted to bc found, that was. More often than not he didn't.

Not that it had stopped him from posing for that insane calendar of local island men that had been organized to raise funds for the clinic. *Ooopaa!* Theo's eyes followed that very calendar's trajectory across the room as it slid to the floor behind the reception desk. It was his month anyway. No great loss.

Again Alida tried to pull her son away from him and run. "It's gone on too long!"

"It's nearly over now," he soothed. *As if he knew.* Earthquakes could last for seconds or minutes. There'd been tremors on the island before, but nothing like this. The Richter scale would be near to double digits. Of that he had no doubt.

He tuned in to the chaos, breaking it down and putting it back together into some sort of comprehensible order. Rattling. Sharp cries of concern. Sensory discord.

As much as Alida struggled against him, pleaded with him to free her and let her run from the building, Theo's instinct was to stay put and work through it. These were *his* patients. *His* clinic. He'd promised them solace and care from the moment they entered the bougainvillea-laced doors and he'd meant it with every pore in his body.

The need to launch into action, preparing for the storm bound to follow in the earthquake's wake, crackled through his body like electricity. It was likely only seconds had passed—a minute or two at most—but each moment had shaken the island to its core.

He heard a woman cry out in pain.

"Get in a doorway!" he shouted, his broad hands cupping the child and Alida's heads.

Not being able to control what was happening made Theo want to roar with frustration.

"Is it over?" Alida's voice was barely audible amidst the rising chaos of human voices.

Theo shook his head, tightening his grip so that she didn't leave until he was positive it was safe.

How soon were aftershocks? Immediate? The next day?

This was the cruelty of nature. You simply didn't know.

The same way you didn't know if the parents who gave birth to you would act like Alida—protectively—or like his—abandoning him at the first opportunity.

He shook his head clear of the thought. They didn't deserve one second of his attention. The people here did. The people he'd vowed to care for.

He shouted out a few instructions. Their clinic was a small one, but there must be at least fifty people there. Doctors, nurses, patients, a few older patients who needed more care in the overnight wards.

Another crash of waves and the howl of the earth fighting against the manmade buildings upon her surface filled his senses.

Please let the clinic be spared.

He tightened his grip on the mother and child, wondering for just an instant what it would be like to hold his own wife and child. What lengths would he go to for them?

Another tremor gripped the ground beneath them.

All thoughts other than survival left him.

Theós. Let us be spared.

CHAPTER TWO

FOLD, FOLD AND TUCK.

Just the way her mother had taught her.

Perfect.

Cailey gave a satisfied grin at her swaddling handiwork, popped a kiss onto her finger, then onto the baby's nose, all the while imagining her mum giving her a congratulatory smothering hug before pulling out a huge plate of *souvlaki* for them to share. Or *bougatsa*. Or whatever it was she had magicked up in her tiny, tiny kitchen. Miracles, usually.

She ran her finger along the infant's face. "Look at you, little *mou*. So perfect. You've got your entire life to look forward to. No Greek bad boys breaking your heart. That's my lesson to you. No Greeks."

"Are you trying to brainwash the babies again, Cailey?"

Cailey looked across, surprised she hadn't even noticed that her colleague Emily had entered the nursery. The more time she spent with the babies, the more she was getting lost in cloud cuckoo land!

"Yes." She grinned mischievously, then turned to the baby to advise her soberly, "No Greeks. And no doctors."

"Hey!" Emily playfully elbowed her in the ribs. "I've

just started dating a doctor, and I won't mind admitting it's a very welcome step up in the world."

Wrong answer!

"And what, exactly, is wrong with being a nurse?"

"Not a thing, little Miss Paranoid."

Emily's arched eyebrows and narrowed eyes made her squirm.

"Looks like *someone's* had her heart broken by a doctor. A Greek doctor, to be precise."

"Pffft."

Emily laughed. "All the proof I needed."

She moved to one of the cots and picked up an infant who was fussing.

"C'mon. Out with it. Who was the big, bad Greek doctor who broke our lovely Cailey's heart?"

"No one."

Someone.

"Liar." Emily laughed again.

She shrugged as casually as she could. Maybe she was a liar, but leaving her small town, small island, and archaically minded country behind for the bright lights of London had been for one purpose and one purpose only—to forget a very green-eyed, chestnut-haired Adonis who would, for the purposes of this particular conversation, remain anonymous.

Cailey lifted the freshly swaddled infant, all cozy in her striped pink blanket, and nuzzled up close to her. *Mmm. New baby smell.*

Life as a maternity nurse was amazing, but rather than mute her urges to hold a child of her own it had only set the sirens on full blast.

Twenty-seven wasn't *that* old in the greater scheme of

things. And Theo wasn't the only man in the universe. Definitely not *her* man. So…

"Cailey?"

The charge nurse…what was her name again? Molly? Kate…? Heidi? There had been so many new names and faces to learn since she'd started at this premier maternity hospital she'd become a bit dizzy with trying to remember them all… She ran through the names in her mind again…

High on the hill was the highest nurse… Heidi!

She squinted at her boss's name tag.

Heidi.

Ha! Excellent. The memory games she'd been playing were paying off. She knew she'd battle her dyslexia one way or another. She'd done enough to get this far in her medical career, though it would never take the sting out of the fact that she'd most likely never become the doctor she'd always dreamt of being.

"Sorry to interrupt, love, but I think you might want to see this."

Cailey gave the infant—Beatrice Chrysanthemum, according to her name card—a final nuzzle before settling her back into the tiny bassinet and following Heidi along to the staffroom, where a television was playing on a stand in the corner of the room.

It was a news channel. The ticker tape at the bottom of the screen was rolling with numbers…casualties? Cailey's eyes flicked back up to the main news story. There were familiar-looking buildings—but not as she was used to seeing them.

Out of the corner of her eye she saw Emily walk in, reach for the remote and turn up the volume. At first the English words and the images of a Greece she didn't quite recognize wouldn't register. They were a series of disconnected phrases and pictures that weren't falling into place.

"Isn't that the island you're from?" Emma prompted. "Mythelios?"

Cailey nodded in slow motion as everything began falling into place.

An earthquake. Fatalities. Ongoing rescue efforts.

Her heart stopped still. The pictures of devastation had switched to a live interview being conducted outside the clinic in the fading daylight.

Of course it was him. Who else could command the world's attention?

There, front and center, more breathtakingly gorgeous than she'd allowed herself to remember, was Dr. Theo Nikolaides, appealing for any and all medical personnel who could help to come to Greece in its time of need.

She tried not to morph his entreaty for help into an arrogant call for "the little people" to come and do the dirty work while he took the glory. This was a crisis and all hands were helping hands—not rich or poor, just hands.

She stared at her own hands…her fingers so accustomed to work…

"Cailey?" Heidi touched her arm. "Are you all right?"

She turned her hands back and forth in the afternoon light as the news sank in. People were hurt. Her mother could be hurt. Her brothers…

A flame lit in her chest. One she knew wouldn't abate until she was on a plane home.

No matter how much she hated Theo, hated the wounds his words had etched into her psyche, she would have to go home. Islanders helped one another—no matter what.

"I'm fine. But my island isn't. I'm afraid I'm going to need some time off."

CHAPTER THREE

IT WAS ALL Cailey could do not to jump off the ferry and swim to shore. Flights to the island had been canceled because of earthquake damage to the runway, but it hadn't put her off coming. The same way a childhood crush gone epically wrong wouldn't stop her from helping. Not when her fellow islanders needed her. And this time she would be able to do more than help with the clean-up.

Ducking out of the wind, she pulled her mobile out of her pocket and dialed the familiar number. She wanted to hit the ground running—literally—but if her mother found out she'd come back and hadn't checked in first it would be delicious slices of guilt pie from here on out.

"Mama?"

Static crackled through the handset. She strained to listen through the roar of the ferry's engine's.

"…seen Theo?" her mother asked.

Theo?

Why was her mother asking about *him*? She'd come back to the island to *help*, not answer questions about her teenage crush. Surely ten years meant she'd moved on enough in her life for people to stop asking if her heart had mended yet?

"Mama. If you're all right…" she parsed out the words slowly "… I'll go straight to the clinic."

"Go…clinic… Theo…love…brothers…getting by…"

Cailey held out the handset and stared at it. She'd spoken briefly to her mum before she'd boarded her flight last night, so she knew her brothers were unhurt and, of course, already out working. As was her mother who—surprise, surprise—had already gathered a brigade of women to feed the rescue crews and survivors at the local *taverna*.

A Greek mother, she'd reminded Cailey time and again, was nothing if not a provider of food in times of crisis.

But…*love* and *Theo* in the same sentence?

Had her mother gone completely mad or was the dodgy reception playing havoc with her sanity?

"See you soon, Mama. I love you," she shouted into the phone, before ending the call and adding grumpily, "But not Theo!"

She glared at the handset before giving it an apologetic pat. It wasn't its fault that everyone on Mythelios was trapped in a time warp. But she'd moved on, and working at the clinic was as good a time as any to prove it.

She moved back out to the ferry's deck and squinted, trying to make out the details of the small harbor she'd once known like the back of her hand. By the looks of all the blinking lights—blue, red, yellow—it was little more than a construction site. Deconstruction, more like, she thought, grimly stuffing the phone in her bag and shouldering her backpack.

The news footage she'd seen at the ferry terminal in Athens had painted a pretty vivid picture. Some people's lives would never be the same. Two tourists had already been declared dead. Scores injured. And the numbers were only expected to rise as rescue efforts continued.

The second the boat hit the shoreline Cailey cinched the straps on the backpack she'd so angrily stuffed with clothes she'd hoped would suit the British climate all those years ago, and took off at a jog.

Some buildings looked untouched, whilst others were piles of rubble. There was a fevered, intense buzz of work as the dust-covered people of Mythelios painstakingly picked apart the raw materials of the lives they had been living just twenty-four hours earlier. Window frames. Cinder blocks. Stone. It was clear the earthquake had been indiscriminate, and in some cases brutal.

"Cailey!"

She stopped and turned. Only three voices in the world made her feel safe, and this was one of them.

Kyros!

Before she had a chance to give voice to her big brother's name she was being picked up and swirled around.

"Cailey *mou*! My little starfish! How are you?"

Despite the gravity of the situation, Cailey laughed. She never would have believed hearing her childhood nickname would feel so good. Or simply *smelling* the island, her brother's dusty chest and, miraculously, the scent of baking bread.

Together she and her brother looked across the street to the bakery. All that was left was the building's huge and ancient stone-built ovens. And there, undeterred by the open-air setting, was Mythelios's top baker, pulling loaves out as if working amidst rubble was the most normal thing on earth.

Cailey's brother smiled down on her. "I'm so glad I

saw you. We're just about to go up to the mountains—
see what we can do up there to help the more isolated
houses." He squeezed her tight. "How is the family success story? Does that London hospital know how lucky
it is to have you? Have you seen Theo?"

Cailey did her best not to let her smile falter as Kyros
held her at arm's length and waited for answers. What
was it with her family and all the Theo questions?

Kyros's eyes narrowed. "You don't look like you eat
enough over there."

"I'm fine!" She batted away his concerns. She ate
plenty. There was no keeping her curves at bay no matter how often she ate like a rabbit. "You must be boil-
ing in that suit."

"This?" He did a twirl in his firefighter's gear. "I suit
it well, don't I?"

"Still the show-off, I see."

"Absolutely!" He winked, then just as quickly his
expression turned sober. "And now I'd better show off
how good I am at helping. There are still a few dozen
people unaccounted for. Tourists, mostly."

"Is it as bad as they say on the news?"

He nodded. "Worse. The more we dig, the more fatalities we find. There are a lot of injuries." He tipped
his head down the street. "The clinic was heaving when
I was there last. Have you spoken to Theo yet?"

She ignored the question. "How's Leon? I tried to ask
Mama a minute ago but the line went—"

She stopped talking as a very large, very exclusive,
four-by-four, outside just about any mortal's price range,
pulled to a stop beside them. The back window was
rolled down centimeter by painstaking centimeter to
reveal silver hair, icy cold blue eyes...

Oh, goodness. Theo's father had aged considerably since she'd seen him last. One of the most powerful men on the island seemed to have been unable to hold back the hands of time.

Just about the only thing Dimitri Nikolaides *couldn't* do, Cailey thought bitterly.

"Ah! Miss Tomaras. How…*interesting* to see you back here."

Shards of ice shot through her veins as her brain tumbled back through the years to that day when he'd made it more than clear what he and the rest of his family thought of her.

Nothing but a simple house girl. That's all you'll ever be.

Her brother leaned in over her shoulder. "Cailey's here to help, Mr. Nikolaides. She's a Class-A nurse now."

"Oh?" A patronizing smile appeared on the old man's face. "You're planning on going to the clinic?"

"To *help*, yes."

She caught her knees just as she was on the brink of genuflecting and stopped herself.

What was she *doing*? Was her body trying to *curtsey*? Good grief! The man wasn't a king and he certainly didn't run the island. Even if he behaved as if he did. And yet there was a part of her that still worried she would never be smart enough, good enough, talented enough to come home and do anything other than fulfil the fate Dimitri Nikolaides had outlined for her.

"I'm sure there's some little corner you'll be able to help out in. Plenty of cuts and scrapes to tend to."

Mr. Nikolaides eyes scanned the length of her, as if assessing a race horse. Working class mule, more like.

That was how he viewed her family and it was how he always would.

Cailey's spine stiffened as she forced her static smile not to waver.

"Maternity, wasn't it?"

"S-s-sorry?" *Noooooo! Don't stutter in front of the man.*

"I heard through the grapevine that you help other women with their children. Sweet."

Coming from his mouth, it sounded anything but. Not to mention bordering on pathetic. Women on Mythelios were expected to do nothing less. Cook. Clean. Bow. Scrape. Sometimes she wondered if the island had ever been informed that the twenty-first century had arrived—an era when women were allowed to be smart and have opinions and love whomsoever they chose!

She stared at the lines and wrinkles carved deeply into his face. Saw the cool appraisal of his unclouded eyes. *What made you so mean?*

Once he'd successfully bullied her off the island the man should have had all he wanted. A son to matchmake with the world's most beautiful heiresses. A daughter at an elite medical school. No doubt he knew exactly who *she'd* marry, too. The daughter of his housekeeper was safely out of the picture, so as not to sully his daughter's circle of friends or, more importantly, his son's romantic future.

She forced a polite smile when the silence grew too awkward. "My family usually bundles in wherever help is needed. Leon's police squad is out saving lives this minute."

"*You* don't look too busy," Mr. Nikolaides glanced

at Kyros. "And your mother? Is *she* doing anything or simply enjoying her retirement?"

Cailey almost gasped at his effrontery. Her mother had *earned* her money at the Nikolaides mansion just as she had earned her retirement. And Kyros? Why wasn't *he* saying anything? Why wasn't *she* saying anything?

She'd never let anyone speak to her like this in London. Not after the years of work she'd poured into becoming a nurse. And definitely not after her years of living away from the island to "protect" a billionaire's son. As if Theo needed *protection* from all the European heiresses she'd seen dangling off his arm in the society magazines she might have read accidentally on purpose at the hospital gift shop. On a regular basis.

"Oh, yes. You know us, Mr. Nikolaides," she eventually bit out. "We Tomarases love helping clear up other people's messes."

Mr. Nikolaides blinked. Then smiled. "Yes, we *do* miss your mother's deft touch up at the house. I trust she's well?"

"Couldn't be happier," Cailey snapped.

"Mama's very well, thank you Mr. Nikolaides." Kyros's hand tightened round Cailey's arm. "We're just off now, sir. Glad to see you weren't hurt in the quake."

He turned his sister around and frog-marched her away from the dark-windowed four-by-four, now weaving its way through the rubble strewn along the harborside road as if it had been thrown down by a petulant god.

"What was *that* all about?" Kyros growled.

"Nothing."

He wasn't to know Dimitri had all but packed her bags himself all those years ago. Demanded she never enter the Nikolaides house again. Not as a friend to his daughter Erianthe. Not as a "helping hand" to her mother. And especially not as anything whatsoever to do with Theo, his precious son who was prone to develop "a bleeding heart for the less fortunate."

She launched herself at her brother for a bear hug. It was the easiest way to hide the lie she was about to tell. "I'm just tired after the overnight flight. Once I get to work I'll be fine. It's just weird seeing the island like this."

"I know, huh?"

She could feel his voice rumble in his chest and cinched her arms just a little bit tighter around him. Once she let go of him she'd have to go and face the other Demon of Mythelios.

Full points to Dimitri for pipping her to the post. But she wouldn't have been surprised if he was stalking the harbor for interlopers. *Huh*.

He looked old. The worn-out kind of old that came from emotional strain rather than physical. Proof he was human? Somewhere in there?

Besides, he'd only put a voice to what Theo and his mates had already been thinking, and no doubt Erianthe too, who hadn't even had the guts to say goodbye to her before winging her way off to her fancy boarding school...

Bah! Enough of putting blame at other people's doors. She'd believed everything Dimitri Nikolaides had said about her because there had been some truth in it. She *wasn't* as smart as the others. She *did* have to work twice as hard to understand things. Finally figuring out she was dyslexic had helped. A bit. But it hadn't made all the medical terminology easier to read. She'd just had to face facts. She wasn't up to Nikolaides standards and no amount of teenage flirtation would change that.

A siren sounded and shouts erupted from a fire truck as it pulled to a stop beside them.

She gave her brother a final squeeze. "Go out there and save some lives." She went up on tiptoe and gave each of Kyros's ruddy cheeks a kiss.

"Same to you, Cailey." He scrubbed a hand through her already wayward hairdo, if you could call stuffing her curls into submission with an elastic band a hairdo. "Welcome back."

She smiled up at him, praying he wouldn't see how their run-in with Dimitri Nikolaides had shaken her to her core. "It's good to be here."

"Is that enough?" Theo was impatient to get back to work. Yes, the media could help. No, he didn't have a moment to spare.

The look on the reporter's face acknowledged the question was rhetorical.

He undid the microphone and began to walk away, ignoring the pleas of the other reporters. They'd be better off showing footage of the rescue crews hard at work while he figured out how to help patients and simultaneously order the urgently needed helicopters to get the worst cases over to Athens.

He could call his dad.

He could also saw off his own hand. Lifting up that phone would come at a cost. It always did.

"Dr. Nikolaides?"

"I'm sorry, I don't have time for any more interviews—"

"No! I'm not with the press. I'm a doctor. My name is Lea Risi."

He stopped and turned. The woman was wearing holiday clothes. Chinos. A flowery top. Her accent was not local, but she spoke flawless Greek. Useful, considering there was a heavy mix of tourists and locals pouring into the clinic.

For just a nanosecond he rued the appeal of this gorgeous port town that drew holidaymakers from all around the world. If only they were on a rocky outcrop with a diminished population...

"Dr. Nikolaides!" A paramedic was calling him from the hastily put-together triage area off Reception.

He beckoned to Lea. "Come along, then."

"Don't you want to know my credentials?" She ran a few steps to catch up with his long-legged strides.

"Not particularly." He scrubbed a hand through his hair, then pulled the shoulder-length mane back under control with an elastic band he'd picked up somewhere during the course of the day. He didn't know when, exactly. Sixteen hours' straight trauma work did that to a man. The details blurred.

"I'm a psychiatrist."

He nodded. *Fine*. That meant she had medical credentials. "What do you want? Old or young?"

"Sorry?"

"We've got patients coming in from a care home and a school. Both were hit hard. We're triaging on site and transporting to hospital with limited resources."

He stopped and wheeled round, holding out his hands to steady her when she lost her balance trying not to collide with him.

"Apologies." He shook his head. "I'm a bit short on manners today."

"I totally understand. I just want to help."

Theo put out a hand. "Good. Help is what we need. Theo Nikolaides." They shared a quick handshake as he rattled off the necessary facts. "I run the clinic. With the help of some friends. Doctors."

He silently reeled through the cities in the world where they might be. Was Deakin in Paris or Buenos Aires this month? And Christos…? New York. Definitely New York. Ares? Only heaven knew.

Burn specialist.

Neurosurgeon.

Miracle-worker.

If only they were all pilots. He needed them here. But they'd come…they would come.

"Put me wherever you think I'll be best placed—"

Lea was about to say something else when his eyes latched on to a set of unruly curls weaving its way through the crowd jamming up the entryway into the clinic.

Christos!

A jolt of lightning would have affected him less.

What was Cailey Tomaras doing here? The last time he'd seen her—

"Doctor?"

"Sorry. I'm a bit frazzled." He tapped the side of his head. "What did you say your name was again?"

"Leanora Risi. Lea. Just call me Lea."

Her empathetic smile spoke volumes. She could see he was busy, but she wanted to help—and at this juncture he needed all the help he could get.

His eyes slipped past Lea again. Cailey had left the

island to become a maternity nurse, hadn't she? Good for her. He knew she'd always been interested in medicine—

"If there's someone else you'd rather I speak with…" Lea put a hand on his arm.

"No. I'm your man. Apologies. There's just some-one I—"

Someone I should've kissed ten years ago. Someone I should've taken on a proper date. Someone I never thought I'd see again.

He looked down at Lea's feet and saw strappy sandals not wholly suited to working in a chaotic clinic.

"Here on holiday?"

"I was." Lea tipped her head and tried to capture his attention. "But now I'm here to help. I don't have any equipment but I have these." She lifted up her hands and twisted them as if they were freshly washed for surgery.

"Perfect. Good."

Wholly distracted, he let his attention shift past Lea yet again.

Cailey face had grown…not thinner…just… Well, even more beautiful, obviously. She'd had quite a lead in that department. Her cheekbones had become more elegantly defined…her lips were still that deep red, dif-ficult to believe it was real and not painted on…

Had she finally come home?

"Dr. Nikolaides…?" Lea's expression shifted to one of grim determination. "You obviously need to be else-where. Now, I haven't practiced emergency medicine in a while. But I'm definitely up to the cuts and bruises variety of injury—if you'll just point me in the right di-rection I can get on with helping patients."

"Yes. Of course."

He gave himself a sharp shake. He wasn't here to ogle

ghosts from the past. There were very real, very urgent medical cases that needed help. *Now.*

"Why don't you go grab a notebook from Petra? She's the loving but steel-hearted battleax working the main desk. She'll give you everything you need to work your way through the queue and categorize people. We've got a couple of doctors working just through that archway. It's makeshift, but we aren't really kitted out for intensive care. I'll be there shortly. There are a couple more volunteer doctors from the mainland seeing less urgent cases."

He looked up to the skylight above them as a medical helicopter flew overhead.

"And a medevac. If we're lucky, we'll soon have one very talented nurse on board as well."

Lea gave his arm a quick squeeze, then headed toward Reception to start work. If she'd said something to him, he wouldn't have known. All he wanted to know was what had brought Cailey back to the island she'd sworn never to set foot on again.

CHAPTER FOUR

"WELL, LOOK WHO we have here. If it isn't Little Miss I'm-Going-to-Make-a-Difference."

Theo Nikolaides. As she lived and breathed...barely.

She opened her mouth. She'd prepared for this. Spent hours of her life thinking about what to say when and if she ever saw him again.

Ffzzzzttt! There went her ability to use actual words.

"Come to help out at our little backwater clinic, have you?"

"I...uh..."

Kaboom! An explosion of fireworks she was clearly powerless to resist went off in her chest, then her belly, then her... Well, everywhere, really.

"Cailey? Are you all right? You haven't been hurt, have you?"

Crrrrassssh! Down came the defenses she'd worked so hard to build up.

She batted away his hand as he reached toward her. She wasn't ready yet. For *that* voice. *Those* words. His *kindness*.

Her cheeks burned at the memory of their heated exchange all those years ago. She forced herself to swallow the array of comebacks she could've spat back, and instead shifted the infant she'd been cuddling back into the arms of his mother.

Prove you've grown up. Prove you've made something of yourself!

"It looks like a superficial wound to me. Cuts always bleed a lot. Just keep the pressure on and I'm sure the good doctor here will get to you as soon as possible."

"Absolutely." Theo gave the mum a quick nod in Lea's direction. "Dr. Risi will be down in a minute to log the case, and we'll get someone to see you and this little one as soon as possible."

Cailey watched, transfixed, as Theo ran his index finger along the infant's face. How could someone so incredibly caring leave his father to do his talking for him?

Pffft. They'd both been young and stupid. At least *she* had been. On too many fronts.

Didn't mean they could kiss and make-up, though.

A vivid image of Theo pulling her roughly to him for a hot, heated kiss swept through her body. And then she crushed it. That was all in the past.

"How funny—you remember my goal." She turned on her brightest smile. "Mission accomplished. I *am* here to make a difference, thank you very much. A good one. So, if you don't mind putting one of the 'little people' to work, I'll happily get out of your way."

Sea-green eyes bored into her from a face featuring the strong, evenly planed cheekbones she'd dreamt of tracing with first a finger…then her lips…

He was looking at her curiously. She shifted under his gaze, not enjoying the intense scrutiny.

"Here I was, thinking an earthquake would've reminded you that we're all born equal," he said blandly.

It would've been a hell of a *touché* if she hadn't

known for a fact he thought she was in an intellectual league well below him.

She held her ground, arched an eyebrow that might have looked defensive but was in fact proud and resilient and completely without insecurity. She hadn't knuckled down for years of painstaking study, work and paying off student loans to get this far only to feel belittled again.

"I think you would probably be most useful working alongside me. C'mon." He scooped up her backpack, turned and signaled for her to follow him. "Let's get you some scrubs and then you can show me what you're made of."

He put his hand on the small of her back and began steering her through the crowd, using his own body as a shield against the push and surge of people desperate to see a doctor.

While her infuriated brain shot off in one direction Cailey's body was actively registering Theo's on a much more primal level. All six-foot-something, long-legged, trim-waisted, white-coated package of complete and utter male perfection kept brushing up against her as if…as if they had already shared an intimacy beyond that one perfect kiss…

"I think I can get scrubs on my own, ta." She shot him her best I'm-a-big-girl-now look, eyes sparking as they landed on his amused expression.

"No, you can't. You've never been here before."

"Yeah, but—"

"Yeah, but nothing." He grinned down at her. "You can quit the 'city girl' act, Cailey. You're home now. Time to see what my little *kouklamou* of Mythelios is made of."

It certainly wasn't sugar and spice. Not these days, anyway.

Despite her rising fury, something in her softened as she stomped alongside him to get kitted out in scrubs.

Beautiful doll. He'd always called her that back then. Sure, she'd just been his kid sister's friend. Daughter of his family's housekeeper. But even though they'd never put words to it there'd been *something...* Something *magic* between them.

She'd been absolutely sure of it right up until the moment she'd heard him tell his friends that a Nikolaides would never end up with a cleaner.

And that had been that.

Rage at the memory did nothing to stop her insides from fluttering as his hand shifted on the small of her back. How on earth she'd thought she would be immune to him even after all this time was beyond her.

She stole a glance at him as he stepped to the side to avoid a gurney being wheeled through the packed corridor at high speed.

Theo might not be everybody's cup of tea. He had his flaws. A tiny scar by his eye acquired from daredevil antics in one of his father's olive groves. Hair that always looked as if it could do with a cut. Another small scar just below his nose that only seemed to add to the strength of his unbelievably sensual mouth. Sensual, but male.

Everything about him screamed *alpha*. Masculine. It had since they were young—as if he'd been born vividly aware of the world's mysteries and was just biding his time until the rest of the world caught up. Take it or leave it—that was his attitude. Not cavalier. Or haughty.

Simply *knowing*. As if he'd made a deal with the universe to do his part and in exchange…

That was the mystery. She'd never seen him take anything. Not one single solitary time. That was the Theo enigma.

He might talk the talk of a rich, privileged so-and-so, but she'd always thought the shadows that crossed those sea-green eyes of his betrayed greater depths. Hidden sorrows he'd rather keep secret. He'd never bare the heart behind that insanely touchable chest of his.

He turned back to her with a smile still playing on his lips. Trust him to be all calm and relaxed amidst a level of mayhem that would have rendered any sane person tearing out their hair.

"There's no need for a tour of the clinic. Shall we just get to work?"

"I think you're going to want to get out of that top first."

"I…uh…" She looked down at the white top she was wearing that had somehow magically acquired a layer of grime and rolled her eyes. *Kyros*. Her brother had been filthy.

Oh, good grief. Where's your spine? Your vocabulary? Use them!

"It's not— I'm here to…"

What is wrong *with you?*

A nurse skidded to a halt beside Theo and put a hand on her chest to stop him. *Lucky minx.*

"Dr. Nikolaides, we've got five patients coming in the next ambulance."

"Five!"

Two pairs of eyes snapped to her.

"There are only two ambulances on the island. We

bring in as many people as they can carry," Theo explained.

There was nothing in his voice beyond passing on information. Where was the derision? Why was he taking his time with her? When had he become so…so… extra-perfect?

Her eyes fixed on Theo's lips as he spoke to the nurse. On the tip of his tongue as it touched and retreated from the smooth run of teeth save one crooked one just to the left of center that she'd always liked. Yet another slight imperfection that made him mysteriously even more perfect.

His tongue swept the length of his lower lip before his teeth snagged that lip and pressed down on it while he thought for a moment when the nurse asked where he wanted the patients. It was like being in a slow-motion version of her teenaged fantasies…before the kissing began.

She watched, still mesmerized, as he released his lip and rattled off a list of updates.

A Mrs. Carnosi with a broken arm needed to go to Cubicle Three while her plaster set. A man was in Recovery on the first floor after a heart attack—could someone find his wife down at the harbor? She was helping the baker, he thought. A four-year-old with a head wound could probably do with some crayons to pass the time as the televisions weren't working. All the children, in fact. There were some in a storage locker along with some paper. He was sure of it. Oh, and he'd organized a water delivery so everyone who entered the clinic could be given a two-liter bottle to see them through their waiting time.

Was there *nothing* the man hadn't thought of? All

this while also seeing patients? Where was the young man she'd last seen? Arrogant. Elitist. The one who'd turned against her as easily as kicking a door shut. The one who'd compelled her to scrimp and save and study and learn. To leave her homeland pushed by the towering wave of shame that she would never be good enough for a man like him.

She couldn't have been wrong about him after all of this time. *Could* she?

Theo reached back and gave her shoulder a little pat and a squeeze as another doctor took the nurse's spot and asked him to run his eye across some X-rays. A compound fracture. Were they up to performing the surgery the patient would require?

Vividly aware of Theo's fingers on her shoulder, Cailey was barely capable of lucid thought. Her insides were behaving like electricity cables cut loose in a storm. Sparks flying everywhere. Nothing behaving the way it should.

She squeezed her eyes tight against the warm olive color of Theo's skin. His toned physique. The perfect, capable hands touching her.

Just imagining the man holding a child, helping a *yiayia* to cross the street with her shopping or explaining to a daredevil teen that he couldn't go swimming while his arm was still in a plaster made her insides turn into liquid gold.

Which was all very irritating because she was meant to have become *immune* to Theo Nikolaides.

She forced herself to open her eyes and meet the mossy hues of his irises whilst trying her level best to ignore the fact that the man was in possession of the longest, darkest lashes she'd ever seen. He also had more

than a five o'clock shadow, but that indicated he'd been
working hard and—surprise, surprise—made him look
more like a rock star than an unkempt layabout.

No doubt about it. As a grown man Theo Nikolaides
was a living, breathing example of a mortal embodying
the majesty of the Greek gods of legend. Zeus, Adonis,
Apollo... Eros...

"Shall we get you out of these things?"

Theo was looking pointedly at her filthy top, but her
thoughts and his tone suggested anything but an innocent need to improve her hygiene.

Was he...*flirting* with her?

This was taking being cool in the eye of a storm to
a whole new level.

Just one lazy scan of her dust-covered body and—
poof!—just like that she felt naked. Each sweep of his
eyes drew her awareness to the cotton brushing against
her belly, her breasts, the tingling between her legs that
was really, *really* inappropriate seeing as she'd vowed
to remain immune to the Nikolaides effect. Not to mention the scores of patients waiting.

Seeing him looking at her the way he was...*hun-
grily*...she felt a brand-new array of fireworks light up
her insides and actual electricity crackle between them.

This was all wrong. There was a crisis happening not
inches away. People needed help. Patients needed his attention. *Her* attention.

He'd never looked at her like this before. As if she
were an oasis and he'd crawled in from the desert desperate for one thing and one thing only.

The sun abruptly lit up the clinic's central glass dome,
its rays filtering down to them through a tumble of roof-

top wisteria like film lighting. Dappled. Hints of gold and diamonds.

When Theo tilted his face, green eyes still locked with hers, it was all she could do not to reach into her chest and give him her heart. It had always been his. He'd just never wanted it.

Before she could say anything, though, he held out his arm to clear a path for her toward the rear of the clinic.

Of course the crowd parted. Things like that happened for the Theo Nikolaideses of the world. And the Patera and the Xenakis families. Not to mention the Moustakas family. The four families who commanded the bulk of the island's wealth thanks to their business savvy.

Mopaxeni Shipping. The glittering star of the Aegean Seas and beyond. All those businessmen's sons would inherit untold millions—if not billions. So what on earth was Theo doing here in this small town clinic when the world was his oyster?

"Aren't you meant to be—?"

"Right." Theo cut her off, directing her to a green door at the far end of the corridor. "In here."

She turned and tried to take her bag from him.

He shook his finger—*tick-tock, no, you don't*—in front of her lips. "I'm coming with you."

Great. Just what she'd always dreamed of. Death by proximity to the unrequited love of her life.

She pushed open the swinging door to the changing room. Might as well get it over with.

Theo had absolutely no idea where this cavalier Jack-the-lad attitude he was trying on for size had come from.

He was exhausted. Running on adrenaline. He needed

food, coffee, and yet… Was this—? Was he trying to *flirt*? Was this what stress did to him? Or was this what all-grown-up Cailey Tomaras did to him?

There'd been that one time as teens, when they'd all been running around the pool, messing about. He'd grabbed her, and she'd slipped on the grass, and they'd fallen in a tangle of limbs on top of one another and there'd been a moment…a kiss…

Makapi!

There were a thousand other things Theo should be doing besides going down memory lane to find hints of a romance that had never been. A restorative fifteen minutes of sleep. Walking the small wards, filled to bursting wards, and diving in where an extra pair of hands were needed. Helping with rescue efforts.

Not staring at a pretty girl from the past.

She looked good. A far cry from the reedy teenaged girl who had seemed to all but live in the shadows of his father's ridiculous mansion. A full cherry-red mouth. Inky black hair. A deliciously curvy figure he could almost *feel*—as if he'd already tugged her close to him for a passionate embrace.

He scrubbed a hand through his long hair, hearing his father's distinctive voice in his head.

"If you're going to slum it as the island medic, the least you can do is maintain the family reputation. I'll not have you gallivanting round the island with a half-wit cleaner's daughter."

His eyes flicked to Cailey's. Dark. Full of passion and empathy. And, if he wasn't wrong, the smallest dose of fear.

His heart cinched. That she should feel that way around him… His father was a cruel man. Why he couldn't see that kindness, understanding and empathy were far more effective tools for so-called "people management" was beyond him.

Theo had grown immune to Dimitri's tendency to cut a person to the quick, but Cailey...? He'd never subject her to the ego-lashings his *babbo* had dealt out without a second's thought. And for some reason his father had always had it in for the girl. He'd need to keep her close to him. Far easier to keep her out of harm's way then.

"Are you ready to go straight to work?"

Smooth. Nice way to make a woman who's flown overnight to come and lend a hand welcome.

She narrowed her eyes at him. "You're not going to stand there while I change my clothes, are you?"

Cailey's sharp tone brought him back to the present.

He ran his eyes down the length of her. Long legs. Sensually curved hips making a nice dip at the waist. A tug of desire unexpectedly tightened in his groin. *What the hell?* He was supposed to be exhausted, not horny.

"I'll sit with my back turned."

"Yeah." Cailey's hands landed solidly on her hips. "I don't think so. Say what you need to say and then..." She swirled her finger around in an *out-you-go* gesture.

"Fair enough." Despite himself, he grinned. She was setting parameters. The old Cailey would've been too shy to be so feisty. This new Cailey was becoming more appealing by the minute.

Another tug below his belt line broadened his smile. Quite an impact for an unexpected reunion. One of the earthquake's silver linings, he supposed. Maybe she was strong enough now to stand up to his father.

She pursed her lips and tipped her head from side to side in a *when-are-you-going-to-get-going?* move.

Fine. He got the message. "Right. Here's the story. All hell's broken loose. As you probably know, the quake was strong. It hit this side of the island hardest. A lot of old buildings weren't up to the magnitude. It hit in the afternoon—"

"I know. I know all that," interrupted Cailey impatiently. "I saw the news. Late lunch. Quiet time. Lots of people taking naps… Only the Brits mad enough to go out in the sunshine. You should probably know I specialize in pediatrics and maternity nursing, so if it's—"

"You'll be working with me in urgent care," he cut in. He didn't care how bolshie she was. He was going to look after her, and the easiest place to do that was in his trauma unit.

"I haven't done trauma for over a year."

"But you've done it. And that's where I need you. Case closed," he said firmly before she could protest.

Her shoulders shot up, her mouth opened, but when she saw his stance go rock-solid she dropped the challenge with a flick of a shrug.

"Casualties? Any idea of the scope yet?" she asked.

"Hundreds." Theo shook his head. "I don't know. Several hundred at the very least. The island's got…what?… fifteen or twenty thousand people on it, so it could be more. Patients are presenting with injuries hitting every level of the spectrum, from cuts and bruises to…well…" His mood sobered at the thought of the older gentleman who'd had a fatal heart attack earlier in the day. "Worse than cuts and bruises."

Unexpectedly, Cailey reached out and took his hand. "Are you sure you don't need some rest? You look awful."

"Ha! Thanks. Don't beat around the bush anymore, do you, Cailey?"

She gave him a sad smile. One that said, *I think you might know why.*

The door to the locker room swung open and with it came the chaos and mayhem of the quake's aftermath.

"Dr. Nikolaides?" The nurse was halfway out through the door already. "There's a helicopter on approach to collect a couple of patients. We need you to sign off on them. And the ambulance is pulling up now."

"Of course."

He brusquely pointed toward a cabinet. "There are spare scrubs in there. All sizes. Report to trauma when you've changed. You're working with me. And that's an order."

CHAPTER FIVE

CAILEY STARED AT the empty space Theo had just occupied.

What on earth…?

Bossy so-and-so.

Hadn't changed a bit. Still lording it about as if he knew everything which—well, in this case he probably did.

You're working with me. And that's an order.

Typical Nikolaides privilege. Just because she was a nurse, and had failed to get into med school, and had taken twice as long as anyone else to get her nursing degree—

Stop! She didn't need to keep raking it all up again. The all too familiar pounding of her heart suddenly leapt into her head, drowning out everything else as she forced herself to take in a deep, steady inhalation and then breathe out again.

You're a nurse, she told herself. *There are patients. This isn't about you. Or Mr. Bossypants.*

She was scared, that was all. The trauma ward wasn't her optimum work zone. But she'd done it before—admittedly getting one teensy-tiny panic attack on her score card. Never mind. She could do it again—minus the panic attack part. There was no way she was leaving this island with her tail between her legs a second time.

A quick wash and she'd get her priorities back in order. She'd returned to Mythelios to help, not to swish around Theo Nikolaides praying he'd notice her. That ship had long since sailed.

When Cailey entered the trauma area it was sheer madness. The number of people had doubled. The volume was higher. The urgency of tone was even more shrill.

A shot of fear jettisoned through her bloodstream and exploded in her heart. This was a far cry from the calm, hushed corridors of the maternity ward she'd left behind in England. There the serene environment helped her stay calm—particularly when she struggled with writing up notes and tackling new medicines and...well... any new words. They all took extra time. Her brain processed things differently.

For the most part she'd beaten her dyslexia into a new, workable form of submission. But this?

This was bedlam. She was going to have to shore up every ounce of courage and nursing know-how she had to avoid falling to bits. It had happened before and she never wanted to go back there again. Especially not in front of—

"All right? Ready to go?"

Theo.

Theo was putting his arm round her shoulders and giving her a squeeze. Everything faded for an instant as she just...*mmm*...inhaled the scent she hadn't realized was all but stitched into her memory banks.

Could he sense her fear? Had he seen the blood drain from her face when she walked into the trauma unit?

Spotted the tremor in her hands before she wove them together to stop their shaking?

He squared himself off in front of her, one large, lovely hand on each shoulder. "Just remember: I'm a humble country doctor and you're a big city nurse. You can do this, *koukla mou*. Okay?"

Surprisingly, the term of endearment wrapped around her like a warm blanket. She looked up into his rich green eyes and drew strength from them, felt her breath steadying as he continued.

"I know it seems crazy in here. It is. But this situation is new to all of us and we will each do the best we can. One patient at a time is how we're going to deal with it. All right? One patient at a time."

When their eyes caught she felt her heart smash against her ribcage. The man was looking straight into her soul, seeing her darkest fears and assuring her he would be there to help no matter what. She stared at his chest, half tempted to reach out and touch it, to see if his heart was doing the same.

When their gazes connected again he was all business. He steered her over to a gurney that was being locked into place by a couple of rescue workers.

"Right! Cailey, this is Artemis Pepolo. I've known *this* feisty teen since she was born."

The dark-haired girl nodded a fraction, the rest of her body contracted tightly in pain.

"Artemis has just been rescued after a pretty uncomfortable night under a beam—but you hung in there, didn't you, my love?"

Artemis's breathing was coming in sharp, staccato bursts and her lips were rapidly draining of color. She tried to smile for Theo but cried out in pain. Her arm lay at an odd angle and one touch to the side of her throat revealed a rapid heart-rate.

"Pneumothorax?" Cailey asked in a low voice.

Theo gave an affirmative nod, his gloved hands running along the girl's ribcage as he spoke. "Good. Yes. Traumatic pneumothorax, in this case. The beams of her house shifted when they were getting her out and broke a couple of ribs. No time to get her X-rayed before we relieve the tension. Can you snap on a pair of gloves, get some oxygen into her and clean her up for a quick chest tube?"

Cailey clenched her eyes tight, forcing herself to picture the chart she'd made for herself on how to go through the procedure. Images always worked better for her than words. Miraculously it came to her in a flood of recognition.

And then, as one, they flew through the treatment as if they'd worked together for years.

After snapping on a pair of gloves from a nearby box, Cailey swiftly pulled an oxygen mask round the girl's head and placed it over her mouth, ensuring the tube was releasing a steady flow. She then took a pair of scissors from a supplies trolley, cut open the girl's top, applied monitors, checked her stats and covered her with a protective sheet, leaving a mid-sized square of her ribcage just below her heart exposed. She swabbed it with a hygiene solution as Theo explained the protocol he was going to follow.

"I'm using point-five percent numbing agent to numb the second intercostal space and then a shot of adrenaline-epinephrine before we insert a pigtail catheter, yes?"

"Not a chest tube?" she asked.

The doctor she'd worked under during her stint in the London trauma unit had been old school. *Very* old school. She wouldn't say it had been entirely his fault she'd had her...blip...but he most certainly hadn't helped.

Theo put the tube over a tiny metal rod. "Most hospitals are using the pigtail catheter now. Far less painful for the patient."

She looked for the sneer, listened for the patronizing tone, and heard neither. Just a doctor explaining the steps he was going to take. But better. A doctor saying his patient's comfort was of paramount importance to him.

And then it was back to business. Cailey gave the region around the fourth and fifth intercostal space of the girl's ribcage a final swipe of cleansing solution and then stood back as Theo expertly inserted the needle into the pleural space, his fingertip holding just above the gauge for a second. Their eyes connected as he smiled.

"Ha. Got it. I can feel the air releasing." He turned to his patient and gave her a gentle smile. "Hang in there, love. We're almost there." He attached a syringe to the needle. "I'll just do a quick aspiration to make sure we get all that extra trapped air out."

Once he was satisfied, he expertly went about inserting the thin wire and tube as if he had done it a thousand times. Within seconds the tube was in, the wire was pulled out and Cailey had attached the tube to a chest drainage system.

"Right, Artie. We'll just leave you here to rest up for a bit and then see about moving you somewhere a bit more peaceful where we can check out that arm, all right?"

He pulled off his gloves, smiled at Cailey and tipped his head toward the main trauma area. "Ready for the next one?"

She was impressed. For a man who professed to be a humble country doctor, he knew his stuff.

"Did you study trauma medicine?" She couldn't help but ask the question after pulling the curtains round Artemis and watching Theo give notes to the nurse who, he'd explained, was in charge of moving patients out of the trauma area.

He nodded. "I thought if I was going to be running this place on my own sometimes I'd better be prepared."

"You're here alone ?"

"Well, not *alone*, alone. There are interns who come in from Athens to have a spell, but they usually get bored with island life eventually and want to get back to the mainland. And the lads come back on and off at certain times of the year in a sort of unofficial rotation; they're just not here at the moment."

She nodded. He must mean Chris, Deakin and Ares— the other Mopaxeni *malakas* he'd set up the clinic with. She wasn't so sure *malakas* was the right word for them anymore. Miracle workers, more like. This place was a far cry from the crumbling old clinic she'd gone to as a girl. And Theo was completely different from the elitist snob she'd been expecting.

"Right." He rubbed his hands together as if preparing for a fantastic adventure. "How are you with broken bones?"

Broken bones. Fractures. Lacerations. Internal bruising. Heart palpations. A massive blood clot... The list went on.

And no matter what he threw at her Cailey stayed bright, attentive and, much to his surprise, willing to learn. There were holes in her knowledge—as to be ex-

pected for someone whose specialty wasn't trauma—
but she seemed capable of everything short of reading
his mind, and even that was sometimes questionable.

Whatever he needed—a particular gauge of needle,
a certain type of suture thread, the correct scalpel—she
already had it ready before he could ask for it.

As he opened the curtain for their next patient he
stopped. *Ah.* Marina Serkos. They'd gone to school together until his father had deemed the local primary
unfit for purpose and shipped him off to boarding school.

"Looks like someone's due soon."

This was his one bugbear. The baby checks. He knew
he should be happy for others. Share in the joy of a new
innocent life being brought into the world. But all he
could think each time he saw a pregnant patient was,
Good luck. You'll need it.

Not exactly a ringing endorsement for "happy families". But happy families hadn't been the remit in the
Nikolaides household. Appearances were everything.
No one outside the family knew he wasn't his father's
success story. Nor did they know he was adopted. And
no one—not even his sister—would ever know his silent
vow never to bring a child into this world.

Pawns. That was what he and his sister had been.
Pawns in a game that hadn't seemed to have any rules.

"Theo?" Cailey had helped Marina up onto the exam
table and was wheeling a sonogram machine into place.
"Do you want to do the exam?"

Both women were looking at him a bit oddly. If they'd
been exchanging information he hadn't a clue.

He scrubbed his hands over his face and forced a
smile. "Apologies, Marina. It's been a long day."

"Marina's worried about her baby," Cailey explained in a confident voice.

Ah! Of course. This was her terrain. He nodded for her to continue. It was a relief not to have to *ooh* and *ah* each time a fist curled, or a hiccough came halfway through an exam. In his darker moments he sometimes wondered if the only thing his fellow islanders could think to do during the slow winter months was procreate.

"She's not experienced any blunt trauma, thank goodness, but when the quake struck she was taking a much-needed nap, I presume…"

Both women smiled at Marina's large bump. She was probably near full term by now.

"Are you at seven months, Marina?"

"Eight," she answered, her brow creasing with worry. "The baby used to kick all the time, but when the bed collapsed, I just— Ooooh…" She blew out a steadying breath as tears popped into her eyes. "I haven't really felt the little one move since."

"Well, then." Cailey pulled on a fresh pair of gloves. "I guess we'd better take a look at the little one."

Her tone was bright, efficient, and exactly what a worried mum needed to hear at a time like this.

She held out the scanning wand to Theo. "No, no, you go ahead. This is your terrain," he said.

"You're a maternity doctor?" Marina asked, her eyes brightening.

A flash of something crossed Cailey's eyes before she answered. Frustration? Sadness? But when she turned back to Marina it was as if he'd imagined it.

"No, no. I'm a nurse working on a neonatal ward in a London hospital."

"No chance you want to stay here, I suppose?" Marina asked, then threw an apologetic glance at Theo. "Apologies, Dr. Nikolaides, but sometimes it's nice to have a woman to speak with about...you know..."

He nodded. He knew. But they were a small, charitable clinic running on a limited budget on an island few doctors wished to call home all year round. He'd tried to get female obstetricians to come in at least once a month, but with weather, budget constraints, people's busy schedules—things didn't always pan out.

He didn't blame them, those doctors who refused his invitations to take a massive pay-cut and cope with small-town life complete with an unlimited supply of Mythelios Olive Oil.

Big-city hospitals, well-funded research clinics... those were the places that drew talent. Look at Cailey—she'd gone to London and stayed there. And his best friends had left. Add to that an earthquake, and... Oh, well. No need to go down *that* rabbit hole again.

Obstinacy—or something like it—was the only reason he stayed. Whether it was a relentless showdown or a twisted truce he and his father were engaged in...

He shook his head and forced himself to tune in to Cailey's exam. There were no answers when it came to his father. But there were in medicine. Which was why he all but lived in the clinic. Long shifts were a damn sight better than "family time."

Cailey had just slid up Marina's top to expose her swollen belly, complimented her on her lack of stretch marks—something he would have felt like an idiot doing—and was about to apply a huge dollop of gel when she pulled it back.

"Have you eaten or drunk anything in the past few hours?"

Marina shook her head, then stopped herself. "I did drink a lot, because I remember from my last scan they needed me to have a full bladder. It doesn't take much these days!"

"I'm not surprised." Cailey laughed, then put the gel tube above Marina's stomach. "Ready for the cold?"

Marina flinched as it hit her skin and gave a nervous laugh. "This is my third pregnancy. You'd think I would be used to it by now."

"Skin never gets used to a sudden hit of cold," Cailey soothed as she placed the baton on the far right of Marina's stomach and began the scan. "So…let's see what your little one has got up to."

Theo rocked back on his heels and crossed his arms. It was nice to take a backseat for a change, to watch Cailey slip naturally into a role that obviously suited her. He'd never known why she hadn't followed her dream of becoming a doctor and had instead opted for neonatal nursing, but if her complete calm and confidence at this moment exemplified her professionally he'd bet that London hospital would be holding on to her for dear life. Dedicated quality nurses were like rare jewels—something you kept close.

Soon enough, the tell-tale rush of a liquid-sounding heartbeat was accompanied by the whooshed release of air from everyone's lungs.

The women's eyes connected and together they laughed, then returned their attention to the screen. where they could see the curled-up form of a baby sucking its thumb.

Theo picked up Marina's chart, which Petra had somehow magicked out of the mayhem despite the ongoing chaos at the clinic. "Want me to take notes?"

The women turned to him, almost surprised to see him still there.

"Sure. Feels like a luxury to have a doctor take the notes," Cailey said with a smile.

"Consider it payback for all your excellent help today."

Cailey's brows contracted together briefly, as if she were trying to divine something deeper from his words before turning back to the monitor. "The good news is we have a steady, regular heart-rate. One-thirty."

"Isn't that a bit low?"

"Mmm...it's at the lower end of the spectrum, but well within what we would expect. Anything below one hundred or above one-seventy would be of concern." She winked at Marina. "Your baby is obviously made of stern stuff! Now, I presume you're up to date on all your antenatal scans?"

"Yep. Dr. Nikolaides makes sure of that."

Theo nodded and lifted up the clipboard as a reminder that he was here to take stats. These lapses into chit-chat with mothers always made him nervous. There were the inevitable questions—when are you planning on tying the knot? Starting a family of your own? Bringing a little shining star into the world for your parents to spoil? Conversations he normally actively avoided.

Cailey threw him a *hold-your-horses* look, but gave him the baby's BP in the same steady voice she'd been using with Marina.

She checked the baby's growth, matched the results with the previous figures and pronounced them excellent. She measured the blood flow between the placenta and the baby, and checked the amniotic fluid.

Cailey pointed at the screen, then clamped her fingers over her mouth. Her fingers dropped to her chin and she threw an *uh-oh* look in Theo's direction before asking Marina, "Do you know if it's a boy or a girl?"

Marina nodded her head. Yes, she did. "It's another boy! I'm going to be officially outnumbered when this one is born." A look of panic crossed her face. "If everything's all right?"

"Well, he's moving around just fine, from what I can see. You probably received a big shock yesterday, and perhaps he was sensing your need for stillness. It sounds pretty scary."

"It was," Marina said. "But now that I know my baby's safe I can relax." She smiled at Cailey. "Have you got any of your own?"

Theo's eyes snapped to Cailey. He knew how well *he* responded to that question...

"No," she said simply, taking the baton off Marina's belly and wiping it clean.

Irritation lanced through him as he finished off the notes.

No. That was it? No, *Maybe one day.* No, *Yes, I've left him back in London with my lover.* No, *Perhaps when I meet the right guy...*

What the hell? What did it matter to him if she wanted children or not?

They all started as shouting erupted beyond the curtained cubicle. There were calls for the defibrillator, for more blood.

Theo didn't need to hear more. "Apologies ladies, I'd better get out there."

"All right if I finish up in here?" Cailey asked, clearing the monitor and scanning equipment to one side.

"Yeah. Fine. You wrap things up then I'll see you out there?"

She nodded.

"Good."

Just a few hours in and already he was growing a little too used to having Cailey by his side.

Which was not good. Because whoever came too close into his orbit would also come into his father's orbit…and that *never* went well.

CHAPTER SIX

"AND IT LOOKS like we're back to a normal BP. Heart-rate is steady."

The team around Theo clapped with relief. Their sixty-five-year-old patient, a local schoolteacher, had been helping rescue crews to pull away rubble when a lifetime's worth of deep-fried squid and a love of the honey-soaked sweets brought to him by his students had caught up to him.

Despite her fatigue, Cailey was riding high. She hadn't helped on a cardiac arrest in ages, and this had been a resounding success. Theo had been amazing. A cool, calm and collected doctor in the eye of a pretty crazy storm.

As an orderly wheeled the patient to a recovery room Cailey couldn't help but express her admiration. "That was *amazing.*"

Theo smiled down at her, green eyes alight with the satisfaction that came with a high-adrenaline, high-stakes treatment. He'd never looked more attractive to her than he did at that moment.

All of a sudden her knees went weak and everything flew off balance. Theo's arms were around her in an instant, swirling her into the doorway in a fluid move that would have put a tango dancer to shame.

When she opened her eyes all she could see were his lips. And that teensy little scar her tongue itched to reach out and— *Stop it!* She sucked in a shallow breath, horrified to notice that her breasts were pressing against his chest. They obviously had a mind of their own. Little minxes.

Theo didn't move. *OMG.* Did he…did he *like* it? Like *her*?

Her brain went into overdrive. Was she going to have to rearrange a thousand vows never to succumb to the likes of Theo Nikolaides for the very clinical and reasonable sake of finding out just once what it would be like to…? *Oh… Oh, my…* His thighs were pressed against hers. His hips… He was very, very close. She felt the soft exhalation of his breath against her mouth and wanted more than anything to part her lips and taste him.

She risked a glimpse up into his eyes.

What she saw in them conveyed a thousand messages. Hope. Interest. Desire. A bit of confusion.

Little wonder! She was feeling about as confused as they came. For starters…why was he holding her in this doorway after she'd swooned like an idiot?

"Aftershocks."

"I'm sorry?" Cailey shook her head, only to hear a collective gasp come from the trauma unit as another one hit.

Theo's hold tightened around her, his tall, lean form curling protectively over her, his hands cupping her head against the rigid doorframe as they waited for the tremor to pass.

When it did he stood back and, as if nothing had happened at all, reached out to tuck a few strands of her disobedient hair behind her ear.

"Are you all right, love? Do you need to take a break? We've got relief doctors coming in from the mainland in about…" his eyes traveled to a nearby wall clock "…twenty minutes or so."

Love? Since when did he call her "love"?

He stifled a yawn.

"I think if anyone deserves a break it's probably you," she said, pleased with her stern tone. Then she reached out to give his arm a *you've-worked-hard* squeeze.

Big mistake.

Go away, tingles and butterflies!

"You look tired, Cailey."

"No, *you* look tired."

He rolled his eyes. *No kidding*, the gesture said. *Of course I'm tired, but I'm in charge.*

A strange need to coddle him seized her. He was great at looking after others, but who looked after him?

Good grief. She wasn't letting herself fall for him again, was she? But then perhaps she had never actually got up again after the first time…

"Cailey…"

"Theo?"

He crossed his arms and fixed her with a classic big brother look. "You should get some rest."

She crossed her arms too, beginning to enjoy this back and forth banter. Never mind the fact that being sassy helped her hide the wave after wave of emotion pummeling her mind, her guts, her heart.

Longing. Desire. Heartache. Lust.

She'd thought she'd lain all those things to rest when

she'd boarded that plane bound for London all those years ago.

"Tell me, Cailey, who exactly do you think is going to look after the clinic if I leave?"

His expression of triumph spoke volumes. He thought he'd nailed it.

She glanced past his shoulder and smiled as a group of a dozen-plus doctors shouldering medical kits walked through the double doors leading into the trauma area. Fresh-faced. Ready to work.

"They will."

"What?" Theo turned around and registered the change of events.

"So I guess that's settled, then. We'll *both* take a break."

"Where are you staying?"

Theo was as surprised as Cailey when the question popped out.

She glanced at him, and their eyes caught and held tight.

She was always more than your kid sister's friend.

"I haven't really organized things yet. My brothers are crazy busy with the rescue crews." Cailey looked away, a slight flush blooming on her cheeks as she mumbled, "And I don't really think there's room at my mum's now that—"

"What?" Theo took Cailey's shoulders in his hands, forcing her to look at him. "Is Jacosta all right? Is her home intact?"

Cailey shrugged, tears filming her dark eyes. "She says so, but I've not seen the flat myself."

"Flat? I thought you lived in a house?"

"We did, but…" Cailey looked away, a few poorly hidden tears falling from her eyes as she turned.

"But what?" His chest felt restricted against the strain of his lungs. "Has my father not been paying her retirement pension? Do you want me to speak to him?"

Bloody man! The most tight-fisted billionaire he'd ever come across. Not that he knew scores of them, or anything, but he knew enough to know that money made a man more of who he was at heart. Good, greedy, kind, cruel…it didn't matter. Money was an enabler, and if he thought that for one second—

"No, it's not that. When I left for London she sold the house."

She swiped at her eyes, her expression one of pure defiance. There was a story there, but Cailey wasn't pausing for him to ask any questions.

"The place she's in now is diddy. But it's fine. *She's* fine. We're all fine. The Tomaras clan is, as it always has been, perfectly happy. Earthquake aside."

She quirked an eyebrow, adopted a faint smile and looked up at him, unable to hide the shadows of the past shifting across her features like a slow-moving storm.

Clearly not *all* of the Tomaras clan was happy.

"All right, then. If there's no room for you to stay with her, you'll stay with me."

"What? No." She took a step back and held up her hands. "*No*. Completely unnecessary. You've got—"

"Pish-tosh."

He plucked the old-fashioned English expression from his days at medical school in London. Why had their paths never crossed there? She should have called him. Or Erianthe, who was still there.

He swore silently under his breath. He should have

kept a closer eye on Cailey. From now on he would. "You're my responsibility."

"Er...and why *is* that, exactly?"

"Because I said so."

Winning answer, Romeo.

Unsurprisingly, Cailey looked unconvinced.

What was he going to say? That he didn't want his father to see her without him there to protect her? It was true. It was also true that he wouldn't be able to live with himself if he thought for one second Cailey's family had been forced to downsize because of anything his father had done.

Somewhere deep inside that sinewy heart of his, he knew his father loved him. Even if he was "just adopted." But he also knew Dimitri's vow to make him pay for not becoming the son he'd wanted when they'd adopted him all those years ago still held strong.

Anyone might think the man would be *proud* that his son had become a doctor. Healing and supporting the very islanders who had helped make his family rich. But, no. He was meant to have followed in his father's wake, taken up the helm at Mopaxeni Shipping and filled the family coffers even further.

"'Because I said so' doesn't really cut it with me, Theo."

He tipped his head back and forth. Fair enough. Cailey was a spirited, passionate woman. No surprise tht she wasn't falling for the dominant male tack.

"You've worked hard, and tomorrow will be more of the same. *Please.* Come to mine and get some rest."

Better.

"I'm not staying."

He barked out a disbelieving laugh. How could he have forgotten how stubborn she was?

"Yes," he ground out in a non-negotiable voice. "You are. My clinic. My rules. You work for me, and if you want to continue to do so you need some rest. I've got a spare room and a perfectly good bed for you to sleep in. As far as I'm concerned you need to be in it. *Now.*"

Cailey's cheeks streaked with red. "Yeah, I don't *think* so."

Theo squared himself in front of her. Rolled his shoulders back. Pulled himself up to his full height.

What was he doing? Presenting himself like a prize stallion?

Idiot. She's exhausted. So are you. Act normal.

He cleared his throat and started again. "Get your things. I'm taking you home."

Way to go caveman. Real smooth.

"Theo, really. I'll be fine."

He smiled, caught by surprise at the way she'd said his name. It sounded like a…a verbal caress. Just the chink in her armor he needed.

"I'm afraid it's non-negotiable, Cailey. Bed. Sleep. I can throw some hot chocolate into the mix, but that's where I draw the line."

What was he? Twelve?

Cailey pressed her feet to the ground, obviously gearing herself up to protest, and then, much to his surprise, suddenly wilted.

Raising her hands, she said, "Fine. You win." She turned her surrendering hands into pistols, "But we need to stop by Stavros's *taverna* so I can see my mother. And after that just a few hours' sleep then I'm back here, just like everyone else."

"Deal."

He put out his hand, and when she placed hers in his to shake on it he stunned them both by raising her palm to his lips and giving it a kiss.

Cailey virtually ran to the changing room to get her backpack. She wouldn't have been surprised if sparks were flying out of the soles of her trainers.

What was going on?

An earthquake wasn't the only thing that had shaken up the island.

Theo was not the man she had decided he would be. In her head—and in truth she had devoted far too much time to this—he had become a mini-Dimitri. No. Worse. A *Monster* Dimitri. A: because he stood about a foot taller. B: because he was a thousand times more commanding when he chose to be. And C: Theo was a million more miles off-limits and a gazillion times more gorgeous than his father.

But other than that...? Exactly the same.

She pushed into the changing room, ran to the sink, stared at the back of her hand for a minute, debating whether or not to kiss it back, then threw handful after handful of cold water on her face willing her brain to try and match Bad Theo with—well...with *Real* Theo.

The real Theo posed a much greater threat to her. The real Theo, in just one day, had teased apart each of the perfect tight stitches she had carefully inserted over the wound in her heart and burst them wide open again.

The man was an infinity of little perfections.

Never mind the tug-your-fingers-through-it hair, the ridiculously green eyes, his athletic physique and utterly kissable mouth... He was an incredible doctor. And she found that about as sexy as it came. He was thoughtful. Empathetic. Resourceful. He was a generous colleague. He hadn't once patronized her or tried to catch her out when she'd hesitated over a medicine vial or which scalpel to pick up when he needed one. Not that it had happened much. From their very first patient he'd actually managed to bring out her A-game.

And now she was going to spend the night at his house.

Her powers of resistance were pitiful. She stared at the mirror above the sink and mimicked herself, "'Okay, Theo. Yes, Theo. Whatever you say, Theo.'" Pathetic!

She'd always imagined her return to Mythelios would be more...*triumphant*, in a dignified and grown-up way. She'd wow him with her cool professionalism and make him realize exactly what he'd lost.

Not fall into his arms at the first sign of an aftershock and then agree to curl up in his guest bedroom only not to sleep because he'd be right next door.

She stared at herself again.

Serious face, this time.

Had she tarred Theo with the same brush as his father? Theo had never told her to get lost. Or to steer clear. Okay, so she had heard him laughing with his mates about a Nikolaides never marrying a housemaid once, and that had stung—singed itself into her psyche probably for ever—but it was *Dimitri* who'd told her to stay away from Theo, not Theo himself. And she wasn't a housemaid anymore.

Besides, there was definitely chemistry between them. No denying that. There always had been.

But what if this was just a tease only for him to push her away again? She knew Theo would never marry her, but she had come back sort of triumphant. She was a nurse in an exclusive hospital. She'd done some cracking good work today. Her mother was free of her need for a Nikolaides paycheck so there'd be no more dangling that fear factor over her head. It still shocked her that Dimitri had said he'd fire her mother if Cailey didn't leave his family alone.

A flame lit sharp and bright inside her. She *would* take Theo up on his invitation. The bed. The hot chocolate. She deserved it.

It might not have been his fault her mother had decided to sell the family home to help Cailey with her nursing school fees, but it *was* his fault for being so ruddy nice she couldn't find a reason to say no to staying with him. And if Dimitri found out about this and tried to exact any kind of vengeance the blame would fall solidly on Theo—and then she'd leave the island and never think of either of them again.

"Ready?" Theo strode into the changing room, scooped up her backpack with one hand, slung it on his shoulder and opened his other arm to create a protective arc around her shoulders as he steered them through the crowds to the front door.

Oh, swoon. Wrinkly scrubs suited him. Then again, being naked probably suited him too. Not that she'd imagined that. *Much.*

He pushed open the front door, his arm still round her and whispered, "Out of the frying pan…"

At first she didn't get it—and then just a few footsteps beyond the clinic a whole new raft of sensations bombarded her.

Discordancy. The shrill sounds of heavy machinery hammering away at centuries-old rock and beam. The savaged spot-lit remains of homes and businesses that had virtually disintegrated when the quake had hit.

A wash of guilt rushed over her that she could have been thinking naughty thoughts and having saucy tummy-flips while all this mayhem was still happening across the harbor town.

This was the reason she was here. Not to play out some revenge fantasy against one of the island's richest men.

She shivered beneath the weight of Theo's arm, which was still resting lightly on her shoulders protectively, the way a boyfriend or a husband might touch a loved one who'd had a rough day and was feeling a little fragile.

"You warm enough?"

Theo's voice was soft, a balm against the harsh sound of saws on metal and jackhammers rat-a-tat drumming against concrete.

"Mmm…" She was *confused*, maybe, but not cold. Not with his arm wrapped around her.

Another shiver rattled down her spine at the thought of his father seeing them. He'd warned her off once and this was stark disobedience of the "stay away from my son" remit she'd promised to obey.

But that was years ago.

"Want my jacket?"

"No, no. I'm good."

Scared. Excited. A little bit more lusty than she should be. But strangely…*whole*. As if coming back to the island and finding herself walking side by side with Theo Nikolaides had been the one thing missing from her life.

"Sure?"

He slid his hand to her waist and steered her round some debris that had fallen from a shop front they were passing. The owners sat inside. Their folding chairs flanked an empty crate holding a candle and a half-empty bottle of ouzo. The pair, who must be husband and wife, lifted their glasses when they saw Cailey and Theo passing.

"Yasou!" the pair called out in tandem, then downed their drinks, wincing against the angelica and mace-flavored liquor.

Cheers? Seriously? With their house fallen to bits round them?

"Yasou!" Theo called back, smiling warmly at Cailey, then quickly tightening his fingers at her waist and tugging her out of the path of a couple of smashed watermelons that had been squirted out beneath a collapsed canopy.

"Making the best of a bad lot?" Theo called over his shoulder.

In Greek they called out the age-old saying, "Everything in its time, and in August...mackerel!"

Despite herself, Cailey giggled. "They're certainly optimistic."

Theo shrugged. "They've probably seen worse."

Cailey pulled back, and the warmth of Theo's fingers shifted easily to the small of her back as if they'd been a couple forever. "Worse than their shop crashing to bits when they both look on the brink of retirement?"

Theo stuck out his lower lip and tilted his chin. "First: people like them *never* retire. Second: a bit of patient-doctor privilege sometimes gives an insight into how people prioritize what is bad and what is worth raising a glass for."

Ah. A "big picture" response. She got it. Theo was saying a mashed-up shop was nothing to what that couple had already faced on a personal level. They might have lost a child. Battled cancer. Survived a serious accident. Whatever it was had already put this couple face to face with their mortality—and this time, after the huge quake that had taken over a dozen lives already, they had survived. So why not toast one another?

She glanced back at the couple, merrily refilling their glasses and laughing quietly to one another. Bad things happened, but it was how you responded to them that mattered.

Like deciding whether or not to be frightened of a man who no longer held her family's purse strings. Or of his son who, when you looked at him "big picture" style, was little short of perfect.

CHAPTER SEVEN

"CAILEY-OULA!"

Theo retracted his hand from Cailey's waist at the sound of her brother's voice emerging from the rising and falling chatter across the street at Stavros's *taverna*.

It wasn't strange at all for Greeks to show one another physical affection, but it was now that disaster had struck that Theo realized his protective older brother feelings had morphed into *I really want to kiss you* ones.

At the sound of Leon's voice Cailey unleashed the fullest smile he'd seen since her arrival. Bright, full of energy, eyes sparkling as if she *hadn't* just spent the past twelve hours working her heart out.

A swift tug and a tightening right where it counted hit him hard and fast. Oh, yes. His intentions toward her were definitely romantic.

"Kyros! Leon!"

Cailey was up and being hugged in a big brother sandwich before he'd even had a chance to get his head round the fact that she wasn't standing next to him anymore. The crowd was so thick at Stavros's it would have been no surprise to find half the island's population were there on the flower-laced veranda. A veranda miraculously untouched by the quake.

A rapid-fire exchange of information passed between the siblings in a shorthand he almost envied. Wives? Great. Where were they? Serving food—just like everyone else. Stavros and Jacosta had organized it. Where was Mama? Serving her famous *souvlaki*.

Cailey moaned, kissed the tips of her fingers and lifted them to the starlit sky. Theo's stomach rumbled. He too had moaned with pleasure over Jacosta's *souvlaki* on days when his father had been out of town and he'd "slummed it" in the kitchen.

Shouts were being launched in the direction of the *taverna*. "Theo! What are you doing standing over there by yourself?"

Jacosta appeared next to her children and beckoned for him to join them, her arms wide open. As ever she was non-judgmental, welcoming, loving.

For the first time in his life he hesitated. How strange to suddenly feel like an outsider on his own island. This had never happened before.

Neither had wanting to completely rip the clothes off a woman he'd known since childhood.

The earth wasn't the only thing that had shifted that day.

"Come! Come!"

Jacosta had him in a warm embrace before he had another moment to think. Kisses were exchanged. The standard questions peppered him: "Are you all right? Is your home all right? How is your *mama*? Is her ankle elevated? I heard she twisted it. Your father? I saw him driving past, so I took it as a good sign. Cousins? Aunts? Uncles? Are you hungry? Eat. Eat. Look at you. Skin and bones. You must eat!"

He laughed and succumbed to the hug she pressed

him into. It was pointless to resist Jacosta's entreaties for a hug from her "third son."

Wouldn't life have been different if only he'd been adopted by a family for love, not power. He stiffened at the thought and, as if sensing his conflicted feelings, Jacosta let him go.

It was his body protecting his emotions. Protecting them from the inevitable hurt that would come if he so much as *thought* of having a family of his own one day.

"Theo." Jacosta crooked a finger, indicating that she wanted him to come closer. Not that Cailey and her brothers, who were still in the full flow of information exchange, would overhear.

"I hope you are keeping an eye on my daughter." She tapped the side of her nose and smiled gently. "Look after her. She may act the brave one, but she's tender inside."

A huge cheer erupted from the overspill of villagers at Stavros's, followed by an excited gabble of conversation.

Jacosta gave Theo a knowing look. One that said, *I know you know her as well as I do...so be kind.*

Cailey twirled round toward them with a huge smile on her face. "They've found Stavros's cousin's daughter!"

"Wonderful." Jacosta pressed her hands into the prayer position and lifted her eyes to the clear sky up above.

"Mama!" Cailey gave her mother a huge squeeze. "Why are you crying?"

"I'm just so happy. So relieved to have all my children here." She reached out her hands, and a sob of relief filled the air around them as she pulled Cailey closer and then called her boys over for a big, tight family hug.

Something that would never happen in my family, Theo thought darkly. His father had only called to say he'd chartered a helicopter to come to the mansion and fly his mother to the mainland for treatment on her ankle and her nerves, and then asked if Theo was "keeping up appearances" with the clinic.

He couldn't believe his father still didn't get it. That he loved being the island doctor. No, he wasn't a specialist surgeon like his mates—the other "golden boys" of the Mopaxeni founders—but he loved it. Loved helping carpenters and fishermen and cherished ever-aging *yiayias* and even billionaires. Not that his father would deign to receive treatment from *him*. Too personal. Too much like needing the son he claimed was nothing but a disappointment to him.

He scrubbed his hands through his hair. *Enough.* He was tired. Hungry. No point in getting all emotional over a family who liked to hug just because his didn't.

"Come! Theo." Jacosta waved him over to their small group. "Give me a kiss, then go in and make yourself useful. Fetch this poor girl some *souvlaki.*"

She turned to her daughter and they had a swift, low-voiced exchange. He caught the words "sofa" and "extra blankets". Cailey's eyes flicked to his, then guiltily back to her mother's. Jacosta shot him raised eyebrows, clearly went through some mental calculations then offered him an *aha-you-sly-dog* smile.

"I've got food at home, Jacosta," he said.

"What's wrong with the food we have here?" Jacosta's smile shifted to a frown. "You've never turned down my *souvlaki* before."

She lowered her gaze to half-mast and tilted up her chin, her expression wreathed in suspicion. He'd seen this look before. Mostly when his father had exploded about something ridiculous and Cailey had been present. Jacosta had always swiftly shifted Cailey behind her, literally protecting her from the verbal lashing, bowing her head, apologizing, taking every blow he unleashed.

He didn't like being on the receiving end of that look. He wasn't his father. The last thing he wanted to do was hurt Cailey.

"Mama, it's fine. Volunteers have brought food to the clinic. Why don't we eat together later? As a family, when this is over. Then we will have a reason to celebrate, yes?"

"Paidi mou!" Jacosta threw her hands into the air in disbelief. "It's not reason enough to celebrate that my daughter has come home? That her brothers still have life coursing through their veins? That your *mama*'s *souvlaki* is being devoured by all these good people who have escaped with their lives but my own flesh and blood won't take even the tiniest of bites to add some flesh to her body?"

"Yes, of course, Mama, but…" Cailey pressed her thumbs above her eyes and gave her forehead a rub, surreptitiously appealing to Theo for help with a sideways grimace.

Theo swept a hand across his mouth to hide his smile as a glimpse of the teenage Cailey emerged.

"It's been a long day," he said placatingly to Jacosta.

"So she should *eat*!"

"I need to *sleep*, Mama!"

"Mama, let her go." Kyros appeared through the crowd with two takeaway packets wafting the alluring scent of Jacosta's *souvlaki* in their direction. He kissed his mother's cheek, then handed the boxes to Cailey with a wink.

"Now, go!" Kyros made shooing movements with his hands as if he were clearing the area of chickens. "Get some rest, then come back and fix more people. I'm not going to bust my gut rescuing people only to find the clinic staff falling asleep on the job."

His grime-streaked face turned from teasing to sober.

"My wife's nephew is still missing. He went off to play before the quake and they haven't seen him since. There's a crew out there searching right now."

Cailey reached out and gave his arm a squeeze. "I'm so sorry. How old is he?"

"Six."

They all stood for a moment, weighed down by the ramifications. The weather wasn't yet obscenely hot, but spring often saw the temperature gauge fly up unexpectedly, and the longer someone was trapped the more likely it was they'd suffer from severe dehydration. What happened next wasn't worth considering.

"Fine." Jacosta wiped her hands together as if she'd been behind the decision for Theo and Cailey to leave all along. "Off you go. *Shoo*! Get some rest. I'll bring you some yoghurt and fruit in the morning."

Cailey took a deep breath as if to protest, then clearly remembered it would do no good and surrendered to the hug her mother was drawing her into.

Another round of kisses were exchanged and then they were back on their way.

"Your mother is a force of nature."

"That's putting it mildly," Cailey replied dryly, then sucked in a sharp breath as first her spine and then her whole body responded to Theo's touch when he replaced his hand on the small of her back to steer her onto a small tree-lined street that led away from the village's main thoroughfare.

Who *was* this man?

He was much more comfortable with the villagers than she'd anticipated. No lofty heights. No clear social barriers up between him and them.

Had he really changed from that arrogant teen she'd overheard telling his friends about the heiresses his father had lined up for him to marry into this...this kind, generous-hearted, self-effacing man?

There weren't any heiresses in sight now. And—not that she was obsessed or anything—but the pictures of Theo with some willowy blonde on his arm had dried up in the society mags of late.

She chanced a glance at him as he ruffled a child's hair after the little one had run out to show him the bandage he'd applied earlier to her arm. He knelt down and gave it a studied look, then praised her for looking after it so well.

Crikey, that was sweet. *He* was sweet.

Just feeling Theo's broad hand reassert itself on the small of her back relit a flame in her core she now knew had never really been fully tamped out.

As they continued walking she couldn't stop the niggling thought that ten years ago she'd blown the whole "Nikolaideses don't marry housemaids" thing out of proportion. Had she, a teen herself, taken umbrage for something she should've just laughed off? Or, better yet, should she have flounced out of the pool house she'd been cleaning, flicked a hip in his direction with a saucy follow-up that he didn't know what he was missing?

Instead she'd been upset, hurt and offended. Leaving had been an easy way to protect her heart from feelings she'd thought would never be reciprocated.

Theo slowed his pace and dropped his hand from her back. She missed his touch instantly. How quickly she'd grown used to something she thought she'd never know.

He stopped in front of a large wooden gate and dug his hand round in his pocket, presumably for a key, his shaggy hair falling forward across his darkly stubbled cheeks.

Theo must have felt her gaze on him. He raised his eyes to meet hers and dropped a slow, dark-lashed wink in her direction as he pulled something out of his pocket with a flourish.

"Ta-da!"

She stared at the object in his hand. A mini-screwdriver?

"Man's best friend."

"A screwdriver?" she deadpanned.

"Absolutely." Theo gave her a quick nod, then turned to the gate. "I lost the key about three years ago, and last winter it started jamming, so…"

He fiddled a bit with the screwdriver at an area on the doorframe that looked as if it had borne this routine more than a few times, then gave the door a swift kick. "*Voila!* Your boudoir awaits, *mademoiselle!*"

Trying to push aside images of Theo sweeping her off her feet and carrying her to said boudoir, she tried to wrangle her backpack off his shoulder.

"No, you don't." Theo swept his arm out, indicating that she should enter the small but incredibly lush garden where a smattering of golden sandstone slates led to a modest-sized whitewashed traditional home. "In you go." He pulled the gate shut behind them as she entered the garden. "So. What do you think?"

What did she *think*? She thought it was the last sort of place a Nikolaides would live in. More to the point, she thought it was perfect.

The small house was precisely the type of a home she'd dreamt of living in before she'd left the island. Draped in bougainvillea, shaded by palms and…was that a pomegranate tree? It felt…cozy. It was about as far as you could get from the ostentatious steel beams, floor-to-ceiling glass and columns of the neo-classical mansion he'd grown up in.

There went a few more of her hypothetical conjectures about The Life of Theo.

"I think it's beautiful."

He squinted at her, the corners of his lips tweaking up into a quirky smile. "Excellent. And it looks like the chaps who did the stonemasonry all those years ago knew what they were doing."

"What?"

"No cracks from the earthquake."

"Haven't you been—?" She stopped herself. Of *course* he hadn't been home yet. He'd been at the clinic yesterday afternoon when the quake struck and hadn't been home since.

In lieu of throwing herself at him and telling him how selfless and wonderful he was, she shifted her weight on her heels and gave the house a studied look.

"How old is it, exactly?"

"Hmm…" Theo drummed his fingers on his chin and stared at the house as if someone would pop out of the front door and tell him.

My goodness, he has a lovely jawline. Had she ever even noticed a man's jawline before?

"Not very. Three hundred years old? Maybe four? Not dawn of civilization stuff."

Cailey couldn't help but laugh. She'd always held a deep affection for the neglected and often abandoned stone structures dotted about the island. How funny that Theo seemed to share the exact same level of enthusiasm. He took a few long-legged steps past her and opened the thick wooden door to the house.

"You have the key to this one?" she teased, feeling a strange new store of energy coming to the fore.

"Never locked." He looked back at her and gave her another one of those butterfly-inducing winks. "Wait here for a minute while I check the structure. It would be a bit embarrassing if your bedroom had been swept out to sea."

Double swoon!

There was no doubt about it. Theo was flirting with her and she was falling for it hook, line and sinker. Just as she'd warned herself not to.

Then again… If this whole "get some rest at my house" thing was leading where she thought it might, it could lay a few old demons to rest.

Yes. Definitely. They'd have their night of carnal bliss and then *poof!* She'd lend a hand for a few more days at the clinic, maybe throw in a bit of a showdown with Dimitri, then get back to her job in London, put an end to the evil glares of the gift shop lady every time she leafed through the society mags, and get on with the rest of her life.

And maybe monkeys wearing tiaras would fly out of her backpack.

Theo appeared at the doorway. "It's safe. Still no power so I've lit some candles. Just a couple of broken plates." He laughed. "Typical Greek, eh? Breaking plates in the best and worst of times. C'mon. In you come."

He crooked his finger, beckoning to her like the wicked wolf luring little Red Riding Hood into his lair.

Goosebumps skimmed across her skin as she stepped inside. Like the outside, the interior had the gentle glow of whitewashed stone walls. Theo had lit several candles set in traditional wall stands complete with mirrors, so a soft, warm light flickered around the room.

The ceilings were higher than she'd expected. The odd exposed support beam added character. Wooden, of course. A small kitchen was tucked at the back of the large open-plan area, so that there was room for a circular dining table opposite a pair of French windows. In the living room area, where they stood, a pair of over-sized sofas, perfect for napping or reading on, were dotted with blue throw pillows. The sofas faced another set of French windows, leading to a covered veranda, beyond which she could just see the white effervescent foam of the sea—still a bit choppy, though there had been no aftershocks since the one a few hours ago.

"It's beautiful."

"Not as beautiful as you've become, Cailey."

Theo was right behind her, his voice low and weighted with intention.

She wheeled round and stumbled back a few steps. Being so close, inhaling his scent—amazingly pure and clean after such a long day—was suddenly too much.

"Why are you being so nice to me?"

Theo actually looked shocked at her question. "Why shouldn't I be?"

Cailey was about to launch into a rather detailed explanation of exactly *why* this was all rather peculiar when he closed the space between them and put a finger to her lips.

"Cailey *mou*. I've always felt we had a connection, you and I. Don't you know that?"

She shook her head against his finger, fighting the urge to open her lips and draw it into her mouth. Any connection they'd had had been more master and servant than anything. She'd grown up working in his house. Scrubbing, cooking and cleaning alongside her mother, who had spent her entire adult life serving as the Nikolaides housekeeper.

Sure, she'd played with Erianthe when they were kids, and sometimes with Theo when he and his gang were in the mood to torture or tolerate his kid sister, but a *connection*…? She'd thought that kiss they'd shared all those years ago had been a dare. A cruel one at that. For it had been only a day later when she'd overheard him telling his friends he'd never marry a housemaid.

She was surprised to see him looking hurt. Genuinely hurt. Furrowed brow. Eyes narrowing. A sharp intake of breath. The whole caboodle.

"Not in the strictest sense," she whispered against his finger.

"We're peas in a pod. You must know that. And today, working together, wasn't that proof?"

"No. It only proves we work well together. Our lives…we're so different."

She wanted to hear him say it. Say he'd held himself apart from her because of her background. That he'd soared where she had failed even to get into medical school, let alone become a doctor.

"You *are* different from me," he said, lowering his head until his lips whispered against hers. "You're better."

Before she could craft a single lucid thought they were kissing. Softly at first. Not tentatively, as a pair of teenagers might have approached their first kiss, more as if each touch, each moment they were sharing, spoke to the fact that they had belonged together all along.

Simply kissing him was an erotic pleasure on its own. The short walk to Theo's house had given his lips a slight tang of the sea. Emboldened by his sure touch, Cailey swept her tongue along Theo's lower lip, a trill of excitement following in the wake of his moan of approbation.

The kisses grew in strength and depth. Theo pulled her closer to him, his lips parting to taste and explore her mouth. The hunger and fatigue they'd felt on leaving the clinic were swept into the dark shadows as light and energy grew within each of them like a living force of its own.

Undiluted sexual attraction flared hot and bright within her, the flames licking at her belly, her breasts, her inner thighs, as if it had been waiting for exactly this moment to present itself. Molten, age-old, pent-up, magically realized and released desire.

CHAPTER EIGHT

"COME, *KOUKLA MOU*."

Theo pulled one of the candles off its stand and took Cailey by the hand. He led her to a doorway on the far side of the living room, barely knowing where his energy was coming from. A stress release after such an intense day? A primal need to remind himself of his mortal ability to weather such an extreme act of nature?

Or was it something much more simple? Like fate?

He turned to her and released the riot of curls from the wooden hairclip barely managing to hold her inky black hair in place. She flushed and looked to the floor as silky waves cascaded around her shoulders.

"Are you sure this is what you want?" His voice sounded hoarse. A sure sign that his emotions had taken over.

She turned her head and gave looked at him askance. It was a look that said, *Are you?*

"*Thee mou*... I've thought about you—about this—all day. I just want you to be sure. If this is your first time—"

She cut him off with a shake of her head. "This isn't my first time. But..."

He swept his fingers along her face. "But what? You can talk to me, Cailey."

She looked him straight in the eye and said, "You're the first man I ever wanted."

Her words roiled through him like molten lava.

"Come here, you."

He tugged her to him, blood pounding through his veins, powering the need to taste, touch, taunt…and fulfil her every desire.

Cailey tutted playfully. "I've waited twenty-seven years for this…let's take it slow."

She pushed his hands down, then began with trembling fingers to unbutton his shirt.

He lifted her hands to his lips and kissed each of her fingertips. "Don't be scared. It's only me."

Her cheeks pinkened. "That's precisely why I'm shaking, you fool."

"I don't frighten you, do I?" He almost laughed at the absurdity of it.

"No." She shook her head. "It's how I *feel* about you that frightens me."

She looked so vulnerable the only thing he could do was pull her to him and whisper into her ear that she could trust him. He meant it, too. And couldn't imagine making the promise to anyone else.

"How do I know?"

He held her away, so he could look her straight in the eye as he said, "Because I feel exactly the same way as you do."

"What? Excited, terrified and itching to get naked all at once?"

He laughed softly. "That about captures it."

She tipped her head to the side, as if ascertaining

whether he meant it. "You're not quite who I thought you were, Theo Nikolaides."

"Oh? And who exactly *did* you think I was?"

She shook her head, "I'm not really sure anymore, but…" She lowered her lashes then opened her eyes with a teasing flash of a smile. "Do you think we should just go for it?"

"I think that's a most excellent idea." He laughed again, before weaving his fingers through hers. "Come on." He led her to the big sprawling bed he'd indulged himself with when he'd bought the place. "Let's spend as long as we need to get to know one another all over again."

She held her ground. "Sorry. Just one more little thing. Can we have a no-strings-attached rule? Like, what goes on at the earthquake…stays at the earthquake?"

"If you wish." He shot her a sidelong look. "Unless it's to keep this a secret from a boyfriend back in London?"

"No." She sucked in a quick breath. "No boyfriend. Just big brothers…and a mother who seems to find out everything anyhow and…well…your father."

"My father?" He barely recognized his own voice it had hollowed out so quickly. "What's *he* got to do with anything?"

"I don't really think he likes me."

"Well, I don't like *him* very much." The bastard. If he'd so much as said a single word to her…

Cailey's eyes widened. "Really?"

"Really."

He flicked a switch in his head. He didn't want to be talking about his father right now. Or anyone else, for that matter.

"C'mere, you." He pulled her over to the bed and straddled her before pressing his lips gently to hers. "What goes on at the earthquake…stays at the earthquake."

He took Cailey's hands and put them back on his chest as he dipped his lips to hers for another deep, erotically charged kiss. Feeling her breasts press up into his chest, her nipples taut with anticipation, sent a surge of blazing heat straight to his groin.

He gave the hem of her scrubs top a gentle tug. "May I?"

She nodded, her eyes sparkling in the candlelight.

He slowly lifted her top up and off her, his fingers lightly grazing the bands of lace cupping her breasts as he did so. By God she was beautiful. Olive skin. Full breasts. Dark nipples, taut and tempting.

He put the top on a chair by the bed and knelt in front of her. Unable to resist, he softly cupped her breasts, relishing the sensation of lace and warm skin as Cailey wove her fingers through his hair and tugged his head back for an urgent kiss.

Enough with the niceties, her kiss told him. *It's time to get down to business.*

All he could absorb in his overwrought brain was that he wanted more. To touch. Caress. Give her every ounce of pleasure he could.

He curved an arm around her waist and pulled her to him, his fingers cupping one of her breasts as he licked the other one through the gossamer lace barely containing it. He shifted the fabric to one side and gave her nipple a hot, wet lick. Her fingers dug into his hair again, giving him all the permission he needed to continue. Swirling, tasting, touching, caressing…

He forced himself to adopt a more luxurious pace, relishing the soft shudders of approbation as Cailey's body reeled and recovered from the erotic journey of his tongue and lips across her breasts, down to her belly. Shifting across her hips. Making the most of the luscious dips and curves along the way before lowering his lips to her waistline.

His fingers worked slowly, tauntingly, at the butterfly bow she'd tied in her scrub bottoms. Before releasing it, he encouraged her to lie back as he teased two of his fingers over the gently rounded surface of her belly, stopping only to draw in a deep breath of her skin. Vanilla? Or was it honey? The sweet and pure scent of olive oil? Enchantingly indescribable aromas all designed to drive a man wild. Drive *him* wild.

Centimeter by centimeter he lowered her scrubs…then her panties…adoring the shivers of excitement buzzing across her skin as he dropped kisses, little nips and licks, along the swoop from hip to hip and lower until she wove her fingers into his hair and cried out to be with him.

"Not yet. Not yet, *koukla mou.*" He spoke the words and his lips whispered against the delicate skin just above the thin strip of hair leading to the soft folds between her legs. "If you have waited this long, I want to make it worth it."

He thought he heard her say, "It already is!" and "Now!" but then her words melted into moans as he slipped his fingers between her legs and stroked the honeyed response to his caresses.

He was as fully erect as he had ever been, and sustaining this level of control was going to be a challenge, but she was worth it. Especially if it was true that she had wanted him all along…

* * *

Cailey felt drugged with pleasure as Theo slid his warm, assured hands between her legs and parted them.

She'd had sex before, but she was certain she had never been made love to. And they hadn't done anything much beyond kissing yet!

All the blood in her body surged and collected at the pulsing triangle between her legs as Theo cupped her buttocks in his hands and began to lick her. The level of pleasure he elicited was electrifying. She felt so sensual, so alluring—it was as if he was drawing an inner goddess out of her she'd never known existed. Each of his touches inflamed a deep-seeded pulse from her very essence that grew and hummed until she dug her nails into Theo's shoulders, pressed closer to his lapping tongue and cried out to him to let her release. She tried and failed to stem a wail of sheer ecstasy as her body tightened and arced as wave after wave of pleasure luxuriously swept throughout her body.

Theo held her tight to him after climbing up onto the bed alongside her. "Feeling better?"

"I was never feeling bad," she managed to murmur as she pressed herself to him, seized by the spirit of a tigress.

She'd forgotten he was still wearing clothes. Nerves completely eradicated, she swiftly undid his shirt buttons, then just as quickly unhooked and, in one extraordinary move, whipped off his belt. To their mutual astonishment she gave the length of leather a sharp crack before flinging it to the far side of the simply furnished room.

"My goodness, little one…" Theo said approvingly. "You're full of energy tonight."

Cailey moved her hands to his thick erection. "I'm hardly little, and it's not exactly as if you're running on empty. Shall we see what we can do for *you* now?" She gave the length of his shaft a playful lick.

Where did that come from?

She didn't do sexy talk. Or crack leather belts like a dominatrix. Or demand sex, for that matter.

Being with Theo was dangerous. On far too many levels. But at this exact moment she had no inhibitions— and no ability to stop herself from wanting more. She pushed him back on the bed and crawled on top of him, straddling him with a provocative twitch of her lips.

"Tell me, Doctor. Would you like to have your own turn?"

For a nanosecond he looked confused. When her hand began to stroke the velvet-soft length of his shaft the dawn of realization came quickly. He grinned, clearly amused at the she-woman he'd unleashed, and raised his hands in a move that said, *Do what you will. I'm yours for the taking.*

Cailey pressed herself up onto her hands and knees and swept her breasts along the smooth surface of Theo's well-defined chest. Not weight-lifter bulky…just strong and perfect. She gave each of his dark aureoles a lick and a quick suck before slowly working her way south.

When she first touched his erection with the tip of her tongue he inhaled sharply. When she took him in her mouth he cried out her name, fingers reaching out to touch her hair before falling helplessly to his sides as she had her wanton, wicked way with him. As his pleasure increased, so too did Cailey's. The two-way exchange of pleasure wasn't something she'd considered in all these years of wondering… Yes, she'd had sex before, but this felt different. Powerful. Captivating. Like an awakening.

A heated thrill thrummed to life in the very kernel of her femininity. Giving Theo pleasure was as erotic as receiving it. The more he responded to her touch, the more energized she became. The more she gave, the more he craved.

Abruptly Theo pressed himself up and pulled her alongside him. "I want you, Cailey. *Now.*"

His voice was urgent, full of longing. It was the most uninhibited she had ever seen him. Being the reason for it sent fresh ribbons of pleasure through her. In the clinic Theo was the picture of a man in control. Here, beneath her fingertips, he was vulnerable to her lightest touch. Power and protectiveness wove together as one as she kissed his neck, his throat, his lips.

"I want you," he said again as their mouths parted after another all-encompassing kiss.

There wasn't a single cell in her body capable of saying no. She'd imagined this moment for years…and the reality was light years better than any fantasy she had conjured.

"I'm all yours," she said, meaning each of the words with a totality that came from realizing she'd loved him all along. If this was her one chance to love and be loved she was going to take it. Even if it meant returning to London on her own, she'd have this moment locked in her heart as proof that for one night she had been everything he wanted.

Theo slipped an arm across her belly, then gently shifted her onto her back. "You're sure?" His green eyes were almost black in the flickering half-light the candle afforded them.

She'd barely finished saying yes before she felt the

tip of his shaft tease at the heated entrance to her womanhood. She parted her legs in response. Never before had she been so aroused.

Theo moved slowly at first. Teasing the tip of his erection in and out of her until she was nearly mad with euphoria and longing. And then he began to press into her more deeply, each penetration bringing with it another layer of fulfilling pleasure. It wasn't until she begged him that each measured stroke became lost in a shared desire to meet one another thrust for thrust. Restraint was abandoned. Her hips became fine-tuned to his untethered thrusts. Her hands wove tight round his neck, then shifted to his back as she wrapped her legs round him, wanting him to bury himself as deep within her as their longing would permit.

Their shared desire lifted them outside of human constraints and into a timeless eternity. When the rhythm of their lovemaking reached a mutual crescendo, as one they gave themselves to the all-consuming joy of a shared climax before collapsing in a weighted tangle of limbs and desire.

As their breathing began to steady Theo rolled off her, pulling her with him so that they were still joined together.

"My goodness, little one…" He dropped kisses on each of her cheeks and her forehead, "Welcome home."

Cailey gave him a deep kiss in return, then began to giggle as she slipped away from him so they could snuggle under the covers. "I have to admit this is not *quite* the homecoming I was expecting."

"You and me both," Theo teased, wrapping an arm around her shoulders and pulling her close to him so she was nestled against the warm, solid length of his body.

"Little Cailey Tomaras is all grown up." He swept a hand along her curves as if to prove it.

"Worth the wait?" she asked.

"And then some."

They lay for a moment in silence, their breathing leveling out, shifting into a cadence matching the susurration of the waves just beyond the bedroom windows.

"That's never happened to me before," Cailey said eventually.

"What? Getting hit on in the midst of a humanitarian crisis?"

"Well, that too." She giggled, still a bit shell-shocked at the dichotomy of the day. And how natural it all seemed.

Work hard. Love hard. *If* that was what this was. It was so easy to be with him. Intuitive, almost.

"I mean the…you know…" Shyness washed over her despite the raw intimacy they'd just shared. "The butterfly magic." She pulled her arm out from under the sheet and pointed to below her waist, whispering, *"Down there."*

Now it was Theo's turn to laugh. He pulled her closer to him and pressed a soft kiss on her forehead. "Is that what the cool kids are calling an orgasm these days?"

"Well, no. But for me it was…"

"Virgin territory?" he countered, a slightly incredulous tone in his playful voice.

"In a manner of speaking."

She looked away, slightly horrified that she'd brought it up at all. He was obviously experienced and she was a virtual neophyte. One boyfriend. A few rounds of terrible sex. She'd ended the relationship once she'd convinced herself that being alone was better than pretending she was loving it. Loving *him*.

In truth, no one had ever really stood a chance of winning her heart when—love him or hate him—it had always belonged to the tall, olive-skinned, unconventionally handsome doctor now lying naked as a statue of Adonis right next to her, lazily tracing his index finger along her collarbone.

"It's true." She decided to own her history. "This is the first time I've truly experienced pleasure during sex."

Theo propped himself up on his elbow, his mouth curving into a warm smile. "In which case, *koukla mou*... I am both honored and humbled to have brought you that pleasure."

She pressed a soft kiss on his lips, grateful he hadn't crowed about his prowess. But that wasn't the Theo she'd always been attracted to. *He* was truly a kind-hearted, generous man.

Raw emotion scratched at the back of her throat as she took on board the impermanence of what they had just shared. Sheer happenstance had brought them together today. Day-to-day life would surely push them apart. Not to mention his family.

Not wanting him to see her mood shift, she turned around so that they were spooning. Beyond the windows the stars sparkled brightly above the sea. She'd forgotten how clear the sky was here...how nourishing the sound of the waves could be.

She'd always dreamt of living close to the sea. On her mother's salary they'd never been able to afford it. At least her mum could see the Aegean now, from the small balcony of her flat.

Silver linings were everywhere, she reminded herself as Theo's arms tightened around her and eventually they drifted off to sleep as one.

CHAPTER NINE

CAILEY WOKE WARM and nestled in Theo's arms. The early dawn light that was so particular to the island was just reaching its tendrils through the windows, hinting at a sunny day ahead and then, a few moments later, promising one.

She shifted gently in his arms, relishing his scent, the feel of his skin, his...

Oh, no.

Oh, no, no, no, no, *no.*

Her eyes popped wide open as she realized what they had done last night. And more to the point what they hadn't.

Protection!

Years of medical training should have drilled into each of their heads that if they didn't want a baby they should use a condom.

Her skin turned clammy as instant panic took hold. She trawled her mental calendar to remember when she'd had her last period, where she was in her cycle. Her skin went prickly as she counted out the days to her peak fertility zone.

Out the blue she remembered a joke she'd heard someone tell in the maternity ward, when one of the nurses had asked another what you'd call couples who practiced the rhythm method.

The answer?

Gulp.

Parents.

Her mouth went dry as the Sahara as she slid herself as fluidly as she could out of Theo's embrace. She grabbed a pair of fresh scrubs from her backpack and tiptoed to the bathroom. Mercifully the earthquake hadn't affected the island's water supply.

Another aftershock might easily change that small mercy. Could another aftershock send her back in time and help her make better decisions?

She glanced back at Theo, all peaceful and perfect-looking.

Oh, no, no, no, no, no. This was very, *very* bad.

Work.

If she took a shower, downed a coffee...or seven... snuck past Theo and went to work she could get her head screwed on straight and think about what she should do in between the inevitable flow of sutures, bandage applications and blood pressure tests she'd be performing... alongside Theo...her boss.

"Hey, there, beautiful."

Cailey yelped in surprise and whirled around, hoping her mad morning hair and wild-eyed look would send him running for the hills. That way she could sort out this mess on her own and never have to admit she'd been—*they'd* been—so idiotic. Why she felt the need to protect him from any fallout was a bit strange, but then *life* was being strange at the moment.

"You're looking ready to take on the day."

Theo's morning grin was slow and lazy. Dreamy,

actually. If her stomach hadn't been full of a squad of high-octane piranhas it would have enjoyed the gentle swoop and swirl of butterflies.

How on earth was she going to tell him that they might have just made the most permanent, life-changing, baby-shaped oopsie?

"Want me to jump in the shower with you before we head back to Chaos Central? A little delicious morning escape before the storm?"

Um... Of course.

But it wasn't as if a bit of soap and water would help her forget the work that awaited them. Or the baby they might have made last night.

The brain knocking around in her skull was Chaos Central. Not to mention the heart pounding against her ribcage. The arterial pulse popping along the side of her throat.

Couldn't he see it? Didn't she look tachycardic or anything? Ashen? A bit breathless? Or was that the same thing as looking totally in lust for a guy she'd just gone Aphrodite over the night before?

He wove his fingers through her tangle of hair and gave her a soft kiss on the lips. "Mmm...morning breath."

"Theo, sorry, I just—"

"It's all right, *kouklamou*." He swept a finger under her chin and then popped it on the tip of her nose. "Good to know your only need is for a toothbrush and some toothpaste. That much I can do."

He turned to the bathroom, then threw her a grin and a wink.

"It's an airplane amenities bag, FYI. Not a Lothario's stash. Trust me—last night broke a long drought. But it was worth the wait," he quickly added with another kiss. "Absolutely worth it."

"Good. That's great. I mean, I have my own tooth-brush in my bag. It's just that—" Cailey tipped her head into her hands and drew a deep breath.

Just say it. Just say it, you idiot.

"You want a coffee?"

Theo's brow was furrowed. He was clearly not quite understanding why his invitation for a shower *à deux* should cause such consternation.

"No!" She squeaked, about an octave higher-pitched than she'd intended, and then she all but shouted, "I need the morning-after pill!"

A loud, insane buzzing took over in her brain. That wasn't strictly what she'd planned to say, or entirely what she'd *wanted* to say—but, hey…maybe Theo had always hoped and dreamed of a shotgun wedding with a bride whose stomach was the size of a watermelon. Not that she even knew if she was pregnant yet…

"Ohh-kaay…"

Theo clearly thought he was humoring a crazy woman—and then she saw him go through his own ver-sion of revisiting the night. His brow furrowed again. Eyes drifted up to the right. Fingers drummed along his chin.

It was easy enough to see the wheels turning behind those beautiful green eyes of his. Narrowing at first, then widening. *Not good.* A flash of something dark and dan-gerous swept across the bright spheres, leaving them a shade darker than forest-green in its wake. A flash that read: *This wasn't meant to happen.* Rapidly followed by, *This is definitely not going to happen.* Not on his watch.

What a fool she'd been. To let herself get swept away

like Cinderella at the ball only to realize princes didn't go for girls who rode to parties in pumpkin carriages.

A coolness overtook Theo's entire demeanor and it chilled her to the bone. *This* was the Theo she'd been expecting to see after all these years. The one she'd deluded herself into thinking had been a figment of her imagination.

"Right. Fine. That's what you want to do? Not a problem."

His voice was clipped. All business.

If there was a way to feel invisible and yet like the elephant in the room all at once, Cailey was certainly experiencing it right now.

"Well, it's not exactly what I *want* to do," she snapped. It wasn't like she'd made love to *herself* or anything. "It's just the first thing I thought of."

"Aren't you *on* anything?"

She shook her head. "Like I said, jumping into other people's beds isn't really my *modus operandi*."

"What? You think it's mine?"

She shrugged. "Maybe. What do I know?"

Her insecurities leapt to the fore and against her better judgment her entire body became a hot shield of defensiveness.

"Lately you haven't been the regular player on the society pages you once were. Forced to slum it with the local talent these days, Theo? Is *that* what's got you so het-up? That you went low-rent?"

Theo started to say something, then stopped himself. "Fighting about this isn't going to fix anything," he said instead.

Everything in her crumbled. He hadn't denied it.

Hadn't said anything to convince her she wasn't just common riff-raff to him.

It took all her power to maintain eye contact. "So, what do you suggest we do?"

"Are you sure you're all right with taking the morning-after pill?"

His tone spoke volumes. He wasn't asking the question because he thought it was a bad idea.

She nodded, still clutching her clothes to her naked body. About as exposed and vulnerable as it got. It certainly wasn't the way she'd wanted to have this conversation. Not that she'd wanted to have this conversation in the first place!

She didn't really know if she wanted to take the pill. But she *did* know she was absolutely not going to corner Theo into anything he didn't want. It wasn't as if he was jumping up and down for joy, plucking names out of the ether for their unborn child.

"Absolutely. Not a problem." She kept nodding, as if her neck had turned into a spring. "I'll just jump in the shower, shall I? Then get down to the clinic."

"You'll need me to prescribe it for you."

His voice sounded like cold steel. And there was no meeting her gaze. His eyes looked past her intently, as if she were no longer the woman he'd murmured sweet nothings to all night.

Ha! Those sweet nothings were exactly that. Intangible bits of fluff as useful as a dust mote.

She fought the sting of tears at the back of her throat, silently waiting for the follow-up. The accusation that although she clearly thought she'd risen a rank after her time in London, back here on Mythelios a Nikolaides was still in one league and a Tomaras was decidedly lower.

When none came she slunk off to the shower and scrubbed herself to within an inch of her life, wrestling with an internal tennis match of recriminations.

Why had she come here in the first place? Why hadn't she just stayed with her mum? The sofa wasn't that bad. Besides, her family were the ones who had always been there for her. Helped her find ways to fight her dyslexia. Found the fees for nursing school. English lessons. Private tutors. And yet here she was, years later, still following Theo round like a lovelorn duckling, kidding herself that she was doing it to help her family.

A curl of disgust at her own behavior snapped against her conscience, leaving a vivid mark. She'd done it again. Let her feelings for Theo override her pride. Her dignity.

After her shower she toweled off quickly and pulled on scrubs and trainers, desperate to run to the clinic and get to work—help out as much as she could until the crisis had abated and then hightail it straight back to London, where life as a celibate was looking pretty fine to her right about now.

When she opened the blue wooden bathroom door Theo was leaning against the wall, a towel wrapped round his waist, a steaming cup of coffee in his hand. Thick and dark—the way real Greeks liked it. Her mouth watered. And it wasn't for the coffee. Was this just an additional splash of torture? Showing her what she couldn't have anymore?

He looked up, his expression a mix of contrition and agitation. *Damn*, he was beautiful.

"I was a bit of an ass." He handed her the coffee.

"I didn't want to be the one to say it," she managed,

in as light a voice as she could conjure. The last thing she'd been expecting was an apology. If that was what this was.

She accepted the cup and took a grateful gulp of the inky black coffee. Mmm, she'd missed this. She'd missed *him*.

"I should've sorted out protection last night. Things just got…"

"A bit weird?"

"A bit *wild*," he corrected, the corners of his mouth twitching against a smile. "This whole…" he waved a finger between the pair of them "…whatever it was… *is*…it's uncharted territory for me. And it's certainly not 'slumming it,' as you so elegantly put it." His voice took on an edge. "Don't treat yourself that way, Cailey. It's not how I think of you and it certainly isn't how you should think about yourself."

His admonishment silenced her. Just as well, considering he was sucking in another breath for part two.

"The point is, however great last night was, children are definitely not on the cards for me—and I'm guessing they're not for you either, with your big-city lifestyle. You're focusing on your career. I'm trying to keep the clinic afloat. So…" He gave his hands one of those *here-goes-nothing* claps. "We'll get you the pill and everything'll be sorted. By tonight it'll be as if the whole thing never happened."

He gave her a solid nod, as if that was the end of that. Something in her bridled. As if it had *never happened*? Seriously? *That* was how much last night had meant to him?

What a Class-A wazzock he was being—as one of the nurses in London liked to say. She wasn't a hundred percent sure what it meant, but it didn't sound good. Not that *she* was much better, though.

She was an idiot to have thought last night was anything other than just a life-affirming connection in the wake of a crisis. Sure, they'd both worked their guts out. And, yes, working together had been as organic as if they'd been doing it all their lives. But she was the only one who had dreamt of being with Theo. That much was clear.

He wanted to forget all about it? *Fine*. Two could play at that game.

"Thanks so much for the coffee," she said with a saccharine smile. "It was lovely."

She took a step forward, a bit annoyed there wasn't enough room in the corridor to swish past him. There wasn't a chance in hell—or on earth either, for that matter—that she was going to cry in front of him.

"Glad you liked it."

Theo put his mug down on a small table and clapped his hands on her shoulders. It wasn't sexy. Definitely more older brother to kid sister than lover to lover.

Why couldn't he just move, so she could finally exhale the epic sigh trapped in her lungs?

The little flicker of hope he'd lit when he'd appeared with the coffee and a sort of apology was completely and utterly tamped out. It had been one night. One amazing, sensual, madcap, lusty night, to be lodged in her memory banks forever.

"We'll sort this out at the clinic, yeah? I'll meet you there in ten…maybe twenty minutes. I have a couple of phone calls I'd like to make beforehand. Just introduce yourself to whoever's on duty and they'll sort you out.

I'm sure the overnight crews will be desperate to get some sleep."

She stared at him. Really? That was it? *Thanks for the sex, glad you liked your coffee, now beat it*?

He blinked, then looked away.

Oh, yeah. That flicker of hope was well and truly extinguished. He was probably going to call Dimitri. Get him to call out the cavalry to herd her off the island.

She turned on her heel and left. No chance, no way, no how was she going to let Theo Nikolaides crush her heart all over again. She was going to go back to that clinic and show him what he was really missing.

Then she'd leave. On *her* terms.

"Cailey!"

Theo called out her name a second time, but the heavy slam of the door drowned out his voice.

Fix it, man! Bloody *fix* it.

He punched the wall, instantly regretting it. What the hell was a fist going to do to a wall that had withstood a few centuries, not to mention an epic earthquake? And since when did he take things out on stationary objects?

What a terrible mess.

He liked Cailey. Always had. Seeing her again had reawoken something in him he'd never really put a name to. Something beyond desire.

He scrubbed a hand through his hair. What an idiot. For a doctor he really could be oblivious sometimes. From the moment she'd appeared at the clinic it was if... as if he'd been made whole.

Typical.

The answer both to his dreams and his worst ever

nightmare was all wrapped up in the same dark-eyed, black-haired, sensual, kind-hearted package.

He'd handled things with Cailey about as well as he'd handled Dimitri push had come to shove. The day he'd told his adoptive father he'd have to make a choice. Show him some respect or face the consequences.

He'd well and truly thought Dimitri would choose the latter.

That showdown had been the single most terrifying and empowering moment of his life.

He pressed his thumbs to his eyes as if it would erase the memories, but until he drew his last breath he would remember each second of that day to within a particle of its essence.

His sister had just been unceremoniously shipped off to boarding school in England and tensions had been simmering between him and his father ever since.

"Why not just man up and do what you've been bred to do?" his father had roared when Theo had come to him with a proposal.

"What? Like a stallion?" Theo had retorted, drawing himself to the fullest height his nineteen-year-old self had allowed. "A bull? Is *that* why you pulled me off the streets? To ensure the Nikolaides line continues exactly as you imagine? Three-piece suits, an heiress of your choice for a bride and lording it over the rest of Mythelios as if I were amongst the Chosen Ones?"

He'd run his eyes the length of his father, unable to conceal his contempt.

"Not a chance in hell."

His father's eyes had narrowed and crackled with a deep anger Theo had never seen flare so bright. This fight wasn't their usual flare-up over some trivial social gaffe—Theo wearing the wrong outfit, saying the wrong thing, shaking the wrong hand, pouring the wrong cocktail. This one had begun over the dream Theo had shared with his best mates: to become an island doctor at a clinic they would create to fill the void now the state-run hospital had reluctantly closed its doors.

He'd thought he'd made all the right steps. He'd had perfect grades. The best manners. And, as his father had hoped, Theo had forged deep and lasting friendships with the sons of Dimitri's business partners...the four men who'd had an idea for a local Greek shipping company and turned it into a global phenomenon: Mopaxeni Shipping.

Their wealth had surpassed all their expectations. But it hadn't changed who they were at heart—and that day Theo had learned who his adopted father really was.

A man so fearful of losing his status he would go to any limits to keep it. He'd grown up poor. He'd known hunger. He'd known loss. He'd endured fear and pain. And he'd vowed never to feel any of those things ever again.

Being forced to adopt a child had been a critical blow to his ego. A virile, powerful man, unable to impregnate his own wife? A billionaire powerless to have a son of his own?

He'd solved the problem by literally buying Theo from an orphanage. Money meant privacy. No paper trail to expose Dimitri's one weak point.

And then had come Erianthe. The miracle baby. Perhaps his adoptive mother had felt less stress to "produce" after they'd adopted Theo. Perhaps Dimitri had. Either way—they'd had their own child and Dimitri had never lost an opportunity to remind Theo of just how lucky he'd been to be adopted by a wealthy man.

When Theo had asked to use his trust fund to establish the Mythelios Free Clinic his father had actually laughed.

"That's no sort of business," he'd howled, virtually wiping away tears of disbelief. "You *do* understand what the word 'non-profit' means, don't you, Theo?"

"I understand that Mythelios has no physician. No hospital."

"No son of *mine* will become a common island doctor. It's no better than being a vegetable merchant or a mechanic!"

"And what's wrong with that?" Theo had countered. "Who fixes your car when it breaks? Who feeds you? Who grows the food you eat? Clothes you? Cleans your house? *People!* Living, breathing people, with hearts beating in their chests!"

"What do I care for other people's hearts?"

"Nothing, from what I can see!" Theo had spat in response.

His father had moved as if to hit him.

Theo had caught his wrist tight and said, in no uncertain terms, "If you continue down this path, one by one the people of Mythelios will come forward and tell you to your face just how little they respect you."

"The people of Mythelios *do* respect me." Dimitri had growled, his fist still encased in his son's palm. If there was one thing Dimitri prized more than money it was respect.

"*Do* they?" Theo had dropped his hold. "You can't *buy* respect. Or loyalty. Those things have to be earned. Tell me...was it Spiro, a humble plumber, who became mayor, or you? What about the island's public service awards? Are any of those plaques hanging on *your* walls?"

The questions were rhetorical and they both knew it.

His father had turned white with rage. So Theo had reached out an olive branch. The point of their discussion hadn't been for his father to suffer. He'd just wanted Dimitri to feel compassion. Some innate empathy for those less driven to increase his bank account. But more than anything he'd wanted the man who had given him so many opportunities to be proud of the path he'd chosen.

"Funding a clinic to help people who began life just as you did—with only the dreams in their hearts—would go a long way to improving that precious public image of yours," Theo had declared.

So they'd agreed.

Once Theo was qualified Dimitri would give him the money to start up the clinic, and in turn Theo would laud his father for his largesse. After that Theo's trust fund—and those of his three friends—would be enough to keep it going. In short, it would be a business agreement disguised as familial love—and it had worked, even if Theo had thrown every penny he had at it, leaving little over for himself.

The jangle of Theo's phone broke through the wash of memories threatening to consume him. He pulled the handset out of the trousers he'd discarded the night before and stared at the screen.

Erianthe. She had a second sense, that one. Always knew when he needed a dose of real love. Loving his sister seemed to be the only thing that came naturally to him. Maybe because it had always been protective. Protecting her from Dimitri's rages. From her own tempestuous ways. Boarding school seemed to have done the same thing to her as it had to him. Focused her drive and ambition.

"Eri *mou*!"

"Hey, big brother. How's my island? Still holding together with sticky tape and a bit of elbow grease?"

Despite himself, he laughed. She'd called yesterday and asked the exact same thing. It wasn't entitlement in her case. It was her heart. She was a true Mythelonian. So he repeated what he'd said yesterday. "We're managing. Stay where you are and finish getting that medical degree. *Then* you're allowed to come home."

"Thanks, Mr. Bossy."

"Hey! Big brother knows best." He tried to tack on a laugh, but he wasn't feeling it. Not today. He just felt… bossy.

"It feels pathetic to stay here while you're shouldering the load," Erianthe play-protested. She knew she was just a couple of months away from getting her specialist degree. Dropping it now would be a fool's errand.

"Don't worry. The lads are coming in soon."

He looked round for his coffee mug, found it and took a fortifying swig, relieved to be able to think about work again. Much safer territory.

"All of them?"

He thought he heard a note of anxiety in her voice but dismissed it. With him, she was a straight talker. If she wanted to ask something, she asked.

"Yup. We've got quite a few relief doctors in from Athens until they can come. Chris is coming as soon as his contract ends. Two or three weeks from now. Deakin…not sure, exactly. I think he's stuck in New York for a couple of months but he has promised to do a stint."

"Anyone else?" Her voice was quiet and a little strange.

"Not sure. I've been trying to get hold of Ares, but you know him. International Man of Mystery and Medicine. I can't locate him. I think he might be in Africa somewhere, but he tends to be where mobile telephone signals are *not*."

"Oh. Good. Fine."

Now her voice sounded strangely bright. Since she'd passed through her teens Erianthe didn't really *do* emotional, so the happier she sounded, the more worried she usually was.

"It *is* fine, sis. Everyone's fine. Why did you ring?"

"Just to check up. I tried talking with Mum and Dad and that went about as well as expected."

Theo huffed a mirthless laugh. "I heard he had his driver take him on a tour of the destruction yesterday. Still haven't heard if he plans to help anyone."

"I thought that was *your* job?" Erianthe parried.

Yes. Well. He supposed it was. Dimitri earned the money. Theo wrestled some of it out of him to do good. That was how they rolled. One big happy do-gooding family.

"Hey! You'll never guess who turned up yesterday." Now it was *his* turn to sound unnaturally chit-chatty. "Cailey Tomaras."

"Cailey?" Erianthe whooped. "That's great. I haven't heard from her in years. Is she well?"

"Didn't you two stay in touch while you were at boarding school?"

"Nope."

"Why not?"

"Dad."

Ah. Enough said, he thought with a mental eye-roll. Dad's money, Dad's rules.

"How is she?" Erianthe asked. "Did she ever get into med school?"

"Med school? No. She's a nurse. Neonatal. She works in some fancy maternity hospital in London."

"Oh. I never realized she was so close or I would have got in touch. But that's funny... She always told me she wanted to be a doctor. Guess she got smart and figured out a much faster route to helping people was to become a nurse."

"Not long now and you'll be doing just the same, Eri."

He smiled as his sister gave a melodramatic sigh. "I know... I just wish... I just wish I was there now with you. Helping."

"You will be. Soon. Now hang up the phone and let me get to work, okay?"

"Okay. Love you."

"Love you, too."

He stared at the phone as he disconnected the call, wondering if he'd ever hear those words from his father.

Maybe not.

Just as he'd never say the words to a child of his own. Too much history to inflict on an innocent. Too many conditions.

He stopped himself punching the wall again. He hated that what had happened between Cailey and him had been slashed in two by a foolish oversight. Chances were slim to nil she'd ever want to speak with him again.

But perhaps it was best to have it all nipped in the bud now. The day he'd bullied that money from Dimitri was the day he'd vowed never to trust himself as a father. And Cailey deserved to live the life she wanted. Not walk the tightrope of conditional love he'd chosen for himself.

CHAPTER TEN

"HELENA FAIRFAX?" CAILEY called out the name, scanning the crowd for a hint of recognition. Though it was still early morning, the crowd at the clinic had grown.

"Here!" an English voice called out, and Cailey caught sight of a hand waving above the sea of heads clustered in the reception area. "Here, it's me!"

The crowd shifted and moved as the woman worked her way forward. Cailey had to stop herself from gawping when the woman emerged from the crowd.

"Mrs. Fairfax?"

The woman nodded, gingerly holding a barbecue fork inside her mouth…its tines visible on the outside of her cheek, "Dat's me!" Incredibly, she managed to smile. "I didn't know if I should try to pull it out," she mumbled around the utensil. "Thought I might leave that bit to you."

For all of the things she *didn't* love about the British, Cailey certainly loved their pluck! She didn't think *she'd* be smiling under the same set of circumstances.

"Good. Smart thinking." Cailey held her arms wide to show Helena where to go. "Let's take a look at that in an exam room, shall we?"

"I see you've begun without me."

Cailey's spine shot ramrod-straight at the sound of Theo's voice. *Terrific.* Just what she needed. Theo's presence had felt reassuring yesterday. And now, just a few hours of lovemaking later, it felt…really, really unnerving. He boss. She underling. He man… She frail woman who just might be pregnant.

How could he sound so…so calm, cool and collected after what had happened?

She might be carrying his child, for heaven's sake! Okay. So it wasn't a baby just yet. Biologically speaking she knew that would take a day or so…or maybe not happen at all…but—

"Nurse Tomaras? Any chance you're going to take Mrs. Fairfax into an exam room?"

"Why, yes…" she ground out.

So it was *Nurse Tomaras* now, was it?

"There most certainly is, *Dr.* Nikolaides." She smiled warmly at Helena. "Please. Do follow me."

She showed her to a curtained area at the far end of the bustling clinic and settled Helena onto the exam table before pulling a bright light round—all of which she did without giving "Dr. Nikolaides" so much as a glance.

Puncture wounds were mostly tricky if they were near organs or key arteries. Luckily the cheek was a relatively safe area in so far as acute damage was concerned.

Cailey snapped on a pair of hygienic gloves hard enough to sting, which served only to irritate her more as she pulled up a wheelie stool to take a better look. She glanced at Theo, who had just finished pulling the curtains around the cubicle.

"I'm just taking a look. Unless you'd like to examine the patient first, *Doctor*?"

"Um…" Helena flicked her eyes between the pair. "Is everything all right between you two?"

"Perfect!"

"Couldn't be better."

They glared at one another as their words overlapped.

Cailey knew she shouldn't be angry. Taking the morning-after pill was a perfectly acceptable solution to their dilemma—she just wished he hadn't gone so… so Robot Man on her. It wasn't as if she'd been trying to trap him, or anything.

Sternly she reminded herself that she shouldn't put words in his mouth. He hadn't said anything of the sort. He'd been perfectly civil.

"Would you *like* me to take a look?" he asked, more mildly.

She glared him again, and then pushed her stool backwards. It wasn't as if she had a vast amount of experience in pulling barbecue forks out of women's faces.

Theo put his hands on his knees, readjusted the light and took a look. "Well, the good news is it doesn't look like there's any structural damage to your cheek. Puncture wounds, if kept clean, are pretty good healers, so you won't need stitches. But before— Whoops!"

The wheels of the supplies trolley Cailey had been preparing started to slide across the floor as another aftershock hit.

"No!"

Theo was falling toward Helena and Cailey leapt behind him and pulled him back, furious with herself for enjoying the feeling of his tight bum pressed against her. Last night she would have given her hips a bit of a shift and grind. If there wasn't a patient in front of him now…

"Oops!"

Cailey lost her balance and Helena yelped as Theo's hand bumped against the fork handle as the aftershock sent the pair of them tumbling to the floor.

"Sorry! *Sorry!* Aftershock."

Cailey scrambled to her feet, cheeks streaked pink with embarrassment. She'd landed right on top of Theo and for a split second had considered kissing his Adam's apple.

Helena rolled her eyes. The woman was clearly made of stern stuff. Or else she thought the two of them were completely insane.

After Theo had levered himself back up and shot Cailey a peculiar look, he moved the light again and took a good look. "I heard on the way in they're going to get the electricity back on soon, so you won't have to barbecue your breakfast for much longer."

Even Cailey laughed at that. Staying grumpy around a man who embodied the word *congenial* was tough. Not to mention a man who was funny, kind, an excellent doctor and stupidly gorgeous.

But other than that…? Total. Jerk.

"Thank you so much, Dr. Nikolaides. You're a star."

And he had been. After a numbing agent haad been administered in one swift, effortless move he had released the fork.

Helena didn't mention the exacting care with which Cailey had applied the small bandage over the two perfect tine marks. It was all, Theo, Theo, Theo.

"Serves me right for being such a greedy cow!" Helena laughed. Flirtatiously. As if she wasn't married. Which she clearly was. A rock the size of marble flashed on her finger.

Theo, who was washing his hands at the sink, shot the patient an amused look. "Oh?"

"There was a bit of sausage left on the fork and I decided I'd gobble it up before my husband and the boys saw it, but then an aftershock hit. *Ooh!*" She gingerly pressed her hand to her cheek. "Talking too much should probably be off the menu."

"Right, *Mrs.* Fairfax." Cailey indicated that she could get off the exam table. "Take the bandage off after half an hour or so. It's just there to catch anything we haven't managed to tidy up. I know it seems counterintuitive, but it's actually better for puncture wounds to let them breathe."

"Nothing like the fresh salty air of Mythelios to help heal me!"

"Is this your first time here?" Theo asked, clearly enjoying his patient's obvious coquettish looks.

You'd think he would be a bit more concerned about the queue of patients waiting out there.

"Not at all. We're from Britain," she said, in her cut-glass accent. "Obviously."

"Not tempted to go home, given the quake?"

"Not yet! We've got a jolly good tale to take home. This place is like a second home to us. Been coming for years. My husband and I had our first…well…" She feigned embarrassment, fluttered her lashes, then lowered her voice to a sultry bedroom tone. "We had our first proper assignation here."

Cailey's cheeks instantly flared with heat. Good grief! They'd asked for the woman's medical history, not a blow-by-blow account of her sex life!

"The island does that to people," Theo replied factually, before latching eyes with Cailey.

Her heart skipped a beat. *Maybe...*

"All right then, Mrs. Fairfax." Theo returned his attention to the patient. "Do let us know if the wound starts to feel anything out of the ordinary. Heat. Tingling. You'll want to do your best to prevent infection. But we like to try and avoid antibiotics if we can."

"Oh! Heavens. Don't worry about anything like that. I'll keep it clean. Do a little saltwater gargle every few hours or so. Ta-ta for now!"

And with that she scooped up her handbag, swirled past the curtains and was gone.

"Right, then, Nurse Tomaras." Theo closed the door behind him and turned around to face her.

"Please don't call me that." Cailey scowled. "I think it's probably fair to suggest we're on a first-name basis by now."

He arched an eyebrow at her.

She tried to arch one back and failed, so turned around and started cleaning up everything from Mrs. Fairfax's treatment instead.

Cleaning, her mother had always insisted, was a cure-all.

"Cailey. Can you stop that for a minute?"

"Not really, no. It needs to be tidied and there are loads of patients out there waiting. Maybe you can make yourself useful by asking Petra who's up next?"

"Not until you stop disinfecting everything in sight and look at me."

He wasn't enjoying this any more than she was. And probably found talking about it twice as hard.

She pointedly laid down the spray bottle and shoved

the paper toweling she'd been using into the bin, put her hands on her hips and gave him her best attentive face.

"I thought you might want this." He dug into his pocket and pulled out the single tablet encased in garish bright orange plastic packaging. "Subtle, huh?"

He laughed, but his words fell between them like lead. It wasn't funny. And he wasn't handling this well. Surprise, surprise. His bedside manner only seemed to come to him when a patient was actually a patient.

Cailey's hand snapped out to grab the packet.

He held it up out of her reach.

"Seriously? C'mon, Theo. Just hand it over."

"You don't look very happy about it."

"I'm not."

"Why not?"

"It's just…it…" She huffed out an exasperated sigh. "It's hardly the stuff of romance, is it?"

"So it's a lack of romance that you're worried about rather than having a baby?"

Nice one, mate. Way to show Cailey support.

"So far, according to my humble nursing classes, there *is* no baby. This little pill will just make certain of it."

She snatched the orange rectangle from him, stuffed it in her pocket and looked up at him with defiance written across her features.

"Happy? Can I get back to work now?"

"No. And no. Not until we talk about this."

"What's there to talk about?" she whispered angrily. "We had a one-night stand. It was just about the sexiest thing that's ever happened to me in my entire life and now it's over. So, if you would kindly leave me to it, *Dr.*

Nikolaides, there's a rather large crowd gathered outside hoping for some medical treatment."

"Cailey, if you don't want to take that pill, don't take it."

Her hands shifted from balled-up fists on her hips to a protective criss-crossing over her chest.

"And what? You'll suddenly discover a deep-seated desire for a picket fence lifestyle and become a father to a baby we don't even know exists? Yeah. I don't think so."

Her entire body radiated defensiveness. A reaction, no doubt, to his clinical approach—which was only making this bad situation about a thousand times worse.

"You're right." He forced himself to keep his voice low and steady. His father's would be up at about nine decibels by now.

The cubicle curtain was hardly soundproof, and if there was one thing he valued it was privacy. Honesty was on a par with that.

"If you'll forgive my bluntness, a child is the last thing I want. Cailey— Oh, please don't cry…here."

He pulled a tissue out of the box on the supplies trolley and handed it to her. He should pull her to him. Hold her until the tears stopped. Kiss her until the fear abated. But he wasn't built that way. Wasn't equipped to absorb her fears. Stark evidence, if he needed any, that he didn't have what it took to be a father.

But he wasn't having her run out into the clinic with tears pouring down her face either. Facing up to his father had, at the very least, given him the courage to face situations head-on.

He tipped his head toward the exam table. "C'mon. Take a seat."

"There are *patients* waiting, Doctor," Cailey growled, swiping furiously at the tears escaping from her eyes.

"Yes. And they're going to have to wait for two more minutes. The trauma team is fully staffed. *You're* what's important right now."

She shot him a dubious look as she hoisted herself up onto the exam table. "And how exactly do you come to that conclusion, Dr. Nikolaides?"

"Well, *Cailey*…as you noted earlier, I think we're on an intimate enough basis that we can go with first names from here on out—yes?"

She nodded and reached across to grab more tissues, but not before throwing him another dark look.

"Right." He sat on the exam table beside her. "I think we can both agree neither of us is happy with this solution." He pointed to the pocket where she'd put the pill.

"Look who got the high scores in med school!" Cailey poked him in the thigh with an index finger.

He took solace from her stab at black humor. "I work all the time. Your life is in London. So, I think we can also agree we're not really in the best place to have a baby."

"Just like that?"

She didn't want *a child now, did she?*

"I thought you wanted to focus on your career. That sort of commitment takes time. Time you won't have if you have a child."

"We don't even know if I'm pregnant yet, Theo!"

"So what are you saying? Do you want to wait and find out if you are and *then* make a decision?"

"No." There wasn't the slightest hint of a waver in her answer.

"What, then? Tell me what you want."

She glared at him, her face a picture of resilience and strength—before her features crumbled and a solitary tear snaked down her cheek.

"Just… I'll take the pill and in a few days, when you don't need me anymore—when the *clinic* doesn't need me anymore—I'll go back to my 'big-city life', as you call it, and you'll never have to think about me again."

"Cailey. *Koukla mou.*" He swept away the tear with the pad of his thumb. "That would be impossible."

She sniffed and batted his hands away. "It's not exactly as if you're offering a red carpet invitation to stay on the island and see what would happen if—" She sucked in a big breath and pressed her fist to her mouth.

"If what?"

She shook her head. She wasn't going to answer, but instinct allowed him to fill in the blanks. She meant see what would happen between them if she lived here. If they dated. If they went about their lives like all sorts of other young couples did—exploring the possibilities of love.

Damn. This was one area he couldn't go.

His phone buzzed in his pocket. He tugged it out and looked at the screen. A message from his father.

Dinner. Tonight. Nine p.m.

Typical Dimitri message. Commands. All the man did was tell people what to do.

Precisely what he *was doing with Cailey.*

"Why don't you sleep on it?"

"What?" Cailey looked at him as if he'd just pulled magic pine cones out of his ears.

"Sleep on it. You have time." He took her hand in his. "*We* have time."

Her palm lay limp in his and she said nothing, so he continued.

"You can take the pill anytime in the next seventy-two hours. That gives you—"

"Three days," Cailey completed for him. "I know. I may not be a doctor, but even a nurse knows how this medicine works."

Theo's eyes widened. "I wasn't suggesting—"

"Yeah. I know. A good nurse is like gold dust," she recited in a monotone voice as she gave her hair a shake, pulled an elastic band out of her pocket and bundled her curls into submission.

"Cailey." He bent down and picked up the pill packet that had fallen out of her pocket when she'd retrieved her hairband. When he handed it to her again their eyes caught and locked tight. A jolt of invisible electricity crackled between them as their fingers touched.

He closed his eyes against it and sighed. What a mess. If only he'd been raised by a normal, loving family he might have the skills to deal with this better. Or if Cailey were a patient... Patients were easy. In the door—out the door. A few minutes of understanding, advising and then they were gone. Nothing personal...nothing lasting.

When he opened his eyes again Cailey's entire demeanor had turned prickly again.

"So..." She pushed the packet back into her pocket and straightened her scrubs top. "What do we do in between?"

"You mean for the next seventy-hours? Well... We could behave like ten-year-olds and pretend we don't know each other, or we could just carry on as we did yesterday."

Cailey's eyes widened.

"Working together."

"Ah. Yes. Good. And I'm totally looking forward to sleeping on my mum's sofa."

"There's always my spare room—"

"Nope! *No*. No, thank you. I am all about the sofa." She gave him a grim smile and hopped off the exam table.

A wave of protectiveness swept through him. As insane as it seemed, this scare made him want to spend *more* time with her, not less. And yet he knew intimacy, love without conditions, selflessness...those weren't skills he had in his arsenal.

He got down off the exam table too, and did a few boxing moves. Cailey's bewildered expression had told him all he needed to know. Handling anything more intimate than a one-night stand was definitely *not* his forte.

"We're in this together, right, buddy?" he said. *Buddy?*

"Yeah..." Cailey took a step back, grabbed her stethoscope from the supplies tray and yoked it round her neck. "Whatever you say, Doctor."

Then she whipped open the cubicle curtain and headed to Reception to find their next patient.

CHAPTER ELEVEN

"YOU SURE YOU'VE had enough to eat?"

Cailey pulled her mother into a tight hug. "Yes, Mama. I've had enough for two!"

The second the words were out of her mouth she realized just how right she might be.

The pill.

It was two weeks since Theo had given it to her… and she had completely forgotten to take it. No doubt he assumed she'd done the sensible thing and had taken it.

It seemed sheer madness that something so huge had simply slipped her mind. She hadn't thought of anything else for the first couple of days. Each time it had popped into her mind she'd tried to reasonably weigh out the pros and cons. Then the enormity of the decision would begin to engulf any sort of common sense she had, so she'd give herself a couple more hours to think about it.

She'd decided to prioritize. The first thing she needed to do was block Theo from her radar. Forcing herself to remember the day Dimitri Nikolaides had made it more than clear that she would never be good enough for his son was all she'd needed to do to start burying her feelings for him. She'd done it once, she reasoned, and she could do it again.

But last time she hadn't made love to him. Last time there hadn't been the slightest chance she was carrying his child.

Oh, no, no, no. This wasn't happening. This couldn't be happening!

Things had been so busy at the clinic she'd barely seen Theo, let alone spoken to him. And the doctor she'd been working with instead, Alex Balaban, had proved to be a much-needed distraction from her problems. He worked at a teaching hospital in Athens, and clearly loved sharing his years of experience with anyone who would listen—unlike many of the doctors she'd encountered, who thought nurses were merely there to tidy up and wipe away a patient's tears.

Dr. Balaban had sensed her eagerness to learn and over the past two weeks…had it been a *fortnight* already?… Cailey had been completely consumed with learning, helping, and caring for each of the patients who came through the clinic doors. If Theo didn't want her, the patients certainly did.

Popo! How *could* she have forgotten something so important?

"Cailey *mou*! My love. Let your mother breathe!"

Cailey instantly dropped her arms, whipped around and grabbed her backpack off the freshly tidied sofa. She made a big show of finding her trainers, getting just the right pair of socks. *Busy.* She needed to keep busy until she could wrap her head around this.

"Do you want me to do some laundry for you today?" her mother asked, in a voice that actually meant, *What are you hiding from me?*

She could feel her mother's eyes burning holes in the back of her head. Or perhaps it was her own guilt for keeping something so huge from her mother. Not that her mother had questioned Cailey when she'd told her she'd decided the sofa was fine, as Theo was now hosting a load of the visiting doctors from Athens at his house.

She'd raised a dubious eyebrow but she hadn't pressed. Softly, softly was her mother's technique, and usually…always…it worked in the end.

"No, Mama. That's fine. I'll do it when I get home. To London," she qualified.

"What? Leaving so soon?"

The fact that she hadn't jumped on a plane the same day Theo had handed her the morning-after pill had been a minor miracle, but things had truly been busy at the clinic, and when she'd suggested she assist one of the out-of-town doctors, seeing as she knew most of the locals, Theo had put up scant resistance.

"Things are slowing down at the clinic. I think some of the volunteers from Athens will be heading back soon. I'm sure they don't need a lowly nurse clogging things up once the Mopaxeni lads start coming in."

"Cailey!"

Her mother's tone was so sharp she turned to face her.

"Don't you *dare* speak of your achievements in that way."

"Being a nurse wasn't exactly my original plan, though, was it?"

"And being a housekeeper wasn't mine," her mother reprimanded. "I planned to be an astronaut. Did you know that?" She smiled, her eyes flicking out the window and up to the cloudless sky. "We may not always get what we think we want, but we usually get what we need."

Cailey bit down on the inside of her cheek. Hard

enough to draw blood. Her mother rarely played the "fisherman's widow" card. Or the "housekeeper to an ungrateful billionaire" card. Her mother was grace personified. And the reminder of all her mother had lost and fought for humbled her.

"I'm sorry, Mama."

"There's absolutely nothing to be sorry for, Cailey. And remember I am *proud* of the work I did for Mr. Nikolaides. I am even more proud of you and your brothers. You've soared beyond anything I hoped for you."

"What *did* you hope for us?" Cailey had never asked. She supposed she'd always been too busy being wrapped up in what she *didn't* have to think about what she did.

Her mother looked her square in the eye. "I wanted you to be healthy. And I wanted you to be happy."

"What if I would've been happier if I was a doctor?"

"*Would* you? It would mean you'd still be in some university somewhere now. It would mean all those children you've helped bring into the world would not have had you to clean them, swaddle them, give them a goodnight kiss. It would mean you wouldn't have been able to help all the people here these past two weeks."

Cailey tipped her head back and took a deep breath.

"You *tried*, love," her mother continued. "You tried with every ounce of your being to get into medical school. Is it fair you didn't get in? Probably not. Is it fair we didn't have enough money for special tutors or private schools or whatever else might have helped you with your dyslexia? Absolutely not. But you are a wonderful nurse, at an incredible hospital, and I bet each and every one of your patients thinks the world of you."

"If I was a doctor I'd be able to afford to give you

back the money you lent me for nursing school and you could get a bigger place."

"What makes you think I don't love it here in my flat?"

"Well…it's—"

"It's absolutely perfect. I spent my entire life cleaning up after you and the Nikolaideses—and took pride in it," she added, before Cailey could jump in. "But now that I'm retired I'm loving looking after just me. I barely have to dust. There is no silver to polish. No chandelier crystals to wash. It's perfect. I'm happy. And all I want now is to make sure you are, too."

Cailey opened her mouth to say that of course she was happy, but nothing came out. Coming home had opened up her very own Pandora's box of insecurities and they seemed to be flying at her like a swarm of locusts.

Theo.

Being in his arms and then being pushed away in a matter of hours.

Unprotected sex.

It all proved yet again that she wasn't worthy of being a Nikolaides bride—because who behaved this recklessly?

Worthy? What was *worthy* at the end of the day?

She'd carried more than one baby out of the arms of a mother who'd opted to give her child away rather than take on the responsibility of parenthood herself. Were those women unworthy or were they just scared? Had they been rejected at some point themselves?

She understood the soul-destroying path of self-destruction that could lead to. She thought she'd tackled the way the Nikolaides family had made her feel. Got back up on her feet and made something of herself. But now…

Now she felt as though she'd been split into two very distinct parts. The pragmatic part that was wishing for a time machine. She should have ripped open that packet in front of Theo and swallowed the pill there and then. Problem solved. And the other part of her…the huge thumping, powerful ache in her heart…was utterly relieved she had done no such thing.

"You're right, Mama. I'm sorry."

"No." Her mother cupped her face in her hand. "Don't apologize for being human. Just promise me you'll look after this big heart of yours, all right?" She put her other hand on Cailey's sternum. "Listen to it. It's wiser than you give it credit for."

Cailey nodded and gave her mother a quick, tight squeeze. "Well, I guess I'd better go see some patients. Doctors are absolutely useless without a good nurse backing them up."

"That's my girl."

Her mother gave her a quick kiss, handed her a bag filled with homemade almond biscuits and shooed her out the door.

The clinic was strangely quiet when she entered.

There were a few patients waiting in the trauma section and the general reception area, but there didn't seem to be as many staff scurrying around.

Then she heard the motor of a boat shift into low gear at the back of the clinic.

Petra spied her from the central reception desk and pointed toward the dock area. "New patient coming in. Out you go!"

Cailey couldn't help but smile as she obeyed. Petra ran the clinic as if it were her own. What she said went.

So Cailey scuttled out through the back door and on to the short pier, where a fisherman was pulling up in his boat. There wasn't any official ambulance vessel, so the local fishermen had been bringing in anyone they could if it meant a shorter trip for the patients.

As the forty-something man threw his rope toward the dock she caught it and smiled. Though her memories of her father were hazy, the ruddy complexions and bulging muscles of the men commanding this particular boat reminded her of him. She'd thought he was the most powerful man in the world, and when her mother had told her the sea had taken him...

It had been a profound reminder of how precious life was, and that each rescued soul represented a triumph against Mother Nature's might.

She knelt and secured the rope to the dock cleat, just as her father had taught her. If she was pregnant she'd teach her child just as her father had taught her... First one swoop of the rope—

"Cailey?"

She whipped round at the sound of Theo's voice. How he still managed to take her breath away when he'd been nothing but the consummate, cool professional over the past couple of weeks was beyond her.

Pffft. No, it wasn't. She'd been told to stay away from him years ago. And she had. But those years apart hadn't made the slightest bit of difference. In the very first moment they'd laid eyes on each either other again a love that had never died had blossomed once more in her heart.

Her hands instinctively swept to her stomach. She'd have to tell him. But how?

"Are you up to date on what's happened to these patients?" Theo asked, all business.

"No, Petra just said to come out here. Is Dr. Balaban on his way?"

Theo shook his head. "He went off with the fire crew."

"Is Kyros all right?"

"Yes, he was driving the rig, I think. It's a house fire. Someone moving in before the gas company had a chance to check the lines and—" He made the sound of an explosion, mimicking the incident with his hands.

"Bad?" She couldn't hide her wince. Burn patients suffered so deeply.

"We'll know soon enough. They're going to try to bring them back here and treat them. No choppers to Athens for a few more hours. Until then you're with me."

Before she could react one of the fisherman was helping a young boy wearing a backpack step across to the pier. When he put his hand on the boy's elbow the boy screamed in pain.

Theo, with a complete lack of self-consciousness, quickly took the boy's right hand in his. "Cailey, meet Nicolas. Nicolas, meet the best nurse Mythelios has on offer." Theo glanced down at the boy's other hand and sucked in a sharp breath.

"She'd better have the patience of a saint!" A heavily pregnant woman held out a hand for Cailey to help her off the boat.

"And this is Nicolas's mum—Georgia Stephanopolous."

"Nicolas shouldn't be taking up your time," Georgia snapped, her features taut with distress. "Not when there is so much else going on."

Cailey gave Georgia a nod of acknowledgement, then looked at Nicolas. The boy's hangdog expression had grown even deeper.

"Perhaps *you* can knock some sense into him," she said when she caught Cailey's confused expression.

"It was an accident!" The boy looked up at her with wide, pleading eyes.

All other thoughts dropped away as Cailey absorbed the scene. Tense mother. Young son—maybe six? Seven years old? He was wearing a backpack. He had scraped knees. And what was that stuck in his hand? It looked like *needles* of some sort.

She looked to Theo to explain as they all began walking to the clinic.

"So, Nicolas here was being a bit of a hero—"

"A bit of a *fool*!" his mother interjected.

Theo didn't respond to the comment so Cailey followed his lead. When parents were distressed their fear often manifested itself as anger. Rage, even. Any comment made to placate or suggest otherwise was often adding fuel to the fire. A hurt child was already a tense situation.

"Nicolas," continued Theo, in a strong, steady voice, "was trying to rescue a kitten that had been trapped in some rubble, and he managed not only to dislocate his elbow, but also fell into his mother's cactus garden in the process. Bad luck, little chap." He tousled the boy's hair and gave him a smile.

Poor kid. Cailey gave his thin shoulder a squeeze. A sting of sadness seared her heart when tears appeared in his eyes. "Did you manage to rescue the kitten?"

The little boy nodded, fat tears plopping out onto his cheeks and rolling through the streaks of dust he'd acquired during the rescue. "His name is Zeus," he whispered, his shoulders hunching against the anticipated response from his mother as they all went into the exam room.

Cailey closed the door, seeing Georgia's eye-roll, and then, unexpectedly, the woman burst into tears.

"Zeus is his father's name," she sobbed.

Cailey threw Theo a bewildered look. He calmly handed her a box of tissues, lifted Nicolas up to the exam table and nodded at Cailey to go with her instincts and give the poor woman a hug.

"That's a *good* thing, right?"

"No!" Georgia wailed, her body dissolving into shudders and low moans which had the knock-on effect of eliciting a fresh wash of tears from her son.

Cailey held the woman as tightly as she could and looked over her shoulder at Theo, mouthing, *What happened?*

Theo made a quick check to see if Nicolas was looking. His big brown eyes were solidly focused on his feet, swinging limply from the exam table. Then Theo looked grave and shook his head.

The minute gesture spoke volumes.

Nicolas's father had been killed in the quake.

Blackness shrouded her heart as the weight of the revelation pressed the air from her lungs. She knew exactly how this little boy felt, and for the first time she was getting a glimpse of how incredibly brave and strong her mother must have been in the wake of her own father's death.

Seeing the situation from an adult perspective—as a cruel, senseless death—instantly deepened the love she had for her mother.

As Cailey held Georgia in a tight hug she watched as Theo talked the boy through each of the steps he was taking. A quick injection for pain relief. Then they would get to the elbow as soon as he had plucked the evil-looking cactus barbs from his hand. Not that Theo *said* they were evil. Instead he used words to describe Nicolas like "brave" and "strong" and "selfless."

All words she could use to describe Theo.

How could a man this amazing not want a child of his own?

She concentrated on the weight Nicolas's mother was letting her accept as she wept and grieved. When Cailey had first seen her Georgia's face hadn't been tear-stained, nor bearing the tell-tale red puffiness that followed in the wake of one of her own crying jags. Despite her sharp temper the poor woman must have been holding back her grief-stricken tears in order to be brave for her little boy.

No wonder she'd erupted once help was at hand. Seeing her little boy crawling amidst the unstable rubble, then hurting himself as he had, must have been terrifying. Especially in the wake of such a harrowing loss.

A small meow broke through the taut atmosphere.

Cailey froze, and felt Nicolas's mother go completely still too.

Theo took a step back from the exam table and gave Nicolas a sideways look. Stern, but not frightening. He clearly knew his way around children. What on earth had him so dead set against having his own? The man was a natural with them.

"Nicolas…" he began slowly. "Did you maybe bring a furry friend along to the clinic?"

Fear widened the little boy's eyes and he shot a panicked look toward his mother. Aware that everyone was looking at her, Georgia took a few tissues, blew her nose and tried to steady her breath. "Nicolas Georgiou Stephanopolous…"

"Meow!"

All eyes were drawn to the purple backpack Nicolas was carrying as something inside it began to wriggle frantically.

Cailey gave Georgia's hand a squeeze and took a step forward. "Nicolas, do you mind if we try and take your backpack off?"

The little boy shook his dark hair back and forth and then cried out in pain.

"Why don't we get that elbow back in place first?" Theo suggested, pulling out the last cactus barb. "Then we can take the backpack off and see who might be stowing away in it."

"I didn't put him in there," Nicolas blurted. "He crawled in when it was accidentally open."

The mewing grew in volume.

Georgia was the first to make a decision. She took two quick steps toward her son, unzipped the backpack and dipped her hands in. When she drew out the tiny ball of mewing fluff and turned it round to face her, everything in her softened.

"He has his eyes."

Theo sent her a questioning look.

"My Zeus. He had bright blue eyes like this."

She nuzzled the kitten, then pressed it to her cheek as once again tears cascaded from her eyes. A couple of moments passed and then she looked up at them all, ruffled an affectionate hand through her son's hair, dropped a kiss on the top of his head.

"You've done the right thing, love. You've done well." Choking on the next words she continued, "Your *baba* would be so proud."

Holding back tears of her own, Cailey helped Theo as he deftly saw to the dislocated elbow, explaining in his calm, steadying voice as they proceeded that Cailey was going to hold on to Nicolas as… One, two, three and *ooopa*! Look what they'd done. Put his elbow back in place!

"Now your funny bone will work again," Theo said moving his own arm back and forth.

"If I move my arm it will work now?"

Theo laughed. "Of course it will work. Give it a try."

"Right now?"

"If you're up to it."

Nicolas gave Theo a shocked expression which quickly turned to awe when he tried bending his arm and found it didn't hurt.

"Cailey, would you mind fitting Nicolas with one of our neoprene splints while I explain a few things to his mum about aftercare?"

Cailey shook her head, still as impressed as Nicolas was at how Theo had dealt with an intensely emotive situation.

"We'll just be out in the corridor when you're done." Theo bent down so he was eye to eye with Nicolas. "You look after Zeus, all right? But more importantly always, *always* listen to your mother. Especially now. The island is still healing. It's not made of strong muscles and bones like you."

Theo pointed out where the splinting supplies were to Cailey, then lowered his voice as Georgia opened the door to the busy corridor. "I'm going to recommend she takes Nicolas out to the garden to play with his kitten and have a chat with Dr. Risi."

"The psychiatrist from Canada?"

"Greek-born, Canada-reared—yes. Lea specializes in trauma, and I think Georgia could probably do with a few coping skills..." He glanced across at Nicolas, who was staring glassy-eyed at the kitten nestling against his mother's chest. "The neoprene splint should do the trick. All right?"

She nodded, trying not to lean in and inhale him. This man had absolutely everything right...except the desire to commit.

Well...the desire to commit to *her*. And that was the nub of it.

She watched Theo leave the room, then turned on her brightest smile for Nicolas. "Let's get this splint on you—just for a bit of padding."

"I thought it was fixed?"

"It is, but sometimes things take a bit longer than we like to heal properly."

"Like Mummy's heart?"

"Exactly like Mummy's heart. And yours, too."

Cailey remembered her brothers, so brave after their father had died, stepping up without being asked. She couldn't remember either of them shedding a single tear.

After she'd eased on the neoprene splint and explained to Nicolas about giving his arm some rest, Cailey sat up on the exam table beside him.

"You want to look after Zeus, right?"

Nicolas nodded, his lips thinning in preparation for bad news.

"Sounds like a pretty good idea. Just make sure you save some extra care for your mummy too, all right?"

Unexpectedly Nicolas's face lit up from within. "She's the *best* mummy!"

"Good to hear." Cailey grinned, hopped down from the table, then lifted Nicolas down to the floor. "She is *definitely* raising a great little boy."

"Thank you, Cailey. I promise to be good."

Cailey got down on her knees, felt her heart aching for him and his mother as Nicolas threw his arms around her for a huge hug.

She took a deep breath of little-boy scent, vividly aware of how lucky Theo was to work at this island clinic. He'd get to see this little boy as he grew up. Perhaps the next time he saw him he'd be on the island's youth football team, then he'd have a girlfriend, maybe even get married himself one day and have a child of his own.

Her hand slipped to the soft curve of her belly. There wasn't a soul in London who would want the same for *her* child. If there was one, she firmly reminded herself.

She'd have to sneak a pregnancy kit out of the supplies cupboard when she had a moment.

A knock sounded on the door and Theo's face appeared while she was still hugging Nicolas.

"Apologies for interrupting!"

When Nicolas turned around, his face a huge grin, Theo smiled. Not the tear-fest he'd clearly been expecting.

"Ready to go out into the garden now?"

Nicolas nodded and ran to accept his mother's outstretched hand.

"Well done." Theo nodded toward the pair as they headed out to the courtyard garden, where Dr. Risi was holding informal talks with anyone who needed it.

She could probably do with a chat herself, Cailey thought wryly.

"You too," she said, realizing Theo was waiting for a response. "You're a good doctor."

"You're a good nurse."

She blushed. She knew she was good at her job. She'd almost literally worked her fingers to the bone to reach the top of her class. But hearing it from Theo, who'd actually become the doctor he'd vowed to be all those years ago, meant a lot.

"We could use someone like you around the clinic."

"I'm right here."

"But for how long?"

Good question. Nine months? Eighteen years? Forever?

She parted her lips to ask him if he had a few minutes to talk.

"Dr. Nikolaides?" A thirty-something doctor from Australia, whose family was originally from Greece, approached the pair of them.

Cailey had seen him coming in and out with the rescue crews working out of makeshift ambulances, but hadn't yet spoken with him.

"A bunch of us are going over to Stavros's *taverna* tonight. It'll be a good chance to wave off the crews heading back to the mainland in the morning. Fancy joining us?"

The Australian doctor looked at Cailey, did a quick double-take, then gave her a very slow, very obviously appreciative head-to-toe scan. "Well, g'day. *You're* most welcome to join us too, young lady. Dr. Alexis Giantopolous at your service—and you are…?"

"A very qualified, very respectable nurse, born and

bred right here on Mythelios, who doesn't take kindly to being patronized," Theo answered for her, through obviously clenched teeth.

Cailey's eyes popped wide open and she only just managed to stop her jaw from dropping. Was Theo *jealous*?

Theo slung a proprietorial arm over her shoulder. "We'll see how we go, Alexis. After the shift."

Cailey dropped her eyelids to half-mast and gave Theo a sidelong look. Two weeks of being pretty much ignored by him and all of a sudden they were a "we" when a bit of competition presented itself?

There had to be more to it than that. Nothing was that simple. If only she'd dreamt up an imaginary boyfriend or paid one of her study buddies to invite her to a dance in front of Theo all those years ago...

It still wouldn't have stopped his father from bullying her off the island.

And it still wouldn't make up for the fact that she'd completely forgotten to take the morning-after pill and could very well be carrying his baby.

"Right, then. I can see my extra-curricular talents will only go to waste here." Alexis took a very stagey step backwards and dropped a saucy wink in Cailey's direction. "Looks as though I need to find someone else to share this hot Australian bod with."

He stepped back again and "shot" them both with his index fingers.

"But you'll both be there, right? It's meant to be a ripper of a gathering!"

Cailey laughed and Theo grumbled.

"C'mon..." She gave him a little nudge and ducked out from under his arm. "It just might be fun."

CHAPTER TWELVE

"*GIGANTES PLAKIS?*"

Theo took the bean dish from Cailey and smiled. "*Ef-haristo*. Thank you."

"I still speak Greek, Theo. No need to translate."

Cailey took a long drink of water. There had been a bit of bite to her comment.

"Yes, of course. I know, it's just..." He sighed and scrubbed a hand across his face, feeling the fatigue as he spoke. "These long hours must be taking their toll."

"You've really worked hard."

He sought her face for any signs of derision. Animosity. There were none, but neither was there the usual light in her eyes, nor that ready laugh he'd heard brightening up the clinic when she worked with Dr. Balaban.

"You've worked hard, too. It's great to see you putting all your nursing training to use."

She shot him a look but said nothing.

"I mean, it's been nice to see you."

"Yes, well...next time there's an earthquake I'll be sure to come back and lend a hand."

"Do that, yes. Wait! You're not leaving, are you?"

"'Fraid so. I mean...unless you need me to stay. But things seem to be largely under control now."

"Yes, they are, but there's always room for a good nurse with excellent language skills."

Damn! He was being a complete and utter idiot! This was what he had in his casual banter arsenal? Platitudes that sounded as if they were straight out of a human resources manual?

Little wonder he was single. He had the panache of a sea slug. But couldn't she see he cared? That he was trying?

"Would you mind passing the salt, please?"

He handed it to her. "Local salt," he said. "Delicious."

She nodded her head as she took the salt shaker and began to put much more than any health professional would have ever recommended for daily consumption on her food.

Stop. Being. So. Thick.

She was trying to get his attention. Those angry shakes of the salt obviously had nothing to do with Stavros's ability to season calamari and a whole lot to do with the man sitting next to her.

A bolt of understanding hit him in the chest. Unless he stopped compartmentalizing he was never going to be able to give Cailey what she deserved. A peaceful resolution before she went back to London.

So it was either suck up the fact that she was going to leave this island with a subterranean opinion of him, or find some way to stick a crowbar in his heart and prove to her he cared.

Until now he'd only been thinking of things in black and white. He lived here. She lived in London. He couldn't do relationships.

But she didn't seem to *want* a relationship. Not anymore anyway.

It wasn't as if you gave her much of a chance, you idiot. Try again. Don't let her leave the island thinking you're a complete ass.

"Do you enjoy working with Dr. Balaban?"

"Yes."

Her answer was solid and genuinely positive. *Good.* Traction.

"I've really learned a lot from him."

"He's an excellent doctor."

"That he is."

"Enough to inspire you to try for med school?"

Her eyes did a few rapid blinks. He was losing ground. Touchy territory, from the looks of things.

"I think I'll stick with nursing, thanks."

"Good. Yes. You're great at nursing."

He was back-pedaling at a rate of knots but not entirely sure why. How did everything he said to her seem to morph into ramming each of his feet straight into his mouth?

Cailey nodded in acknowledgement, her eyes firmly glued on the plate of calamari working its way down the table.

Excellent. Not only had he clearly insulted her choice of career, but he was now officially less interesting than the island's most common food. Or, more to the point, less reliable.

He hadn't exactly made much time to speak with her over the past fortnight. If she were a patient he would have insisted on clearing the air. Making sure she understood.

His chest tightened as she stabbed a ring of calamari and squeezed juice from a wedge of lemon on to it.

He *had* made things clear to her. Crystal-clear. He

didn't want a relationship. He didn't want a child. And he didn't bend those rules for anyone. But he'd just left her to take that wretched pill on her own and not given it one more moment's thought.

They were crowded onto a bench jammed with people, but it felt as if the two of them were completely isolated. From the group. From each other.

He scanned the two long tables butted together in the courtyard area of the *taverna*, where the group had made a decision to eat family-style. Everyone seemed to be having a great time. Everyone but them.

When he looked back at Cailey her focus was still firmly on her plate.

"Everything okay?" He gave her a gentle nudge and a smile.

He knew he wasn't going to come out the good guy here, but he could do better than this. Cailey deserved more than a one-night stand and a cold shoulder when she had been nothing less than open and honest with him.

"Yup," she answered eventually, her voice tightly polite. "Stavros has outdone himself. Yum."

She pointed her fork at her plate and proceeded to rearrange her food. From what he'd seen she hadn't taken so much as a mouthful. Hardly the behavior of someone digging in and enjoying her meal.

He scanned the tables full of medical and rescue professionals, reliving their days, plucking stories from their pasts to dazzle one another with. Many of them had been to earthquakes before. Turkey. Tibet. One—the ever flirtatious Dr. Giantopolous—had even been to a quake in New Zealand. Everywhere the stories were the same. People coming together in times of adversity.

He could do it for his patients. He simply didn't have it in him to expose anyone to the insane dynamics of the Nikolaides family household.

The word "babies" started being bandied about regularly enough that he couldn't help but tune in.

"Elevator!" one of the ER techs shouted out.

"Been there, done that!" A redheaded nurse from Ireland pursed her lips. "Easy-peasy."

"Back of a taxi!" yelled another nurse.

"We've *all* done the back of a taxi," shot back Dr. Balaban from the far end of one of the tables.

"Twins? On your own? When it's you giving birth?" she challenged.

Dr. Balaban laughed, raised a glass and rose to make a bow of respect to her.

"I've helped deliver triplets." Another paramedic threw his hat into the ring.

"Quadruplets!" Cailey called.

Her eyes had become bright and her cheeks were pinkened up from the lively atmosphere. When the crowd cheered and pronounced her the winner they made her stand up and receive a full round of applause.

She was, Theo forced himself to acknowledge, the most beautiful woman in the room—both inside and out—and he was letting her just walk away from him.

Stavros arrived with a couple of flagons of red wine. Local, of course. He always championed the island's producers as much as he could.

When Theo began to dig into his pocket Stavros waved him off. "On the house," he said. "For everything you do."

He also received a rowdy round of applause and cheers.

Before he could leave, Theo stopped him. "How's the cut?"

"Good, good," the older man replied, his fingers lifting to the bandage on his head that looked freshly applied. "Cailey has been changing the plaster for me every day after her shift. The headaches come and go."

Theo's eyebrows knitted together. "What type of headaches?"

Stavros shrugged. "Don't you worry about it, young man. Bad in the morning...better by lunchtime. I'm fit as a fiddle right now." He tipped his head in Cailey's direction and lowered his voice. "You are looking after our Cailey *mou*?"

How on earth—?

Cool it. This was just one islander looking after another.

"Absolutely. She's doing an amazing job at the clinic."

"Yes." Stavros gave Theo a meaningful nod. "She is a true asset to the island."

Theo glanced at Cailey, her smile finally at full mast, engaged in a lively conversation with the Irish nurse across the table about the quadruplets.

"Yes, she is."

"Are you going to do anything about it?"

"Me?" Theo nearly choked on his wine. He had feelings for her, yes, but...

"Yes, you." Stavros looked at him quizzically. "Who else could offer her a job at the clinic?"

"Ah, yes. The clinic. Of course. Well, we are always happy to consider bringing local talent into the fold."

Stavros hadn't missed the *aha!* moment. A sly smile worked its way across his lips.

Theo opened his mouth to protest but Stavros waved

it off. "No, no, my boy. None of my business. None of my business at all."

Theo knew as well as anyone born and bred on Mythelios that "none of my business" meant that by morning the whole island would know Theo had set his hat at Cailey's door.

He turned back to the table of doctors, praying that he was about to become absorbed in a rigorous discussion about gall bladders.

"What about best excuses for surprise pregnancies?" a raucous EMT who was here on holiday from the States asked through a huge guffaw. "I bet I've heard 'em all."

The list swept from miracles to madness. Divine intervention took a lot of credit. As did numerous "secret tonics," blindfolds and sexy nurse costumes. All the nurses around the tables took a lot of ribbing at that one.

Cailey dipped her head, her expression hidden behind the spill of curls falling round her shoulders.

"Nobody's mentioned earthquakes," one doctor said when the table fell silent.

Everyone nodded for a moment, as if giving his statement its due weight—and then burst into hysterics.

"No, no. Seriously," the fifty-something doctor continued. "I've been to a lot of conflict zones, natural disasters—the lot. And without fail nine months later there's a rush in the maternity ward."

"What else are people going to do with no television to distract them?" Alexis asked. "Rhetorical question, obviously."

He scanned the table until he caught Cailey's eye and dropped her a slow, meaningful wink.

Theo swallowed hard. He told himself he wasn't about

to punch the guy...but his fingers had curled instinctively into fists.

"Well," cut in a seasoned nurse from Athens, "an earthquake is a *much* better excuse than faulty protection or forgetting to take the morning-after pill! I mean, *seriously*! Who has ever met someone who has *genuinely* forgotten to take the morning-after pill?"

Theo forced himself to chuckle along. It had been a far from ideal solution, but at least he and Cailey had managed to cover their bases after their own "accident."

Instinctively, he turned to Cailey.

All the color had drained from her face.

And as he registered what her ashen complexion implied he felt the blood drain from his own.

Cailey couldn't get out of the *taverna* fast enough.

The look of horror on Theo's face had told her everything she needed to know.

She'd made the biggest mistake of her life.

Her feet picked up the pace and before she knew what was happening she was running down the main street toward the beach, as if there wasn't enough air in the busy thoroughfare to fill her lungs.

When she'd taken the pregnancy test after her shift all she'd wanted to do was go home. Then Theo had stopped her in the hallway and all but insisted she come along to the *taverna*.

Trust him to want to keep up appearances when curling up in a ball on her mother's sofa was what she would rather be doing. It was the Nikolaides way, it seemed. Showing one face to the world and hiding the real one in the shadows.

But really? This time she was no different.

She was carrying his child after having pretty much agreed to take the morning-after pill.

It had been an honest mistake, but it was one Theo would very likely never forgive her for.

She ran and ran until she reached the beach, where she kicked off her trainers, tied up the skirt she'd pulled on after changing out of her scrubs and waded straight into the sea.

As the surf hit her feet and then her shins she forced herself to time her breathing with the cadence of the waves. In and out. In and out. Hyperventilating and fainting into a high tide wasn't going to help anything. Not with a baby growing inside her.

She offered the ocean a grim smile. See? Proof positive that she could still be practical about *some* things.

Too bad she hadn't been so sensible with her heart.

When she'd seen those two pink lines appear on the pregnancy test her heart had flipped...with *joy*.

She loved Theo. She always had. Yes, he was flawed. But who wasn't? She had a Mythelios-sized chip on her own shoulder because she'd never be a doctor. Surely Theo was allowed foibles of his own.

Did it break her heart that he didn't love her back? More than she would probably ever admit. But when it came down to it every cell in her body was over the moon that she hadn't taken that pill. She *wanted* this baby. *His* baby. And she would do everything in her power to make sure it was healthy and happy.

As if on cue a full moon came out from beneath a pile of clouds, its powerful light hitting the sea like a fistful of silver glitter. An endorsement from the heavens if ever there was one. Her hands folded protectively over her stomach. Her first proper maternal instinct. Made to assure the life growing inside her that she would do everything she could to protect it.

Right. If she was mature enough to have a child on her own, she had to be mature enough to talk to Theo and confirm his suspicions. He had a right to know for definite that he was going to become a father, whether he liked it or not. And she had a lot of thinking to do.

She turned around and made her way up to the beach, grabbed her shoes and headed back toward the clinic.

No point in delaying the inevitable.

She needed to start putting her exit plan into place as soon as possible.

"Dr. Nikolaides!"

Lea Risi was running out of the clinic, waving her arms at him. Agitation coursed through him. Couldn't she see he was busy?

"It's Georgia Stephanopolous. There aren't any doctors at the clinic and she's gone into early labor!"

Theo did an abrupt about-face. He was about to say, *You're a doctor—you fix it.* But Lea had made it clear that psychiatry was her specialty, and she had already been unbelievably generous with her time and skills. He had no doubt she would have seen Georgia through the birth if she could. But a truly talented doctor knew when to ask for help—and Dr. Risi was one of the best.

He shot a look down the darkened street. No sign of Cailey. Whether she had fled the *taverna* out of guilt or fear was beyond him, but it hurt him to the quick that she had run away from him.

"How early is she?"

"Four weeks."

Dammit.

However much he wanted to get to Cailey, talk to her about what was going on, he couldn't leave a patient.

Thirty-six weeks wasn't so early that the baby's health would be dramatically compromised, but it was still moderately premature. A mental list of possible issues started to fall into place. Low birth weight. Blood sugar. Breathing problems. Jaundice. Trouble latching on and feeding.

And on it went. There were enough variables that he needed to be there.

"Right." He knew he looked as grim as he sounded. "Let's go."

When they reached the clinic Lea pointed him toward the makeshift resus area, where he could hear a nurse encouraging Georgia to breathe through the contractions.

"I've put her in here. It seemed to have the most equipment in case—" She stopped, unable to put words to the unthinkable. *In case it all went wrong.* "I'm really sorry, Dr. Nikolaides. I know you've hardly had an hour outside of the clinic, but…"

"Don't worry. Honestly. And thank you." He gave her arm a quick squeeze. "You've done the right thing. Upstairs there's a room with a neonatal cot in it. Would you mind bringing that down?"

She shot an anxious glance toward the courtyard garden. "I've left Nicolas on his own…well, with his kitten…in the garden. We were all having a bit of a play together when the first contractions hit."

His phone rang. He swore under his breath. Didn't he have enough on his plate? He pulled the phone out of his pocket.

Cailey. The last person he'd expected to be on the other end of the line.

He showed the phone to Lea. "Cailey Tomaras. She's a neonatal nurse."

And she was very likely pregnant with his child.

He took the call. "Cailey?"

"We need to talk."

"Absolutely. We do. I'm just at the clinic. Georgia Stephanopolous is in labor."

"But that's too early!"

The instant concern in her voice told him all he needed to know. She would come if he asked.

Get over yourself, your issues with your father, and ask her to help you. The best doctors know when to ask for help.

"Can you come straight here?"

"Of course."

Relief flooded through him. He'd delivered babies before, even preemies, but never when he was wondering about the welfare of the mother of his *own* child.

"I'll just go and get Nicolas, shall I?" Lea was already heading out to the garden. "I'll ask Cailey to fetch down the cot when she gets here."

"Good—fine. Thank you!"

He popped into the screened-off area where Georgia was pacing from window to exam table and back again like a caged tiger. When she turned to face him her expression was frantic with fear.

"He should be here!"

He knew who she meant. Her husband. The man who had fathered her child and who had been so cruelly taken from her. No doubt the trauma of losing him so tragically had brought on her labor early.

And you should be there for Cailey.

Unable to find the best way to answer, he gave her a

nod. "You just keep telling us everything you're experiencing and we'll do the best we can for you and your baby. I'll go and scrub up and be back with you in a minute." He looked at the nurse who was busy setting up the monitors. "Cassandra, do you have everything you need?"

"Everything but the cot," she said evenly.

Cassandra was in her early fifties. She'd had four children of her own, so this was familiar territory for her.

"Georgia's not too far from the active phase, so you go on and scrub up. We'll be just fine."

He gave her a nod of thanks and headed to the supplies cupboard to get a surgical gown to cover his street clothes.

Out of the corner of his eye Theo saw a familiar tangle of dark curls working its way through the smattering of people still seeking refuge in the clinic's large foyer.

His heart leapt and crashed against his ribcage.

"Cailey!"

She turned at the sound of her name and quickly picked up her pace. In the opposite direction.

He jogged through the triage area and caught up to her, grabbing one of her hands.

She yanked it away as if she'd been branded.

There were countless things he should be saying to her. *Are you really carrying my child? What can I do to help? Can you believe me when I say that I care for you but that I am not the man you deserve?*

Instead he pulled a surgical gown out of a nearby cupboard and asked, "Are you happy to scrub in?"

A glaze of tears sprang to her eyes but her voice was cool. "Of course. Dr. Risi has asked me to get the cot from upstairs, which is where I'm headed, and then I'll be right down."

A sharp, intense battle lit up his heart. Was he going

to choose his father's path of ignoring anything emotional? Anything painful? Or was it time to man up and
face reality—no matter how painful?

He reached out and took hold of her hand again, held
it firmly. "Are you carrying my child?"

"*Our* child," she retorted, fireworks flaring in her
eyes in a series of bright sparks. "*Our* child."

She leant in close, so that a passing nurse wouldn't
overhear her.

"And before you have a chance to launch into any recriminations—yes. I was an idiot. Yes. I forgot to take
that wretched pill. Do I regret it?" She didn't wait for him
to answer. "*Not. For. A. Second.* But don't worry. I won't
be trying to get anything from you. So let's just make this
simple, shall we? From now on we'll call this baby *mine*."

He was so much caught by surprise at her fierce claim
on the child he released her hand.

She massaged her wrist with her other hand and eyed
him almost clinically. For someone who had gazed at
him before with something little short of love—

Christos.

She *loved* him.

Which made admitting he didn't believe he was capable of the depth of love she deserved all the more painful.

"Dr. Nikolaides?"

Cassandra was calling from down the hall and beckoning to him.

"On my way."

He looked Cailey straight in the eye. One way or the
other he'd do right by her.

"This isn't finished. We'll talk about it later."

"Fine." She gave him a curt nod and headed off to
the lifts.

CHAPTER THIRTEEN

"YOU CAN DO THIS, Georgia." Cailey pressed a cold cloth to her forehead and gave her hand a squeeze.

"I don't want it to come out yet! I'm not ready!"

"Of course you are."

"No!" Tears streamed down Georgia's face as she fought the intensity of another contraction. "I can't bear that my husband won't ever see him!"

"Her blood pressure is increasing." Theo's voice was calm. Steady.

Cailey nodded her acknowledgement. She knew what he was saying. Georgia's emotions were getting the better of her, and any distress the mother was feeling would transfer straight to the baby.

"We're here for you, Georgia," Theo said. "You have everything you need right here."

If only "Dr. Theo" was on a par with "real-life Theo," thought Cailey Then she wouldn't feel she had to shoulder the guilt for getting pregnant.

Give yourself a break. It was an honest mistake. And you're going to deal with it. On your own.

Cailey gave Georgia's forehead another wipe and smiled at her. Her heart ached for the woman. Widowed so young. A little boy to look after. No income now that her husband was gone. A baby about to come into the world and yet…

"I've got an idea." She positioned herself so Georgia could see her face. "What do you say we get Nicolas in here to hold your hand? Dr. Risi can come, too."

Georgia shook her head back and forth. "Not like this. I don't want him to see me like this."

"Your little boy is made of courage. He wants to help you."

"But it's my job to look after *him*," Georgia sobbed. "How can I do that now that my husband is gone?"

"You can and you will," Cailey said with conviction. "I've seen how you two are together." She softened her voice. "Let your son help you through this. He wants to help."

Despite her vow not to look at Theo, her eyes crept toward him. Above his face mask she met his unwavering gaze. She was almost shocked when he didn't look away.

Was that what he'd been trying to say out in the corridor earlier? That help might not be coming in the way she wanted it to but he would try?

"Get him. Get my boy."

Cailey nodded and handed the cloth to Cassandra. "Back in a minute."

A few minutes later Nicolas had his mother in stitches as he mimicked her howls of pain.

"You sound like a werewolf," she gasped as another contraction hit.

"You *do*, Mama!" His eyes widened. "Ooh. That one sounds the worst."

"It's the most powerful so far," Theo said, his eyes focused beneath the blue drape over Georgia's knees. "Cailey, can you come here for a minute?"

"Absolutely."

"Georgia, we need you to give another big push."

Just as Cailey reached Theo's side the head emerged. Cailey deftly suctioned the mouth and nose.

"Just one more push now...and it looks like you have become a big brother, Nicolas. Well done!"

"Boy or girl?" Georgia asked, wilting back against the pillows with equal parts relief and exhaustion.

Theo nodded at Cailey to hold the newly delivered baby while he made swift work of clamping the umbilical cord.

"You have just had a beautiful little girl."

Cailey didn't look at him, but she could have sworn his voice had cracked as he'd delivered the news.

She swiftly wiped the baby clean. "We're just going to dry her off, to help keep her warm."

"Why does she need to be warm? It's almost summer outside," Nicolas asked.

"Little babies can't control their temperatures as well as you can, so it's important for her to be warm and right here on your mummy's chest."

Cailey lowered the baby into Georgia's arms relishing the moment. This was one of her favorite parts of being a neonatal nurse.

"Cailey?" Theo's voice was questioning.

She bristled. She knew what he was asking. Why haven't you suctioned her again? Why haven't you swaddled her yet? Or taken the blood tests? Or done the thousand other things neonatal nurses were meant to do?

She could feel Cassandra staring at her. Waiting for her to take the lead. This was, after all, her specialty.

And then it hit her. This *was* her area of expertise. Her mother was right. She loved her job. Loved what she did. Being a doctor had been a dream, but so had being a princess and if the gossip magazines were anything to go by being a princess wasn't all it was cracked up to be.

"I tend to let new mums have a moment with the baby before all the tests begin," Cailey explained. "And leaving the umbilical cord for a few minutes gives extra blood-flow, which should help reduce the chances of anemia and iron deficiency."

She noticed Nicolas reaching out toward his little sister and then pulling his hand back when he saw her watching him.

"Go on. It's all right to touch her."

Everyone stopped and watched as Nicolas reached out his small hand toward his sister's even tinier one. When their fingers touched the baby blinked, her blue eyes connecting first with Nicolas and then Georgia before closing again.

Cailey's heart squeezed tight and then all but exploded. This was what it was all about. Pure, organic love.

She glanced at Theo, who was preparing to deliver the placenta. "Are you happy for me to do the Apgar assessment?"

Theo nodded. Was his lack of verbal response an emotional reaction to the birth? Or just further proof that he didn't want children of his own?

Heaven knew she was feeling all sorts of emotions. Joy, relief, fear, excitement. And that was just for Georgia! If she was going to do her job properly she couldn't even *begin* to address what she was feeling. She looked across to Cassandra and smiled. The seasoned nurse wasn't even bothering to wipe away the tears freely rolling down her cheeks.

"She is an absolute beauty."

"I'm really sorry to have to do this." Cailey reached out and took the little girl. "We just need to run a few tests."

"Why? Is something wrong? Is this because she was born early?" Georgia pushed herself up and reached out for her child—her mother's instinct to protect at its highest level.

"She looks fine to me," Cailey soothed. "She's pinking up nicely. If you remember when Nicolas was born, the medical staff would've done all of the same tests."

"I was born in a boat!" Nicolas beamed.

Georgia gave a light laugh and fell back to her pillows. "Nicolas's father thought he would help me go into labor by rowing me around in a boat. It turned out to be too good a tactic. Nicolas was born about one hundred meters from the shore."

"Sounds like quite a surprise," Cailey said as she began quickly checking the baby's heart-rate and taking notes on her breathing, muscle tone, and gently turning her head to the side to check her asymmetrical tonic neck reflex. Her right arm flexed and the left arm reached out from the body as her tiny fingers began to uncurl. Perfect.

"It *was* a surprise," Georgia said, pulling her son to her for a hug. "*He* was a surprise."

"Oh?" Cassandra asked.

"Let's just say my husband and I hadn't exactly planned on being parents so soon."

"Ah, well…" Cassandra laughed. "It happens to the best of us." She smiled at Georgia, then looked to Theo and Cailey for their smiles only to find none.

"Hmm." Cassandra sniffed as she shrugged off the lack of response from her colleagues. "I guess it's just you and me, then."

* * *

About an hour later, after the placenta had been safely delivered and Cailey had finished the rest of her tests and put the baby in the warm neonatal cot as Georgia snuggled up with Nicolas for some sleep, their work was done. Cassandra had to head home so Cailey volunteered to stay with Juno, the newborn little girl, until the morning shift arrived.

Sitting quietly with the infant—small at two and a half kilos, but in perfect health otherwise—was every bit the tonic it had been at the hospital in England.

She was so absorbed in watching the little girl's fingers as they twitched and curled in her sleep that she hardly noticed Theo walking in.

"Everything all right?"

Something about his demeanor said he needed to be here as much as she did. She pulled a chair up alongside the incubator and patted it.

"I owe you an apology—" she began. He made a move as if to interrupt, but she held up a hand to stop him. "Sit. Relax. And before you ask—which is your right—I didn't do it on purpose."

His eyes were on Juno, just as hers were, but she was sure he could feel the energy buzzing between the pair of them.

"I never thought that, Cailey. Not for one second. But you know how I feel about becoming a father."

"I know, and I'm so sorry, but..." She'd wanted to scream and yell, but just as quickly the urge left her. She squeezed her eyes tight and drew in a breath. Shouting at him wasn't going to change anything, let alone help the situation. "I'm sorry. It was a genuine oversight."

"Wasn't the pill in your pocket?"

"It was," she conceded. "It must've fallen out when I took my clothes off, or got tangled with a tissue or something. Whatever it was…things were so busy, and I guess it was out of sight, out of mind because—"

"Life took over," he finished for her, nodding along, as if the same thing might have happened to him, given how chaotic things had been over the past fortnight.

It had really only been in the last day or so that life at the clinic had begun to feel less like a crisis and more like a recovery.

Cailey put her hand on the clear dome of Juno's crib and spread her fingers wide, then yawned.

"Do you want me to stay?"

"No, no. I'll be all right. I texted Mum and she said she'd bring over some coffee and baklava in a bit."

"She's a good woman," Theo said.

"She's a good *mother*," Cailey countered, and instantly regretted the clarification. It wasn't like she was trying to rub it in. She was just shoring up all the time with her mother that she could before she went back to her life in London.

"And you will be too."

She turned and looked at him, but said nothing. She wished it didn't hurt so much that Theo's voice was tinged with sadness. Sorrowful or not, it was the words he *didn't* say that sat between them like an untethered lion.

She forced herself to put a voice to the thoughts they were both thinking. "I'm guessing you don't want to be involved at all."

He looked at her for a moment, his cheeks hollowing as he considered what to say. In the end he shook his head. "But I won't leave you to pay for everything on your own, obviously."

"Obviously," she repeated with more than a hint of acerbity. "After all, it's the Nikolaides way, isn't it?"

Theo's forehead instantly crinkled into deep furrows.

She held up a hand. "Please. Don't bother. I don't want your money. I never wanted anything from you. Not a free pass to medical school. Not a leg up on the society pages. No matter what your father told you, I never took so much as a cent from him. When he ordered me to leave Mythelios ten years ago I did as I was told. Just like a good little servant girl. Don't worry. I'll do it again. Only this time I'm going to do it with my head held high."

He shot her a look of disbelief and something deep within her bridled.

"What? A person can't just love another person for themselves?" She didn't give him a chance to answer when she saw him raise his eyebrows in surprise. "As if you didn't know. C'mon, Theo. I know you weren't born yesterday. I thought leaving Mythelios would be enough to cure me of you, but then I was stupid enough to open my heart to you a second time. But now that I know you're just like your father—solving all your problems with money—I'm pretty sure I'll be able to get over it. Over *you*."

His lack of response was like swallowing broken glass.

So. That was that. She was going to be raising a child on her own.

Was it in the circumstances she'd thought? Not at all. But she'd do everything in her power to give this baby the best life possible.

She was going to have to take a leaf out of the Mythe-lios islanders' book and rise above it, even if her heart was breaking.

It would mend.

Mostly.

"Well, then." She crossed her arms over her chest and leaned back in her chair. "If you don't mind, I guess it's time I heard why you did what you did ten years ago."

CHAPTER FOURTEEN

THEO STARED AT HER, his heart pounding against his rib-cage in double-time.

His father had tried to *pay* her to leave? The sheer audacity of it all but blindsided him. Pieces in the jigsaw puzzle he'd never known he was putting together began to fall into place.

Erianthe's departure... He'd been told she needed better schooling, but afterwards she'd never been the same, carefree, fun-loving wild child that she'd been before then.

And Cailey's departure had been fairly sharpish after Erianthe's.

Her mother had said it was to do with nursing college and he hadn't even thought to question it. People chose paths and followed them. Just as he'd followed his own. And in so doing he had clearly been completely oblivious to everything happening around him.

"I never asked my father to talk to you."

"Yeah, *right*." She actually laughed.

Cailey deserved the truth, so he sucked in a sharp breath, looked her straight in the eye and said, "I'm not my father's son."

Cailey drew back in surprise. "I'm sorry?"

"I'm adopted," he clarified, before realizing that the look on Cailey's face was more relieved than horrified.

It had never occurred to him that people might see it as a *good* thing.

"So…what exactly are you saying? I'm supposed to feel sorry for you for being adopted by a billionaire and given all of the opportunities in the world?"

"Hardly. Pity is the last thing I deserve. Or want. You're right in some ways, but not in others. I hit the jackpot. I had everything I wanted as I grew up…everything but love."

Cailey sucked in a breath, no doubt about to say something along the lines of *Boo-hoo, you poor little rich kid.*

He held up a hand, vividly aware of the small baby lying in the incubator right in front of him.

He could have this if he wanted. A child. A woman who loved him… Though he had a lot of apologizing to do if he was ever going to get her to trust him again.

Just tell her the truth! Tell her what you feel.

"I lack the power to connect. With anyone."

"What?" Her nose crinkled as she looked at him in disbelief. "That's utterly ridiculous. You're amazing with your patients. And you and Erianthe were always close."

He tipped his head back and forth. "Until she went away, yes. Afterwards—not so much."

"So why didn't you stay in closer contact?"

"That's not what Nikolaides *do*!"

He stopped himself short of slamming his hand down on the counter running alongside him. He was raging against the wrong person. Taking it out on the one woman who deserved to be treated with kid glove tenderness. But he'd never voiced any of this before, fearing the thoughts he'd long suppressed would do one thing and one thing only: manifest themselves as rage. The one emotion that came so easily to the Nikolaides household.

Determination obviously flourished in the Tomaras family, because Cailey was still sitting there. Waiting. She wasn't going to let him off the hook. Not easily.

The silence between them hummed with tension.

He felt fearless when it came to medicine. And utterly defenseless in the face of becoming a father. It was a responsibility he was simply incapable of fulfilling.

History had taught him that.

Protecting Erianthe and his mother from his father's rages had been the only thing stopping him from running away as a boy. But his instinct had been to run. Not to stay.

And the only reason he stayed now was a little boy's pitiful need for his father's love. A love he would never receive. A love he would never be able to give to his own child.

Cailey stared at him, her dark eyes unwavering. In a completely dispassionate voice he'd never heard from her before she asked, "So what is it the Nikolaides 'do'?"

"What do you mean?"

Her upper lip twitched, as if she was resisting the temptation to sneer. "I'm already very aware of what they *don't* do. Marrying housemaids, for example."

"What do you mean?" He felt as if he'd been slammed against a wall.

"That little gem came straight from the horse's mouth," she said almost casually, as if telling him the island was due for yet another sunny day.

He huffed out a hollow laugh. "If that's something my father said, I wouldn't be surprised."

"Actually, your father said a lot of things. He said I wasn't worthy of you. He said I'd be nothing more than a housemaid. He said he'd make sure I never so much as put a toe inside any hospital you worked in so long as he drew breath. He was willing to pay me, of course. To protect you from my evil clutches."

"What are you talking about?" Theo could barely hear above the roar of fury raging in his head. He'd never heard any of this.

"Didn't he tell you?" Cailey asked, as if they were discussing the days of the week milk was delivered. "He told me if I didn't leave his house, leave Erianthe to her studies and, more to the point, leave you alone he would make sure my mother, my brothers and me never found work on this island again."

"But we weren't together."

"No. But he must've sensed there was something between us. Chemistry. The possibility of something developing."

"And then he told you a Nikolaides would never marry a housemaid?" Theo could hardly believe he was hearing this.

"Not exactly." She spread out her hand in front of her and looked at her fingernails. Her expression was maddeningly indecipherable when she eventually looked up at him. "You said it."

Frustration crashed through his intentions to do this rationally, calmly. Proof—as if he needed more—that he was right to step away now. He *never* would have said such a thing to Cailey. His mind reeled back through memory after memory, trying to find the moment—

any moment—when he would have said something so reprehensible and came up blank.

"No. Sorry, Cailey. You know me better than that. I would never have said something like that."

Cailey shook her head sadly, as if trying to reason with an unruly child. "I'm afraid I heard you say it to your friends."

"Not a chance. I don't feel that way. Only pure luck meant I didn't grow up in an orphanage. My father reminded me of that again and again, just as he—"

Ah. His father. Of course. Where else would such a hateful, divisive thought come from?

It all came back to him now. His father had just sent Erianthe off to boarding school and Theo had been putting his foot down over his plans to be a GP rather than some globally lauded heart surgeon.

His father had been railing at him about not wanting to throw good money after such pathetic goals. He wasn't paying for Theo to waste away his life in a backwater clinic and marry a housekeeper, he'd shouted. He wasn't paying for Theo to be common. Not on *his* watch. Not with *his* money.

It had been the precursor to their final stand-off. Though he thought he'd won at the time, he could see now that his father had been the victor after all.

Sure, Theo had become a GP. But at a cost…

He'd never have a family of his own. Never love and live with any sort of freedom of the heart.

The bitterness he'd always directed at his father threatened to consume him. He'd worked so hard to be a better man. A kinder man. But one look into Cailey's disappointed face told him his worst nightmare had in fact come true. He'd become exactly what his father had hoped for. A cool, distant, impartial bastard.

A thick, steel rod of pain shunted through him as he accepted the mantle. It was the only way he could get Cailey to see he should never parent a child.

"You asked what us Nikolaides do instead of caring?"

She nodded, blinking against the obvious threat of tears. He swallowed down an urge to console her, pull her into his arms and try to wash away the cruel words he'd already burdened her with. Instead he ploughed ahead—just as his father would have done.

"They work. They create fiefdoms where they can wield power. They're better off living alone."

Cailey blinked again and swiped at her eyes, absorbing his blunt assessment of his own family. "I see."

The coolness in her voice wrapped round his heart and twisted it with sharp, unrelenting force.

"Well, then." She pushed up from her chair and looked up at him. "If you don't mind, I'd like to watch Juno on my own tonight. In the morning I'll be gone."

He nodded. He understood. "That's fine. We've got enough staff to cover the clinic now."

She winced and he didn't blame her. She was the mother of his child and all he was concerned about were staff rotas.

It might be painful as hell, but all of this was for the best.

"And don't…" she cautioned as he turned to leave. "Don't you ever try to get in touch with me or my child once I'm gone. Understood?"

He neither nodded nor protested. In the long run she'd see he was right to do this.

The moment he'd left the room, the depth of his loss

hit him with Mach force strength. After a quick check on Georgia and Nicolas he walked out to the pier and stared out into the black night.

Knowing he would never have Cailey in his life felt akin to someone reaching into his chest and pulling his heart out of his ribcage. Without his having even noticed it, she had *become* his heart.

How could he not have seen it?

When she smiled, his world was brighter.

When she laughed, people glowed. *He* glowed.

She was passionate. Committed. Loving. Warm. Generous-hearted. Everything he could ever imagine wanting in a woman. A wife.

Cailey Tomaras. The one woman he had never let himself truly love. And yet here it was...love. Standing up proud like a soldier prepared to go into battle to fight for what it most valued, what was most vital in his life.

He loved Cailey.

Yes, they had shared one perfect night together, but in reality it could have been a million. That was how deeply she was embedded in his heart.

He couldn't believe he'd been so blind to the role she'd played in his life. They'd known each since they were children. Played together. Scraped knees together. He knew what made her laugh. What songs made her jump up and dance. That even the slightest bit of a breeze would untether one of her curls and let it frolic in the wind. And yet...

He hadn't remembered she'd always wished to be a doctor. It hadn't even occurred to him that her career as a nurse might feel like second-best to her. How could you know so much about one person, ache to know so much more, and still let them go?

The day Erianthe had been sent away sprang to mind. Cailey had come over, mystified that her best friend had left without so much as a goodbye. He'd had nothing to offer by way of an explanation. Dimitri had his ways, he'd said. He'd done his best to be a shoulder to cry on. She'd thrown her arms around his neck after he'd dried her tears and he'd wanted nothing more than to kiss her again, like he'd done that one time by the pool, but he hadn't.

Two days later she'd left and he'd never seen her again until recently.

He could blame Dimitri all he liked, but he'd let her slip through his fingers then and now the full depth of his love was being slashed in two as reality slammed into him.

Once again he was letting her go.

For a good reason, he reminded himself.

Their child would live a happy life. Cailey had enough love in her heart for the two of them. Her family would no doubt close ranks around her with the fathomless love and support he'd seen them offer one another through the years.

Any salve to his conscience evaporated.

And he would be no better than the parents who had abandoned him. He was choosing the coward's way out.

He would never forgive himself for it, but he would pray that one day Cailey would understand that he had done what was best for all of them.

Cailey stared out the window of the hospital staffroom, vividly aware that the dull, lackluster British summer sky mirrored her own mood.

Listless was a better word.

Ever since she'd returned to London a fortnight ago her entire body had felt out of sync…as if she'd gone through a time warp in Greece and was unable to get herself back to reality. Back to the life she had vowed to lead.

"Everything all right, Cailey?"

One of her favorite colleagues, Elise, handed her a cup of tea with a grin.

"Minty tea with a drop of honey. I don't know how you do these long days without caffeine." She raised her own glass of tar-thick coffee and gave a sheepish grin. "It's like I tell all my patients. Do as I say, not as I do."

Cailey smiled and accepted the warm mug. "Thank you, Elise. It smells great."

"It must've been tough."

"What?" Cailey hadn't said a word about Theo or the baby. How did Elise know?

"Working there after the earthquake. I've never done anything like that. You're very brave, Cailey."

And very stupid, she thought, willing herself to squash the image of Theo that inevitably popped into her mind only about a hundred thousand times a day.

"Well, cheers to you, love. May we all learn from you and your incredible strength."

They each took a thoughtful sip of their drinks.

"Biscuit for your thoughts?"

Elise jiggled a biscuit tin in front of Cailey. She shook her head. She hadn't been all that hungry lately. She took her vitamins, but each time she prepared a meal and sat down to eat it her hunger just vanished.

"Go on. I've not seen you eat a proper meal since you came back."

Cailey took a biscuit and made a show of enjoying a small nibble.

Elise beamed and gave her back a rub, instinctively sensing her friend's need for a bit of comfort.

"It'll be all right, love. I'm sure everyone back home was ever so grateful for all of the work you did over there."

Everyone but the one who counted most.

"Right." Elise tucked a couple more biscuits into Cailey's front pocket and gave her cheek a friendly peck. "I've got to get back on the ward. Take as long as you need."

As Elise disappeared out to the busy ward Cailey reminded herself these were the moments she needed to latch on to. Small, to be sure, but even the tiniest of reminders that she was building a life here in the UK was a positive step forward.

After she'd made it more than clear that her intention was to stay in London—no matter how much she longed to be with her family—her mother had promised to come over when the baby was born. A smile crept to her lips. As if she'd be able to keep the headstrong *yiayia* away.

Her brothers had been equally inflexible about their travel plans. And her sisters-in-law. They'd all piled on their promises of help, refusing to listen to her protestations that she'd be fine. Building cradles, changing tables. Knitting caps, jumpers—whatever she required. They'd promised her everything she needed, but they were unable to deliver on the one thing she wanted.

Theo.

None of them had pressed. None had pushed.

There was no need for them to ask questions about the father, she'd realized. Her heartbreak had been written all over her face.

She reached up to touch the necklace her mother had

pressed into her hand when they'd walked to the ferry dock together. Her finger traced the tiny gold phoenix. It was a gift her father had given her mother to wear when he was out at sea.

"Put this on, love," her mother had said, tears sparkling in her eyes. "I know you think things are impossible now, but…like me…you will rise like the beautiful phoenix who lives in here."

Her mother had put her hand above Cailey's heart, then pulled her daughter to her for a deep, strong hug, as if trying her best to transfer the strength she'd gained from surmounting life's deepest sorrows.

If her mother could raise three young children on her own and stay as positive and loving as she had, then so could she. She was a Tomaras! And she would do what Tomarases had done from the beginning of time: rise from the ashes life had thrown in their path and fly.

"Are you ready to bring another baby into the world?" Elise's voice jolted Cailey back into the present.

The question was far more pointed than Elise could ever know.

Her hand shifted to the tiny life only just gaining a foothold.

"Yes." She nodded, feeling something shift inside her, as if the first flutterings of the phoenix were those of the very child she was carrying in her womb. "Yes, I am."

CHAPTER FIFTEEN

THEO LOOKED UP from the stack of paperwork he'd been trying to plow his way through when the singing began.

What the…?

How had the entire staff managed to circle around him at the reception desk without his even having noticed?

Instead of "Happy Birthday" they were singing "Happy Anniversary."

Petra was standing in the center of the staff members, now whittled down to the people who regularly worked at the clinic as the need for clinicians from the mainland had abated.

As their song peaked he finally registered what they were singing for.

The clinic.

The four candles atop the ridiculously enormous cake Petra was sagging under were for each year the clinic had been up and running.

He should feel pride.

He should feel happy.

All he felt was a bone-aching sorrow that the woman who should be by his side was gone.

Petra, who seemed to know everything without having it spelled out for her, saw his expression shift from confusion to understanding to pain.

She hoisted the large cake onto the counter. "Make a wish," she commanded.

He opened his mouth to protest, only to have her cluck away his attempt to kick up a fuss.

Petra, like Cailey's mother, knew how to keep Theo in line.

The thought brought a smile to his face.

He could see Cailey doing the same. Reprimanding a toddler for wanting more cake or ice cream before gathering it in her arms and giving it a huge kiss. It was the Greek mother's way. Firm but unconditional love.

"Go on." Petra nudged the cake across the high counter. "Wish."

He scanned the smiling faces of the people who had helped bring this clinic to life.

The doctors, nurses, technicians…everyone who had stepped through the clinic doors…all of them had not only offered their services to improve the welfare of their fellow islanders, but had done so from their hearts.

His eyes flicked to the calendar hanging over the reception desk, no longer turned to "his" month, but flicked over to Cailey's brother Kyros now, posing in his firefighter's uniform. Next month was Deakin's photo. He'd be arriving soon, from whichever African nation he'd been traveling in most recently. Then Ares. Then Chris. As they'd promised. In their own ramshackle way they would all manage to be there. Lend a hand when he needed it most.

Not a single one of them shared his blood, and yet… they were his brothers.

He lifted his gaze from the cake and stared at the staff

in wonder—as if seeing them for the very first time. These people believed in him. They had all forsaken high-paying jobs on the mainland to help him bring quality medical care to the islanders. Without question, they had invested their futures in him, believing him to be dependable, kind, a man of moral integrity. A leader.

And he *was* those things. For the staff. For his patients.

But not for Cailey. And not for his father.

Today was the day that would change.

Every face looking so expectantly upon him now deserved for him to be the man they already believed him to be.

Having a child wasn't a problem. It was an opportunity. A chance to prove again and again that he had it in him to become the man he had always wanted to be.

He smiled at his team, and then at the flickering candles. He knew what he was going to wish for. And he knew what he would spend each and every moment of the rest of his life trying to do.

"Thank you," he said, feeling more indebted to the clinic staff than he could ever express. "If anything, I owe a debt of thanks to each and every one of you. Without your help—your tenacity and your faith—we wouldn't have made it through the first day the clinic doors opened, let alone been able to help the people of Mythelios when the earthquake hit. You have all helped to make this clinic the success story it is and will continue to be."

He looked down at the candles, then up at Petra. "It may have taken me a while to catch on, but I think you know what I am going to wish for."

She nodded.

Of course she did.

Petra knew everything.

"In which case…" Theo's lips parted in the first genuine smile he'd given in the weeks since Cailey had left Mythelios "…let's all make sure this works."

He gestured for everyone to gather in close and—as with most things in the clinic—on a three count they collectively blew the candles out.

"You're not leaving the hospital already, are you?"

Theo pulled himself up short. He knew that commanding tone. And, of course, the accompanying blade of disappointment that made it cut deep.

"Dad? What are you doing here?"

"I want my stats checked."

"What? Why?" He glanced at his watch. He had a plane to catch. "We did your physical last month. There's nothing wrong with you."

"I want you to check again," Dimitri snapped, his eyes zigzagging round the reception area. "Or go get a doctor. One from the mainland. Stay. Then you can watch and learn."

He'd never stop, would he? Never stop belittling the choice Theo had made to be a GP.

Theo briskly guided his father to an exam table and yanked the curtain round them.

"I *am* a doctor," he said putting the blood pressure cuff on his father's wrist and briskly inflating it. "The last time I checked you were absolutely fine. Now, unless some strange new symptoms have presented themselves…" He stopped and looked at the results as the cuff peaked and deflated. "For a man who's been around the block a few times you are healthy as a horse. Happy, now?"

He hadn't spoken to his father like this since the day they'd gone to war about the clinic. He'd been filled with rage that again and again Dimitri had put barriers in the way of his living a life that was, at its heart, a good one. It might not be powerful. Or commanding. Or lucrative. But it was a good one. And *he* was a good man. And he was damned if Dimitri was going to stop him from fighting for the good woman who should be by his side.

His father was eyeing him, then he asked, "What kind of horse?"

Theo threw up his hands. "What the hell does it matter what kind of horse?"

Much to his shock, his father began to laugh. "Oh, Theo. You should see your face. You look—"

"What?" Theo was furious. "*What* do I look like?"

"You look just like me."

The thought sobered each of them. Of course it was impossible that they would physically resemble one another—but the rage, the hot flares of temper…those things were learned. And in that moment they both saw stark evidence that those lessons had in fact been handed from father to son.

"Dad…why are you here?"

"I heard you were leaving."

Theo would have asked how, but word always traveled fast around Mythelios.

"Yes. I'm going to see Cailey."

He braced himself for the inevitable explosion, the admonishment. The scorn.

Instead his father nodded, stared at his hands for a moment, then looked up into his son's eyes and asked in a cool, clear voice, "Would you like some money?"

Disbelief flared inside him with a white-hot rage. The

protective walls he'd built round his heart came crashing down. Shame that he'd let Cailey return on her own swept through him, and just as quickly formed into an immovable rod of resolve.

"Is that how you plan on making your grandchild disappear? With money?"

His father looked at him, confused at first, and then pale as comprehension dawned.

"That's right, Dad. Your son has gone and done it again. Brought shame to the house of Nikolaides. What do you want to do this time? Try to pay me off to leave the island like you tried with Cailey?"

"No, I—" He reached out to Theo. "I thought we had an understanding."

"No, *you* had an understanding. I just agreed to it because, like a fool, I thought one day you'd see things the way I did. I thought you'd grow to like the clinic and see yourself as part of this community. But you still don't get it, do you?"

"What exactly am I meant to get?"

"That I am every bit the same as these so-called commoners. Flesh. Blood. With a heart beating in my chest that, no matter how much I try to deny it, has feelings. But I may as well face facts. No matter what I do, I'm never going to be enough for you."

"That's not true."

"Really? Where's the pride you should feel for me, Dad? We both know I'm not your true flesh and blood. That I didn't follow the path you wanted me to. I get it. I've been nothing more than a really expensive disappointment. Well, let's just call it quits now, shall we? Whatever it takes."

He was ranting now, but he couldn't stop himself. It

was as if the floodgates had finally opened in his chest and there was no chance of closing them.

Unblinking, his father stared at him as he continued, "Shall we shut the doors of the clinic? You've done your bit. Seen the island through an earthquake. Your reputation will stay intact. We'll close it now and I'll spend the rest of my days working to pay back what you put into the clinic. Sell a kidney. Become the overpriced specialist you always dreamed of. And while we're at it why don't we dispense with the whole 'family' ruse? I'll address you as Dimitri, or Mr. Nikolaides, from here on out."

"What? No! I'm your *father*."

"Then why don't you ever act like one?"

They both stopped and stared at one another. Theo was shocked that he'd even asked. His father was pale.

Much to his amazement, his father sank onto a chair and dropped his face into his hands.

Theo fell to his knees, fearing his rage had gone too far, and pulled his father's hands away from his face. "Dad? Dad, are you all right?"

"I only wanted you to be happy."

Theo exhaled heavily. "I *am* happy. *Was* happy," he qualified. "This—" He spread his arms wide to show he meant the clinic. "This all made me very happy."

"Until *she* came back."

"Cailey? Yes. Cailey coming back made me even happier. It was when she went away that I realized what I'd lost." He sat back on his heels. "Why did you threaten her ten years ago? Why did you make her leave the island?"

His father sat back wearily in the chair. "It is the only way I know how to do things. With power and money—

the two things I never had as a boy. The same two things you never seemed to want."

"All I wanted was for you to love me."

"And I do."

"So...what? You show it by telling a girl from the wrong side of the tracks you'll put her mother and brothers out of work if she doesn't leave me alone?"

"I thought she would hold you back. That her...her learning difficulties, her desire to be here with her family, never to leave the island, would keep you from your dreams."

"*Your* dreams, you mean."

His father shrugged, then gave Theo a sad smile. "I think I got that part wrong."

"Yeah. You did. I truly love my job. I'm sorry I'm not what you wanted me to be, but this is what I love doing. And Cailey is the woman I should be jumping on a plane for and begging forgiveness from."

"What? Why do you need her forgiveness?" His father sat upright.

"I told her I didn't have it in me to be our child's father."

"Ridiculous. Of course you do. You're a Nikolaides."

Theo couldn't help but laugh. "That's exactly why I told her I didn't know if I had it in me."

Dimitri gave him a considering look for a long, uncomfortable minute, then abruptly shrugged the kind of Greek shrug that spoke a thousand words. It said, *You're right. I was wrong. You're my son. I love you. I support you.* It said all the things Theo had hoped to hear his whole life, and in one fell swoop gave him the belief that, although it was a tentative beginning, he and his father just might have begun a journey to heal a relationship that had never really had a chance to grow.

"Son…" His father grabbed hold of his arm and pulled himself up to stand. "When you get back from England…with Cailey…perhaps you can ask her to give an old man another chance."

"Perhaps you can ask her yourself."

"Perhaps I can." He nodded. Then lifted his blue eyes to his son in a swift move of impatience. "So, go." His father flicked his hands at Theo. "Go! Go and get this girl carrying my grandchild and come back soon. Your mother will be wanting to start knitting, or whatever it is grandmothers do."

Theo's expression turned sober. "I may not be successful in bringing her home, Dad."

"What? Don't be ridiculous." He clapped his son on the back. "You're a Nikolaides. You can do anything you set your heart on."

"From your lips—"

"I know, I know." His father looked upwards along with his son. "This one may be in the hands of the gods. But remember." He thumped his hand on his son's chest. "What you have in here is every bit as powerful."

Theo reached out and pressed the buzzer on the traditional English doorframe. Trust his sister to "go local."

Not that he'd expected to find a whitewashed, stone home with a blue door in the center of London, but… He turned and looked down the street and smiled. Black cast-iron gates. A perfectly manicured central square. People walking along the street avoiding eye contact. It was all so… *English*!

Then again, she'd never been one to do things by halves so why start now?

The door opened and an unexpected knot formed in his throat as his eyes lit on the sister he hadn't seen in far too long.

Was this proof he'd made the right decision?

"Theo?" Erianthe didn't bother hiding her astonishment and quickly threw her arms around him.

He folded his arms around her and enjoyed the unchecked emotion.

"Hey, sis," he murmured into her hair. "Fancy giving your old brother a bit of Dutch courage?"

A few minutes later, after his overnight case had been safely stored in the central hallway and his sister had plumbed a few key facts about his unexpected appearance from him, Erianthe handed him a strong cup of coffee.

"It's not exactly Dutch courage, but it'll have to do. No way am I sending you out on a mission this important with booze on your breath."

He grinned at his sister. She was so…*vital*! And focused. Everything about her spoke of the strength and determination she'd poured into the final years of her medical training as she honed in on her specialty. A far cry from the rebellious teen his father had shipped off to boarding school years ago.

"So!" Erianthe folded herself into an armchair across from the sofa where Theo had settled himself. "You've gone and got your teenage crush pregnant."

Theo whistled. "Don't bother mincing your words, will you, Eri?"

"No point," she parried. "Sounds to me like you've got a lot of making up to do. And if I know Cailey—"

"Have you seen her?" he interrupted, his heart skipping a beat.

"No." She shook her head. "I haven't seen her since I left Mythelios. Hey! Don't look at me like that. From what you've said, you didn't exactly stay in touch with her either. Not that you didn't make up for it during the quake." She laughed as only a kid sister could. With pure non-judgmental affection.

He nodded. "Fair is fair. I deserve your jibes…*and* hers."

"Oh, don't you worry." She batted away his concerns. "If she's anything like she used to be, I'm sure she'll let you know exactly how she feels."

Eri was right. Cailey had been nothing less than honest with him. And all he'd done was cloak himself in a protective shield of lies. Well, no more. Now that he'd begun to clear the air with his father he'd do his level best to be as honest and open with Cailey as he could.

He took a sip of the coffee and gave his sister a thoughtful look. "You've changed a lot since I saw you last."

She put her coffee cup down on the table beside her and traced a figure of eight on her knee. "It's easy enough to do when the motivation is right."

"What do you mean?"

She looked at him as if he'd asked the most inane question in the universe. "There was getting out from under Dad's thumb for one. Not letting him make decisions for me anymore. Proving his way of living life isn't the *only* way…" She raised her coffee cup to him in a "cheers" gesture. "Well done you, for getting the clinic built. I am still astonished he gave in."

Theo shifted in his chair. It hadn't been easy. But

he'd stood up to his father and made his point. Now he needed to face his fears head-on.

Fears that he wouldn't be the father he knew his child deserved.

"You're wavering," Erianthe observed drily. "Stop wavering and start doing. Or, if you prefer, I can keep on reminding you about all of the lovely lessons our father taught us through the years."

She lifted her hand, as if in preparation to talk him through each point, and Theo laughed.

"I get it. Point made. Like I said, you've changed. And, believe it or not…he's beginning to as well."

Erianthe threw him a dubious look.

"Honest. He'll probably always be a crotchety, bull-headed businessman, but as a dad… He's trying. And that's something I have to learn from." His expression sobered as he looked across and met his sister's clear, intent gaze. "I want to be a good father."

"So?" She gave him a pointed look. "Why are you sitting here with me? Go out there, hail a taxi and get yourself over to the hospital—where I hope you'll drop to your knees and beg that girl to forgive you."

"That's your prescription?" He grinned and rose from his chair.

"As a doctor and a sister, yes." She smiled back at him and pushed him toward the door. "That's exactly my prescription."

CHAPTER SIXTEEN

"SHE'S A REAL BEAUTY."

Cailey smiled at the new father, his eyes misted over with the wonder of holding his daughter in his arms for the first time. Two weeks ago a moment like this would've sent her fleeing to the Ladies' to have a quiet little sob, but she'd had a stern talk with herself.

She'd worked in the maternity ward before she'd so much as had a boyfriend, let alone a chance at having a child of her own. Now she was perfectly placed to prepare for what lay ahead. Love, tears, pride. She'd seen all those things and more in the parents who had come through the ward, and she would continue to see them again and again.

Up until her own maternity leave, she thought, her hand giving the slightest hint of roundness on her belly a soft caress.

"I'd better get to the florists before they shut." The father reluctantly handed over the infant to Cailey. "Her mum deserves all the flowers in London for this. More."

Cailey gave his arm a rub with her free hand and spent a few moments cuddling the little girl after he'd left. It was a miracle, she thought. The gift of life.

"Just look at your little nose." She popped her index

finger on its nose. "And your two tiny eyes. And two teeny hands... And one day you'll be all grown up."

"She's a real beauty."

Cailey started at hearing the exact same words she'd just heard coming from a very different voice. A voice she hadn't banked on hearing ever again.

Taking a moment to collect herself, she stroked the baby's cheek with the back of her hand, then gently placed it into its bassinet.

"Hello, Theo."

She resisted the urge to cross her arms over her chest to hide the pounding of her heart. "Are you here to see anyone in particular?"

Playing coy wasn't her usual remit, but she had to protect herself somehow. Why hadn't he just stayed away, as he had all but promised he would?

"I think I made some very serious mistakes recently."

"Oh?"

She swished past him and began walking toward the staffroom. Having this conversation, or *any* conversation, in front of these newborn babies felt like...treason or heresy or...*ugh*! She didn't know. It was hard to untangle one thought from the next, knowing the man she loved was doing his level best to catch up to her.

She whirled around and tumbled back a few steps when he nearly collided with her. Flailing for balance, she felt Theo's hands on her arms, steadying her.

She wrenched herself free. "Don't. Touch. Me."

"Cailey, please. I need to talk to you."

"Oh, really? Well, about two weeks ago I needed a father for my child. But we don't always get what we want, do we?"

The words hit their target. Theo looked as shocked as if he'd been hit by a car.

Her heart twisted against conflicting emotions. There was no pleasure in hurting him.

"I'm sorry." She took another step away from him. "I can't do this, Theo. Please, can you just go?"

"What if I said I was here to be that man?"

Her mind fuzzed. She'd built a wall around her heart over the past few weeks and in little less than the blink of an eye Theo had decimated it. She felt raw and exposed.

"You *aren't* that man," she choked out. "You told me as much."

"I said a lot of things," he agreed. "And most of them were about as wrong as they could be."

"Everything all right here, Cailey?" Elise appeared by her side. "I can call Security if you need me to."

Theo took a step back, his green eyes solidly on her own. "Ten minutes?" he begged. "Ten minutes…"

"Ten minutes for what?" asked Elise.

Cailey would have laughed if she hadn't been trying her best to control the jitters that had turned her nerves into a fistful of dancing crickets.

"To convince this beautiful woman to become my wife."

Elise's eyes widened. "Cailey Tomaras, you dark horse, you. Why didn't you tell me you were hiding this Adonis away in a corner?"

"He is a Theo, not an Adonis," she replied, instantly feeling her resistance wearing away.

His wife?

"Actually, I'm pretty busy," she said breathlessly.

She couldn't do this—melt at the first opportunity. It was what she'd done in Mythelios and look where that had landed her. Pregnant and alone.

Not. A. Chance.

"If you need medical help, sir, I think you will find A and E on the ground floor."

"Cailey."

Theo reached out for her hand and she pulled it away.

"Can we at least talk?"

"No." She pretended to look at a patient's form, but all she could see were blurry letters. She knew for a fact it wasn't her dyslexia this time. It was her body going into survival mode.

"Cailey, love." Elise took hold of both of her shoulders, dipped her head and looked her in the eye. "If you don't accept this man's proposal, d'you mind if I jump in there and accept for you?" She gave him a hungry scan then stage-whispered, "Just...*look* at him! Eye candy for life."

"Candy can give people cavities."

"And stress can give people ulcers," Elise retorted, completely immune to the simmering emotions roiling between Cailey and Theo.

"It's a good point." Theo adopted the manner of a wise old physician. "We wouldn't want stress hurting the baby, now, would we?"

"Baby!" Elise shrieked, and swiveled on Cailey. "You didn't tell me you were pregnant."

"I also didn't tell you that this big Greek meatball broke my heart."

Elise gasped and swatted at Theo's arm. "You scoundrel!" She stood next to Cailey and crossed her arms, clearly thrilled to be part of this living, breathing soap opera. "What did you do and how are you going to make up for it?"

"I didn't step up when I should have."

"Why not?" Elise was indignant.

"Because I was a fool. I was afraid I'd lose something I'd fought for, but now I realize absolutely nothing matters without Cailey in my life."

"Swoon!" Elsie did a dramatic dip of her knees and sent Cailey a look of sheer disbelief. "Why are you not throwing yourself into this man's arms?"

Cailey threw her friend a sidelong glance. However much she loved her bolshic attitude, this really was her battle to fight.

"Elise...do you mind if we have a few minutes alone?"

Elise looked between the pair of them, as if deciding whether or not there would be any danger in leaving them alone. "Right. I'll give you fifteen minutes in the on-call room and if I hear shouting I'm calling Security. If I hear nothing I'll presume you've made up and I'll put up the 'Do Not Disturb' notice. Are we clear?"

Cailey couldn't help but giggle at Theo's baffled expression. This was utterly ridiculous. Was he really here to try and win her hand in marriage?

She tipped her head toward the on-call room. "Fifteen minutes."

She drew in a deep breath, hoping it would give her the strength she'd need to say no regardless of whatever appeal he made. She'd made her decision. She wasn't prepared to endure any more heartache.

He could say what he needed to and then go home.

She was going to raise this child on her own.

The second the door closed behind them Theo took Cailey's hands in his. "I owe you an apology."

"You don't owe me anything."

"Yes, I do."

"What exactly is it you think you owe me?"

Theo looked her straight in the eye. "My respect, for one. I hadn't realized just how vile my father had been to you."

Cailey sucked in a sharp breath and pulled her hands out of Theo's. "I'm not here to talk about him."

"We have to."

"No 'we' don't. 'We' aren't a 'we.' You've made that very, very clear, Theo."

"I was wrong."

She shifted her jaw, almost as if she were chewing the words over. The admission hit her straight in the heart. She wanted to believe him. She really did. But there wasn't a chance she was going to let herself be dependent upon someone else's emotional or financial whims. Not with her child's welfare on the line.

"And what exactly does that mean for me?"

"It means I hope with all of my heart you will let me spend the rest of my life showing you just how much I respect you and honor you and cherish you."

"Those are all just words, Theo. They're worth about as much to me as the money in your father's bank account. Absolutely nothing."

Which, of course, was a lie. His words meant the world to her—but she couldn't show him that. Not with so much at stake. There wasn't a chance in the world she was going to open her heart to him again.

"Dad can't wait to meet his grandchild. He told me to tell you that."

Oh?

"You told him I was pregnant?"

That came as a surprise.

"Yes, I did. I also told him I was in love with you. And that if he wanted the clinic he could have it."

Her eyebrows shot up.

Theo shot her a sheepish smile. "I did also offer to pay for it."

"How?"

"I haven't strictly worked that part out yet, but with you by my side I am convinced anything is possible."

"And how did Dimitri take this news? That you're willing to throw it all away for a housekeeper's daughter?" She narrowed her gaze. "Are you here because you've been banished, too?"

"No. Quite the opposite."

"Theo, if you're doing this just to put your conscience at rest, you can leave it—really. There are two things I learned about myself during the earthquake. The first is that I really love my job and I know I'm good at it. That gave me a sense of pride I've never really let myself feel before. And now that I have that I know I can be a perfectly good mother on my own. You made it explicitly clear you had no interest in following in your father's footsteps—"

"Which is why he and I had it out. Why I told him I needed to come here. Apologize. Win you back. I love you, Cailey Tomaras. With every cell in my body, I love you. And I am hoping you will do me the honor of being my wife."

"And the baby?" she asked softly.

"I *want* the baby. I've always wanted the baby. I just want to be good enough for it. And if you're willing to trust that I will do the very best I can we can make another baby after this one, and another after that one…"

Cailey giggled as she let him pull her to him. They kissed softly. Lovingly. Transferring the affection in their hearts into touches and caresses.

"What was the other thing you learned about yourself?" Theo asked.

"What? After the earthquake?"

"Mmm-hmm." Theo nuzzled into Cailey's neck, loving her scent, her touch.

"I learned how important family is. And how I'd really rather live in Mythelios than here in dreary old England."

Theo laughed. "I'm very happy to hear that."

"You are?"

He cupped her face in his hands and lowered his lips to hers. The kiss that followed embodied the perfection and timelessness of true love. Soft. Passionate. Tender. Powerful. She felt his love transfer directly to her heart, knowing that as each day passed it would only grow stronger and more resilient, no matter what life threw their way.

The sound of approaching footsteps halted their kissing. Through the doorway they heard Elise's muffled voice.

"It's been seventeen minutes. I'm putting the 'Do Not Disturb' sign on. You have half an hour. Start your watches!"

They stared at one another, then burst out laughing.

"Will you come back to Mythelios with me, Cailey?"

She nodded. "I will. But make me one promise."

"Anything," he said.

"I can work at the clinic."

"Done."

"Well, then..." She gave her watch a quick glimpse. "We've only got sixteen more minutes before I'm due back on. Fancy making good use of them?"

"It would be my pleasure."

CHAPTER SEVENTEEN

"WHAT ARE WE going to do?" Cailey was still staring at the monitor in disbelief.

"Build bunk beds, I guess." Theo laughed as he retraced the path of the monitor over his wife's gently rounded belly.

"Leda isn't going to take kindly to no longer being the Princess of the Cottage."

Cailey shot her husband a knowing look. Their daughter was glorious, but she had each of her parents wrapped firmly round her little finger.

"I suspect she shall take on the role of Queen with little prompting," Theo said, humor warming his voice like sun-drenched honey.

He handed his wife a few tissues to wipe the gel off her tummy after they'd spent a few more minutes gazing in wordless wonder at the new lives they had created.

Theo looked up at the wall clock. "We'd better get up to Mum and Dad's house soon."

"Lunch?"

Theo nodded, a wry smile on his lips. "Dad's got some new inflatables for the pool he wants to show off to Leda."

"He loves being a grandfather, doesn't he?" Cailey giggled. "What is it this time? A huge swan?"

"Flamingo," Theo answered. "He knows Leda loves pink."

"Can we stop by the *taverna* beforehand?"

"Why's that?"

Cailey slid off the exam table and shifted her top back into place. "I just thought perhaps we could let a certain someone know he might be a godfather soon."

Theo's eyes lit at the suggestion. "And that, my dear..." he crossed the room to give his wife a deep kiss "...is one of the many reasons why I love you."

She pulled back and smiled broadly, laughter rippling through her every word. "I *am* rather marvelous, aren't I?"

"The best," Theo answered without a moment's hesitation. "The absolute best."

* * * * *

TEMPTED BY
DR PATERA

TINA BECKETT

MILLS & BOON

To my family.
You *are* my home.

PROLOGUE

THE IMAGES FLASHING across the television screen were…
horrific.

Deakin Patera's gut became a tight ball of fear as he
strained to make out the words. He couldn't hear the
newscaster's voice over the noise in the bar, but he knew
that landscape—that shoreline—by heart. And the text
crawling along the bottom of the screen told snippets
of the story: *Eight point one earthquake rocks Greek
island. Hundreds injured. Death toll not yet available.
A few still missing.*

Who?

Hell! Who?

Pulling out his phone, he checked for text messages.
He had one from his aunt.

Safe for now. Will advise about aftershocks. No damage on the house, thank God. Where are you?

No damage on the house. Unlike that other time. His
palm scrubbed over the rough skin on the side of his
neck, even though that particular damage had faded
long ago.

He typed a quick message back.

Glad you're safe. I'm in Africa on medical mission. Any word from the others?

She would know who he was talking about. His best friends from childhood. They had all partnered together to open a much-needed clinic on their home island— just as their parents had all partnered together to found Mopaxeni Shipping, the company that had made them all rich.

Deakin rarely saw the clinic nowadays, but Theo kept him apprised of how it was doing. Their joint trust funds paid the bulk of the expenses, but a crisis like this one was going to stretch its finances to breaking point.

He kept half an eye on the reports as he scrolled through the contacts on his phone.

There were worries over tsunamis rolling in from the sea. His aunt hadn't said anything about that, and nor had she texted back about his friends.

He sent off another question.

Tsunamis?

Within seconds he had a reply.

So far, no, thank God. But we're on high ground. Should be okay. I have a message out to Theo. Chris and Ares aren't on the island. Haven't heard of damage to the clinic. The airstrip is a wreck, though. No flights in or out at the moment.

No flights. Well, at least they were able to get messages in and out—although that could change at any moment as more and more people tried to get a hold of loved ones.

His aunt hadn't heard from Theo. Where was he?

Even as he thought it, his phone began to vibrate in his hand. The readout was exactly what he wanted to see. *Thank God!*

He shot off a final text to his aunt.

Will write more soon.

Then he answered the call.

"Theo, glad to hear from you."

"Don't be glad. Not yet. You've heard?"

Was his friend injured? The clinic decimated?

"I'm just seeing the news. Is it as bad as it looks?"

"If you mean does the island look like it's been through a meat grinder...almost. Where are you?"

The same question his aunt had asked.

"Africa. I still have a bit more than a month left on my contract."

"Find a way to get out of it, then. Mythelios needs you."

"No, it doesn't. It's done fine without me—*better* without me."

A sigh came over the phone. "Stop with the tired excuses, already. That was ages ago. Everyone who matters has already forgotten."

His parents were dead, so *they* certainly had. But everyone?

"*I* haven't forgotten. And I bet if you asked Ville neither has he."

He scrubbed a hand over his neck once again. Even without the obvious reminders looking back at him in the mirror he would never be able to erase those images from his head. Of his best friend's grin right before the world exploded before his eyes.

"Ville's family moved off the island ten years ago. Besides, it doesn't matter."

Before he had time to draw enough breath to throw another excuse at his friend Theo brushed it aside with a sharp expletive.

"No buts, Deak. We've had this argument before. Mythelios is suffering. So put aside your self-pity for once. It's time for you to do the right thing. Come home. The sooner, the better."

CHAPTER ONE

THE CRUSH OF people in the inner sanctum of the clinic made Leanora Risi wince. Just over a month since the earthquake and the flow of those emotionally and physically wounded had not completely abated.

Many were drawn to the steady presence of the clinic and its outside garden. It had gotten so it was hard for her to find a quiet corner in which to hear from those who were still having problems dealing with the after-effects. She was well past the end of her vacation and her savings were slowly dwindling. She was going to have to make a decision about whether to leave or not...soon.

But not right now.

A man with dark shaggy hair and a jaw shadowed with what had to be a three-week growth of whiskers made his way to the front desk. There was an exhaustion about him that went beyond physical tiredness. It was in the way his eyes shifted slowly from one person to the next. He greeted several of them, shaking their hands, but it was a rapid clasp and release. Not the hearty greeting most of the islanders gave each other.

He reached the desk, but didn't take the pen to sign in. Instead he flipped over the top sheet with his right hand and started studying the entries.

An internal alarm went off inside her. While it wasn't against the rules for patients to glance at the list of other patients to see how long the wait would be—at least she didn't think it was—the way he was acting was odd, making her gut tighten.

The number of patients they'd had right after the earthquake was staggering, and they had ended up just stacking new sheets on top of the old ones, since they hadn't had time to sit down and collate the data and put the sign-in times on charts yet. Even though things had evened out quite a bit, there were still things they hadn't completely caught up with.

When those long fingers flicked another sheet over, it was Lea's signal to move. Murmuring an apology as she accidentally brushed shoulders with an older woman, she hurried forward, arriving beside the man and firmly placing her hand on the first couple of sheets, trapping his beneath them.

"Can I help you with something?"

His gaze swiveled from the stack of papers to her face. Up went dark brows, a hint of irritation marring his rugged features. "You can let me see how many patients have been treated today."

That inner alarm became less certain. Those low growled words didn't sound apologetic. At all. No sign of the nosy-neighbor-caught-with-binoculars-up-to-his-eyes syndrome. Instead he acted as if he had a right to look at those pages. But she didn't recognize him. She would have remembered those high cheekbones, that bump in an otherwise straight nose.

Although...wasn't there...?

What?

Despite the whiskers, his strong jaw was clearly visible. This was a man who wasn't easily deterred from something he wanted. She just wasn't sure what that something was.

She blinked to bring the room back into focus. Still filled with people. A few of them were on the list, waiting to be seen, but many just needed the solid presence of the clinic to ground them.

She lifted her hand from the papers, although she probably shouldn't. He still hadn't explained who he was.

"May I ask what you're looking for, specifically?"

"I believe I already explained that, Ms....?"

Her chin tilted. "It's Dr. Dr. Risi."

"I wasn't aware the clinic had hired a new doctor." His voice downshifted, becoming a little less gruff. "Where is Petra?"

"Petra's mom hasn't felt well since the earthquake. She's been going home during her lunch break to check on her."

How did he know the clinic receptionist's name? Although most of the islanders in this area seemed to know each other.

And now he was flipping through those patient sheets once again. "I don't see a list of symptoms or injuries."

"There isn't one. Things got too chaotic, trying to separate them out, so we just did triage, taking the critical patients first. We put the ones who were stable but needed a specialist in a secondary waiting area in the Serenity Gardens."

Facing the ocean, the courtyard led to a spacious garden that faced the sea. Lea's tiny treatment area had been carved out of a dead-end path, shielded on two sides by vine-covered trellises.

It was the perfect place for her to see patients who

needed to work through what they'd experienced during the quake. It was wonderful, and restful, and despite the tragedy she loved what she was doing there. More than she'd ever dreamed possible.

The people in the waiting area weren't the only ones who needed to be grounded. She'd come to Greece to do just that. And had ended up on the island just as the quake hit. She'd stayed to help.

Her attention came back with a bump when the man in front of her made a slight scoffing noise.

"What?"

"Nothing."

It was then that she realized she still didn't know who he was. He could be a psychiatric patient for all she knew. "Do you need to leave a message for Petra?"

He frowned. "Is Theo—Dr. Nikolaides—back yet?"

Theo had just gotten engaged. His whirlwind romance with Cailey had been a bright spot for the clinic, and probably one of the reasons why there were more people than normal here. It was as if folks wanted to catch a glimpse of the couple—live vicariously through those who had been able to find happiness in the midst of tragedy. Cailey was also nearly two months pregnant, and the baby had become a symbol of hope.

"He's taking a much-needed personal day. Did you have a consultation scheduled with him?"

Maybe he actually *was* a patient.

"Not exactly." One side of his mouth went up in a half-smile that sent her pulse tripping over itself. "He called me. Basically said I was an emotionless so-and-so if I didn't come home as soon as I could."

Home…

Home?

Then she swallowed—hard—an awful suspicion crashing like a boulder in the pit of her stomach. "You *live* here?"

His smile widened and he let the papers fall back into place as he turned toward her. "I don't live *in* the clinic, if that's what you mean."

"No, I don't mean that, I just…" She was at a loss for words—which was unusual, since talking was what she was paid to do. What she loved to do. No, it wasn't the words. It was the listening…the empathizing…the *helping* that she loved.

Although she couldn't help everyone.

Her eyes closed as a shot of pain punched through her chest.

No, don't think about that. Not now.

Something touched her hand. "Hey. Are you okay?"

"Yes." She forced herself to smile. "I'm just tired. And I forgot to ask who you are."

"Of course. Sorry, I just always assume that everyone knows who I am." Something dark slithered through his brown eyes. Then it was gone again as quickly as it had come. "I'm Deakin Patera. I'm one of the four founding partners of the clinic."

Ack!

God, she should have realized. Theo had said Dr. Patera was due to arrive in the next couple of days. She just hadn't expected someone who looked like he'd stepped straight off the cover of a wilderness backpacking magazine. He could have told her who he was sooner. Emphasized his medical title like she had.

She wasn't even sure why she'd done that. Maybe because she'd expected him to talk down to her like a few colleagues had over the years. But those people had been few and far between.

"I'm sorry. I didn't recognize you."

He dragged a hand through his hair. "It's okay. It's been a long flight, and it's not like our portraits are on the walls or anything. Thank God."

What an odd thing to say. She smiled. "Maybe they should be. Your reputations seem to be known far and wide."

The softness to his eyes disappeared. "I'm sure they are."

Those four words might have come across as arrogant boasting if not for the strange tone in which they were said. It was as if he despised that fact.

"I don't understand."

"It's nothing." His glance turned to the occupants of the room. "Where do we begin?"

The words to a famous old musical song came to mind, but there was no way she was breaking into song. Not around *this* particular man. Besides she couldn't compete with the likes of Julie Andrews.

"A lot of these people are just meeting friends and family here." She nodded at the foursome who were even now passing through the wooden and glass doors off to the left. "The clinic seems to have become almost as much of a meeting place as Stavros's *taverna*. And, since the bar is within walking distance, it makes it ideal."

With its traditional white stucco exterior and well-manicured gardens to the side of it, the clinic was a beautiful building, combining old-world charm with all the modern amenities of a medical facility. The Serenity Gardens boasted many nooks and crannies, ideal for intimate conversations, and benches were sprinkled along a curving walkway which was wide enough for wheelchairs and yet rustic enough to invite exploring. A white sea wall and a boat dock were newer additions.

"I can see that. Theo always did want this place to be more than just a medical clinic. Hence the so-called Tranquility Gardens."

"They're called the *Serenity* Gardens, and it doesn't sound like you approve of the addition."

He shrugged, his dark shirt pulling tight over muscular shoulders. Shoulders her eyes had no business lingering on. She hauled her attention back to his face.

"It's not that I disapprove," he said. "I just don't believe a manufactured place can bring tranquility. *Serenity*," he corrected. His smile came back, although the left side of his mouth didn't quite lift as high as the other. "Although Theo is convinced it can."

"I think it can as well. It's where I see most of my patients."

"How does that work? Did Theo put an exam room out there?"

The image of a hospital bed nestled between the flower pots made her smile back. "No. Not yet, anyway. I use the exam rooms, obviously, for physical investigation, but the garden is much more conducive to talking things through."

"Things? Such as unfavorable diagnoses?"

"Not exactly. I guess this is where I should say that I'm a psychiatrist." She held up her hands. "No couch jokes, please."

His head jerked back, a muscle in his jaw twitching for a second before going still. "Couch jokes are the farthest thing from my mind at the moment. Theo hired you?"

She bit her lip. Maybe the Serenity Gardens wasn't the only thing Dr. Patera would disapprove of. "I just happened to be on the island when the earthquake hit. I stayed to help. It's on a volunteer basis at the moment."

"The quake happened over a month ago. What about your own practice?"

It was her turn to shrug. "I'd already given notice at my hospital, so I'm kind of between jobs."

"And where was that? In Athens?"

Ah, he thought she actually lived in *Greece*. One of the perks of having parents who had immigrated to Canada from Greece when she was a kid was that she was bilingual. The fact that he hadn't heard any trace of an accent made her happy. As did the ease with which the islanders seemed to have accepted her.

"No, I lived in Canada. Toronto."

"Your family is Greek, though."

It wasn't a question. "Yes. They moved there when I was young."

Someone came up on his right and said something to him. Dr. Patera turned his head to give the man his attention and Lea's breath stalled in her lungs at what that shift of position revealed.

Scars. Big ones.

Wickedly thick, they began at the lower half of his strong square jaw and formed twin streams that coursed down the side of his neck, disappearing beneath the collar of his shirt. Continuing on to those shoulders she'd just been admiring? Probably. The scars were paler than the rest of his skin. So they were old.

How old?

God. Those wounds must have been agonizing when

they were fresh. Debriding. Skin grafts. Therapy to allow for movement. All part of third-degree burn treatment.

What had caused them? An explosive device? Some kind of caustic agent? Maybe he'd been in the military or something. She had a feeling that what she'd thought was an attractive lopsidedness to his smile might be due to the contracture of skin and muscle drawing everything down. Her gaze traveled to his chest. How many more scars were hidden beneath his clothes?

Her mind tossed an image of a very naked Dr. Patera at her—one who aimed that scrumptious crooked smile right at her and sent her brain into overdrive. She swallowed hard, feeling a weird shifting sensation burrowing through her midsection. Her teeth dug into her bottom lip.

Oh, Lord, what was once seen could not be unseen.

Except she hadn't *really* seen him naked. She'd just—

His attention shifted back to her with a suddenness she hadn't expected. She released her lip in a hurry, but it was too late. She knew it the second his eyes flickered to her mouth and back up.

She'd seen them. His damned scars.

He gave an inner grimace. They were kind of obvious. His tendency to keep his right profile to a person was ingrained from years of trying to keep the damage to his skin out of sight. Hidden, but not forgotten.

Along with his sense of shame?

Probably. The two things seemed to go hand in hand. It was one of the things that had kept him from wanting to come back to the island. Almost every person on Mythelios knew what he'd done. Or at least they thought they did.

Except Dr. Risi, here. And now even *she* had seen
the evidence—she just didn't know the reason for it.

He wasn't even sure why he'd participated in the
founding of this clinic. He'd wanted to leave after medical school and never come back. And for the most part
he'd done exactly that. But his three best friends in the
world had been determined to take their parents' tar-
nished legacies and turn them into something good. And
as long as he could give his input from a distance he
was good with that. His traveling did the trick for the
most part. He was able to give his nods of approval from
afar, except when they absolutely needed his physical
presence.

Like now.

If he'd expected to see a quick show of pity on this
new doctor's face, though, he was sorely disappointed.
She met his gaze with steady green eyes that gave nothing away.

That was probably the psychiatrist in her. She was
trained to listen without judging. Not to seem shocked
or horrified, no matter how ugly the story. Or how hid-
eous the outward appearance.

His dad—after a rare crack had appeared in his chilly
demeanor—had once sent him to a shrink in Athens,
six months after the accident. But Deakin, his scars still
fresh and painful, had refused to say anything. After
four sessions of sitting there in sullen silence they'd
given up. All of them—including the psychiatrist.

He tried to recall what Lea had been talking about
moments earlier, working to forget the way those white
teeth had captured that full bottom lip in a way that was
far too sexy for a psychiatrist.

He switched to English so those around would be less

likely to understand them if she tried to ask about his scars. "So, what part of Greece were your parents from?"

"Athens—like you thought. My dad was a welder and went to Canada to help with the building of one of the Orthodox churches. He ended up staying." She sent a lock of long dark hair spinning over her shoulder with a flick of her wrist. "He sent for me and my mom a few months later, and we went, sight unseen. But we love it there now."

The switch in language hadn't thrown her for a loop. In fact her English was as flawless as her Greek. He knew himself well enough to know that his Greek accent was still fairly strong, even after years of speaking English in other countries.

"You don't ever get homesick for Greece?"

"Not really. I was a kid when things changed."

That he understood. He didn't get homesick either. And he'd also been a kid when things had changed. Only, unlike for her, the change hadn't been a good one for him.

She went on. "Besides, you can find Greeks on almost every street corner."

"You can, indeed." Deakin had found pockets of Greek communities almost everywhere he'd gone. "Well, shall we get started? Are you only seeing patients who need counseling?"

"No, we've been kind of short-staffed, as you can imagine, so I've been helping wherever I can. The immediate injuries from the quake have been taken care of, but there are still issues—broken bones, lacerations that have become infected... Burns. But I *have* been seeing patients who are struggling to cope with the after effects of the earthquake. It's what I specialize in. People dealing with PTSD."

He tried to ignore the way she'd hesitated before saying the word "burns."

"PTSD from time served in the military?"

"No, civilian for the most part. Trauma comes in many forms."

Yes, it did. He wasn't sure if she was subtly trying to dig into his past struggles, but he wasn't going to take any chances. He didn't need someone probing where they didn't belong.

Time to get to work.

Just then Petra came back from wherever she'd been and glanced his way. She did a double-take, her eyes widening.

"Deakin!"

She rushed through the door to the waiting room and grabbed him in a strong, matronly embrace.

Her graying locks were scraped back into a bun and dark-rimmed glasses were pushed on top of her head. The combination gave her a no-nonsense appearance. One that was well-deserved. She could be formidable when she wanted to be.

"It's about time you came home."

He stiffened at that word. This wasn't his home. Not anymore. But at least her presence took Dr. Risi's attention off him.

"I'm sure you're keeping the clinic running like a well-oiled machine."

She dropped her glasses onto her nose and peered at him over the top of them. "It's not easy, let me tell you."

"I'm sure. Did Chris or Ares make it home yet?"

"No. Not yet. But I'm hopeful you will all be reunited soon. It's been too long."

"Yes, it has."

While he didn't miss the island, he did miss his friends.

"So, Theo has been handling the crisis alone?" He'd thought maybe the others would have made it back sooner than him.

"Well, he has Cailey now. She's been a huge help. And Lea has been *aprosdókito kaló*. She's very organized. And beautiful, don't you think?"

Color bloomed in the psychiatrist's face. Petra had called the doctor a godsend. And beautiful.

And Petra was right. She was very attractive. Dark-lashed eyes gleamed with purpose beneath arched brows. And with each upward curve of her lips high cheekbones appeared.

And yet there was something lurking just beneath the surface. He'd caught glimpses of it when she'd talked about PTSD. Did her patients' pain affect her on a personal level? He knew from experience that as much as you tried to maintain an emotional distance there were some patients who touched something inside you.

His own throat tightened whenever he was called on to treat a child who'd suffered horrific burns or who had lost limbs from incendiary devices or from IEDs. It was why he did what he did.

"I think you've embarrassed Dr. Risi, Petra."

"It's okay. I'm fine. And please call me Lea. We all tend to be informal around here."

The way she said that make him take a closer look at her. She didn't *sound* fine. Did she think the older woman was trying to set them up somehow? Well, she needn't worry. He wasn't about to start a romance with anyone—especially not someone with ties to this island.

But she didn't have ties—had said she didn't get homesick for Greece. She was a temporary visitor, that was all. She wasn't staying on the island for long.

The image of those teeth gripping that lip in a tight embrace sashayed across the backs of his eyelids, playing peekaboo with a neglected part of his anatomy. He could think of a way to make her do that all over again. For very different reasons.

He stopped that thought in its tracks. *Not happening*. She could be leaving tomorrow for all he knew.

His job didn't lend itself to relationships. And that suited him just fine. Theo might have found true love, but that was something Deakin neither wanted nor needed. Because relationships meant exposing the worst of yourself to someone else.

Lea pushed that errant strand of hair over her shoulder once again and glanced out over the waiting room, which was gradually clearing out.

"It may not look that way, but this is one of our slower times." She looked at the sign-in sheet. "It'll stay that way until after lunch."

Deakin was having a hard time understanding why exactly he was even here. Could he fly out before Theo realized he had arrived?

"Are you still seeing new injuries?"

"Some. There are a few buildings that still aren't stable. So we're seeing crush injuries. And with those unstable buildings come gas lines and electric wires, so there's a chance of electrocution and burns—"

She was still talking, but that last word was all he

heard in that moment. It was the second time she'd said it.

Deakin's father had replaced his boat. It was right there in the rebuilt boathouse. Leaving it to Deakin in his will had seemed like the ultimate slap in the face, but since they'd left everything else to him as well it probably hadn't been meant like that. But Deakin had kept it, taking that vessel out for a spin every time he came home—which wasn't often. But the guests that booked his home were granted full use of the grounds—including his Jeep and the boat.

"Hello?" Lea snapped her fingers in front of his face. "Are you okay?"

He frowned, hating being caught thinking about his past. "I'm fine. I'm just dealing with a serious case of jet lag. I need a shave and a shower."

"You must be exhausted. Did you come straight here after landing on the mainland?"

"Yes, but I'm fine." He wasn't, but it had nothing to do with being tired.

There was no way he was going to share any of that with her. *Temporary visitor, remember?*

Petra interrupted. "I talked to your aunt this morning. She was sure you were arriving today and said to send you straight over to the house. She's put a moussaka in the fridge for you."

His Aunt Cecilia was in charge of renting out his parents' house and his cottage to tourists. It seemed better than letting them sit empty and untended.

"Great." He glanced at the wall behind the reception desk, frowning when something caught his eye.

Dammit. What was *that* doing there?

He shook his head and tried to continue his thought. "Where did you end up staying?" he asked Lea.

"At a private cottage a few miles from here."

Petra laughed. "A few miles from here in *that* direction." Her hand waved a few times in the air before pointing to the west.

There probably weren't all that many bed and breakfasts operating right now. Not that the damage to the island was horrific, but he could pretty much guarantee that tourist income was down. Hadn't his aunt said that his house had been sitting vacant ever since the earthquake? Who wanted to vacation in a place torn apart by a natural disaster?

He couldn't think of anything on the west side of the island except for the expensive houses owned by people like his parents. Although... His house was in that general—

"*Whose* cottage?"

The receptionist smiled wickedly, while Lea looked thoroughly confused. "Theo, Cailey and your aunt figured it was the best place to house her, since the hotel she was staying at was damaged by the quake. So she's staying in the cottage, Deakin. *Your* cottage."

CHAPTER TWO

THIS WAS *DEAKIN'S* HOUSE?

She set a skillet on a burner to heat and gritted her teeth.

Why hadn't Theo told her? She'd assumed it was a relative's house or something. But the tiny white building behind the opulent house was perfect, and she loved staying there. The formal manicured grounds here made the Serenity Gardens look like something out of a dollhouse, although it was a gorgeous setting. The clinic's grounds were informal, while the house she was staying so close to screamed money. Even the boathouse had a tiny apartment over it.

She had never really stopped to think about who on the island could afford something like this. Theo had said he and his friends' parents had been part of something called Mopaxeni Shipping. They'd all been wealthy. She didn't know the whole story, and although the clinic was state of the art she had gotten the impression that they were only scraping by and looking for fundraisers.

Like that calendar over the desk in the main entryway at the clinic that boasted photos of twelve very hunky locals. Some of them were doctors, or employees of the clinic, and others were firefighters or involved in other lines of public service.

Deakin was somewhere in the main house at this very moment. It had been more than obvious that he wasn't happy with her being here. The look on his face when he'd realized exactly which cottage Petra was talking about had been priceless…and embarrassing. But unless she just wanted to leave the island there wasn't much she could do about it. And she was enjoying the work far too much to let Deakin's grumpiness drive her away.

The property was usually rented out when Deakin wasn't there, Theo had finally admitted when she'd called him and confronted him about the cottage. He hadn't been positive Deakin would come back when he'd offered it to her, and they'd needed her at the clinic. And for that to happen she'd needed someplace to sleep. It had been the only logical solution.

That didn't make it the most comfortable one now that Deakin was home. He'd claimed it didn't bother him to have her staying there, but his voice told another story.

Cracking an egg, she listened to the satisfying sizzle as it hit the heated oil, the earthy scent filling the air, making her mouth water.

She made her way to the refrigerator for some orange juice, pulling a small glass from a cupboard on the way. She could *do* this. From what she'd heard about Deakin, a plastic surgeon who specialized in treating burns victims, he didn't stay in one place for any length of time. He probably wouldn't be here for more than a week or two. As soon as he could Deakin would be on his way.

He didn't like the island. She wasn't sure how she knew that, but she did. It was in the way his eyes shifted

from thing to thing, that ever-present frown on his face.
Something here held bad vibes for him.

Maybe he'd been injured on the island?

It didn't matter.

She hadn't come to the island to speculate on its residents, past or present. She'd come here to escape.

No. Not to escape. To start over.

There was a difference. Starting over involved staying here on this earth, not—

Dammit.

A piercing shriek shattered her thoughts in an instant, and her brain struggled to locate the source.

A smoke alarm, just behind her.

Why…?

Oh, no! Where there'd once been the satisfying crackle of a cooking egg there was now billowing smoke coming from the stovetop.

But that alarm…

God! Her ears!

The racket was huge and dramatic, with flashing strobe lights and a screeching caterwaul that reminded her of a seagull. Or maybe a million of them.

The hot oil wasn't actually on fire, thank heavens, so she rushed over and grabbed the pan. She was hurrying toward the sink with it just as the front door burst open.

Deakin appeared, stopping in his tracks as his eyes jerked from her face and landed on the pan, which was now safely under the tap.

He came over, putting both hands on the edge of the counter, his breath seesawing in and out. "What happened?"

She could barely make out the words over the alarm.

"I was trying to cook dinner, but…" She had to yell, her vocal cords straining. "Can you turn that thing off?"

He pulled a remote from the front pocket of his chinos and aimed it toward the still blaring siren.

She sucked down a deep breath, her ears ringing in the sudden silence that followed. "Wow. Why didn't you just turn it off from the house? I think you got an industrial-sized alarm by mistake."

"No mistake. It's safer."

Her head tilted. *Safer?* Okay…whatever he said.

She gave a rueful gesture toward the skillet. "I'm sorry. I'll reimburse you, of course, if the pan is ruined."

"It's nothing. I thought the whole cottage was on fire."

It was then that she realized his upper lip was damp with perspiration and the tight lines running down the side of his face weren't from irritation but from something far worse. *Fear.*

Of what?

A smoke alarm went off, Lea, that's what.

He didn't want to lose his home to her stupidity. But she had never seen an alarm like that. Actually, when she looked closer she also saw ceiling sprinklers, jutting down at regular intervals.

"I guess I'm lucky the sprinklers didn't go off and give you water damage on top of everything else. I really am sorry."

He brushed aside her words. "It's nothing. I'm just glad you're okay. The sprinklers are set with a delay. If the alarm isn't shut down in ten minutes they engage, and then the fire department is notified."

There was a tense element to his voice, that made her take a closer look at the way he was perspiring.

A warning tingle started at the back of her head and

traveled up over the top. She shut off the faucet. Maybe that was what those scars were from. A house fire. It would explain a lot. His apathy toward the island. His reluctance to return, according to Theo.

Bad memories?

If it had been the big house or this particular cottage, they had been rebuilt to perfection. They looked like they'd been standing on this rocky crag for the last century. Except for the boathouse. That was different from the main house and the cottage, even though it still blended in. It just seemed *newer*, somehow. But there was no way she was going to ask.

"I'm fine." She forced another smile. "Unfortunately my meal didn't fare quite as well."

"The smoke detector certainly didn't approve." A *beep-beep* accompanied a few more manipulations of the remote control. "There. I've reset it for you."

Just in case his panicked reaction *wasn't* all in her imagination, she decided to put his mind at ease. "Thanks. I'll stay far away from the stove tonight so I don't trip it again. Cold cuts it is."

He paused for a few long seconds before glancing at her, and sure enough his muscles seemed to relax all at once. "My aunt's moussaka is heating in the oven at the main house. There's more than enough if you want to share."

She tried to ignore the way her mouth watered. Moussaka was one of her favorite dishes. "Are you sure? I don't mind just making a sandwich."

If he was as uneasy about having her at the cottage as she thought he was, it was up to her to make sure her stay was as discreet as possible. Especially since there wasn't anywhere else for her to stay. At least not now. Maybe in another week or two something would open up and she could leave Deakin alone in his cottage on the hill.

"I'm sure. I was going to offer earlier, but I wasn't sure what your plans were."

"My plans are a bit charred now," she said, nodding at the sink. "You rent the house out, Theo said? The cottage as well?"

"Yes. Since my parents are both gone it's the best way I can think of to keep them occupied, so their upkeep is not left completely up to my aunt."

His tight jaw said that his parents were "gone" as in deceased. She was surprised Theo hadn't mentioned that.

"I'm sorry about your parents."

"It's been a while, but thank you. They died in a car accident on the mainland."

They died together.

She closed her eyes for a second, trying to suppress a wave of grief. At least one of them hadn't left the other wondering where they'd gone wrong. Or if they could have done something—*anything*—differently.

Not a healthy avenue to pursue.

With as much PTSD as she'd treated, you'd think she'd be able to recognize it in herself. The problem was, she *did* recognize it. There just wasn't anything she could do about it. Things were the way they were, and no railing against fate was going to change it.

Mark was dead. His life cut short in a single defining moment.

Six months before they were supposed to be married.

"It's hard losing someone you care about."

The words came out of their own volition, making her frown. She needed to change the subject before it brought back even more memories. Ones that were better off left behind her.

"So, your aunt is a good cook?"

He pushed away from the counter, his tenseness evaporating. "One of the best on the island. Besides managing this place, she caters special events here on the island."

"Wow. I think I remember Theo saying something about the caterer being related to you. Is that your aunt?"

"If he called her Cecilia Patera, then, yes. She's really the only woman on the island who cooks for a living. Her moussaka is out of this world. They even serve some of her *meze* at Stavros's *taverna*. You've been there?"

"Only once. The owner was a little gruff."

Deakin's head tilted. "Really? That doesn't sound like Stavros. But I guess everyone can have an off day."

The man hadn't been mean, he'd just answered someone a little more curtly than she'd liked and that had been enough for her. She hadn't been back since.

"I'm sure that's what it was. Anyway, since I have destroyed my sense of hearing as well as your frying pan, I think I'll take you up on your offer of moussaka, if it's really okay. I can just bring a portion home and eat it here, though. I don't want to inconvenience you."

"I wouldn't have offered if it was an inconvenience. Or I could make you a quick omelet if you have your heart set on eggs."

"I actually love moussaka, so no. Eggs just seemed quick and easy."

The right side of his mouth went up. It was then she realized that she couldn't see his burns at all. Because that side of his face was angled away from her. But even if that crooked smile *was* a result of whatever had happened to him, it didn't make it any less sexy.

"Not so quick and not so easy, from the looks of it."

"Only because I was distracted," she protested with a smile.

He glanced toward the television, which was off. "Oh? By what?"

By thoughts of orange juice and…and her mysterious neighbor. But she was not going to say that out loud. He would kick her out if he suspected she was daydreaming about him.

She wasn't. She was just…thinking about life and the strange ways that paths intersected. And sometimes came to a dead end.

She shifted as a familiar heaviness in her chest made itself known.

There was nothing you could have done, Lea.

The voice inside her head came back with its customary rejoinder: *How do you know that for sure?*

She couldn't know. She would never know. And even if she became convinced she'd missed a whole barrage of symptoms—which she hadn't—it was too late now.

Deakin was still waiting for her response.

She glanced out the window over the sink and caught sight of the gorgeous sunset. "By that." She motioned toward the sight, mentally crossing her fingers.

He put his elbows on the counter to get low enough to look out the window. "It is beautiful. I have the same view from the kitchen in the main house."

He might think it was a pretty view, but it didn't go deeper than an objective observation. How did she know that? There had been no emotion in the statement. No softening of his eyes. No smile the way he had when she'd changed the subject a few minutes ago.

"It's pretty breathtaking." She tried again to prod him lightly, not even sure what she was looking for.

"Yes, it is. Are you ready?" He had already turned away from the window, was coming around to the other side of the counter and checking the knobs on the stove.

"I already turned them off."

"Sometimes they stick."

No, they didn't. She'd heard the click as they snapped off.

Rather than be offended by his double-checking, she felt a rush of sympathy go through her. More and more she was convinced that something bad had happened to him very close to home. And those scars were old, so it had been a while ago. Long enough for him to have stopped needing to check knobs on a stove. Or was it…?

Leaving the cottage, he indicated the way down a cobblestone pathway that led to the main house. The harsh heat of the day was giving way to cooler temperatures now that the sun was going down. Even so, she was very glad the cottage was air-conditioned.

"Have you been in the house itself yet?" he asked.

"No, but it's beautiful from the outside."

"Yes, my parents did a nice job on it when it was built."

Her eyes skipped to the white boathouse near the shore. "You're very lucky to live so close to the water. It's a shame you aren't here very often to enjoy it. I would be in that boat every chance I got."

His steps faltered for a second, before he continued on. "I go out in it every time I'm home."

"I bet it's gorgeous out there on the water."

"I guess it is." He glanced back at her. "I'll probably go out at least once while I'm here. You're welcome to join me if you'd like."

"Oh, I wasn't angling for an invitation. I'm sorry if it came across that way."

"It didn't."

Lea wasn't sure how she felt about going out on the water with him. There was something about him that made her uneasy.

She decided to sidestep the subject without making it too obvious. "Did you grow up in this house?"

"Yes."

She waited for him to elaborate, or tell her how long he'd lived there, but he didn't. By the time she tried to think of something else to break what was becoming an uncomfortable silence they were at the front door. Dark and heavy, it loomed over the small porch.

Or maybe it was her thoughts that were dark.

The main house hadn't seemed ominous before.

He opened it, motioning her through the entryway, and the feeling instantly went away. White tile flooring blended into equally white walls. It might have come across as spartan and cold except for the touches here and there of an azure blue that reminded Lea of the warm ocean waters that surrounded the island. It was there in a painting. In the pillows she could see through the arched doorway of the living room. It had been professionally decorated.

"I didn't expect the inside to look like this."

She couldn't stop the words. She thought the cottage was lovely and homey, but this was head and shoulders above the quaintness of where she was staying. It was ultra-formal and elegant. And somehow it didn't match Deakin at all.

He should be surrounded by brown furnishings and dark shadowy corners.

No, he shouldn't. That would be depressing.

Except it wouldn't. It would match what she sensed was inside him: hidden recesses that he revealed to no one.

She tensed. Hadn't she come across that before? Looking back, she wasn't sure how she could have missed those signs in Mark. Only she'd been young and in love, and Mark had had a way of flashing that care-free smile of his in a way that had seemed so genuine.

Wasn't that how emotional scars in people were over-looked until it was too late?

As if on cue, Deakin turned back, his scars appearing in stark contrast as the light from the doorway poured over them. "How did you expect it to look?"

"Don't get me wrong…it's extremely elegant." There was no way she could give voice to her thoughts from a moment earlier. *No way. No how.* "It's just very differ-ent from the cottage."

"My aunt had a hand in decorating the cottage. It's where I normally live when I come here. The house is rented out most of the year. The people who were going to rent it this month backed out because of the earth-quake."

"Your aunt didn't help decorate the main house."

It was a statement. Not a question. There was no way the same person had had a hand in *this* house, although a skilled interior decorator could probably pull off two such divergent spaces.

"No." He swept a hand around the foyer. "This was all my parents' doing."

He said it as if it was not the way *he* would have done things.

"Are you going to redo it?"

"No."

The single word answer didn't invite discussion. Instead she studied the textured paint on the walls and the pricey rugs on the floor and changed the topic to something a little more neutral.

"Your guests must love staying here."

His eyes closed for a split second. In gratitude? She had no idea.

He tossed a set of keys and the remote he'd had at the cottage onto a nearby console table. "They seem to like it."

"Is there another remote for the alarm at the cottage?" She allowed a glimmer of a smile to play across her face. "In case I decide to cook again at some point?" The scent of something warm and inviting curled around her nostrils. "Although if that heavenly aroma is what I think it is I may have to hire your aunt to cook all my meals for me."

"I'm sure she would be happy to."

Lea had a feeling *he* might be happy if she did that as well.

"Seriously, do you want the cottage stove to be off-limits? Just say the word. I don't want you to worry about me setting the place on fire every time I'm in the kitchen."

"I'm not."

He wasn't what? Worried? Because the stiff set of his

posture as he walked in the direction of the living room said something different.

"I'll give you a quick tour while dinner finishes heating."

They went through the archway, and her eyes tracked from thing to thing.

"This space is pretty obvious…"

The blue pillows she'd noticed earlier were set in precise rows along the back of the couch. It reminded her of suture lines. She did her best to hide the shiver that went through her. It was only her imagination. Or maybe just a reaction to the whole smoke alarm encounter.

She almost hadn't noticed that he'd shaved the stubble off his face sometime this evening. His hair was still on the longish side, but it was thick and glossy now, and her fingers suddenly itched to touch one of the dark wavy locks as he came to a stop. The man looked like a Greek god out of a legend.

She dragged her gaze back to the room when he turned to face her, and tried to shut the door on the shot of pure hormones that jetted through her.

Dust. Look for dust. A cobweb. Anything!

The perfectly square coffee table in front of her held a stack of magazines about boats, a white plaster lighthouse and a tray that held three blue candles. Not a speck of dust.

"Does your aunt clean the place after guests leave?"

"No, I hire a service to come in once a week. My aunt must have asked them to come in for my arrival."

So he'd known exactly when he was coming home? Why had no one warned her before he arrived? "Does Theo know you're here?"

"Not yet. I didn't give him my exact itinerary. I figured I'd stop in at the clinic and then come straight home if it wasn't overrun with patients. I hoped to catch him there, but obviously not if he's taking a personal day. I'll call him in the morning."

"Patients seem to come in spurts. Some days we can hardly keep up. Other days we're twiddling our thumbs—like this afternoon."

"How are you getting to and from the clinic?"

She shifted her weight to the other foot. "Well, there's a...um...a bicycle stored behind the cottage. I hope you don't mind I've been borrowing it?"

"Why don't you take the car? It's there for guests—surely Cecilia told you about it?"

"She did, but I was worried about aftershocks right after I vacated my hotel. I figured I could navigate a bicycle off the road in case of a car accident or a traffic jam. And then, once that danger had passed, I'd just got used to riding in. It helps me enjoy the beauty of the island."

"It's not quite as beautiful as it once was."

"You should have seen it right after the quake hit. It was awful."

The memory of the ground shuddering beneath her feet, of plaster cracking and sheeting off the walls in her hotel room, stopped any lingering feeling of attraction in its tracks. She'd crawled under the bed, hoping the roof wasn't going to cave in on top of her. It had seemed like forever before the ground tremors had subsided, when in reality it had probably only lasted a few minutes.

"I'm sorry you had to go through that."

Her brows went up. "I'm sorry *anyone* had to go through it. It was terrible."

"I'm sure it was." He dragged a hand through his hair.

"There was no way I could have come any sooner—my contract was unbreakable. I saw the reports on the news when I was sitting in a bar in Africa. Theo called as I was watching, and once I got off the phone with him I called everyone I could think of to see if they were okay."

They walked through the door to the dining room—another opulent space, where a huge glass-topped table crouched beneath a low chandelier. The surface, like the coffee table in the living room, was devoid of dust or even a single smudged fingerprint.

It bothered her, somehow. This didn't look like a place where a family might recount the minutiae of their day. Or where a child might spill a glass of milk and not live in fear of messing up something. Instead it reeked of formal place settings and expensive crystal. A place where business negotiations were hammered out.

Had Deakin eaten here as a child? God, she hoped not. She could just picture him eating a bowl of breakfast cereal all by himself. But maybe it hadn't been that way at all. Maybe he was from a big family who laughed their way through life.

"Do you have more family on the island?"

"You mean siblings?" He shook his head. "Nope. I'm an only child."

So no under the table kicking of a little sister or brother. No food fights or handing non-tasty morsels to the family dog. There was no sign that a pet of any kind had ever lived in this house.

Lea's childhood home had been messy and chaotic, with dogs and rabbits and horse shows through the local club. But she wouldn't trade it for the world. Medical school had been too grueling for her to have pets, but she certainly planned on having one or two once she got settled. In fact she and Mark had visited a shelter one time, just a week before he died.

Thank goodness they hadn't adopted a pet that day.

A fresh bout of anger went through her, even though he'd been gone more than a year. Ten years from now she would probably feel just as bewildered, could understand the grief and anger of other loved ones who'd been left behind just as suddenly.

"I'm an only child as well."

She wasn't going to delve beyond that, because she didn't know enough about him to trade childhood snapshots. Not yet, anyway. And probably not ever, since she wouldn't see him again once she'd left the island.

A pang went through her at the thought of going back to Toronto. As much as she loved her parents and her adopted city, she had put down the first tiny threads of roots on Mythelios. The second she'd stepped onto the island there'd been a sense of home. Of belonging. Maybe because of her Greek heritage. But her savings would eventually run out and she would have to go back to work.

The question was where.

He stopped in the doorway of the kitchen and turned toward her, propping his left shoulder against the door frame and crossing his arms. "It must have been quite an adjustment moving to Canada, then."

She had to backtrack for a second to realize he was talking about her being an only child.

"In some ways. But I think it made it easier for me to adapt. Toronto has a lot of immigrants, but I went to school. I had to learn English quickly in order to survive. Sink or swim. I swam."

And Mark hadn't.

He pursed his lips. "You've left your position there, though. Where are you off to next? Back to Canada?"

It was as if he'd read her mind. "I'm not sure yet. I haven't thought that far ahead."

Her parents were there. And yet the last thing she wanted to do was face her and Mark's old apartment. She'd have to, though, even if just to pack up her things. *His* belongings were long gone. Mark's mom and dad had been tasked with the heartbreaking job of sorting through everything and deciding what to do with his personal items. She'd spent the week in a hotel to give them some privacy. That had been many months ago, but the sharp sting of those days still remained.

"I understand how that is."

His arms dropped to his sides, his posture opening up as if he really did understand her uncertainty.

Glancing over his shoulder, he said, "I think dinner is probably just about ready. Are you okay with eating out on the back deck? It should be cooling off outside by now."

"Outside sounds wonderful." She hoped her tone didn't give away how relieved she was they were not to be seated at opposite ends of that enormous table.

The right side of his mouth kicked up in a way that said he was just as glad. "Good. Then if you'll get the plates out of that cabinet by the sink, I'll get the pan out of the oven."

Opening the glass-fronted cabinet, she pulled down two ornate pieces of china, giving a quick wrinkle of her nose that she hoped he wouldn't see. Maybe their conversation would be a little less brittle than the dinnerware. Maybe they could even put that awkward first meeting behind them and get off on a better foot. For as long as they both were here.

She grimaced at how close that was to another sentence. If Mark had lived they would be married. But he hadn't. And they weren't. And Lea had no plans to leap into another romance anytime soon.

Right now she just needed to focus on putting that painful period in her life behind her. While she never would have wished Mythelios's earthquake on anyone, it had served to take her mind off herself and focus on doing good for those on the island. Didn't she always tell her patients that giving back to others was a great way to derail self-pity? She should have taken a page from her own book months ago. But she hadn't been ready to let go of the apartment which was a last connection to her fiancé.

She took a deep breath and accepted the steaming plate Deakin handed her with a murmured thank-you.

One thing was for sure, though. She was never getting involved with another man who carried a truckload of baggage. If she dated again, she was picking someone fun. Someone full of sunshine and light.

No brooding. No past trauma.

She gave a mental pinky-swear…to herself.

Happy, cheerful, and an eternal optimist. That was the best prescription she could think of.

And what better place to start than with herself?

CHAPTER THREE

"WHY DIDN'T YOU tell me you were arriving yesterday, Deak? Cailey and I would have picked you up. Did you fly in or take the ferry?"

Theo stood in the doorway to the exam room his patient had just exited, his frowning countenance not fooling anyone. His friend was glad to see him.

"I flew. It was a pretty bumpy landing. I guess they'll resurface the runway eventually. My aunt said it got damaged pretty badly."

"It was cracked in half. They did what they could to get it up and running again." He grinned. "I'm glad you could finally join the party."

Setting his laptop on the counter top, he walked over and gave Theo a quick brotherly slap on the back. "From what I've heard you're doing quite a bit of partying. I didn't want to disturb your love-nest."

Theo was one of the few people he'd never felt judged by. As kids he, Chris and Eri had never ogled his scars, but they hadn't tiptoed around them either. They'd accepted them, just like they'd accepted him—something his parents had never seemed able to do after the fire.

He'd never told them the whole truth. It wouldn't have helped the situation and it would have just made life harder for Ville, whose home life had been a million times worse than his. At least Deakin's parents hadn't *hit* him. They'd just frozen him out emotionally instead.

"Love-nest? Really?" He paused. "Cailey's pregnant. I wasn't sure if you'd heard."

Deakin's brows went up and he slapped his friend's back again. Hard enough to make Theo grunt this time. "No, you conveniently omitted that fact during our first phone conversation."

"Well, since it happened sometime *after* that call…" He chuckled. "Oh, you've met Lea Risi, haven't you?"

Deakin picked up his laptop, setting it on the table near the door. "She's living almost under my roof, so it's kind of hard to miss her. Another thing you cleverly omitted to mention."

"We can move her somewhere else if having her there bothers you. Cecilia kind of insisted when the hotel was evacuated. I could always check with Cailey and move her into our house."

"No. I'll survive. It's not like I'll be here for a year or anything."

"You never know."

His chest tightened. "Oh, I *know*."

Better change the subject before they got into it. He and Theo had already gone round and round enough times on this particular subject.

"So, what about this whole fundraising bachelor auction thing Cecelia has told me about? *I* don't have to do anything for it, right?"

"Well, since I'm out of the running, being an expectant father and all…"

Deakin made a sound that was half-grunt, half-laugh. "You must have wanted out of that auction really bad."

"Um…no. That's not quite how things worked. I never expected to meet someone and… Well, anyway, now that you're here you can take my place in the auction. The earthquake decimated our funds. And our CT scanner is on the fritz. It has to be repaired or replaced."

"Not interested. I already did that freak show of a calendar. Besides, I wouldn't bring in enough for a photocopier, much less a CT machine."

The thought of standing on some stage having people bid—or not bid—on his "worth" gave him the heebie-jeebies. Or, worse, having some little old lady place a pity bid on him that had him scrubbing her kitchen sink or something.

"I'd also appreciate it if you'd ask Petra to take down that calendar hanging in the reception area. At least for the month of July."

"Ha! That would be a negative, since that calendar has already brought in several thousand euros. If you want it down, *you* ask her."

And risk getting on Petra's wrong side? Although it might be worth it this time. Deakin's picture on the calendar was for the month of July, which was just over a week away. He didn't want *anyone* seeing that snapshot, especially not Lea.

He wasn't sure why that thought bothered him more than having other people see it. Maybe because he'd grown up on this island and they all knew him—knew his history. She didn't, and he didn't want her asking anyone about the incident which had seared a roadmap of scars into the left side of his chest.

There were areas of it that had never regained sensation, the nerves permanently damaged. He would never again feel the scrape of a woman's fingertips on those parts of his body. His throat tightened. Not that he routinely invited women into his bedroom, for the very same reason that he didn't want that calendar out there for the world to see.

Lea would probably think he'd been on some kind of ego trip during that whole photo shoot. That was the furthest thing from the truth. He hadn't wanted to do it, but their trust fund money from Mopaxeni Shipping had been running short for the year. So they had concocted the stupid scheme to get some local guys on a calendar, figuring some of the islanders might be keen to help fund the clinic.

One of the subjects had had a gall stone attack the day of the photo shoot, so Deakin had been an emergency substitute to save the day—such as it was. He hadn't even looked at the actual shot when it had been sent over—had just checked the "accept" box and sent the envelope back to the photographer.

The thought of Lea seeing how far down his scars went made him queasy. He'd caught her studying his neck when she thought he wasn't looking. Several times, in fact. He'd even almost balked about getting his hair cut this morning, because the longer it was, the more it covered. But that would have been admitting that Lea's curious glances disturbed him on some level. So he'd gone to his aunt and asked her to do the deed. She had, and four inches of shaggy growth had ended up on her kitchen floor.

He hadn't seen Lea since it had been cut. Would her glance skate over him like it had before? It didn't matter. His scars were a reality he dealt with every single day. No amount of hair was going to change that. He was damned lucky his arm and his hand had been spared. He'd turned to the side just in time.

Ville had been even more fortunate. He'd been standing on the far side of him during the explosion and his burns had reached second degree, missing third by a narrow margin.

"Well, the calendar was my first and last hurrah. No auction for me. No one would bid on me anyway."

Theo sighed. "Give yourself a little credit, Deak. There are plenty of women who would *love* to have a chance to place that winning bid."

"No way. Besides, I'm not staying on Mythelios long enough for anyone to put in a claim."

His friend laughed. "It's a bachelor auction. Not a mail order husband scheme."

That made Deakin grin. He'd forgotten how much he enjoyed these exchanges with his friends. "Well, I'm sure there are plenty of other guys who would jump at the chance to be raffled off."

"Auctioned," Theo corrected.

"Same thing."

Theo snapped his fingers. "I just remembered. I called in to the clinic at Naxos to order supplies. Any chance you could do a boat-run over there and pick it up in the next couple of days? Sending it by courier will just up the cost, and we're trying to pare down expenses as much as possible."

"Sure—not a problem."

"Take Lea with you, if you can. She's been on this island since the earthquake and she could probably use a little time away."

Great. He wished Theo had relayed that little tidbit *before* he'd agreed to go. "She's welcome to come if she wants to. But if she doesn't..." He forced a shrug that he hoped showed indifference.

A woman he recognized appeared in the doorway. Cailey Tomaras. Always a beautiful woman, she practically glowed now. Pregnancy hormones? Or was this what love did to you?

It took one touch of her hand on Theo's arm to answer that question. His face was totally transformed, with a smile crinkling the corners of his eyes. Deakin couldn't help but stare. His friend was *happy*. Truly happy.

Hell. What was that even like? He wasn't sure he knew anymore. Traveling from one outpost to another left little time to dissect his feelings. Or anything else.

Which was what he'd wanted when he'd left his parents' home, leaving it as a mausoleum—a reminder of all the reasons he'd moved away from the island.

His aunt had been bugging him to revamp the place for ages. When her requests had begun to show concern he'd let her do the cottage. He'd gotten into the habit of staying there. Until it had been occupied by a certain beautiful psychiatrist, forcing him back into the main house.

And he hated it there just as much today as he had when he'd lived in it as a teenager. Maybe it was time to let Aunt Cecilia have her way with it.

Theo turned toward him, forcing him from his thoughts. "Deak, you remember Cailey?"

"Yes, of course. Good to see you again."

"You as well." She shook his hand. "It's been a while. Theo talks about you a lot."

He tensed for a moment before he realized she probably wasn't referring to his past. There was no condemnation in her eyes, nor any hint of unease. Her eyes had skipped over his scars, but they hadn't lingered the way Lea's had.

Smiling, he tipped his head toward Theo. "All bad, if I know this guy."

"Actually, it was all good. Theo thinks a lot of you, Ares and Chris."

Cailey's fingers reached for Theo's, linking them together. Another shaft of unease went through Deakin's gut and then was gone.

She looked up at Theo. "Are we still on for lunch?"

"Of course. How are you feeling?"

"Better. Hungry." She glanced at Deakin. "You've heard our news?"

"Yes, congratulations."

"Thank you. We're pretty excited. Do you want to join us for lunch?"

And have their happiness remind him of all the things he would never have? Not likely. He knew that was unfair to Theo, and he was genuinely happy for his friend, but it was a shock to have the first one of their group travel down *this* particular path. He certainly hadn't seen it coming.

"Thank you, but I think Lea is entering the sign-in sheets into the patient records and she wants to ask me about some of them." It was only a half-lie.

Theo nodded. "I asked her to take that over for a while."

A while? That sounded a little too open-ended for his peace of mind.

"How long is she going to be here?" he asked, aiming for casual interest but not entirely sure he'd nailed it.

Theo shrugged. "I haven't thought that far in advance."

Weren't those almost the exact words Lea had used when he'd asked about her plans?

"Maybe she'll stay. She seems to really like it here." Cailey smiled.

The pain in his gut was back. "I doubt it. She was at a huge hospital in Toronto. I'm sure she's got better places to choose than Mythelios."

"You never know. Stranger things have happened." Theo's fingers squeezed his wife's. "Hey, when you get a chance can you go by the *taverna* and have a drink for me?"

"You normally have to drink yourself in order for it to do any good."

"I'm serious. Stavros hasn't been feeling well recently, but whenever anyone tries to talk to him about it he basically tells them to go to hell."

Stavros's *taverna* was a local legend, visited by islanders and tourists alike.

"Not feeling well is a pretty vague description."

Theo let go of Cailey's hand and wrapped his arm around her waist instead. "He's been having headaches. And I've been hearing over the last week or so that he's also been really grumpy."

"Lea mentioned that he'd rubbed her up the wrong way. She didn't use those exact words, but it was the idea I got."

"That's definitely not like him." Cailey leaned her head on Theo's arm.

These two had it bad. But he guessed since they were having a child together that was probably a *good* thing.

"Okay, I'll check on him. And I'll get those supplies. Does it have to be today?"

"There's nothing we need right this minute, no. Just

whenever you get to it. Stavros, on the other hand, worries me. If you can't go I'll make time."

"I'll do it. I kind of like the old man."

"Thanks. And on that note, we're off. Call if you need us. And don't try to take over Lea's job."

"I have no plans for doing that."

He wasn't really meeting Lea to discuss the patient records anyway. He'd made that up to get out of going to lunch. Maybe he'd head over to Stavros' place and get a feel for whatever it was Theo was worried about.

At noon?

Probably not the best idea. The *taverna* would be packed. He'd have to wait until normal business hours.

Well, he would just go out and see if he could scrounge up a patient to treat, then. Anything to get his mind off the thought that Cailey really might ask Lea to stay at the clinic. For good.

Why do you even care, Deakin?

He shouldn't. There was no reason to. *He* wasn't staying on the island, so it shouldn't matter at all to him.

All he knew was that it did. And he had no idea why.

The Serenity Gardens had become almost as much of a haven to her as it was to her patients. This was one of the few places that had been left untouched by the earthquake. It was a calm oasis, with the gentle waves lapping in the background becoming white noise that soothed the senses while helping mute the voices that weren't right next to you. It provided an additional sense of privacy.

Some parts of the gardens were open to the public, with curving sidewalks and shady places where people could gather and quietly converse. There were signs that asked for cell phones to be silenced and conversations

kept low and discreet. The place where Lea and her
current patient were meeting had a thick braided rope
stretched between two trellises to keep visitors from in-
advertently wandering in and interrupting her sessions.

Those two trellises, woven through with flowering
vines, created a natural screen for her makeshift office. It was as private as any of the exam rooms inside
the clinic. But it sure was a whole lot more attractive.
She'd already noticed a difference, compared with the
tiny supply closet she'd used when she'd first arrived.
The natural setting created intimacy and calmed frayed
nerves. Including her own.

"I just don't get why my neighbor's house was totally destroyed and mine wasn't touched. It doesn't seem
right."

She'd had several of this kind of patient. People who
didn't understand the randomness of being spared while
someone else had suffered terrible losses. She knew that
pain first-hand.

"I don't have an answer. But you've reached out and
provided a place for them to stay while they rebuild."

"They should probably be the ones here talking to
you, not me. And that makes me feel even more self-
ish. They seem to be coping so much better than I am."

"You don't know that for certain. People can hide
a lot."

As she'd found out the hard way. And she'd bet the
handsome plastic surgeon she'd met three days ago had
plenty to hide, too.

Why was she even *thinking* about him? She'd only
seen him in passing over the last day or so. He'd been
as gruff during those encounters as he'd been during

their first meeting, making her sigh in defeat. And he'd made no more surprise visits to the cottage.

Of course she'd been pretty careful about keeping an eye on the stove since then. No more burned eggs. No more smoke alarms. And no more Deakin.

She wasn't sure how she felt about that.

Cailey had made kind of a strange comment yesterday. She'd asked how Lea was enjoying working at the clinic, and then shocked her by saying that she'd made quite an impact on the island in the short time she'd been there.

She didn't know about that, but the island had certainly made an impact on *her*.

If she could find a place like this for her next position she would be in heaven. She had a feeling there weren't many islands like Mythelios in the world, though. So she'd better enjoy every second she was there. Because it would eventually come to an end.

And she was beginning to hate that thought.

She turned her attention back to her patient. "It sounds like you're doing all the right things. You're helping your neighbor weather this storm, and I promise you they will remember this. You've eased the way for them. Best of all, you're providing aid you might not have been able to had your own house been damaged or destroyed."

"I know, but…"

"It still hurts?"

A muscle pulsed in the man's cheek as he fought to get control of whatever was going on inside him. Finally, he said, "Yes. It does."

"And that's okay. As long as you don't let it take control of your life."

"That's why I'm here. Just talking about it helps, and

knowing someone else understands. I didn't want to worry my wife by breaking down in front of her."

She did understand—even if she didn't agree with him hiding all this from his wife. And her words about not letting guilt take control of his life had come out of the bitter reality of her own recent past.

"You are not the only one going through this. So take heart."

He took a deep breath and then blew it out, climbing to his feet. "Thank you. I don't think the clinic has ever had a psychiatrist before. Or if it did I never knew about it."

She didn't think it had. There were a couple of psychologists on the island, with private practices, but she'd already had a couple of referrals from them. This patient being one of them. They were overrun with people needing assistance for mental health issues, and since Lea was able to prescribe medication, whereas they weren't, she had gradually shifted from just seeing whatever patient came through the doors of the clinic, to seeing people within her own specialty.

She imagined Deakin and some of the others were now taking up some of the slack in other areas.

"I'm just glad the clinic has allowed me to help where I can."

"I certainly appreciate it." He reached out to shake her hand. "Thanks again. Can I call you if I need you? Or if my wife or neighbors need you?"

"Of course. You have my card. Go home. Talk to your wife. Tell her just what you told me. I bet she'll understand more than you know."

"I'll try."

That was all any of them could do.

"Good."

She walked him out and unhooked the rope to let him pass by. This was her last scheduled patient of the day. The man disappeared around the corner and Lea turned back to write up her notes and put them in his file.

Would he be back? Maybe. If he was still having trouble coping, then she hoped he would.

Head down in her notes, she jumped when someone said her name.

She looked up to find Deakin standing over her chair. And had to do a double-take. Something was different about him. She tilted her head and studied his face, her gaze trailing up the right side of his jaw to where his hair created a shadow. *Wait.* There *was* no shadow.

His hair was gone.

Well, not gone. But it was certainly shorter than it had been.

Her insides dipped. And she hadn't even managed to touch it...

Her face burned with white heat. How had *that* thought gotten in there? And how had she missed the distinctive click as the rope barrier was unhooked? A little warning might have been good. God, was her face as red as it felt?

"I'm glad I wasn't in here with a patient."

That had come out a little gruffer than she'd intended it to, because his appearance—his *changed* appearance—had startled her so much.

She had to admit his haircut suited him. Cut to just above his collar, it retained a tiny curl at the bottom that hinted of the waves he'd had chopped off. The rest was crisp and clean and...

She still wanted to run her fingers through it.

Dammit!

"I checked with Petra. She said your patient left a few minutes ago. Am I disturbing you?"

Yes. But not in the way he meant. If his scruffy appearance at the clinic three days ago had knocked her for a loop, this new Deakin—handsome, sophisticated Deakin—was knocking her into the stratosphere.

To keep him from standing there, she motioned him to the seat across from hers. Maybe if he was sitting she wouldn't have as much to stare at.

Nope. He dropped into the chair and propped an ankle on his other knee. He was now at her eye level. A dangerous place for both of them.

"What can I do for you?"

He uncrossed his legs, leaned forward and rested his elbows on his knees. "I think I might be in need of your services."

Shock rolled through her. "Excuse me?"

There was no way she was taking Deakin on as a patient unless it was a life or death situation. Not with the way her system had heated up just at the sight of him.

"Since we're colleagues at the same clinic, it might be better if I referred you to—"

His elbows came off his knees in a hurry and he went stock still. "Hell, it's not for *me*. What made you think that?"

"Well, you just said you thought you might be in need..." She blinked. "I don't understand."

And she really didn't.

"I guess I didn't phrase that very well."

The tight set of his lips made her wonder if he was going to get up and leave. But he didn't.

After a few seconds, he went on. "You said when you

went to Stavros's *taverna* that he was… What was the word you used?"

Trying to remember a specific word right now was going to be great fun. She cast around in her head, trying to dredge up that conversation.

"I think I said he was gruff."

He'd reminded her of a grumpy old man, even though he wasn't all that elderly. He'd mentioned something about a headache and had downed a couple of pills, but his attitude had persisted, ending with him snapping at someone.

"Yeah. *Gruff.* Theo mentioned that as well. And he's worried about him."

"I'm sure everyone is on edge after the quake. And he has a lot of people coming through the bar. It was packed the day I was there."

He nodded. "Maybe it's just that. But since I was planning on taking some downtime tonight and going over there anyway, I thought maybe you could go with me."

Her teeth caught her lower lip to keep her jaw from dropping. Was he asking her *out*?

As if he knew the direction her thoughts were headed, he narrowed his eyes. "I thought you could give me your…erm…*professional* opinion while we're there. If you don't have plans, that is."

Maybe it was the fact that she'd already misunderstood his motive for asking her to go that made her bristle slightly at the way he'd said it. "'Professional' opinion. You mean you want me to read his palm? Peer at his tea leaves?"

"Of course not."

His hand went to the side of his jaw before scrubbing

over the scars on his neck. She doubted he was even aware he was doing it.

"I just want someone there who can get a read on whether he's struggling with the after effects of the earthquake or if there's something else going on. Some physiological cause."

"Sometimes it's both."

"Which is why I'd like you to be there when I talk to him. Please."

The word tacked onto the end told her Deakin really was worried. Or maybe it was Theo's concern that was coming through.

Evidently the Stavros she had met that night in the bar wasn't the same man the community was used to seeing. Which meant she was going to go. Because there was no way she could ignore a plea like Deakin's. She had a feeling asking for her opinion hadn't come easily for this plastic surgeon.

"Okay. I'll tell you what I think—but if the man doesn't want help nothing in this world is going to convince him to accept it."

"I'm not going to suggest anything." He paused. "He's a friend. I want to make sure he's okay."

"And if he's not?"

"Then I'm going to drag Theo, Cailey and whoever else I can find down to that bar and make Stavros listen. We might not be able to force him to admit something's wrong, but we sure as hell can force him to hear us out."

A wave of admiration swept over her. "That *taverna* owner is a lucky man. Not everyone has friends like you and Theo."

Mark had always been a bit of a loner. That was one of the things that had attracted her to him initially. After the frenetic pace of medical school it had been nice to come home to a quiet house. Looking back, she knew warning bells should have been going off even then. But he'd seemed uncomplicated and easy going. He'd never fought. Had rarely gone against her in anything. And he'd been a loyal and faithful companion.

Until he hadn't.

He hadn't seemed depressed. He'd smiled, laughed at her jokes and had seemed to enjoy life.

But it had all been an act. Or had she only seen what she'd wanted to see? Made him into something she needed him to be?

Guilt sloshed over her once again in a wave that robbed her of oxygen. She struggled to break free of its grip and gulped down a huge breath.

"Stavros is a fixture on this island. I think there are a whole lot of people who would stand beside him. It's just that, from what I've seen, people are so busy trying to make insurance claims and do repairs on their homes that noticing little changes in someone's personality is brushed aside."

Another sliver pierced her heart.

Had she done that with Mark? Brushed aside the little changes that might have signaled her to take action? She would never know. Not now.

Maybe Stavros was no different from any of the other earthquake victims, but something was telling Deakin not to laugh it off as the workings of a grump. So neither would she. Not this time.

"So, are the rest of the clinic's patients covered for the day?" she asked.

"Yes, there are other doctors working the late shift, and they're all here."

"Great." She stuffed her laptop into her large shoulder bag. "I'll take the bike and then leave straight from the *taverna* to go home once we're done. Do you want to meet me there?"

"I think it'll look more natural to Stavros if we arrive together."

"Why?"

"Let's just say that I know how the man's mind works. If a woman suddenly joins me at the bar he's going to know immediately that something's up."

"Maybe he'll think I'm trying to wrangle an invitation to join you?"

"Not hardly!"

Before she could mull over those words, he turned and started walking, throwing over his shoulder, "I'll meet you in the parking area. I'm in the red Jeep."

She knew what he'd be driving, since they had offered to let her use the vehicle when she'd moved to the cottage. She'd refused.

But using someone else's bicycle doesn't bother you?

Three minutes later they were cruising down the main strip that ran across the island, heading south toward the spot where most of the island's restaurants and hotels were. Stavros's place was within walking distance of the clinic, but by parking there they wouldn't have to backtrack once they'd left the bar.

Parking wasn't the easiest, and being in the car with Deakin made her realize how much easier it was just to prop her bike up beside whatever store she was going to and forget about it. As it was, it took longer to find a spot than it had to drive to the bar. But they finally located one that had just been vacated and Deakin turned off the ignition.

"Do you have a drink of choice?"

"Um... I didn't realize I was going to be drinking."

Up went his brows. "Stavros is a smart man. We want to try and catch him off guard so he talks to us."

It went against her better judgment, but she finally said, "A strawberry daiquiri, then."

"I would have guessed rum and Coke. Or Scotch on the rocks."

Why was that? Did he not think she could be a frou-frou girl when she wanted to be? Something about that stung.

Her main reason for getting a fruity drink was so that she could take her time sipping it without looking like an oddball. Especially since she didn't drink all that much. The only time she'd gone to Stavros's had been when she'd had to vacate her hotel room. The bar had been the closest place to get something to eat.

She decided to come back with a quip. "It all depends on my mood."

"Ah. I'll have to remember that." A flicker of dark humor seemed to light up those brown eyes. "And what would your mood be tonight?"

Warmth bloomed in her belly.

He's not...flirting with me. Is he?

She decided to test the waters, even though an alarm louder than his smoke detector was currently going off in her head. "My mood? Contemplative."

It wasn't a lie. She was doing her best to figure this out as she went along. So far she was failing on every count.

"A daiquiri is contemplative?"

"It can be anything I choose it to be." She gave him a grin. Okay, he might not be flirting, but it was kind of fun to sit here throwing quips back and forth. "What are *you* drinking?"

His gaze dropped to her mouth and held for a brief moment. Then he shut his eyes tight. When he reopened them, he said, "Whiskey. I'm drinking whiskey."

His opened his door before she could come up with anything to say to that. She hurried to follow suit, embarrassed heat leaking into her face. Deakin clicked a button on his key fob to lock the vehicle. She tried to dredge up some professional conversation, even though she just wanted to grab his arm and ask him to go back in time to a few seconds ago, when the weight of the world had so briefly lifted from her shoulders.

"Anything more I should know about Stavros before I go in?"

"Just that he's owned the *taverna* for as long as I can remember, and he knows almost everyone who lives here. He's good to the tourists who visit and helps whoever needs it. He's a genuinely nice guy."

That hadn't been the impression *she'd* gotten, but she would take Deakin's word for it. Tragedy did strange things to people.

Like sending them running to another place.

That wasn't what she was doing. Was it?

"It's been a while since you've been here, right? Could he simply have changed?"

"Stavros has been the same for as long as I've known him—which is a long time. And Theo also mentioned something being off, and he *lives* on the island."

She reached for the door handle, pulling back when someone pushed through from the other side. A couple, their arms wrapped around each other, stumbled slightly as they came through, the woman giving a high-pitched squeal that raked down Lea's spine. The heavy door swung shut, with neither person offering to hold it for them. The pair was drunk. *Very* drunk.

Off they went across the street, weaving back and forth as they went. Lea watched them go, hoping against hope that they weren't going to get into a car.

They didn't—just kept staggering down the sidewalk, probably headed home.

Deakin frowned. "See? That wouldn't normally happen."

"What? Someone in a bar having too much to drink?"

"Believe it or not, no. Stavros usually keeps track, and he isn't afraid to cut people off when they're getting too close to their limit."

This time Lea was able to swing the door open without resistance. Deakin wrapped his fingers around the upper part of it and held it so she could go through.

She frowned almost immediately. The atmosphere was darker than she remembered, the lights dimmed almost as low as they would go. But she'd only been there once, so maybe it was her imagination.

Deakin paused as if taking stock of the place and then strode toward the bar, where the same white-haired man she remembered was pouring a drink. Even from where she stood she could see that the liquid had sloshed out of the glass a bit, causing Stavros to grab a towel and wipe up the spill.

He said something to the customer, who took the drink from him and walked to a nearby table.

It was loud. So loud she had trouble hearing the piped in music over the raucous sound of inebriation—which she hadn't realized had a specific sound until now.

Stavros's eyes came up and landed on Deakin. "Deak!

Is that you? When the hell did you get home, and why did no one tell me?"

The man dropped his red towel onto the bar and came around to give him a hug. Lea moved closer, and Stavros spotted her.

"Did you bring a wife back with you?"

It wasn't strange that he didn't remember her, but to be mistaken for Deakin's *wife*…

Deakin chuckled, but it sounded forced. "No. No wife."

There was no *not yet* added to that phrase. It was as if he was never planning on getting married. Maybe he was a confirmed bachelor. Or maybe…

No, a woman would be a fool to let a few scars deter her from getting to know a man like this.

A man like *what*? He certainly wasn't the optimistic fun-loving guy she thought she was looking for.

She *wasn't* looking. Where had that come from?

Get a grip, Lea!

"No wife?" Stavros leaned an elbow on the bar's surface. "Are you crazy? They're fun. Had a few of them myself."

The syllables shot from his mouth in rapid staccato, accompanied by a wide grin.

Okay, this wasn't grumpy Stavros. This was manic Stavros. He had a feverish quality about him that made her look a little closer.

Deakin caught her eye and gave a slight nod. She wasn't sure if he'd read her mind and was agreeing with her, or if he wanted her to try to figure something out.

If it was the latter, there wasn't enough to go on yet. She gave a slight shrug.

"No wife," Deakin repeated. "This is a friend. Leanora Risi. She works with me at the clinic."

"Oh, yes. I thought you looked familiar. You had something to eat. No alcohol."

Deakin's brows shot up. "You don't drink?"

"I do on occasion."

Her face flamed for what seemed like the hundredth time that day. She wasn't going to discuss how much she did or didn't drink—especially since she'd already told Deakin she did.

"I'll have a strawberry daiquiri."

"Of course. And you, Deak? What'll you have?"

"How about a little more light? I've never seen it this dark in here."

"It keeps folks happy."

His words were still tumbling, end over end. And was that dilation of his pupils due to the low level of light? Or something else. Maybe the good bartender did more than just tend bar for the people of Mythelios.

She hooked an index finger and touched it to the inside of her left elbow, giving Deakin a slight raise of the eyebrows.

He shook his head—no. He didn't think Stavros was shooting up with anything.

"I'll have a whiskey, then."

A whiskey. He'd evidently been serious in the car when he'd said that was what he was drinking.

Stavros reclaimed his spot behind the bar and began mixing their drinks. In the middle of doing it he picked up a pill bottle and shook a couple of tablets into his hand. It wasn't a brown prescription bottle—it looked like something from over the counter.

"What are those?" she whispered to Deakin.

"I don't know. But Stavros has never taken anything before. At least not that I've ever seen."

The bartender stuck her drink in front of her. She picked it up and took a quick sip while he finished making Deakin's whiskey and handed it over.

"So, what have you been up to?" Stavros asked him.

"I've been in Africa for the last several months, working with an NGO."

"That's good…that's good. Now, if you'll excuse me…"

He moved away to take care of another customer.

"Is this how he was the last time you were here?" Deakin asked her.

She perched on the nearest barstool and took another sip of her drink. "No. Just the opposite. That evening he seemed sluggish and unhappy. He snapped at a man who had a problem with the way he'd mixed his drink."

Deakin set his glass down and stared across the bar at where Stavros was moving at warp speed. "Can you tell anything by watching him?"

"He's never had any personality changes like this before? No highs and lows?"

"He's always been just… *Stavros*. Unflappable. Unhurried. And that man knows his drinks. There is no way he would have mixed something incorrectly. Or gotten angry if someone had called him on it."

The next sip of her drink went down a little too smoothly. She swirled the contents of her glass. "Maybe you should come right out and ask him if he's feeling okay…see what he says."

Stavros opened a drawer behind the bar and looked for something, digging through the contents of the drawer, grizzled brows furrowed. He took a deep breath and pinched the bridge of his nose. As if giving up, he slammed the drawer shut and came around the bar, stopping in front of Deakin.

"How long are you home for?"

The tone was a little less friendly, this time.

"Not long. A month, maybe. Long enough to help with some of the clean-up."

The bartender's fingers repeated the squeeze against the upper part of his nose.

Deakin leaned closer, looking up into the man's face. "You feeling okay?"

Stavros's head whipped up and he stared at Deakin suspiciously. "What do you mean?"

"You seem a little flustered this evening. I thought you might be feeling under the weather."

Just like that, Stavros's demeanor changed from cheerful to angry. His hands, which had been lying on top of the bar, curled in on themselves, clenching into fists. "Maybe you should mind your own damn business, Deak."

"I'm just concerned about you. So is Theo."

"Well, don't be. I'm fine. Always have been. Always will be. All you guys at the clinic should get off your high horses."

A red flag went up in her mind. It was the same attitude Mark had had any time she'd questioned one of his moods. He got defensive and tried to deflect attention away from himself. Only he had used avoidance, not confrontation.

"Hey, don't take it personally," Deakin said, holding up placating hands.

"You mean like your dad did all those years ago?"

Whoa. Lea had no idea what Stavros meant by that,

but the effect the words had on Deakin was shocking. All the color leached from his face until it was the same shade as his pale scars. A pulse began throbbing in his temple. The bartender had definitely touched some kind of nerve.

Deflecting.

Just like Mark.

Deakin—and Theo—were right. Something was wrong with this man. He either didn't realize it or he was ignoring the problem, hoping it would go away.

But she'd learned the hard way that the problem—whatever it was—not only wouldn't go away, it would grow and grow and grow, until Stavros…or maybe even Deakin…could no longer pretend that things were fine.

She just wasn't sure if that moment would be a month from now, a year from now, or if it was about to happen right before their eyes.

CHAPTER FOUR

DEAKIN'S FIRST INSTINCT was to put his fist into Stavros's mocking face. Theo's comment about no one remembering what had happened in the past was obviously not true. Stavros not only remembered, he'd just thrown it right in his face. Thank God he'd left Ville out of it.

Something warm pressed against his wrist, and when he looked down he saw it was Lea's hand. His own were curled into tight fists, just like his friend's had been a second or two ago.

Did Lea sense what he was feeling, or had she read his body language and decided to intervene?

Whatever it was, it acted like a wake-up call. He had no idea why Stavros would want to open that can of worms right here and now, but the man wasn't a fool. He'd had a reason, and Deakin thought he could guess what it was.

His friend gave him a mocking little salute and sauntered off as if he *hadn't* just ripped Deakin's chest open and squeezed the place where his heart should be. The Stavros he'd known would never have done something like that.

Clear green eyes fastened on his with concern. "He didn't mean it."

"Mean what?"

"Whatever it was that hurt you so badly."

He gave a hard laugh. "It didn't hurt me." It had done something entirely different. "But the Stavros I once knew would have never let himself get that angry."

"You looked pretty mad yourself there for a minute or two. You still do, in fact."

Oh, he'd been beyond mad. If she hadn't physically held his hand in place would he have decked his friend?

Regardless of the fact that he'd been caught by surprise, he hoped not. "So what is your professional opinion? Psychological? Or physiological?"

"I'd say both." Her voice was low. "Something has him extremely upset. And that pinching of his nose is either a terrible headache, pressure from his sinuses, or an overload of stress. It could be something as simple as allergies."

"*Allergies?* Do you find his mood swings consistent with allergies?"

"No, but with the quake you never know what could have been released into the air. A lot of these buildings are hundreds of years old. He could have developed an infection of some type. Or a sensitivity to a toxin. But even if it's none of those things you can't force someone to tell you what's wrong if they really don't want to."

He took a long draw of his whiskey as he studied her face. Hadn't he done that very thing once upon a time? Refused to talk? To anyone? Maybe she'd had experience with patients like him.

"You say that as if you've had that happen before. Did someone refuse to open up to you?"

Her glance skipped away from his for a moment before coming back. "I'm a psychiatrist. I've seen it happen a lot on a professional level."

Why had she emphasized the word 'professional?'

"And on a personal one?"

He had no idea why he'd asked that. He'd have been backpedaling like crazy if she'd asked him to explain Stavros's comment about his father.

He half expected her to get mad, but she didn't.

She just said, "I think we've all experienced that on a personal level from time to time—when you wish you could have helped someone who just didn't want to be helped."

Yes, Lea could definitely be talking about him back in the day. When his parents had insisted he talk to someone he'd clammed up even tighter.

He still didn't like talking about what had happened. To anyone. Not even his closest friends. So who was he to try to force Stavros to open up about whatever was bothering him? What would he have done if the roles were reversed? Probably the very same thing.

So he needed to let this go. If Stavros wanted help he would ask for it. At least he hoped he would. Until then Deakin needed to be available, as a listening ear or a shoulder to cry on. If and when Stavros was ready.

He tossed back the rest of his drink, noting that Lea's was only half gone. He was tempted to order another whiskey, but he was driving—and besides, he somehow doubted Stavros would skip back over to them as if nothing had happened.

"I'm ready if you are." She pushed her drink away from her.

"There's no rush. Go ahead and finish."

"I'm good. I'm kind of a lightweight where alcohol is

concerned." She turned to look across the bar at where Stavros was helping another customer. "Do you want to try to talk him into coming to the clinic and getting checked out?"

"I don't think now is a good time. Maybe when he and I have both had time to cool off."

He glanced around, surprised by how many people were still in the bar this late.

Turning back toward her, he caught her looking at something on the side of his—

Dammit! He didn't want her looking at that.

"What are you staring at?"

He'd never called someone out on their curiosity before, but something about the way those green eyes touched his skin had his blood gumming up his veins in a way that was all too familiar.

"Just wondering how you got those."

She seemed unfazed by his challenge. And there was no need to ask what "those" she was talking about. But he wanted to discuss that just about as much as Stavros wanted to talk about what was going on with his health.

Deakin wasn't used to people directly asking him what had happened. He didn't want to tell her and he had no idea why.

Maybe because she was the only person around who didn't have some kind of preconceived idea of who he was or what he had done. The memory of her teeth sinking into her lower lip that first time she'd studied him flickered behind his eyelids. His blood thickened even more, the drumming of it growing in his ears.

"Deakin?"

Only when her voice came again did he realize how

much time had passed since she'd asked her original question about his burns.

Her eyes were no longer on his neck, but wholly focused on his face—with an intensity that made his chest burn.

"I got them in a fire."

Like the one beginning to ignite in certain regions below...

Cool fingers touched his hand as he continued to hold her gaze, trying to swallow back his unexpected response to her. He had no idea what had caused it. Or what it was going to take to put it out.

But right now he didn't care. He flipped his hand over to grasp hers, saw her thick lashes sweeping down when he tightened his hold.

And sure as the day was long, those white teeth began to worry at her bottom lip. Back and forth they scrubbed, until his nerve-endings stretched tighter and tighter.

The noise in the room faded to black. His focus remained glued to her mouth. Her teeth came off, her lips barely parting as if inviting him to peek at the wonders inside.

His will to resist evaporated into thin air.

He leaned forward. The scent of strawberries clung to her. He'd bet she tasted just like that drink. Only better.

When her lashes lifted and her fingers traced across the back of his hand he knew he was done for. It was darker than sin in here. Who would see?

His hand lifted, his fingers threading through the hair at her nape. Then he moved in to see if he was right. One touch was all it would take.

"You want me to add those drinks to your tab, Deak?"

Stavros's strident voice froze him in place, before

breaking through his mental fog. He reeled back on his barstool, his hand sliding out of her hair in a rush.

Lea's soft gasp made his teeth clench together.

Dammit. What was wrong with him?

The fact that he didn't *have* a tab would have been funny, except that his friend's timing was even more laughable. There was no longer any anger in the *taverna* owner's face, and Deakin found his attention once more on Stavros's mercurial moods.

A coincidence? No. The very rare times that he'd seen his friend angry, he'd stayed that way.

When he glanced back at Lea she was no longer looking at him, but seemed lost in the drink she'd discarded moments earlier. She drew it back toward her and took a long draw on the straw.

He smiled, feeling as shell-shocked as she looked. Since he was currently wishing he still had part of his drink left in front of him, he couldn't blame her. Maybe she didn't realize just how close he'd come to kissing her.

She took another quick sip, looking anywhere but at him.

Or maybe she did realize.

Someone staring at his scars was normally met with impatience. Or irritation. Not lust. And that was what it had been. An explosive, unexpected tightening of body parts and emotions.

On his part, anyway.

Right now, though, he couldn't worry about any of that. Not with Stavros still perched in front of him.

"Since when do you let anyone put a drink on a tab?"

"The earthquake changed quite a few things."

Yes, it had. It had kept Lea on the island longer than she'd planned. And it had brought him back there and made him want to kiss someone who was a perfect stranger.

"Never mind. I'll just pay for it."

He reached for his wallet, a grimace forming when Lea reached in her own purse.

He stopped her with a look. "Consider this a thank-you for consulting on that patient with me."

Her eyes widened slightly, but she didn't argue. "I was happy to do it."

Stavros had no idea they were talking about him—or if he did he didn't acknowledge that he might be acting out of sorts. "Do you want anything clsc?"

He certainly did. But he wasn't gctting it. Or even asking for it. He was going to go home and take a very cold shower.

Except he needed to give Lea a ride back to the cottage before he could do that. Or he could just take her back to the clinic and let her get on her bike...

He ruled that option out in an instant, and he wasn't sure why.

"I don't." He looked at her. "Do you?"

"No, I think I've had plenty, thanks." She set her drink down, and this time there was a finality to the move that said she was done. Probably in more ways than one.

How angry would Theo be if he ran their newest physician off before he'd even been home a week? Pretty mad, probably—which meant he owed her an apology.

And what if she *hadn't* realized what his intentions were?

Oh, she knew, Deakin, there's no mistaking that.

Which made it even more difficult.

Handing Stavros a bill without bothering to look at it, he said, "Keep the rest."

"Okay!"

Stavros smiled and pocketed the money without bothering to write anything on the receipt. Which was about as strange as his mood swings. His buddy was normally a stickler for keeping his accounts clean and above-board. He'd seen the man stress over not being able to account for ten cents, much less a fifty-euro bill.

Maybe it was like Stavros had said. The earthquake had changed a few things. Even though Deakin had not been there the day it had struck, could it be that the quake was affecting *him* as well? Inducing some kind of mass hysteria?

And that near miss of a kiss? Was that a result of that same mass hysteria?

He had no idea, but the sooner he got out of here the better. Before it set in again and he did something he really would regret.

The man had actually *apologized* to her in the parking lot as they'd sat in the car.

The sting of humiliation was as fresh now as it had been a few nights ago, when he'd driven her home in near silence. She would have sworn he was going to kiss her in the bar, and evidently he'd thought so too, since he'd felt the need to say he was sorry for his actions.

Well, what about *her* actions? She was the one who'd put her hand over his. It had started out as a quick squeeze of comfort, but that had all changed very swiftly.

Then just like that, so had Deakin.

She felt nauseous and out of her depth. Talk about mood swings. And he thought *Stavros* was the one having problems! She needed to keep a level head here and make no mistakes.

Her fiancé had been moody and out of sorts for the last couple of weeks of his life. She'd been worried he was getting cold feet about marrying her.

It had turned out he was. But rather than being specifically about her, his cold feet had been related to living his life—to living in general.

And, while she hadn't completely missed the signs, she'd misread the reasons for them. She'd been just about to break off their engagement in an effort to take some of the pressure off him when he'd died.

Her cellphone rang, making her drop the tube of mascara she'd dug out of her make-up bag. She glanced at the readout. A single name flashed there: *Deakin*.

Ugh! Had he somehow sensed she was thinking about him? In the week since he'd arrived she'd been doing more than her share of that. His transformation from scruffy but breathtaking stranger to clean-shaven, competent doctor had put her off balance and kept her off balance ever since.

No, that wasn't true. She'd been off balance since the first day he'd strolled into the clinic in all his scruffy glory.

Her thumb hovered over the answer button.

Maybe he was going to tell her she was no longer welcome to use his bicycle. Or, worse, that he wanted her to move out of the cottage. Had the hotel she'd been staying at opened up? She didn't think she could afford to stay there long-term, since she wasn't being paid an actual salary at the clinic. *Yet.*

She blinked as the phone rang for the third time. Was

she hoping she *would* be paid at some point? That Theo would ask her to stay on the island?

Had what had happened with Deakin changed her mind about Mythelios? No. It hadn't. She still loved it. Just as much if not more than she had before.

Taking a deep, reassuring breath, she pushed the "receive call" button on the phone just as it was getting ready to send the caller to voicemail.

"Hello."

"You knew it was me."

Since her greeting hadn't had a question mark at the end of it, it was kind of a given.

"I did. As we're working together, I figured I'd better enter your name into my contacts. In case of an emergency."

And it would come right out again once one of them left the island.

There was a pause.

"Right."

A few more empty seconds ticked by. Just when she thought the connection had broken, his voice came back.

"I have to make a boat-run to Naxos for some supplies. With the stores here still sustaining damage, and since the airstrip is barely able to handle traffic, we're running short of a few things at the clinic—and here at the house as well."

She had no idea why he was telling her this. Was he asking if there was anything she needed? If so, he wasn't doing a very good job of it.

"Okay…"

She let the end of the word trail on long enough to let him know she was confused. At least she hoped it came across that way.

"Would you like to go with me?"

She'd started to rattle off a generic answer before his words actually registered. "I'm sorry?"

"I asked if you wanted to go with me. Theo says you've been working round the clock and that neither he nor Cailey have been able to see their way free to give you a tour of the neighboring islands."

He paused again.

"I didn't realize you'd been working nonstop for all this time with no pay. That has to be remedied."

"It's okay. I've enjoyed it—even though I'm not happy about the reason for it."

"Having your vacation cut short by an earthquake is probably *not* on Mythelios's list of local attractions."

Was that a smile she heard in his voice? "It isn't. Not in the tour book I looked at, anyway."

"Well, I'm sure Theo, myself and the other partners will meet at some point and discuss things. We'll reimburse you for all your help, of course."

Just when she'd thought he was offering to be her tour guide on a fun outing his real motives for wanting her to go made themselves known. He felt guilty that she hadn't been paid.

Her tummy sank through the floor. So much for that smile.

Theo had offered to pay her early on, and she'd turned him down. But now, after more than a month, her savings account was beginning to show signs of strain, even though she didn't have the expense of a hotel. She still had food and supplies of her own to buy.

"So, do you want to go with me? We should have some time to sightsee a little bit. Are you interested in archeology at all?"

"I love it."

Despite her misgivings over his reasons for asking, something in the low rumble of his voice cast a spell over her and made her want to go with him wherever he wanted. Or at least keep him on the phone for a little while longer.

"I haven't even gotten to see the ruins on Mythelios yet, let alone the other islands."

"Hmm…"

A strange tingling went to work in her midsection. Had that dark shadow crept back across his jawline since she'd last seen him? Was his new shorter hair sticking up at odd angles? Her eyes closed as she tried to draw up an image of just that. Maybe he was still shirtless. Or… even better…lying in bed, one arm propped behind his head as he talked to her, with only a sheet covering his—

Lordy! You need to stop that.

The tingling grew into something a little more volatile. A lot more dangerous. She hadn't fantasized about a man since Mark's death. If she wasn't careful all her self-lectures regarding nice, uncomplicated guys were going to fly out the window. Deakin was definitely not "uncomplicated". Not by any stretch of the imagination. And neither were her current reactions to him.

She shouldn't go. Should she…?

"How long would we be gone?"

Well, okay… Her subconscious had evidently disconnected itself and gone rogue.

But he was right. She hadn't had much of a break in weeks, and when she thought about it she *was* pretty drained. Not tired enough to quit and leave the island, but in the rush of those first couple of weeks of emergencies at the clinic she hadn't really had time to stop and think about her own needs. And here Deakin was, offering to change all that. If she'd let him.

But was it smart? Especially given her thoughts a few seconds ago.

Probably not. It was getting harder and harder to view him as a simple colleague. Especially after that encounter in the bar, when she'd been so sure he was going to kiss her.

Now that he'd held out the offer, however, she was going to have a very hard time turning him down, no matter what his motives were.

"We can play it by ear and see as little or as much as you want. The Cyclades form a rough circle around the island of Delos, a sacred site in these parts. It's not inhabited, but it is open to the public during certain hours. We could see the sights and then have lunch on the boat—in the air-conditioning if it gets too hot."

Her brows went up and she pressed the phone a little closer to her ear. "Your boat is air-conditioned?"

"It was my dad's boat, but yes."

His dad's? His parents were both dead. Deakin had surely inherited the boat. So why didn't he think of it as his? Grief? Was it a reminder of his mom and dad? Or maybe it was like the main house. He just hadn't put his stamp of ownership on it yet.

"Are you sure they'll be okay at the clinic without us?"

"I'm sure between Theo, Cailey, Petra and the rest of the staff they'll be just fine. I did let Theo know about the results of our visit to Stavros. Hopefully he'll change his mind and come in to see us."

She could almost hear his mental shrug. "Do you think he will? Maybe I should stay behind just in case."

"Stavros is pretty stubborn. But we'll only be an hour away, in any case, if he does—or if an emergency comes up that they can't handle, Theo can easily call us back in."

The way he'd asked all the partners after the earthquake? She knew that Theo had tried to contact Chris, Ares and Deakin and had asked them to come back, but so far only Deakin had answered that call and that had taken a little over a month. She knew that work obligations made it very hard, but it had been tough in those first days, trying to juggle panicked earthquake victims and their families.

A lump formed in her throat.

Maybe it would do her some good to get away from the island for a while. It might even help her shake off the sense of guilt and sadness over Mark's death that followed her like the caboose on a long, noisy train. A caboose that followed her everywhere, no matter how hard she tried to outrun it.

With that, her decision was made.

"Well, since seeing the islands was one of the reasons I came to Mythelios in the first place, I would love to go. Thank you."

"You're welcome. Theo has been after me to make sure you see a thing or two while I'm home."

Her stomach, which had just started creeping back to its normal resting place, went into freefall all over again.

"Please don't feel obligated to take me."

She hated the way her voice came out, small and uncertain. But that was how she felt.

A beat or two went by. "I don't, and I'm sorry if it sounded that way. I would have asked you to come whether Theo had suggested it or not. I already promised to take you out on the boat, didn't I? It just made sense to combine business with pleasure."

Pleasure? Oh, the sightseeing portion of the trip.

"It does. And I'm sure I'll love Delos as much as I do Mythelios."

And she did love Mythelios.

She loved the mixture of quaint and sophisticated that was a normal part of life here. And it even helped her understand her parents a little better. They had always been so insistent on following tradition. She had thought the mix of old-fashioned Greek beliefs with living in a modern foreign city was strange when she was a teenager. But she was learning that the very texture of Greek society seemed to be the same way: holding fast to tradition while embracing all things new.

She could hardly believe she'd arrived only a few weeks ago. In some ways it felt as if she'd been here for years.

"Do you?"

It took her a minute to realize he was commenting on her statement about loving Mythelios. He sounded puzzled, as if he had no idea what she found so attractive about the island. Maybe he was inured to the charm of the place.

"I really do. Who wouldn't?"

"You might be surprised."

She moved the phone to her other ear. "You don't?"

"I don't *hate* it."

Said as if there had been a time when he had…

She decided to change the subject in case he decided to argue the point. "I'm glad. What time do you want to leave?"

"Anytime you're ready."

"As in now?"

Ack! She still needed to shower and change. Ducking down, she grabbed the tube of mascara she'd dropped a few minutes earlier and did a quick set of calculations.

"Can you give me about twenty-five minutes?"

"How about an hour? That way I can pick up some things for lunch. Unless you're rather eat on Delos? I have to warn you it'll be hot."

"I'm getting use to the heat, and eating on the boat sounds heavenly. Do you want me to bring anything?"

"Just some sunscreen…and yourself."

With that, he hung up, leaving her looking at the phone in consternation. She *would* bring herself. But it wouldn't be the self who was currently crushing over a certain Dr. Patera.

An hour later she was showered and ready in a white floral sundress and comfy espadrilles. And, judging from Deakin's double-take, she looked a little different out of the casual clinic wear he normally saw her in. Speaking of which… She needed to get another set of scrubs if she was planning on staying for much longer. Her current set was on loan from Cailey, and she really needed one of her own.

How much longer *was* she staying?

She smiled and closed the front door of the cottage. That was something she didn't need to worry about. At least not today.

"I'm glad you wore something cool. It'll be warm. Especially on Delos, if we arrive during the heat of the day."

When else would they be arriving? She had no idea what the maritime rules were for Mythelios, but it might not be wise to be stuck out on the water with Deakin at night. Under a full moon.

Wise for whom? *Her?*

She made an internal scoffing sound. This was not going to be a romantic trip. It was a business outing. He'd as much as said that. Yes, but he'd also said they were going to be combining business with pleasure. She was the one who'd placed special emphasis on the second half of that statement.

The boat house—a tall white structure with a cupola perched over it—had always fascinated her. She'd actually never stepped inside the building. With its black weather vane twisting and turning at each change in the breeze, it had a very nautical feel to it.

Deakin unlocked the door and threw it open, letting a sliver of light into the dark space. A large form rose and fell, and then, with the flip of a light switch, the ghost was gone, replaced with a sleek ship.

Mytheliostocracy II.

She blinked a time or two at the black name emblazoned on the side of the boat. It seemed kind of…pretentious. Like the house across the gardens.

She frowned, then hurried to erase the expression before Deakin saw her reaction. It wasn't disappointment. It was just…surprise.

Deakin didn't fit. With any of it. Especially not the shaggy-haired version of the man she'd met that first day. Maybe that was why he'd said it was his father's boat. He didn't want to be linked with this kind of lifestyle. Maybe that was also why Deakin traveled from place to place, trying to help relieve suffering in other countries. It was a way to physically remove himself from what it represented.

Which was what? Wealth? Extravagance? Deakin wasn't exactly poor, though. From what she'd heard he, Theo and the other two, Ares and Chris, had joined funds to pay for the running of the clinic year after year once Theo's father had made the initial investment to open it.

Mytheliostocracy II matched the color of the building it was housed in, but all resemblance began and ended there. The boathouse was traditional. The vessel ultra-modern. A strange mixture, to be sure.

Just like the clinic. Just like the island. Just like Deakin…?

No, he was traditional through and through. He looked and sounded Greek, but he didn't really seem to feel comfortable in the house—or on Mythelios, for that matter. Or was that just her imagination?

She shifted the large bag she was carrying over her shoulder, and Deakin seemed to shake himself out of some kind of trance.

He took the satchel from her. "Anything you need in here right away?"

"I have some sunscreen I'll need to eventually get to, but I can put that on later."

"Let me show you around and then we'll cast off."

He stepped from the solid expanse of the dock to the vessel's surface, which rocked slightly under his weight. Holding onto one of the railings, he reached for her hand. She grabbed it before hopping across herself.

The deck was made of some kind of light polished wood. It gleamed under the lights. Like the cottage and the house, it looked as if it was cleaned regularly. Another thing Deakin's aunt took care of?

"Why don't you visit the island more often?"

The question came out of nowhere, and she immediately wished she hadn't asked. But it was too late to retract the words.

"I'm busy with my own career."

"Do you only work with one relief organization?"

"For the most part, yes."

If he was upset by the question, he didn't show it, just moved across the deck and motioned her to follow. He gestured up a set of short steps that led to an area perched over the bow which housed a wheel and gear levers. Lots of them.

"That's where we drive it."

"We?"

"Surely you want to try it out?" One side of his mouth kicked up.

"I don't know. It looks very complicated."

"Once you get used to it, it's not that bad."

Kind of like Deakin…

He went down another set of stairs until he reached a door on the left. "This is the kitchen."

Small, but well-equipped, the kitchen had a refrigerator and a stove with several burners. The drawers probably housed pots and pans and other essential items. Deakin crouched in front of the small fridge and unloaded the bag of items he'd brought. Meat and cheese, water, soft drinks. And beer. She smiled at that. Not a very aristocratic beverage.

"How did the boat get its name?"

"Mytheliostocracy?"

She nodded. "I take it that wasn't your idea?"

"No. I think my dad saw his company as the aristocracy of the island. He combined that with Mythelios and came up with the name."

It made sense, but it still seemed like an odd thing to name a boat.

"Oh."

"You don't like it?" He propped his hips against the countertop, long legs stretching across to the other side of the galley.

The space suddenly seemed small. And close. She wouldn't be able to get past him without climbing over his legs—and, depending on which way she faced, either her boobs or her butt would brush against him as she went.

She gulped.

"It's not for me to like or dislike," she managed.

Was it a little hard to breathe down here with the windows shut? Or was it just because every time she inhaled his warm scent filled her lungs and trickled through her bloodstream until it reached her heart, making her pulse race?

The scars on his jaw and neck that he seemed to hate so much did nothing to diminish her reaction to him. It was raw and vital and she wanted nothing better than to bury her visceral response to him deep underground, where it could no longer reach her.

She did the next best thing: tried to prompt him into moving to another location. "So, what other goodies does this old barge have on it?"

He grinned, but pushed away from the counter. "Old barge, huh? That about sums it up."

It didn't. Not at all. But it made her realize something. "You don't like the name your dad chose for the boat."

"Not particularly."

Her brows went up at how quickly the words had

come out of his mouth. "The boat is yours now. Why not change it?"

"I don't consider it mine. Not really. And I haven't changed it because it's what the first one was named."

"The first one?"

"It doesn't matter." He frowned. "I'm not here often enough to go through the trouble of having it repainted. Let me finish showing you around so we can get underway."

He took her to a small powder room, and then to an area at the front of the boat where she could sun herself. *Yeah, right.* She glanced up to where the control room was. Any sunbathing would be done under the watchful eye of whoever was steering the boat.

She shivered at the thought of Deakin looking at her almost naked body.

That wasn't happening.

Good thing she hadn't brought a suit.

"And here are the sleeping quarters."

He opened the last door at the end of the narrow hallway and the opulence suddenly ended. The bed was big and impressive, yes, but the furnishings were not. A simple cotton bedspread was tossed over the bed. There was a lamp. A braided rug on the floor. And a nightstand on either side of the bed.

This was probably where Deakin spent the majority of his time when on the boat. She couldn't see whoever had named the boat choosing such spartan décor. But it fit Deakin to a tee. His need for simplicity. Especially after traveling the world and seeing its poverty first hand. So why hadn't he made the same transformation with the main house?

"I like it."

He smiled. "Better than the name?"

"Much better." She echoed his smile and raised him one. "This looks comfortable. A space you could actually enjoy being in."

Only after she'd said it did she realize how it had sounded. Her daydream from earlier that morning came back to haunt her with a vengeance. The one that had had Deakin lying on a bed as he talked to her. He'd been totally naked, a sheet covering his bottom half. And the sheet had been thin enough that she could make out his form beneath it…the strong legs which came together to form a triangle. And topping that had been a telltale bulge… One that had stirred even as she'd looked at it.

She was suddenly glancing at anything *but* that bed. God, if he knew what she'd been imagining…

"Okay, so where to next?"

The panic flooding her system made its way into her voice. And when she met Deakin's gaze his smile was long gone.

Deakin backed out of the door. "Anywhere but here."

With those enigmatic words he turned and headed toward the main deck.

And safety.

CHAPTER FIVE

"DEAKIN! SO GLAD you came. Would you mind looking at a patient for me before you pick up the things Theo requested?"

Konstantinos Banis, an older doctor who had worked on Naxos for many years, met them at the front elevators at the clinic.

"Of course."

Like himself, Dr. Banis was a plastic surgeon specializing in burns. In fact the man had been here when Deakin was brought in as a teen, his skin charred and weeping after the explosion that had almost cost him his life.

Ville had been treated back on Mythelios, so he'd been the one to recount the story of what had happened.

Or his version of it.

Deakin had only heard it months later in Athens, after he was through the worst of his surgeries. He'd just let it stand. After all, Deakin had been the one to strike that match. And Ville had had much more to lose if the truth came out.

Dr. Banis had followed his case long after he'd left his care and his clinic, coming to visit him through years of skin grafts. The two were now friends. He was also the only person in the world except for Deakin and Ville who knew the whole truth—and that was only because his young patient had muttered odd phrases while delirious with pain. He'd put two and two together and confronted him.

Neither boy had been charged with any crime, so Dr. Banis had also let things stand as that was what Deakin had wanted.

Deakin didn't care about any of that right now. He was still half regretting inviting Lea along for the ride. Yes, Theo had suggested he take her, but Deakin had already invited her to join him on the water soon after they'd met.

Was it so that his normal "penance cruise" could be postponed? He'd never brought anyone with him on one before. And the spartan nature of the bedroom that Lea liked so much was because he didn't consider these trips pleasure cruises. They were to remind himself of the consequences of poor choices and of allowing peer pressure to overrule common sense.

Some of those consequences he carried on his person. And some of them he carried in his head.

His decisions had affected his parents for years afterwards. He never wanted that kind of responsibility to hang over his head ever again. He could have told his dad the truth, but the chilly relationship they'd shared wouldn't have changed.

"Could I come as well?"

Lea's voice broke through his brooding. Another reminder that bringing her might have been a mistake. Because as he'd stood behind her in that bedroom he'd wanted to sweep her up into his arms and drop her onto the bed and do some very un-aristocratic things to her.

He glanced at Konstantinos, who nodded. "It's fine by me."

Better do the introductions, then. He'd hoped to get in, get the supplies, make a quick run to Delos and be home before anything disastrous had a chance to happen.

"Lea Risi, this is Dr. Banis, who also works with burn patients."

He omitted the rest of it, afraid that it might open the door for Konstantinos to talk about Deakin's injuries. And the reasons for them.

The two shook hands. "I take it you're a doctor as well?"

"Yes. I'm in psychiatry—specializing in PTSD treatments."

"PTSD?" The other man sent Deakin a sharp look.

"For the earthquake victims," he clarified, hoping Lea wouldn't read anything into Konstantinos's speculative tone.

Except she had. Her head had that funny little tilt it got when she was trying to puzzle through something.

How did he even *know* that?

"Of course," the other doctor answered, patting Deakin on the shoulder.

Dammit. Why did everyone assume that he had some kind of deep-rooted issues related to his accident?

No, don't answer that.

"What is the issue with your patient?"

"Let's walk and I'll tell you."

They headed up the corridor of the Ierá Lytrotís Clinic. It was much different from their own clinic in that this place was the epitome of efficiency at the expense of comfort. Not that one was any better than the other. They just focused on different priorities.

A few minutes later they stood in front of a patient's door while Konstantinos gave them the rundown on his injuries. "I'm thinking about care-flighting him just like I did—"

"Why care-flight?" Deakin interrupted, even though he didn't care one whit about whether or not he would send this patient to Athens. He'd just been trying to cut his old doctor off before he finished the rest of that sentence, because he knew exactly how the man had planned to end it: *Just like I did with you.*

Why was he so desperate to keep Lea from knowing what had happened to him?

Was it really because she was the one person on Mythelios who was untainted by public opinion?

"Well, Athens sees a lot more of this type of case than we do."

Deakin pushed aside his own issues. "Is the patient critical?"

"Not at the moment, but with third-degree burns massive infection is always a possibility. I'll need you both to scrub up and wear protective gear while you're in there."

"Understood. Where can we do that?"

"Just inside the door. We already have a negative pressure room set up beyond that area."

Deakin's brows went up. "That's a new addition."

"Yes. We only had to do about twenty fundraisers to make it happen."

"Did you do a bachelor auction?"

Dr. Banis frowned. "A what?"

"Never mind—it was a joke."

Kind of like the calendar had been. But, hey, it had actually brought in some much-needed money. If the auction could do the same thing, maybe even get that CT machine they needed, then it would be worth it. Maybe he should let them auction him off after all...

Lea, who had been quiet during the walk to the room, spoke up. "Is counseling offered to burn patients on a regular basis?"

The hair on the back of Deakin's neck stood up. Why had she asked that question?

"Not normally, but if the resultant scars are disfiguring, or we feel the patient's quality of life will be affected at all, we might refer that patient to a psychiatrist."

"Okay. I just wondered... Because burns—especially third-degree burns—can cause mental anguish in addition to the physical injuries. Lives sometimes change dramatically."

"Yes, they do."

The murmured words were out of Deakin's mouth before he could shut them down. He was speaking in general terms. Wasn't he? But when both pairs of eyes shifted to him he knew they had taken them as a commentary on his own life.

And they'd be right.

"All the more reason to talk to an objective party about the experience and receive support," Lea said.

"And some people prefer to keep private matters private," he snapped.

If he'd hoped that would stop the direction of this conversation in its tracks, he'd been wrong. Lea's face darkened, color seeping into her cheeks in a way that said she was angry.

"Even if that choice has a devastating effect on those around you?"

Whoa. Wait a minute. His decision not to talk to a counselor had been the choice of a kid who was embar-

rassed and ashamed of what his actions had cost his
parents financially. And about how they had changed
his looks—something that was foremost on most teenagers' minds. But as far as *devastating* anyone went...
that definitely hadn't happened.

He looked closer at the flashing eyes and trembling
chin and realized that the anger she was feeling wasn't
directed at him. At least not specifically. Then who?

Someone she knew in a personal sense?

Time to shift topic.

"Of course not. And Dr. Banis is right to encourage
people to seek help. But you can't force anyone to talk
about their problems. Just like a certain someone we
visited the other day."

Lea pulled in a deep breath and then let it blow out.
"Sorry. I just get passionate about my job sometimes."

Dr. Banis gave Deakin's shoulder a quick squeeze.
"As do we all. Now, shall we go see the patient I was
talking about?"

And just like that the storm was over. At least for
now. The situation told him one thing, though. He was
going to have to watch what he said once they got into
that patient's room.

Burn patients always affected him, even though he
dealt with them all the time. His profession often trans-
ported him back to a place he would just as soon forget. If he wasn't careful Lea might learn all the secrets
he'd worked so hard to keep anyone from discovering.

And, if what he sensed was true, the beautiful psychiatrist might just have a secret or two of her own...

They opened the door, the slight hiss of air as they
went through designed to keep microbes from coming
in. In the bed was an unconscious fifty-nine-year-old

man, his face swathed in bandages that covered every-thing—even his eyes.

"What was the temperature of the grease?"

The patient had been injured by high-temperature grease in a huge industrial vat. He'd slipped on a mat while leaning over to add chicken to the fryer and his face had been dunked below the surface for a second before he'd come up screaming.

His old friend checked the chart and read off the figure.

Deakin swore softly under his breath. Hot enough to sear meat on contact. "His eyes?"

Konstantinos shook his head.

Hell. At least Deakin had retained his sight.

"He's in an induced coma at the moment."

The surgeon showed him before-and-after pictures—one of what the man had looked like before the accident, and one after he'd been debrided for the first time. The difference was staggering. In the first picture the man, Elias, had a youthful salt-and-pepper look to him, his smile brightening his whole face. A face that was now unrecognizable.

"His airway isn't affected, but we put a trach tube in to make it easier to treat the facial burns."

Deakin had never felt fortunate to have had the burns he had, but at this moment he saw life through the eyes of this patient and swallowed. If he survived it was going to be tough, but as long as he had a good support group, unlike *he'd* had, he would make it through.

And this man's injuries weren't due to stupidity. It had been a senseless accident. Something that could have happened to anyone.

"Does he have a family?"

"Yes. He doesn't have children, but his wife has been here almost nonstop. I had to order her to go home and get some rest. She should be back again in a few hours."

"Do you already have a grafting team set up?"

Konstantinos fixed Deakin with a speculative stare. "I'm working on the best plastic surgeon I know right now."

Deakin shook his head. "I won't be around when he's ready to start reconstructive surgery."

From the way Lea's head swiveled his way, he guessed she was shocked to hear that. She shouldn't be. The whole island knew that Deakin never stuck around for long.

Except she wasn't an islander. Was she relieved he'd be leaving soon?

"How about counseling for him and probably his wife too? Will *you* 'be around', Dr. Risi?"

"I'm not sure, yet."

This man wouldn't be ready to talk about his hopes and fears for months. Did Lea really think she might still be on the island by then?

His friend sighed. "Maybe I *should* care-flight him to Athens, then. I have a good team here, but not enough to give him the twenty-four-hour care he needs. The problem is that his wife is a nurse here at the clinic, and we'll really have a hard time replacing her if he goes—she'll want to be with him as much as possible."

If he'd hoped to guilt Deakin into staying he was going to be disappointed, even though he doubted Konstantino was really trying to do that.

"I'm sorry. I can take a copy of the chart and read over it—give you my recommendations if that would help."

"It would indeed, thank you, Deak. I'll be looking forward to hearing your opinion."

A few minutes later they were on their way. But first Deakin made a quick trip to the restroom, leaning over the sink to splash water onto his face. He'd dealt with some pretty horrific burns during his career, but...*damn*.

And Lea... Something about the possibility of her remaining on the island really bothered him. He couldn't put a finger on exactly why, but there was a niggling in his gut that wouldn't go away.

But it would eventually. Once he was off the island and on his way back to Africa, or wherever they sent him next.

At least he hoped so. Because otherwise he was in a lot of trouble.

And so were his patients if he couldn't get his head screwed back on straight. So he would just work hard to make sure that happened. No matter what it took.

The ruins rose from the earth, their white stone catching the mid-morning sun and creating a dazzling display visible even from their position on the water. It gave Delos an ethereal, magical feel.

Lea glanced over at where Deakin was manning the wheel and saw his face was aimed at the shoreline as well. His shoulders were more relaxed than she had seen them all day. Actually, since their very first meeting back at the clinic on Mythelios.

With sunglasses hiding his dark eyes, she'd had no way of knowing what he was thinking until now, when his psyche seemed to breathe a huge sigh of relief.

He liked it here.

Coming had been the right decision, although after

their tense back-and-forth exchange at the clinic on Naxos she had been kicking herself for agreeing to the trip.

His words about some people preferring to keep private matters private had touched a nerve and she'd erupted. Something she rarely did. But suicide was never a "private" matter. *Ever.* Who knew that better than she did?

But she needed to let it go. This was not about Mark. Not anymore. And if she couldn't move beyond it she was going to need to talk to someone herself. She had no right to criticize Deakin for something she had caught herself doing time and time again since Mark had died: bottling up her pain.

It had also bothered her when Deakin had been so quick to say that he wouldn't be around when that burn patient needed surgery. Wasn't there *anything* he would miss about Mythelios?

"We're getting close. Do you want to take the wheel for a few minutes? I should have asked you earlier."

Even his voice sounded more content.

"I'm good. Just enjoying my first glimpse of the is-land." Perched on the seat next to his in the small wheel-house, she admired the view again. "It's beautiful. It's hard to believe a place like this actually exists outside of books."

"Yes. I'm glad the island has remained uninhabited except for some essential staff."

"Mainland Greece has ruins, but I haven't seen any of the ones on the islands."

"Most of them have some. Mythelios has an Apollo's Temple and a few other ruins."

"I'd heard about the temple, but with the earthquake

I haven't gotten a chance to explore much past the village where the clinic is."

"I'm surprised Petra hasn't taken you."

"She's had a lot on her plate, with the clinic and visiting her mom. I don't think she has much down time."

"Hmm…"

She had no idea what that meant. But if she'd been expecting him to offer to drive her around on a sightseeing tour of his home island she was sorely mistaken. Not that she did. Expect him to do that, that was. It was enough to have the day off to enjoy.

She hadn't realized the exhausting pace she'd been keeping until getting on this boat, actually. She'd found her head lolling a couple of times as she sat beside Deakin. Especially since he'd been so quiet for most of the trip.

He hadn't said anything about it. Maybe he hadn't even noticed her head jerking from time to time. Or maybe he'd been grateful for it. It meant he hadn't needed to keep her company.

"Do you want to eat an early lunch first and then go to the island? We have time if you want to lie down for a little while below."

Her face heated. So he *had* noticed. "Sorry. It's been a little chaotic on Mythelios over the last few weeks. I'm more tired than I realized."

He slowed the boat until the engines barely throbbed. The vibrations rattled her stomach as he turned in his seat to look at her.

"It's the letdown from adrenaline. I get it too. After I've been dealing with tragedies in other countries I feel like I could sleep for a week."

"Yes. I feel that way now. But I want to explore the island first. I can sleep later."

"You can nap on the way back to Mythelios, if you want. It's not a long trip, but I can draw it out a little. There's nothing like sleeping on the water."

Said as if he did that a lot. Maybe he did…

"You must love having your dad's boat."

"I don't think 'love' is the right word. I've been thinking of selling it, actually."

"Why?" If she lived on Mythelios and had something like this she would be out on the water every chance she got.

"I'm rarely on the island anymore. If it weren't for the clinic I'd probably sell the house too, and relocate completely."

That she could understand. She'd stayed in Toronto after Mark had died because of her job and that whole thing about not making radical decisions in the midst of a crisis. She'd held on to her job and the apartment for probably longer than she should have.

Living on Mythelios had showed her that she was ready to move on and hopefully leave the past where it belonged. The heartache would always be there. But hopefully it wouldn't be as sharp and painful after a few years.

"Does it hurt living in your parents' house, surrounded by their memories?"

It took him a minute to answer. "It's uncomfortable at times."

She thought he was going to add something else, but he didn't. "Do you have a practice somewhere else? Or do you only do relief work?"

"I've done short stints on several of the islands, including Naxos and in Athens. I'm beginning to think I'm a nomad at heart, though."

"No thoughts of marriage or kids?"

He gave her a sharp look. "No."

Oh, Lord, had he thought she was applying for the position? Nothing could be farther from the truth.

"I was engaged, but it didn't work out, so I see where you're coming from." The words came out of a place of injured pride—just to show him that she wasn't some desperate teenager hoping for her first kiss.

"I'm sorry. Was he in medicine too?"

"Yes. He was a doctor."

Deakin shut off the engines and hit a button. A rumble from somewhere underneath them had her frowning.

"Just setting the anchor." He swiveled his chair toward her and propped his sunglasses on top of his head, looking at her face. "Is that why you left Toronto? A broken engagement?"

"We didn't break the engagement."

"But you said it didn't work out."

She never should have said anything. But now that she had there was no going back. "He died."

"Oh, hell. Lea, I'm sorry. Was he ill?"

"Yes. He was. Only no one knew it." Suddenly, she knew she was going to tell him. *Needed* to tell him. "He committed suicide six months before our wedding day."

If the words shocked him he didn't let on. He leaned across and wrapped his hand around hers. "What a damned fool."

"Excuse me?" She'd expected sympathy. Pity, even. Not the low angry sentence he'd just gritted out.

"He just left you to deal with the fallout."

"There was something going on inside of him that none of us knew about."

Lea still didn't know what. Mark had left no suicide note, so all she and his family had been able to do was guess as to why he'd done it, which somehow made it even worse.

"He never talked to you about it?"

"No, obviously not. I would have asked him to go see someone."

Deakin's lips tightened slightly, but he only nodded. "I'm sorry to have brought up a painful memory."

"You didn't know. It's why I came to Mythelios, actually. I needed a change of venue. A chance to get away from the apartment we shared and think about everything from a distance."

"Will you go back to Canada?"

"Long-term? I don't know. I will probably have to at some point, though. My folks live there, and since I haven't put out any job applications yet I'll eventually have to start looking. This was supposed to be a vacation. And it's been a good one—despite the earthquake. Or maybe even because of it."

He smiled. "Not exactly *my* idea of a good time."

"Maybe not."

The canopy over the upper part of the boat, provided shade from the brutal sun, and there was a balmy breeze blowing across the water.

She took a deep breath and sighed, looking at his face. "So how do you fit in vacation time since you travel so much?"

"I have a little downtime in between assignments, but work is all the therapy I need."

Who'd said anything about therapy? She'd been talking about holidays. Vacations. Time not spent working. "Everyone should have a way to decompress."

He let go of her hand. "Well, not everyone has access to Serenity Gardens. Sometimes we have to work with the hand we've been dealt in life."

"I like to think we can shuffle our deck and start over with a new hand," she said quietly.

"Is that what this trip was about for you? Reshuffling the deck?" he asked.

She kicked her sandals off and tucked up her feet under her, then rearranged the hem of her sundress so that it covered her legs. "You don't sound like you agree."

"It's not that I disagree, I just don't think you can ever get completely away from the past." He nodded over the surface of the water. "Just like on Delos, there are fragments that remain embedded in us. We can't uproot them, no matter how hard we might try."

"Maybe. But perhaps that's the way it *should* be. Our experiences—good and bad—shape us. Delos wouldn't be the same without those ruins, don't you agree?"

Following her lead, Deakin stretched his long legs out and crossed his arms over his chest, the muscles in his upper arms tightening. "I'd have to think about it."

That was okay. He didn't have to agree or disagree with her. He had the right to his own opinion. She would never be able to say that Mark's death had been a positive experience. It had been horrific, and she still got angry and sad about what he had done. But there was no changing it.

Her trip was supposed to clear her head and help her decide which direction to take for the next chapter of her life. But fate had intervened and she hadn't gotten the chance to do that yet. Deakin coming home might have forced the issue, though. She couldn't stay in his cottage forever. Maybe it was time for her to start applying at hospitals in Canada and see where it took her.

Vacations were meant to be temporary. This hadn't been a typical getaway, but it had given her a chance to be immersed in medicine—not just psychiatry—and feel truly useful. Maybe she should try to do what Deakin did. Travel from place to place and find work wherever the wind carried her.

Except she liked being settled in one spot. She didn't think she was the world-traveler type. And when she'd arrived on Mythelios there had been a sense of rightness that she'd never felt before. Maybe she could find another place that gave her that same feeling.

Deakin sat up, his sunglasses back in place, as if making a decision. "Well, I'm ready to eat if you are. And then afterwards we'll explore the island."

The little bit of sharing they'd done was evidently over, from the sound of it. This was the quiet, solemn Deakin she'd first met. If she hadn't been there to witness his outburst when he'd learned that Mark had committed suicide she might have doubted it had ever happened.

And the hand-holding?

A temporary detour. Now he was back on a road well-traveled and sparsely populated. And it looked like he was on it to stay.

CHAPTER SIX

DEAKIN SHOULDERED THE knapsack filled with their supplies and hopped from the boat onto the dock before
turning to offer Lea his hand. Armed with a floppy
white hat that matched her dress—and the island's many
pillars—she looked cool and touristy, a very different
person from the businesslike woman he'd met in the
clinic lobby.

Her warm fingers landed in his, and she held her hat
on her head with the other hand as she stepped across.
The wind whipped her dress, molding it to her body,
making him move uncomfortably before forcing himself to shift his attention to something else.

"Wow, this is amazing! And incredibly windy! I'm
glad my hat has a tie."

She took a moment to take it off and pull the ribbons
from inside, before knotting them under her chin. Then
she gazed around the hills, where the ruins were scat-
tered as if a huge hand had swept across the hilly terrain
and sent things flying in different directions.

A large tour group ambled by, cameras at the ready,
blocking their view for a minute or two.

She frowned. "Do we have to do the guided thing, or
can we look around on our own?"

"Whatever you prefer. I'm familiar with most of the sights, and I have a tour book with me if you want to read more about any specific ruins."

"You came prepared! And, yes, exploring at our leisure would be great."

She trusted him to take her around. That fact shouldn't have sent a flicker of anticipation through him. But it did. He was just as happy to avoid the tourist scene, with up to fifty people all jostling for position to get the best photos. Besides, this way no one would ask awkward questions or assume they were a couple.

Her comment on the boat about reshuffling life's deck of cards had hit him like a ton of bricks. But it wasn't possible. At least not for him. Every time he came to Mythelios and stayed in his parents' house he was reminded of what had happened that day...of what life had been like afterwards. Ville could have been killed, or ended up like Konstantino's patient, and then he would have more than just a boat and a boathouse on his conscience.

The times he felt the most relief were when he pulled out of that boat dock and headed away from the island where he was raised. Like today, coming to Delos with Lea. Then he could be himself, rather than the person he thought everyone saw when they looked at him.

He led the way from the boat ramp, pausing as another large group passed them on the right. Lea's attention was already shifting from place to place, her eyes alight with interest.

The tense muscles in his shoulders relaxed. As much as he hated to admit it, he liked the idea of just the two of them strolling through these ancient areas.

She'd balled up the side of her dress to keep it from blowing up Marilyn Monroe style.

"I thought wearing this was going to keep me cool, but I guess I should have rethought that."

No, she shouldn't. With its spaghetti straps holding up a snug bodice and the skirt flying around her legs, the floral print dress provided a bright spot of color among the white buildings. It was sexy and free, and he liked it a little more than he should have.

More than one guy had glanced their way—probably wondering what a beauty like this was doing in his company.

He shook off that thought.

"There's not much shade, so let me know if you get too hot. We can take a break and go back to the boat."

"I'm fine for now." She gave a quick smile and flicked the fluttering brim of her hat. "And I brought my own shade…and a built in fan."

"I brought some water and snacks." He shifted the backpack to his other shoulder.

The midsummer heat could crush the most exuberant explorer and send them packing back to their tourist boat—if it was still docked. Another reason to go it on their own. They could easily go back to *Mytheliostocracy II* and cool off for a while.

She nodded. "Let me know if you want me to carry it for a while."

"I'm good, but thanks."

Yet another group came by and someone jostled Lea, almost knocking her over. Deakin grabbed her hand and hauled her close to let them pass. Instead of pulling away, her hand curled around his in a way that was comfortable and familiar. Something else that he liked.

They started up the footpath, past some crumbling buildings. "What are these?"

"This is the residential area. The wealthier homes had marble floors and pillars. And a built-in bathroom."

"Built in?"

He grinned. "Well, after a fashion. There was no plumbing. Just a trough." He motioned to a long, narrow dug-out section of the floor that was lined with marble stones.

"You're kidding?"

That made him laugh, giving her shoulder a nudge with his. "Not interested in time-traveling back to that era, then?"

"For a visit? Yes. To live? *No.* Although I often think it might be nice to live without the constant barrage of messages on our cell phones. Or is it just mine that's constantly pinging at me?"

"It's not just yours."

He'd caught himself glancing at the screen of his phone more than once this morning, although he wasn't expecting to receive messages from anyone in particular. It was a habit. And not a good one. Holding Lea's hand, though, took care of that. Not to mention taking care of him being aware of anything except the feel of her skin against his.

"Where to next?"

Lea stood next to a wall that blocked the majority of the wind. She tugged her hand from his and readjusted the strings of her hat, tipping it off her head so that it hung down her back. Her dark locks gleamed in the light.

"There—I think that might be easier, actually."

He'd kind of liked her in the hat. Then again, he liked her with it off too. Their hands found each other once again, fingers linking this time.

"We can head up the hill toward some of the more

impressive ruins. There's the amphitheater and Apollo's temple."

"Have they restored any of the ruins or are they just left natural?"

"They've restored some of them, but not all. The four remaining statues on the Terrace of the Lions are replicas. The originals are in the museum. We can see them on our way out."

They started walking, the easy camaraderie they'd suddenly developed making his defensiveness on Naxos fade away. Leaving it behind was hard. Because if there was one thing he knew how to do well it was defending his emotions from anything that might get too close.

Lea was definitely stepping nearer, and it had nothing to do with their holding hands.

Not that it made him let go. Or made him stop their arms from swinging back and forth in time as they walked up the narrow curving path. The warm, stiff breeze was now at their backs as they hiked up the hill toward the first of the ruins. The higher they went, the closer he had to lean to be heard over the wind.

He'd been to Delos many times, so he could almost recite the spiel of the tour guides by heart, but he knew that probably wasn't what Lea wanted to hear. And it wasn't what he wanted to say. He wanted to talk about the magic of the island. About the refuge he'd found here as a young adult, still struggling with the effects of his injuries.

But he didn't say any of that.

They came to the Terrace of the Lions and Lea's fascination was evident as she strained her neck to see the top. These statues—each perched on a stone rectangle—had seemed much larger when he was a child, but in reality, standing next to them, he saw that Lea's head reached the nearest lion's chest.

"I can't believe these aren't the originals."

The stone work was very good, and unless you were an expert in sculpting you'd probably never guess.

On impulse, Deakin took out his phone and snapped a picture of her. With her face tilted up, the wind catching the darks strands of her hair and sending them whipping around her face, she looked as if she belonged there. The urge to put his arm around her waist and haul her against him had been toying with his mind for several minutes. Maybe that was part of what was behind his sudden interest in photography. Anything to keep from scratching that other, more dangerous itch.

He could always send the shot to her as a keepsake of her day on the island. And then he would promptly delete it from his phone. He wasn't in the market for a wife, or even a girlfriend, but he could certainly appreciate a beautiful woman when he saw one.

And be affected by her. As evidenced on several occasions. Like now…

"What's next?" she asked, coming to stand beside him.

There was that itch again. Getting stronger all the time.

Stuffing the phone back in his pocket, he didn't even need to consult his map. "The sacred lake is just over there."

She turned her head and scanned the terrain in the direction he indicated. "Just over where?"

"There's no water in it anymore—it's been drained."

The natural bowl formed at the bottom of a depression was now dry.

"By the ancients?" Her voice had a breathless tone that he liked.

Hell, what *didn't* he like about her?

"No, it was done in the early twentieth century. There was an outbreak of malaria, and to prevent that from happening again they keep it empty."

"Wow—the sacred lake, done in by a bout of malaria." A choked laugh came out. "I know it's not funny, but..."

"It is—kind of." His fingers touched her waistline at the back of her dress. It was damp with perspiration. "Are you hot?"

"A little."

Deakin dropped his backpack to the ground and crouched beside it, taking out two bottles of water, both still very cold after having been stored in the boat's small freezer compartment. "We need to make sure we keep hydrated."

"Thanks." Twisting the top off, she tilted the bottle to her lips, seeming to caress the rim before tipping her head slightly as she took several long drinks.

From his position on the ground he could see the cords in her neck work as she swallowed. Her tongue then took a quick swipe at a drop of water that had escaped the bottle's opening and started down the side. He almost groaned aloud.

You need to curb that sick imagination of yours, bud.

He gulped some water himself, trying to wash down this unwelcome awareness of her that was steadily getting larger and harder to ignore. A certain part of his body was having the same problem.

He stood up to derail his thoughts. "Let's walk toward the museum. It's just across the way."

Lea screwed the cap back onto her water bottle. He held his hand out for it but she shook her head, holding the chilled bottle to the underside of her throat and closing her eyes.

"I think I'm going to hold onto this for a while. Besides, I know you have more stuff in there. Unless you'll let me carry it for a while?"

"I'm good. Seriously."

And the weight of the pack gave him something to think about. Anything to keep his mind off the way she was touching that bottle against different parts of her neck and sighing. Or the way her dress kept riding up those tanned thighs, despite her best efforts to keep everything battened down and secure.

His phone might not be taking snapshots anymore, but his brain certainly was. And these weren't the kind that could be deleted at the touch of a button.

They made their way past the Agora of the Italians and hiked along the Roman Wall. When they got to the Altar of Dionysus they stopped. Lea looked up at one of the two statues flanking the flat platform, her head tilted sideways as if trying to figure out exactly what...

She got it. And he had to smile. The two phallus monuments were kind of hard to miss.

"They are rather well endowed, aren't they?" she asked, laughter in her voice. "Or is that just wishful thinking?"

"Probably a little of both."

He'd had a few problems with his own...er...monument over the last half-hour or so. If she licked that water bottle one more time he was going to come unglued.

"It gives the idea of *'erecting'* a statue a whole new meaning." This time she giggled out loud.

"Yes, it does."

They finally made it to the museum, and stepped into the first shady area they'd seen on the island. There they found the four original lion statues, along with the Hand of Colossus and numerous other artifacts.

"This is better than some of the places on the mainland that I've visited. There is just so much history packed into such a tiny space."

"I think so too."

The skirt of her dress had been released and was on its best behavior now that the wind wasn't burrowing under it and teasing it away from her legs. *Damn.* Because he was thinking of doing that very thing himself...

Lea turned to look at something and bumped hard against Deakin's side in the process. "Sorry!"

His arm wrapped around her back to steady both of them, and that finally scratched the itch that had been plaguing him ever since they'd dropped anchor offshore. And, hell, if it didn't feel good...

Too good.

Soft green eyes came up to meet his. Her body was still pressed against him.

"Not your fault."

He tried to command his arm to drop back to his side, but since she was making no effort to pull away it was a hard sell. Especially since his own "Dionysus" was showing a whole lot of interest in keeping her right where she was...in the way she felt cradled against his body.

"I practically knocked you over."

"Not a chance."

Was it his imagination or had she turned to face him

slightly, her body fitting against his in a way that robbed his lungs of air?

He couldn't stop his arm from tightening its grip. His body was hyper-aware of every curve and dip of hers. It had been a long time since he'd felt this rush of need, and he was in no hurry to call an end to it. In fact…

His hands moved to cup her face, tilting it up slightly just as a slight movement to his right caught his eye.

Ignore it.

"Deakin?" she whispered.

He hovered, caught between two worlds. The one he wanted to be in—where pink parted lips were wait-ing—and the one that was slowly tugging at the duty center of his brain.

He allowed his glance to stray for just a second and spied a man leaning against one of the walls, right next to an exhibit of some marble busts. Hands on his knees, he appeared to be trying to catch his breath. No one seemed overly concerned, not even the man himself, but something was off.

He scanned the people near him, but either he was alone, or the person or group he was with was looking at something other than the man. His eyes came up at that moment and met Deakin's from across the room, and then his head dropped once again, his fingers gripping his legs more tightly.

Deakin swallowed, then looked back down at Lea. "Wait here for a minute," he murmured, before releas-ing her and making his way over to the man.

If there was nothing wrong with him Deakin was going to be kicking himself into next Tuesday.

The man was a little thick around the middle, and it

could be that he was just out of shape and out of breath, but it wouldn't hurt to make sure.

He reached his side and put a hand on his shoulder. "Are you okay?"

"Can't…c-catch my breath." He paused in an attempt to draw in another wheezy puff of air.

"I'm a doctor. Mind if I check you—?"

At that moment the man's hands came off his knees and he crumpled right where he was, winding up in a sitting position, legs curled, head lolling to the left.

Lea was beside Deakin in an instant, dropping her water bottle and helping him lie the man out flat.

A crowd began forming around them, and he called out to the group. "Anyone know who he's with?"

Deakin's voice carried over the surrounding voices and someone stepped forward.

"I was on the same tour boat as he was, but I think he was alone. He didn't really speak to anyone that I saw. He caught my attention because of his backpack. It's from the same uni that I went to. Is he okay?"

"I don't know yet."

Deakin felt for a pulse and found one. It was quicker than it should be, and the man's skin was hot and dry. Not good at all.

He murmured to Lea. "I need your water bottle, if it's still cold."

"Here."

She pushed it into his hands and he thanked his lucky stars that he'd put them in the freezer on the boat before they'd left Mythelios. He placed the bottle against the man's neck, right where his carotid ran, hoping to cool the blood rushing through his system. He heard the zipper on his own backpack opening and soon three more bottles appeared, to be placed under the man's arms and on his groin—all blood-rich areas.

A tour guide came up and asked if she could help. Deakin quickly explained that he was a doctor and he thought the man might be suffering from heatstroke, and that they needed to get him cooled down as quickly as possible.

"I need to get him back to my boat and take him to hospital. It's air-conditioned."

The tour guide gathered some people who helped form a kind of mobile stretcher by linking hands beneath the man's body and lifting him.

"I don't know if this will work on some of those narrow areas, but if we can just crowd in close..."

They had to try. If the man was suffering from heatstroke he could very well die, since the part of his brain that regulated body temperature was shorting out.

It took fifteen minutes, but in Deakin's head it seemed like forever. He and Lea joined the rest of the group, grasping hands under the victim's legs and doing the best they could to synchronize their steps with those of the other rescuers. They would go through the man's pack as soon as they got to the boat and see if there was anything inside such as a medical alert bracelet, or an identity card listing any medication he might be taking.

Once they had him on board the boat, inside the main compartment on a small cushioned sofa, Lea thanked everyone. Then, with Deakin's help, she switched the air-conditioning on high while he started the boat.

"Can you try to get him cooled down while I drive?" he asked.

"Of course." She had already opened one of the water

bottles and was dousing the man with it. "I'll get some of his clothes off and keep using the water."

Deakin aimed one of the air-conditioning vents so it pointed directly at the patient. "There are more bottles in the freezer. And there's potable water in the tank that runs the taps."

"Go. I've got this."

Deakin went up to the wheelhouse and started the engines, while some of the folks who'd helped them untied the ropes from the cleats on the dock and tossed them onto the vessel.

"Thanks!" he yelled above the engines.

Time to get this man to the nearest capable facility—which was probably their clinic on Mythelios.

For once he felt a sense of urgency rather than dread as he prepared to go back to the island. He gunned the engine and hoped that Lea had everything secured down below as he backed out of the slip on the dock and shoved the gear lever into drive. Then he throttled up, kicking a spray of foam to the side as he spun the boat and headed back the way they'd came.

They'd be bypassing Naxos, though. There was just something in him telling him that Mythelios was the best place for this man to be.

He picked up his radio and called the deck below. He flicked the switch that would allow him to hear what was being said down there, then depressed the call button.

"Lea, what's happening?"

"You can hear me?"

Of course. She had no idea there were speakers downstairs that would pick up her voice. His dad had installed them on the original *Mytheliostocracy* to keep in contact with his mother during trips. And he'd had a duplicate system put on the *Mytheliostocracy II*.

"Yes. There are microphones set up in the speakers. How's he doing?"

"He's still unconscious, but I think cooling him off is working. His pulse isn't quite as thready as it was. Your air-conditioning works great. Too bad the clinic doesn't have its own boat. It could go out on rescues just like this one."

He blinked. They had boats bringing in patients from time to time, but they'd never really discussed having a vessel of their own.

"We're about twenty-five minutes out—maybe a little less if I can coax some more power from this engine."

"I think the important thing is that we arrive in one piece."

A ghost of a smile played around the edges of his mind. "Worried?"

"About the patient. Not about me."

"I'm being as safe as I can."

Which was true. He didn't take as many risks as he had when he was younger. Maybe that made him a boring person. But at least he didn't put anyone else in danger. When he thought about what could have happened to his parents' house, and to them, if that explosion had been any bigger…

Come on, Deakin. Let's just worry about someone you can help.

"I'll keep the intercom on. Let me know if you need anything. I'm going to call ahead to the clinic and tell Petra to be ready with an ice bath."

"Good idea."

He let Lea get back to working on the patient, and

realized as he did so that he had no problem turning the man's care over to her—something that was unusual for him. He was used to being given free rein with his patients, since burn specialists were not a dime a dozen. But this wasn't a burn patient—and, more than that, he trusted her. It was as simple as that. He'd already seen how fiercely she cared about her own patients—it was part of the reason for their little verbal scuffle over on Naxos. She would do her very best for their heatstroke victim.

As soon as he'd alerted Petra, who said they'd be ready when they got there, he put the receiver back up to his mouth to talk to Lea.

"I know we didn't find any kind of medical alert items, but can you go through his backpack again and look for some kind of contact information?"

"Already done. His name is Sam Davidson. He's an American. I only found his mother's name and phone number, so I called and left a voicemail. Hopefully she'll get in contact with me soon."

"Good work. We're getting close. About ten minutes out, I think."

"Sounds good."

He heard her talking to their patient in low, calm tones, asking him to open his eyes if he could hear her. Impatience rose inside him. He wanted to be down there helping, dammit. Not stuck up here driving the boat. He couldn't see how EMT drivers did it.

"He's waking up." Lea's voice came through, then the sound of thrashing and a man's loud voice. "He's a little miffed, I think."

Her voice changed, turning into the bossy Lea he'd met a time or two.

"No, wait. You can't… You need to…"

Then…

"Deakin, we may have a problem down here."

Just then he heard a crash and the sound of glass breaking somewhere below.

"Lea? What's going on? Hey! Answer me!"

A few seconds later, she did. "It's okay. He's just confused. He's lying down again now."

Relief swamped his system. "Do you need me to stop the boat and come down there?"

"No. He broke a drinking glass, that's all. He's fine."

A man's voice came, sounding shaky and weak. "Sorry to be a problem."

"Hey, it's no problem. We're headed to a clinic on our island. They can help with whatever's going on."

"Thank you."

Deakin should be the one thanking *him*. While he certainly hadn't wanted anyone to get sick, their patient had succeeded in doing what all the mental gymnastics in the world hadn't been able to do: taking his mind off his own base desires and putting it on something that might actually do some good.

CHAPTER SEVEN

"YOU'RE GOING TO be fine."

Sam Davidson had spent a few days at the clinic before getting the green light to go home. Heatstroke could cause multiple organ failure, but this particular patient had dodged that bullet. Maybe it was because they'd been able to get those water bottles on him so quickly. Or maybe it was pure luck. Whatever it was, Lea was glad.

Watching Deakin take his vitals at the museum had made something shift in her tummy. She'd been so focused on what she'd hoped was about to happen between them that she'd totally tuned out everything else around them. Until Deakin had told her to wait and quickly headed toward the stranger.

His tan had darkened further since he'd been on the island, making his scars stand out. Those areas had lost all their melanin, either during the healing process or during some of the grafting procedures he'd undergone. But she'd seen them enough now that they just seemed part of what made him Deakin—even though still she wasn't entirely sure who that was.

Just when she thought she was getting to know him, he fooled her and became someone else completely. And that scared her. She wasn't sure why. She wasn't engaged

to this man, like she'd been to Mark. What he wanted
to do with his life should be of no importance to her.

And it wasn't.

At least she hoped it wasn't.

"How long before I can catch a flight home?"

Their patient's voice called her from her thoughts.
Their patient. Theirs. As in his and hers.

Um, *no*. She was not going to start thinking in those
terms.

"Well, if you lived on the mainland we would have already discharged you. But flights from here to the States
aren't the shortest. I just want to wait another day or so.
Surely our food isn't all that bad?"

"Actually, it's pretty good. I just know my mom is
worried and would like me home."

"It won't be much longer," Deakin said with a smile.

Sam lay back against the pillows and glanced at Deakin. "You saved my life."

"No. There were a lot of people who helped—including those who carried you from the museum to the boat."

"I know. I wish I could thank them all."

"We've had a couple of people call and ask about you.
Unfortunately our laws are similar to your HIPPA rules.
We couldn't say much. Maybe once you leave you'll give
us permission to let them know you're okay."

"Of course I will. I'll sign whatever you need."

"Great—thank you."

Petra stuck her head into the room. "Theo wants to
see you for a minute."

"Who? Me?" Lea wasn't sure why he would want to
talk to *her*.

"No, Deakin."

Her voice sounded a little bit ominous.

Deakin must be thinking the exact same thing, because a vein had begun pulsing in his temple.

"I'll be out in a minute. Thanks." He turned back to his patient. "I'll be back sometime this afternoon to check on you again. Hopefully I'll have a better idea of when you can get out of this place."

"Thanks again for all you did. I am very grateful."

"Just be careful out in the heat for a while. There's some evidence that heatstroke can permanently alter your ability to regulate your temperature. So make sure you see your own doctors once you get home. They'll be able to tell you the best way to proceed."

"Why did it even happen? I'm from Florida. It gets plenty hot there."

"Greece has a dryer climate than Florida. You can dehydrate without realizing it." He patted the man on the shoulder. "But it looks like you're on the mend. Just monitor your water intake and make sure you're getting enough even if you don't feel thirsty."

"I definitely will after this." Sam's glance moved to include her. "Thank you both."

Lea smiled at him. "We're just glad you're going to be okay."

"So am I."

Deakin moved to the door and opened it. "Get some rest while you can. I'm sure once you're home you're not going to have much time for that."

They'd discovered, after he'd opened up to Lea one day, that Sam was a stockbroker—it was a job, he said, that ran him ragged. He'd come to Greece hoping to get out of the rat race for a little while. Instead he'd landed himself in the hospital.

Following Deakin out, she wondered what Theo wanted with him. Hopefully Cailey was okay...

And there he was. Waiting for Deakin by the reception desk.

"What do you need, Theo?" he asked.

The other doctor glanced at her for a moment and she backed away. "I think I have a patient coming in a few minutes, so I'm going to run. See you later."

Without looking behind her she turned and hightailed it out of there.

Before she got dragged into whatever was about to go down between the two men.

"All right, Theo, she's gone. Now, spit it out."

It was obvious his friend hadn't wanted to say whatever it was he wanted to say in front of the psychiatrist.

"How do you like working with her?"

His brain went on high alert. Had Theo sensed something unprofessional in his demeanor toward Lea? There had certainly been a few moments on the island when he'd almost stepped over the line of professionalism. But no one knew that except for Lea and him...

"She seems to be good at her job. Patients like her. What is this all about?"

Had he found something bad on her record?

"Do you think she's been valuable to the clinic?"

There was something about the way Theo was asking these questions that made him suspicious. "In as far as her work ethic goes? Or are you talking about her profession itself?"

"Either. Both. Is there something you don't like about her?"

That was the problem. He pretty much liked *every-*

thing about her. Well, her profession itself made him a little uncomfortable, but that wasn't her problem—it was his.

"No. I think she's done a great job—especially since she's a *volunteer.*" Maybe now was the time to bring up the subject of payment.

Theo regarded him for a second. "And if she weren't?"

"Are you thinking of paying her? Because my answer would be that it's about damn time."

"Okay. It's settled, then. I want to call a meeting of the board of directors to make it official. I can at least get Chris online and ask for his input, and I can make another attempt to contact Ares. The clinic is short of funds after the earthquake, but I feel like she's worked hard and has more than earned any proposed income."

"Sounds good. Let me know when the others can meet and I'll clear my schedule."

Theo smiled. "Sounds good. I was afraid you were going to put the kibosh on the suggestion."

"No kiboshing going on here. Do you want me to let her know?"

Great, now he was looking for excuses to talk to her?

"No, I'd like to do it myself, if you don't mind."

"I'm okay with that." Deakin paused. "How's Stavros, by the way? Have you heard anything?"

"Not a peep out of him. I think I may have to pay him a visit…unless maybe *you* want to."

"Ha! Last time we almost ended up punching each other out. It's time for me to say, *Tag, you're it.*"

"Thanks, bud. You never did have much of a bedside manner."

"I never needed one."

"You are a regular riot, Deak."

He laughed. "I do my best." He sobered a bit. "And Cailey? She's still okay?"

His friend's face softened. "She's great. *We're* great."

"I'm happy for you. I really am."

When he'd first heard that Theo had found someone the news had shaken him. It had made his own aloneness feel that little bit sharper. But now that he'd had time to think about it he could congratulate Theo without feeling the world was coming to an end.

"Thanks. That means a lot. I hope Chris and Ares are as happy with their lives—wherever they are."

"Me too. I'm headed out to lunch. If you need something, give me a yell."

"I will."

Deakin decided to stop by the reception desk and see if there were any patients who hadn't been seen and then go grab something to eat himself.

He wasn't exactly sure what else he could help with on the island now the earthquake repairs were well underway. But, like Lea, he was between assignments, so he might as well stick around for a few more weeks before contacting the relief organization and seeing where they could use him next.

Or maybe he really should start looking for something a little more permanent.

Here on the island?

Hell, no. He'd never feel all warm and cuddly about Mythelios—at least he didn't think he would. When he was here all he could think about was how soon he could leave again. With the exception of his aunt, Stavros, and his buddies at the clinic, there was no one he really cared about here on the island. Oh, he would die trying to save any one of the islanders, but he would do that wherever he was.

Petra was seated behind the glassed-in desk, talking to a patient. He waited for her to finish and then went up to her. "Who's next?"

"Hello, Dr. Patera. How *are* you?"

The sardonic drawl was unmistakable. Maybe he *was* a little short with people at times. He held up his hands. "Okay, I'm—"

"Don't tell me the inestimable Dr. Deakin Patera is about to *apologize*." She put her hand over her heart as if having palpitations.

He laughed. "I was going to, but now…"

"Apology accepted."

"I don't remember actually getting that far, but okay."

His gaze went to the wall beside her, noticing immediately the empty nail where the calendar had been. July had hit several days earlier, and he'd been meaning to come over and ask her to take it down. Maybe someone else had gotten to it first, or perhaps Theo had had mercy on him and done as he'd asked. Whatever it was, he was grateful.

"Anything else?" she asked.

"Yes. Thanks for taking that down."

"What down?"

He nodded at the wall.

She looked beside her and her eyes widened. "I didn't do that. But don't worry…" She reached down and opened a drawer and pulled out another calendar. "I have plenty more where that came from."

He groaned. "Can't you just leave it down?"

"Not if I want to eat."

"Sorry?"

"We're running on fumes right now at the clinic, so this calendar has been bringing in quite a bit of money. Having one hanging there is great advertising for it."

When she flipped it open to July he couldn't stand it. "I'm out of here. Unless there are more patients that need to be seen."

"I think Lea took the last one on the list to the Serenity Gardens."

So she hadn't just been making an empty excuse about having a patient a little earlier.

"Okay. Call me if Sam's condition changes." In case she didn't know who he meant, he added, "The heatstroke patient."

"Are you headed home or to lunch?"

He glanced at his watch. Just two-thirty. Theo had said he was headed to lunch, but he hadn't thought to ask if his friend was coming back afterwards or not.

Maybe he should just go grab something from the clinic's little café. Or maybe he should head to Stavros's place to get something to eat and a little something else to drown his sorrows—the sorrows that came from almost kissing your work colleague. But drinking alcohol this early...? Probably not the best idea. Especially if he had to see patients afterwards.

Well, lunch it was. At the small cafeteria. And then he would finish his day, go home, and forget about a certain island and a certain woman and the fact that he'd had fun for the first time in a very long time. And he'd also do his best to forget that she currently lived less than twenty steps away from where he slept.

The smoke alarm went off at exactly nine p.m., its shrill whistle firing up his nervous system like a lightning bolt. He shot up from the sofa, yanking his T-shirt on over his head and grabbing his shoes, then careened through the door and across the lawn.

It wasn't coming from the main house. It was the cottage again. As fast as it had started, it stopped. He stood there in the grass for a moment, waiting. Maybe she'd just burned her eggs again. After all, he'd shown her how to work the remote control to turn the alarm off if it was a false alarm.

Did he go back inside, or did he go over there and make sure things were okay? What if there was a fire and she was trying to deal with it on her own?

The siren blared again, lasting a few seconds longer this time before cutting out. That made his decision. Not bothering to put his shoes on, he finished jogging across the space before banging on the front door. She opened it almost immediately, not saying a word, just spinning around and walking back inside, moving toward the dining room.

He didn't smell smoke. Or see any evidence of it. She turned toward him, picked up the remote and hit a button. Like clockwork, the alarm went off again. This time he went over and took it out of her hand and shut the thing off.

"What the hell, Lea? I don't know what you think you're doing, but this isn't funny. Nor is it a game." His blood pressure had spiked sky-high, and his chest was tight with a familiar stinging fear.

"Do I *look* like I'm playing a game?"

He peered down at her and realized that, while he might have broken out in a cold sweat, Lea was trembling—but not with fear. With anger.

"I don't understand, but if you ever set that off again…"

"You'll what?"

"I'll have to ask you to leave."

Her chin went up. "Then go ahead. Ask."

He was at a loss. Surely she hadn't just set it off to torment him? She didn't even know what had led him to have the system installed.

"Please don't turn it on again."

"Fine. I won't. If you'll do *me* the favor of—" She picked something up off the bar in the kitchen and walked over to where he was standing. She slammed it on the table. "Telling me what the meaning of *this* is."

His eyes tracked to the item. And he groaned. It was the stupid calendar, and it was opened to *his* page.

"Where did you get that?"

"Off the wall in the reception area."

So that was where it had gone. "It's just a fundraiser. I wasn't even supposed to be in it. Someone was sick and I had to fill in."

"That doesn't answer my question." Her mouth was tight with anger. "What is *this*?"

"Listen, I know I don't measure up to the rest of the men in it, but it was either that or scrap the project—"

"Don't measure up? I'm not talking about that, dammit. I'm talking about *this*!" She pushed it closer.

His eyes flicked to the image and then away. It was him without his shirt on. Big deal. Had she tricked him into coming over here to try to humiliate him?

"Tear it out if you don't like it. I don't give a damn."

"God, Deakin. You are dense. *Look* at it."

"No. Just tell me what's wrong with it so I can go home."

"It's been altered. You had all your scars removed. Why?"

What? He allowed his gaze to go back to the picture and forced himself to look at it this time. She was right.

The left side of his face, neck and chest were as clean and clear as the right side of his body. The scars had been whisked away. This was what he would have looked like if the accident had never happened.

He didn't blame the calendar company. *He* didn't like looking at the damage to his body, so why would anyone else?

"Maybe the photographer actually wanted to *sell* some calendars."

"You…" Her nose scrunched up as if trying to contain whatever it was she wanted to say. "Are you saying you didn't *ask* them to remove your scars during the touch up phase?"

"I didn't. But I'm relieved they did."

He hadn't even looked at the photo until now. It was kind of fascinating to see himself without those scars. Without the consequences of a stupid teenaged decision that had changed his life forever.

"They're a part of who you are. They don't look as bad as you probably think they do."

This time it was his turn to get mad. She had no idea what she was talking about. Where did she get off, saying something like that? And to set off that alarm just to force him to come over so she could tell him off… *Not happening*.

"Oh, they're plenty bad, lady."

"Show me."

"Like hell."

He didn't go anywhere without his shirt on. Except to get his damn picture taken for all the world to see, evidently. And even that didn't get him a free pass.

She slung the calendar off the table, letting it hit the ground with a thud. "That's not who you really are."

"Maybe it's who I *wish* I was."

She was mad at him over a stupid picture? Well, he'd see if he could make her even angrier.

"Okay, fine. You're so good at psychoanalyzing people? Analyze *this*!"

His hot breath sawing in and out of his lungs, he reached down and gripped the bottom of his T-shirt, then tore it up and over his head, letting it drop to the ground.

He didn't look down at himself. He already knew exactly what he looked like. Lea did, though, sliding her gaze over his chest, her brows furrowing as she studied him.

All the anger seemed to drop out of her in an instant. Just as he'd suspected. She was shocked. Horrified. Ready to beg him to put his clothes back on.

She didn't. Instead she went and picked up the calendar and opened it to his picture. She looked closely at it. Then at the true image. This time she didn't fling it away from her. She set it carefully down on the table.

"That picture isn't you, Deakin. And if you think the real you disgusts me, you're wrong." Her voice lowered to a whisper. "Oh, *so* wrong."

He swallowed hard. It almost sounded as if she…

He wasn't sure if she moved first or if he did, but they were suddenly gripping each other with desperate hands, his mouth slamming on top of hers with a fervency he'd never felt before. She didn't try to tug free, or even hesitate. Her lips opened wide, her hands going to the back of his head and pulling him closer.

Hell. He groaned, his tongue surging into the vacuum and tasting coffee and her own sweet essence. He'd wanted to kiss her back on Delos, and would have if not for Sam and his heatstroke. But all that was now washed away under a tsunami of need.

Her fingers left his head and trailed down the side of his neck, following something. His scars. Only this time it didn't make him want to jerk away. It made him want to lose himself inside her, to let her touch him and do whatever she wanted.

He frowned slightly when she reached the part of his chest wall that was devoid of sensation. From his shoulder to just below his nipple his skin was completely numb. He fought the urge to stop her, to take her hand and place it where he *could* feel it—feel *her*.

Except this was what she wanted to do. This was what their conversation had been leading up to. Or maybe it had been headed here since that moment in the reception area when she'd mistaken him for a patient. The attraction had certainly been there on his part. And evidently on hers too.

His hands came up and wrapped around her upper arms before sliding up and cupping her face, just the way he had on Delos. Her skin was as soft as he remembered, making him want to do all kinds of things to her.

And she wanted to do things to him too. Easing her head back, she looked up at him, fingers still tracing over his ruined flesh.

"These are part of who you are. And you are very, *very* sexy. Therefore, according to every algebra problem I've ever solved, that must mean these are sexy too."

God, he wanted her. Right now. Before he had a chance to think or reason...or regret.

He scooped her up and carried her down the tiny hallway to where he knew the bedroom was. If she wanted to stop him, she would. He knew by now that she was not afraid of confrontation. Of saying what she thought needed to be said.

She didn't say anything, though. She simply wrapped her arms around his neck and leaned her face against his chest, nuzzling the underside of his chin. His need ratcheted up even higher.

He reached the bedroom and nudged open the door with his bare foot, his soles sinking into the deep carpet of the rug inside. He could lay her right on that floor and be happy. But there was also the bed. And he would be even happier there.

Tossing her onto the silk coverlet, he took the time to look at the way she was splayed out, all soft and sexy, her eyes filled with anticipation.

Bending over her, he planted his palms on either side of her face and leaned in for a kiss. "If you aren't wanting this to go any further, say it now."

"I *am* wanting this to go further. *Much* further."

She linked her hands behind his neck and tugged his face down, urging him to kiss her once again. He was more than happy to oblige. When his chest brushed her breasts the contrast between soft and hard arrowed straight to his groin. He groaned.

Then she was touching him again, stroking places that were numb and places that were not. He pressed a knee between her legs, relishing the way she gripped it between her thighs. Soon she'd be gripping something else...

Suddenly palms went to his chest and she was pushing. He was up and off her in an instant.

"No, no. It's okay."

She came up on her knees, reaching for his hands and pulling him forward again. This time when she shifted him he realized what she wanted and it made parts of him jerk. She twisted until she had maneuvered him onto the bed, flat on his back, with her straddling his hips. Her palms skated down his chest, and when she leaned over and took his left nipple in her mouth he shuddered.

He couldn't feel it, but he could damned well imagine it. And it made other senses come alive. He could still experience the thrill of having her lips on him. The tiny suckling sounds she made, the scent of her hair so close to his nose. The heat of her body on the rest of him.

Then she moved over to the other nipple and his hips surged forward, almost lifting off the bed. Okay, he could feel that, and it was...*electrifying*.

Her pelvis found his erection and ground hard against it.

"Hell..."

If she kept that up, he was a goner.

He gripped her hips, holding them still for several long seconds. It didn't help. They might have stopped moving but her lips certainly hadn't, grazing over the side of his jaw, biting at the joint of his neck.

Like lightning, he flipped her back over. "My turn, honey."

Only he didn't kiss her. He reached for the lightweight knit top she had on and hauled it over her head. He'd half hoped she wouldn't have a bra on, but at least it had a front clasp. He saw the little joiner thing right between those luscious breasts.

He slid a finger beneath it and popped it open before peeling apart the cups, revealing tight puckered nipples. But there was no time to kiss them. Not yet. He wanted her clothes off. All of them. *Then* he would let himself explore.

Climbing off the bed, he noted that her eyes weren't shut. They were watching every move he made, their green irises burning with an inner heat that made him ache.

Off came her bottoms—stretchy exercise pants—gliding over her hips and down her long legs with ease. Legs that would soon be wrapped around his hips as he thrust home.

He swallowed. Things were moving too fast, and yet he was powerless to slow them down. "Promise me we'll do this again."

She didn't ask him what he meant. "I promise."

Taking his wallet from his pants, he flipped it open, hoping against hope that he had something.

Before he could look, she took it from him and tossed it aside. "I'm protected. And clean. And I want to *feel* you."

Damn. She made even condom talk sexy.

He didn't argue—just unzipped his jeans as Lea sat up to watch. That made him hot. The way her attention was fully on what was happening in front of her.

His jeans and briefs went down, and then he was free. Her hands immediately went to the backs of his thighs, just below his ass, and tugged him forward, her tongue moistening her lips in preparation.

"No. That comes the next time. Because first I want… *this*."

He bore her back onto the bed, shuddering with need when she parted her legs and hooked her feet around the back of his calves. He wanted her. Desperately. But he needed to do something first.

Still standing, and with the high bed providing the perfect height, he used his aching flesh to trace along her skin from her knees to her thighs. Her low moan revved him up in a way nothing else could. Over and over he brushed himself along her skin, the sensation taking him almost to breaking point. Then he moved forward to the place where the space narrowed to one tiny point between her legs. He touched the juncture. Then repeated the gesture. Her gasp told him he was in just the right spot.

Planting her feet on the edge of the bed, she lifted slightly so that she could press against him in rhythmic bursts. Her eyes fluttered closed as she continued to pleasure herself. Then she brushed his hand aside and gripped him, her fingers tight and needy as she did the job herself, pumping along him, teeth burrowing into her lower lip in the way that he loved.

And then she was over the edge, her sharp cry tearing through him. He lined himself up in a hurry and thrust home. *Hard.* The squeeze of her body took his senses and focused them into a blurred jumble of heat, wet, and sweet, tight friction. He wasn't going to last. Didn't want to last. She'd promised him more and he was going to take her at her word.

Gripping her ass, he thrust again and again, leaning in and taking her moans into his mouth. Then he finally let himself go, felt a sharp burst of pleasure ripping through him and slashing his world in two. In three. In four. Until it was in tiny pieces that he wasn't sure could ever be put back together.

Satiation snuck in, taking the edge off the furious pace, and his movements slowed, became languorous.

And then he was done, finally allowing himself to press his body fully against hers. She was damp with perspiration, her lids still squeezed tightly together.

A tiny fragment of worry penetrated the bliss.

Open your eyes, Lea.

Was she afraid to look at him? Maybe all that talk

about his scars being a part of who he was had been just that. Talk.

No, she'd been genuinely angry at him when she'd thought *he'd* had those scars on the calendar altered. So it wasn't that she was horrified by them. At least she hadn't been a few minutes ago.

Hadn't she said they were sexy? No. She'd said *he* was sexy.

Wasn't it the same thing?

Right now, he wasn't sure of anything.

He found his voice and used it. "Hey. Are you okay?"

"Mmm…" Green eyes appeared, poring over his face. "Just trying to gear myself up to keep a certain promise."

Relief washed over him and he gathered her in his arms, turning her so they were facing each other. "Regretting that promise already?"

"Oh, no. Not at all."

"That's good—because neither am I. In fact as soon as I catch my breath I think I'll be ready for the second course."

"Second?" Her lips curved. "How many courses *are* there in this particular feast?"

"I would say it's open-ended. There can be as few or as many as we want."

Her fingertips came up and brushed over his temples. "In that case, if you don't mind, I plan on being very, *very* greedy."

Anticipation trickled through him, causing a chain reaction that began to spread its tentacles along him.

"Oh, Lea. I was so hoping you'd say that…"

CHAPTER EIGHT

HE'D MADE HER forget about Mark. At least for a night. As she sat in her little floral alcove in the clinic's garden and tried to concentrate on what her patient was saying she was still thrilled. And terrified.

She'd been so sure he'd asked to have those scars covered up in that picture, so he could pretend they had never happened. But he hadn't. It had been some stupid photographer instead.

But she didn't regret confronting him. It had paid off in spades. He'd made love to her multiple times in multiple positions, each more exciting and different than the last. And when they'd parted ways this morning it hadn't seemed as awkward as it might have. Although Deakin hadn't been particularly talkative. Then again, neither had she. She hadn't wanted to spoil what they'd shared together.

Blinking, she focused again on her patient and put Deakin out of her mind once and for all. Not an easy task. But then she hadn't expected it to be.

She somehow made it through the session, even got some important things accomplished during it, and when she went out to the reception desk she found Theo there.

He motioned her over. "Can I talk to you for a second?"

Her heart stopped for a beat or two, before galloping off at the speed of light. Did he know about her and Deakin? Did she have some big goofy smile on her face or something? Oh, Lord, she hoped not. That would be mortifying.

Why? Hadn't he and Cailey found love in the aftermath of the earthquake?

That was different.

Um...how, exactly, Lea?

"Sure. Here?"

"It's nothing Petra hasn't already heard me say. I just needed to talk to Deakin before approaching you."

Trepidation moved over her. Oh, God, had Deakin told him about what they'd done together? Or, worse yet, maybe they'd decided they didn't need her anymore and were going to ask her to leave.

She didn't want to go to back to Canada. Not yet, anyway. She wanted to stay here—even though she'd told herself time and time again that that wasn't going to be an option. Hadn't Deakin said last night that the calendars were a fundraising tool because of a shortfall in their budget? How exactly did she expect them to be able to pay another staff member when they already were having trouble supporting the ones they had?

"Okay... Is something wrong?"

"No. Not at all. In fact I think we're going to ask you to stay on here at the clinic. Is that a possibility?"

She went from thinking she was going to be fired to going to be hired. Was he serious?

She asked him as much. "I love it here. Are you telling me that I might be offered a permanent position?"

His answer was a smile.

Still not sure she was reading him correctly, she

glanced at Petra, who was nodding vigorously. And smiling too. "Congratulations!"

"Wow, this isn't what I expected to hear today."

Theo leaned a shoulder against the wall. "Oh? What *were* you expecting?"

That was something she wasn't going to tell anyone. Especially not Theo or Petra.

"I'm not sure. You already discussed this with Deakin?"

"I already did. He was in favor of it."

That shocked her. He'd given no indication last night that he and Theo had talked about hiring her. Did that mean he *wanted* her to stay?

A thread of happiness uncoiled inside her before she could stop it. She hurried to wind it back, afraid this was all one big joke.

Would she be able to work with him without imagining him naked? Without remembering exactly what they'd done in bed? She wasn't sure, and that scared her the most.

"Can I think about it for a day or so and get back with you?"

"Of course. I thought this was something you'd maybe already considered, though."

"It's the chance of a lifetime, actually. I was looking to move on from… Well, to move on from my previous location. So I'm having a hard time believing this is actually happening."

"I can understand that. It's a big decision."

Huge. Gigantic. *Gargantuan.*

She would have leaped at the offer a few short weeks ago. But now…?

Actually, now she still wanted it. Deakin or no Deakin. Surely they could learn to work together in a professional way, leaving their private lives in the bedroom? Not that it was even certain they were going to do what they'd done last night again.

But the decision about whether to stay or go had to be separate from her decision about being with Deakin. If she tied them together, making one dependent on the other, then she would be doing herself a disservice. Especially when she didn't really understand what made the man tick. *Yet.*

She wanted to stay. That was the one certainty she kept circling around to.

"I think I've changed my mind. I'd like to go ahead and give you my decision now if I could."

"Of course." He moved his propped shoulder away from the wall as if going on high alert.

"If you're serious about the offer, I'd like to accept it."

"I am *very* serious. I've already called a meeting with the other partners just to make sure everyone is on board, but I'm sure it's just a formality. You've already proven yourself capable and the patients love you. Even the ones who aren't here specifically for counseling."

"I'm glad. I love the people on the island, as well."

He held out his hand and she squeezed it. "I'll get everyone together and get the details hammered out. I'm not yet sure what salary package we can offer you, though."

"As long as I can afford a place to live and food in my refrigerator I'll be fine."

"I'm sure we can find you a few more euros than that. You don't think you'll stay in Deakin's cottage? It's been a rental in the past. And he rarely sticks around for long."

That made her swallow hard. Was he even now getting ready to leave, after only a couple of weeks? Was that why he'd decided that making love with her was safe…because he was already on his way out?

Wouldn't that be easier, though, than having him stay? The second things went south with them she would be out and looking for a new place to work.

He'd only come because of the earthquake—he'd said that himself. And, actually, he had no great love for his home island that she could see. He'd seemed happy to be on Naxos, and even happier to be on Delos. Which was sad. She loved Toronto, despite Mark's death. But his suicide was what had caused her to want to move on to a new place. Maybe Deakin was the same. Because of the fire?

The scars on his chest were worse than she'd imagined, although she'd done her damnedest to make sure he didn't see her shock. The two big scars running down the side of his neck changed once they reached his torso. There the scars looked as if something had landed on his chest and exploded in place. The damage must have been extensive and destructive. No wonder he was so sensitive about it. She would be too.

When she'd touched him there she'd expected a violent reaction, but there hadn't been one. She suspected the nerve-endings in his skin had been adversely affected. And yet, he'd let her stay there and explore, hadn't tried to move her over to where it felt better…to a place he was more comfortable with.

A lump formed in her throat that she couldn't swallow away.

"I don't know what I'll do yet as far as where I'll live. I think that will depend on a lot of things. I expect some of the boarding houses will be opening up for clients shortly."

"I think you're right." He shoved his hands in his pockets. "Well, that's what I wanted to tell you. I'm surprised Petra hasn't jumped in before now to express her opinion." He gave the woman a quick grin that said he knew her well.

She didn't let him down. "That's because you already know what I think. All I can add is that it's about damned time. I've been waiting on you all to do something before we lose her to somewhere else."

Moisture pricked holes in the backs of Lea's eyelids. If she wanted to make a fresh start, far from the tragedy of her past, this was her chance. And she'd be a fool if she turned this opportunity down.

"Thank you. That means a lot, coming from you."

"Well, I'll let you go," said Theo. "I'll get back to you with the details once we have our meeting."

"Okay—thanks again for everything."

With that Theo turned and headed down the hallway toward his office.

She turned to Petra. "Are you sure they'll all want me to stay?"

"I'd say they'd better. Or they'll have me to contend with. And I think they know better than to get on my bad side."

Lea smiled. She had no doubt that Petra's bad side was a place no one wanted to land on. But from what Theo had said she wouldn't need Petra or anyone to plead her case. Asking her to stay was already a done deal. At least according to Theo it was.

Deakin was shoving a screwdriver into a stuck door-lock in one of the exam rooms when a pair of shoes came into view. Worn leather loafers were joined by a pair of faded jeans that had seen better days.

Deakin straightened and frowned when he realized it wasn't a stranger after all. Dark hair and an even darker beard shadowed a tanned face. A familiar face, but one that looked very different from the one he was used to seeing. There had been a time when charm and sophistication had been the cornerstones of this man's life. That charm was nowhere in evidence right now.

"Ares? Is that you?"

The green duffle bag perched on his shoulder was hefted around and dropped on the ground with a loud thud. Several people turned to stare. He was one of their own, but so far no one except Deakin had recognized him.

"Well, it's not my ghost. Not yet anyway."

Ares Xenakis had been part of their tight little circle growing up. Like Deakin and Chris, he had chosen to go through medical school and then get off the island. It looked as if the earthquake really was bringing them all trickling back in. After it was over they would stream back out. At least some of them would—Deakin being one of them.

"Some might argue with that. You look like you've been through hell and come out the other side."

His friend laughed. "Not quite." His face went serious again. "I came as soon as I could."

"Me too." Deakin hadn't been all that polished when he'd arrived either, but Ares might very well have him beaten. "You look like you could use sixty hours of sleep."

"That feels about right. That cottage of yours open? I

could go home, but I've been in the air or laid over for almost thirty straight hours straight. I'm dead on my feet."

Ares had his own residence on a tiny neighboring island, but Deakin could certainly understand being so tired that you could no longer put one foot in front of the other. He'd been there a time or two himself. The problem was his cottage wasn't vacant—and there was no way he was going to suggest Lea share it with Ares, no matter how innocent it might be. Especially since it only had one bedroom.

Why he suddenly felt that way he had no idea. Men were supposed to be able to have sex without it affecting them emotionally, right? Then why did he feel so damned...*affectionate* towards her? A word he had never in his life associated with his personality.

It had to be the time they'd spent together on Delos. It had thrown them both for a loop. Or was it more than that?

"The cottage is rented out at the moment, but the apartment over the boathouse is empty. Or you can stay in one of the guest rooms at the main house."

"If that place is still the mausoleum it used to be, then I'll take the boathouse. With the state I'm in now, I'd probably leave three layers of dirt on everything I touched. Your aunt would have a fit."

"I doubt that. She's going to welcome you like a long-lost son."

Ares glanced around. "She'll be the only one, from the looks of it. My secret agent disguise is evidently working. At least for now. Maybe I'll keep this look for a while."

"Be prepared to be arrested for vagrancy, then."

"That bad?"

"I would say I've seen worse, but…"

"Funny."

Deakin gave Ares' shoulder a quick squeeze. "I'll call Theo and let him know you're here."

"There'll be plenty of time for reunions. Besides, I texted him last night and told him I was on my way. I'm surprised he didn't say anything to you."

There was no way Deakin was going to tell his friend that he'd been too busy last night to have answered *any* call other than the call of the wild…

"Do you want me to take you to the house?"

"No, I've got it. I know where your key is too. That smoke alarm isn't going to go off on me, is it?"

He pointed his screwdriver at his friend's chest. "As long as you don't set anything on fire you'll be fine."

Deakin had already had the scare of his life last night from someone setting off that damned alarm. And then Lea had shocked the hell out of him. In more ways than one.

His teeth gritted when that "affectionate" gene poked its head out again and threatened to spread around some cute little endearments. He had to play whack-a-mole with it a few times before he was finally able to shove it down in its hidey-hole.

"I'll be back when I've had those sixty hours of sleep and feel like a human being again."

Deakin grinned. "In that case it might be a year or two before anyone realizes the island's prodigal has finally returned."

"I'd forgotten just how hilarious you are."

At that moment Lea chose to come around the corner. She froze when she saw Ares. But, since his face wasn't one of the ones on the calendar, she had no way of knowing who he was.

"Lea, I'd like you to meet Ares Xenakis. Ares, this is Dr. Lea Risi. Ares is an old friend of mine. And a friend of the clinic. He's another doctor. He'll be staying in the bedroom over the boathouse for..." He left the last part of the phrase open-ended, giving Ares the chance to set the time-frame.

"Sixty hours or overnight—whichever comes first. Then I'll head for my own place."

Lea smiled. "It looks like you've been on the road for a while."

"You could say that."

"You can give him the cottage, Deakin. I can take the boathouse."

Despite the lines of exhaustion rimming his eyes and mouth, Ares perked up at that. "*You're* the one staying in the cottage?" He shot Deakin a shrewd look.

Oh, don't even go there, bud.

Except he already had, and Lea's face turning a luscious shade of pink wasn't helping any. Was she remembering what they'd done in the cottage the night before?

"I've been staying there, yes."

Deakin was impressed. That cool, efficient tone didn't reflect the color in her face or convey shame or embarrassment. Not that they had anything to be ashamed of. It was just...awkward. And he hated that his first sighting of her this morning had to be in the presence of someone he knew. Someone who could pick apart his motivations and memories and twist them into something they weren't.

Or were they?

"I'm sure there are clean linens ready over at the

boathouse. You know how well Aunt Cecilia likes to keep things tidy."

"I do. And she'd wrap her apron strings around my neck if she saw me going in there and messing it all up."

"Not a chance. She loves you. Probably more than she loves me."

Ares made a scoffing sound. "Well, much as I would *love* to keep using the word love, I'm either going to head over to the boathouse or I'm going to park myself on the floor of this clinic and pass out. And I don't think that would be a cool advertisement for the place."

"Go. I'll see you when you're ready to emerge from your cocoon. Just knock on the door of the house. I'll either be there, or here at the clinic."

One place he would *not* be was at the cottage. Having Ares give him "the look" had knocked some sense back into him. Clearly his perceptive friend had picked up on the chemistry between him and Lea.

What did he think he was doing? He and Lea were not headed in the same direction in life. He was on the road or on the way to catch a plane more often than not. And she was looking for a place to land. She'd said it herself.

Theo and Cailey rounded the corner and Deakin could swear that Ares groaned out loud. Then he gave a grunted laugh.

"What the hell *is* this? All we need next is for Petra to come prancing through, doing aerobics."

Since Petra didn't "prance" anywhere, the thought struck Deakin as funny for some reason. He did his best to change his laugh into a cough, just as Theo recognized their friend.

Not that there was any chance he wouldn't. Other islanders might see a vagrant but, as scruffy as he looked,

Ares was still Ares. Maybe a little more cynical-sounding than he remembered, but from what he'd heard his friend had been in some pretty tough places.

"Ares!" Theo came forward with a grin and clapped him on the back. "Are you in there somewhere?"

"Oh, funny—you all should have thrown your trust fund money into a comedy club instead of a clinic."

"Or maybe a soup kitchen," Theo said with another grin.

Cailey came forward, arms open to give him a hug, only to have Ares wave her off.

"I am a stinking, dirty mess. Let me get cleaned up before you come anywhere near me."

They talked for a few more minutes, but Ares really did look as if he was about to keel over.

Deakin fished in his pocket for his car keys and pressed them into his friend's hand. "Go. I'll catch a ride with Lea."

He stopped her with a look, knowing she was about to remind him that she'd ridden a bike to work for the past month and a half. And he wasn't about to be her biker babe, riding on the back while she pedaled away. Especially not after last night. Although wrapping his arms around her waist and holding on tight sounded pretty appealing…maybe even letting his hands wander up her belly until they reached…

Ah, hell. He would ask Theo to drive him home. Once Lea had left the building.

He went to pick up Ares's duffle bag, but his friend beat him to it, slinging it over his shoulder like it was nothing, despite eyes that were bloodshot with exhaustion and speech that was beginning to slur.

Slapping him on the back once more, he said, "Call

if you need anything, okay?" He paused. "Oh, and Ares...?"

"Yeah?"

"It's good to have you home."

"It's good to be back." He gave a rueful smile. "I *think*. I'll let you know for sure once I'm back in possession of my faculties."

Deakin could understand that sentiment exactly. He'd kind of surprised himself by referring to Mythelios as home, because he hadn't thought of it in those terms for years. Maybe even a decade.

And, as much as he didn't want to admit the reason for that, he had a feeling it was due to the woman standing just a few feet away, observing them with interest.

Was it professional interest or personal? It was something he'd asked himself repeatedly today. She'd slammed that calendar down last night like she really cared. But *did* she? Or had she just been worried, one professional to another, that he was in denial about his old injuries?

And if she did care? Where did that leave him?

He had no idea.

Lea made him want what he couldn't have. What he shouldn't have. And, try as he might, he knew right here and now that it was going to be hard—damned hard—to turn back the hands of time and return to the way his life used to be.

CHAPTER NINE

THE TAVERNA WAS already crowded, judging from the cars jamming the parking lot, and Lea had no idea what she was doing there, other than she'd seen Deakin's red Jeep parked out front and had made a quick U-turn, leaving her bike propped against the side of the building.

Seeing Deakin's old friend in the clinic yesterday, and hearing about his radical change in appearance, had made her think about the reasons someone might make such a huge alteration to their physical appearance. Or their personality. It had also made her think of Mark, and the subtle shifts in his behavior that she hadn't noticed at the time but that had made her go back now and pick apart her responses.

Had it made Deakin want to tackle Stavros again? Maybe he was worried that the bartender might harm himself. Or someone else. He hadn't asked her to come this time, but if she could do anything to help she would.

Pushing open the door and entering the artificially darkened space, she paused to let her eyes adjust to the interior. Stavros was behind the bar, towel flung over his left shoulder, one hand on the polished wooden surface. He was laughing. Laughing hard. His booming voice carrying all the way across the room. No sign of the angry guy from before. That might be a good sign. She would keep her fingers crossed and hope for the best.

She continued scanning the patrons, feeling kind of silly now that she was here.

She saw him. At the other end of the bar from Stavros. His eyes were fastened on her, his jaw tight, and there was some kind of drink in front of him.

Run away. Run away fast.

The internal voice was gradually getting louder and more insistent. But if she left it would look as if she'd run away because of *him*.

And...? Your point is...?

He certainly wasn't waving her over or anything—but, since he was the only one she knew here, and since he didn't appear to have company, she inched her chin up and made her way over to him.

Perching on the empty bar stool next to him, she glanced at his glass and its white contents. He also had a plate of cheese, meats and some other delicious-looking things.

"Ouzo?"

"Yes."

"Is it as strong as they say it is?"

He turned the small glass a couple of times, looking at its contents. "Let's just say it's best not to drink it on an empty stomach." He nodded at the plate of food in front of him. "Compliments of Stavros."

"Compliments? You weren't going to order anything to eat?"

Had he come here to get drunk?

"I was thinking about it."

At first she thought she'd made the comment about getting drunk out loud. But, no. Maybe he was reading her mind. She decided to talk to keep her brain from thinking too much.

She frowned. "How is Stavros? He seems happier today."

"That he does. Would you like something to drink?"

"Actually, I'll have what you're having. I've always wanted to try ouzo. What makes it white?"

He lifted his glass and tilted it slightly. "It's clear in the bottle, but mix it with water or ice and it turns all… misty."

Just like she was feeling tonight. She wasn't sure what it was, but she felt out of sorts. Kind of itchy and dissatisfied. She had no reason to be. Theo had almost guaranteed she'd be offered a position at the clinic. It was everything she'd hoped for and more. Wasn't it?

He motioned down the bar with an upraised hand. "Stavros? Can I get another of the same?"

The bartender made his way toward them, tossing his towel from one hand to the next, his energy surprising compared to the last time she'd seen him.

"You'd better go easy on those."

"It's not for me. It's for Lea. And if we could have some *calamari* to go with that, we'd appreciate it."

"Sure thing."

Grabbing a bottle from the multi-shelved unit behind him, he twirled it in his hand, getting a glass from under the bar. Then he stopped and seemed to sway for a second. It was over so quickly that Lea almost missed it. Deakin *had* missed it. He'd been busy plucking a piece of cheese from the plate.

Stavros poured the drink over ice with a completely steady hand, no sign that he was even aware of his momentary unsteadiness. Maybe she'd imagined it. She was imagining a whole lot of things these days.

The bartender set the glass on a paper napkin in front of her, keeping his hand on it. "Go easy on her. We've carried more than one tourist out of here after they misjudged her. She did *not* go easy on them."

Being called a tourist stung a little, but since the islanders were a close-knit bunch she could understand it. The funny thing was she felt like a bit of an outsider whether she was in Canada or Greece. She wasn't quite Canadian. And she wasn't quite Greek. She was in some nebulous zone between nationalities. What she was feeling was probably what most immigrants felt from time to time.

Only Mythelios was different. It had felt exactly right from the moment her feet had hit the soil.

"I'll be careful. I may not even finish this one."

"Sip it slowly. Ask Deakin if he'll share his *mezedes* with you until your *calamari* is ready. It should be in about ten minutes."

"Thank you."

Once he was gone, she glanced at Deakin. "Have you noticed anything odd about Stavros tonight?"

"No, he seems to be almost back to normal. If he *has* a normal."

She hesitated, unsure of whether she should even mention what she'd seen. "He does seem better. But when he was getting my drink he stumbled…or swayed, or something."

Deakin looked down the bar to where the bartender was handing one of the kitchen staff their *calamari* order. "Really? I should have been keeping a closer eye on him."

"He was laughing pretty hard at something when I came in, too."

"Was he?" Pushing his plate toward her, he handed her a tiny aperitif fork. "He's right. Don't drink it on an empty stomach. An ouzo hangover is bad news."

She smiled. "And you know this how?"

"Don't ask." He waited until she'd speared one of the small tomatoes on the meat and cheese plate. "I'm surprised you stopped in here. I thought this wasn't one of your favorite places."

She shrugged as nonchalantly as she could, swallowing her bite of food. "It's growing on me. Especially now that I know Stavros isn't normally such a bear."

"No...he isn't." The words had a speculative ring to them and Deakin looked down the bar again. "He does seem closer to normal, but I would agree with you that he still seems a little off—although I missed the unsteadiness you saw."

"Could he have had the flu?"

"Flu doesn't normally cause mood swings."

"You're right."

She picked up her drink and swirled it for a second, then took a tiny sip. It was sweet. And there was something else...

"It tastes like something familiar."

"It has anise in it. Black licorice?"

"Hmm...maybe that's it. It's very good." She took another sip.

He pushed the plate at her yet again. "More food."

This time she chose cheese, which was strong and salty and...*good*. So good. "Mmm. This place is definitely growing on me."

She turned to face him as he took a drink from his

own glass, and she noticed he had almost finished his ouzo. One of his fingers reached up to rub at his neck, where the scars were.

"Do they still bother you?"

His hand dropped back to the bar. "No, it's just a habit."

She debated long and hard about asking her next question. It was really none of her business, but she'd *slept* with the man, for heaven's sake. They'd discussed condom use. Surely she was entitled to know a few things about his personal life.

"You said you got them during a fire. Was it at home?"

The smoke alarms told her it had been. Or at least that it had been at a place he hadn't expected to get burned.

Another sip of his ouzo went down. So far she'd only seen him eat one piece from the *mezedes* plate.

"Yes. At home. In my father's boathouse, actually."

"The one where your friend spent last night?"

"No, it was a different boathouse. My dad rebuilt it. And bought a new boat."

Okay, so she was right. The fire *hadn't* been some small, strike-a-match kiddie fire. It had been big. Big enough to cause the extensive tissue destruction she'd seen across his chest.

"What happened?"

His brows went up as another sip went down. "I decided to try smoking for the first time." He gave a humorless laugh. "Let's just say it was an explosive experience."

"The boathouse *exploded*? God! How old were you?"

"Yes. Gas fumes and matches don't play well together. I was fourteen at the time."

"Oh, Deakin. You could have been killed."

"Hmm…"

The way he'd said that… It almost sounded as if he'd *wanted* to be killed.

"Did you set the fire on purpose?" Kids younger than he'd been committed suicide far too often.

"What?" His brows slammed together. "God, no. What made you think that?"

Okay, she hadn't meant to make him angry.

Stavros came and set down the calamari, and then went off to take care of other customers. She was beginning to think she should have kept her wonderings to herself.

"I don't know. I was just asking. A lot of kids play with fire. It's kind of a rite of passage."

"Well, believe me, this was no rite of passage. And, since I almost took out another kid in the process, I'd say I got everything I deserved. I'm sure plenty of folks in Mythelios think the same thing."

Stavros had made a crack about Deakin's father the first time they'd come in here. Had that been in reference to the fire?

"I doubt that. It was a long time ago. I bet most people have probably forgotten."

"Maybe they have. But *I* haven't. My dad was taken to the police station and questioned after it happened. I didn't find out about that until I was in medical school. And my friend Ville got in huge trouble with his parents. They beat him. Broke his arm. Even though he'd been burned as well."

"How terrible. What did the police do?"

"To my dad? Or to Ville's dad?"

"Ville's, of course."

"Nothing. Ville claimed it had happened in the explosion. No one doubted him."

"I'm *so* sorry." She took another bracing drink.

Was that why Deakin stayed away from the island so much? Because he thought people would throw the past back in his face?

"Like everyone keeps saying…it happened a long time ago." He downed the last of his drink. "Eat your octopus."

That sounded like an order. And Lea didn't take orders very well.

"Would you like to try that again? Especially since *you've* eaten almost nothing and finished your drink in less than twenty minutes."

Deakin's half-smile appeared. "Eat your octopus. *Please.*"

He was incorrigible. But appealing.

She picked up one of the fried treats and bit it in half. The crispy coating was delicately seasoned so it didn't overpower the seafood inside. "Oh, this is delicious."

"Stavros has always done a good job with *mezedes*."

"You're not kidding. Try some."

"I'm okay."

He didn't order another drink, which she was glad of. She certainly didn't want him driving if he was tipsy. And she could very easily see how it could happen with this drink. The sugar in the alcohol would keep it from getting released into the system as quickly as it might otherwise. But once it did… Well, you certainly wouldn't want to be driving home.

She popped another delicious piece of calamari into her mouth. "Did *your* dad give you a hard time about the boathouse?" she asked once she'd finished.

He gave a pained grunt. "You mean did he beat me? No. I think my skin grafts and surgeries did that for him. He actually never said a word about it. Just rebuilt his boathouse. And then replaced his beloved boat."

"That's the boat you use now?"

"One and the same."

"I'm sorry that happened to you and your friend." She slid her hand over his wrist, trying to give him a little bit of support.

His eyes came up and speared hers. "Feeling sorry for me now?"

"No. But I think it's time to stop beating yourself up for something that happened years ago." She leaned her head against his shoulder, the act feeling as right as the island did. "And if someone tries to dig up the past just tell them to bugger off."

He laughed, his right hand sliding over her cheek and moving to her nape, his thumb strumming a tune on her jawline. "You surprise me—you know that?"

"I do?"

Each light stroke along her skin sent frissons of awareness spiraling through her belly, the circles slowing spreading outward.

"You do. Every time I think I have you figured out…"

His words trailed off, but the caresses said that he was busy thinking of other things right now. At least she hoped he was.

The hand at her nape moved to her chin, tilting it so he could look at her. "I want to get out of here."

She lowered her voice to a whisper. "I want that too."

That was evidently all he needed to hear, because he dug his wallet out of his pants pocket and peeled off a couple of bills. More than what their drinks and appetizers were worth, she was sure. But he dropped the money on the bar, flashed a signal at Stavros for good effect. The other man noticed it and nodded in their direction.

Then Deakin was towing her out of the bar and heading toward his car.

"My bike. It's parked against the wall."

"We'll throw it in the back of the Jeep."

"Are you okay to drive?"

"Yes. I know my limits."

Did he? Well, he was doing better than she was—because she thought the sips of ouzo she'd had were swirling around in her head and messing with her common sense. She hadn't eaten nearly enough to counter the effects.

He picked her bike up with one hand and tossed it into the back of the Jeep. He then unlocked the passenger side door and pulled it open.

"Where are we going?"

Leaning down, he whispered in her ear. "Does it matter?"

"No…" It didn't matter. All she knew was that she wanted to go with him no matter where he wanted to be.

They made it back to his place and Deakin slid the gearshift into "park" before leaning over and kissing her, his lips pressed to hers in a way that had her heart pounding.

Her body was well aware of where this was headed. It had known ever since she'd sat on that bar stool and asked him to tell her about the fire. He had. And it was pretty obvious that he didn't tell that story to many people. Yes, they might know the bitter facts about what had happened, but Deakin had *lived* it. And it made her sad.

And mad. And, *oh*, so sorry for the two teenagers who had paid such an awful price for being curious.

When Deakin climbed out of the car she noticed he hadn't parked it next to the house or the cottage. It was beside the boathouse instead.

A flutter rippled through her tummy. She scrambled out of the car and onto the sidewalk. "Are we going boating?"

It was already dark, even though the sun hadn't been down long. "We are. Are you game?"

Yes. She was. She trusted him—could tell that while the alcohol might have pried a few secrets out of him it hadn't incapacitated him as far as driving went.

He stopped just inside the dark building. "I want to make love to you. On the boat."

Her throat went dry at the hint of wistful longing she heard in his voice. She turned toward him and slid her fingers deep into the hair at his nape, sighing as his scent washed over her. Rough and masculine, it drove her crazy. *He* drove her crazy.

"I want that too."

His hands went to her hips and he yanked her against him. He was already hard, the edge of his erection pressing into her belly. Holding her there, he lowered his head and captured her lips, his tongue delving in and testing the waters. His mouth was doing what she wanted other parts of him to be doing.

She tugged back. "Boat."

"Your wish…"

Scooping her up, he carried her inside the boathouse and down the plank decking toward where the vessel was moored.

"I can walk."

He didn't set her down. "So can I."

And he could, stepping across the small space between the dock and the boat with ease.

Once aboard, he did set her down, giving her another quick kiss. "Just let me untie and get it ready."

What? She didn't want him to get anything ready but her. "I thought we were just going to stay here."

"Oh, no, *agape mou.* That would be like necking in a car that's parked in a garage. There's no thrill in that."

There was *plenty* of thrill in that. At least in *her* estimation. But she could at least make leaving the boathouse a little more difficult for him.

Walking up behind him, where he was untying the rope from one of the cleats, she wrapped her arms around his waist and pressed herself against him. Her hands slid down his flat abs and ducked below the waistband of his jeans—only to have him grab them and wrap them around his midsection instead.

"Last time you got me too hot and bothered too fast. Not this time."

"I seem to remember that you made up for that as the night went on."

Gripping one of her wrists, he turned around and then pressed it against the hard bulge in his jeans. "This is saying, *Hurry, hurry.* You need to help me say, *Slow down...*"

"But what if I don't *want* to slow down? What if I want the car in the garage?"

He chuckled, pressing her even tighter against him. "That was the wrong analogy to make, because right now I'm having a hard time thinking about anything except driving the car into the garage."

It took her a minute to get his meaning, and then her

eyes widened. "Then what are we waiting for? Let's pull the boat out of its boathouse and put it wherever you want it."

"Wherever I want it? Because boats and cars are all very sexy words right now…" He dropped her hand. "Why don't you go below and check out the bed while I get us underway."

She did as he asked, going down the four steps, moving through the kitchen to where she knew the small bedroom was. She pushed through the door and looked at the bed. What was she supposed to do with it now that she was here?

Ah… She had seen the perfect thing.

Deakin dropped anchor about two miles offshore. There they would be free of anyone possibly coming by—like Ares. His friend had already packed up and gone home after a long, much-needed sleep, but if he'd forgotten something Deakin would have hated for him to walk in on them in the boathouse. Plus the time on the water had given him a chance to cool his body down.

The second she'd wrapped her arms around him he'd been ready to throw her on the deck and have her right there. But he didn't want a rushed affair this time. He wanted it to last. Wanted to actually taste and savor, much like he'd done with the ouzo. No tossing back a couple of shots and calling it a day.

You could learn a lot from the famous Greek drink. Like how to take it slow even when everything inside you was telling you just to chug it quick.

He got up from his seat and stretched, surprised that Lea hadn't come up from below yet. He'd meant for her to check and make sure there were clean sheets on the bed—something he wasn't sure if his aunt would have taken care of like she did the beds in the other residences.

Where *was* she?

Only one way to find out.

He put his hand on the door post and ducked under the low ceiling as he went down the steps. "Lea?"

"In here."

Well, he could have figured *that* out—unless she'd jumped overboard. Actually, maybe she would be smarter to abandon ship than to stay. But she'd asked about his accident in such a matter-of-fact voice. There had been no condemnation in her tones, no horror or shock at what he'd done. Then again, she hadn't flinched at all when she'd seen his chest.

The door to the bedroom was closed.

He frowned. "Everything okay in there?"

"Yes. Come on in."

He opened the door and went inside—and then his body went icy cold. There were candles lit everywhere, including on the bed, where Lea lay on her back, completely naked, a thick squat candle seated in the curve of her belly.

"Put them out. *Right now.*" His voice shook and bile washed up his throat.

Lea sat up in a hurry, setting the candle aside and getting on her knees. She grabbed his hands. "Deakin, they're not real. They're battery-operated. I'm so sorry. I didn't think they looked so realistic, that you might think…"

He *had* thought it, and his abject terror of those things catching everything down here on fire had put out the blaze inside him that he'd been so worried about.

He sank onto the bed, elbows on his knees, hands supporting his chin. "It's okay. I should have realized my father would never have allowed real candles on the boat."

Now that the fear was trickling away he glanced around and saw about ten of the same kind of *faux* candles. He picked up the one in the middle of the bed and rattled it inside its faceted container. It cast a soft, muted light around the room, and his and Lea's shadows appeared enormous on the far wall.

She came up behind him and put her hands on his shoulders, squeezed the tense muscles there, her fingers moving along each row with sure, firm strokes.

His eyes closed as she continued to work her magic, across his shoulder blades and then down his spine. "Feels good…"

"I'm glad." Her lips touched his earlobe. "I'm very sorry for scaring you."

"Not very manly of me, I know."

This time she gently bit his ear. "I can't think of anyone more manly than you."

And that did the trick. The flesh that had receded began to unfurl again, becoming tense and firm. This was one muscle he *didn't* want the tension worked out of. Well, he did. But in a completely different way.

Her ministering hands moved from his shoulders and slid over his chest. A button popped free from his shirt. Then another. It was then that he remembered she'd been naked when he'd walked into this room. Was still naked even now.

He captured her hands and carried one of them to his mouth. "It seems like you always have all the fun." He glanced around the room at the flickering of a dozen artificial wicks. "And I *like* your candles. Thank you for thinking of them."

Standing to his feet, he turned and looked at her. She was on her knees in the middle of the bed, her breasts bare, her belly with its indented waist appearing golden in the low light. He wanted to explore that play of light a little bit more. But first he needed to take the edge off. And since the edge was those wandering hands he needed to do something about them. But what?

"Stay right there for a minute."

"What?"

He slid his hands in between her calves and her knees and tugged hard, tipping her onto her back in an instant. He glanced down and saw his solution. His shirt. He stripped it off and shook out the long sleeves, gripping them and then flipping the main part of the shirt over and over until it formed a kind of rope.

"Do you trust me?"

"Yes."

"Then give me your hands."

Her eyes widened as she realized what he wanted to do. "You have a *bad* side to you…" She put her hands together and held them toward him.

"Do I?"

"I'm thinking yes. But what's good for the goose… I *do* get to reciprocate later, right?"

The thought of her tying him up and running those skillful fingers all over his body made him break out in a cold sweat. To combat the sensation he wound the shirt around her hands and tied it snugly enough that she would have to struggle to get loose. Then he put her arms over her head. Well away from any of his danger zones.

"We can negotiate those terms later on. Right now it's about you lying as still as you can. And letting me do anything I want to you."

CHAPTER TEN

THEY'D STAYED ON the boat all night. And Lea *had* reciprocated.

Deakin had loved every minute of it. Hadn't been able to wait to have her all over again.

He'd slept with other women, and although they'd expressed the same curiosity Lea had about his scars, he'd never opened up to any of them. And in the morning, when he'd parked the boat in its little slip, she'd kissed the back of his neck and told him she needed to go change for work. As if the night they'd shared had been nothing out of the ordinary for her.

Well, it had been for him.

He'd let her go because he hadn't been sure what to do with the swirl of emotions that was making a mess of everything.

She seemed to care about him. In fact she was much less stressed about all this than he was. She just took everything in her stride in that calm way of hers.

So where did they go from here? She was officially still between jobs. Would she be willing to travel the world with him? To see if things between them kept on sizzling like they were now?

And if they did?

Maybe then he'd be willing to take it to the next level. Say yes to a relationship?

Maybe.

The question was, would she leave the island? For him? For them?

He had no idea. What he *did* know was that he needed to get to work and worry about his personal life later.

The clinic's boardroom wasn't big. Then again, neither was the board of directors. Theo had called them in for a meeting about Lea. Deakin waited, a little impatient about this whole production. His friend had already told him that they wanted to pay Lea for her time and he'd already agreed to it. But, since Theo was the one holding down the fort while the rest of them worked elsewhere, he took advantage of the times they *were* here to take care of business. Which meant they would have to vote on it as a group.

Ares and Theo arrived together, laughing about something. The two of them took seats across from Deakin, then Theo opened up his laptop and punched some keys.

"Just calling Chris. I told him that we'd be meeting, and he arranged his schedule so he could join us via online chat."

Okay... Deakin still didn't understand what the big deal was, but he was fine with it. He'd attended few enough of these meetings over the years. And, really, he was grateful for how much time and effort Theo put in to keeping this place running.

Within minutes his friend had the other member of the board on the line. "Hi, Chris, can you hear us?" he asked.

Chris replied in the affirmative.

"Well, let's get down to business. The clinic is running short of funds, due to the earthquake, and the CT scanner isn't working at the moment—so we have expenses coming out the wazoo and no way to pay them. Which is why the bachelor auction will help supplement the money the calendar has already brought in."

That damned calendar. Deakin would be more than glad when July was over.

Chris's voice came through. "I'll do what I can once I get there."

It was then that Deakin noticed Ares was staring fixedly at a spot on the table. Maybe he was as bored as Deakin was. It seemed like the meeting was going on for ages, with them just voting through item after item, like they usually did.

"Last on our agenda is a vote to add a new staff position to our roster."

Last? What had happened to paying Lea for the services she'd been providing ever since the earthquake had hit the island? It wasn't like Theo to forget something like that. But with a baby coming it was understandable that his thoughts might be centered on his unborn child and his fiancée. He would remind Theo of their conversation once he was done talking.

"I've already talked to both Lea and Deakin and they've agreed."

Lea? Why was Theo asking her about adding a staff position? Unless it was to get her professional feedback as they went through the search process?

He hoped she might not be around on the island long enough to be of any assistance. He hadn't talked to her yet about coming with him on his next assignment, but he was planning to. Either today or tomorrow. All he could hope was that she didn't get spooked and take off before he had a chance to explain his thoughts.

"So let's put it to a vote. All those in favor of adding Lea Risi to our permanent staff, say yes."

Chris said yes before Deakin's shocked brain even had a chance to process what had just been said.

Lea was the new staff member?

And she hadn't said a word to him about it?

A throbbing set up in his left temple, the dull ache gaining traction with each second that passed.

"Wait a minute." He held up a hand. "That's not what you and I talked about the other day, Theo. You said something about *paying* her, not hiring her."

"No, I asked if you thought she was a valuable addition to the clinic."

He *had* asked that. But at the time Deakin had assumed Theo was speaking about temporary hired help. Not in terms of a permanent position.

Had Lea already agreed to this?

"I didn't fully understand what you were suggesting."

Theo waited a beat, then continued. "That's okay. Now that I've made it a little clearer, what do you say?"

"I say no."

The words were out of his mouth before he had a chance to really think about them. Ten seconds later the room erupted, with everyone speaking at once.

Theo stood and stared them into silence. "You agreed that she was good for the clinic and that people loved her. *And* that she should be paid for her services. I have no idea why you wouldn't welcome her with open arms."

He already had. But if they voted her in it meant she couldn't go with him when he left. Unless she turned them down.

Was he willing to take that chance?

And why was he so adamantly opposed to the job being offered to her?

He searched his heart. Dug deep and really examined his motives. The events of last night and the previous days played in his mind, the tape running over and over again.

Hell. He knew why. Knew why he'd voted no. Knew why he'd been so anxious to corner her about joining his relief organization.

He loved her.

It wasn't about seeing if the spark in their relationship stayed or whether they could get along outside the bedroom. He wanted her with him because he was already head over heels for her.

That was why he'd voted no.

They all needed to take a breath until he could get to Lea and talk to her. Tell her what he was thinking.

The solution came to him in an instant—and he was going to exploit Theo's own words.

"I don't think we can afford a new staff member at the moment. You said it yourself. The clinic is operating within very narrow margins. We're having to do additional fundraisers to cover the shortfall. And now we're going to hire another doctor? I'm sorry, but I just don't think this is the right time to be making changes like that."

His chest tightened. He knew he was running roughshod over people he cared about very much. He couldn't care less if they hired *ten* new people, as long as one of them wasn't Lea.

Theo's face was tight with anger, but to his credit he didn't explode. "Well, I guess that settles it, then. We've always voted for things unanimously, although in this case I wish we hadn't established that precedent." He looked at Deakin and raised an eyebrow. "Any chance we can convince you to change your vote?"

"Not at this time."

If Lea decided that this was what she wanted—to stay on Mythelios permanently—then he would give her his blessing and catch the next flight out of here. But until he heard the words come out of her mouth he was going to give this a chance to take off.

None of his friends seemed to understand his reasoning any better than Theo did, but they finished up and let Chris go back to what he needed to be doing.

Ares just shook his head and left the room.

Theo stayed a moment longer, giving him a long, hard look. "I'm really disappointed, Deak. I'd hoped for better from you." Then he too walked out.

Deakin slowly sat down in his chair and let out a huge breath. He would make it up to his friends. At least he hoped he would. Once Lea had agreed to continue their relationship, hopefully they would all understand why he'd voted the way he had, and why he'd been so anxious to keep them from talking her into staying.

And if he talked to her and she wanted to stay on Mythelios?

Well, he was leaving.

With Lea or without her.

In the end, the choice was up to her.

"Why don't you want me working at the clinic?"

Lea did her best to keep the hurt from showing in her voice, but it was useless. Everything inside her was shaking. Including her voice. She hadn't believed it when Theo told her Deakin had cast the only dissenting vote, but the look on the other doctor's face had said it all. He was serious. Deakin had voted against her.

His features went blank. "Theo told you?"

"Of course he did. Did you think he wouldn't?"

Her eyes burned in her head, but she refused to give in to the tears. Not yet. Not when she had so much to get off her chest.

She'd trusted this man. Had grown to care about him. And then he'd turned around and stabbed her in the back? *Why?*

"I'd hoped to be able to talk to you before you found out."

"And exactly what were you going to say to me?"

"I was hoping you wouldn't want to stay."

A fresh stab of hurt pierced her heart. She'd held a modicum of hope that Theo might have misunderstood Deakin, that she could bring Deakin to her office and clear this up. She hadn't needed to look for him, though. Deakin had come to her instead.

Thankfully there were no patients around to overhear their little exchange.

"Well, that's pretty damned obvious, don't you think? The thing is, I *did* want to stay. I love this island, and when Theo mentioned the possibility of a permanent position here... Well, I was thrilled, frankly."

"You were?"

"Of course I was. Theo said he'd already spoken to you about it and that you were in favor. So I just don't understand the change in your attitude..."

It went deeper than that. She'd told him on the boat that she trusted him. And she had. She'd trusted him with her life. Her wellbeing. To find out she'd made a mistake was the worst kind of betrayal.

"I just don't think we should make any rash decisions," he said.

His tanned features had paled. His mouth looked pinched and white. Probably guilt over what he'd done.

"*Rash?* Seems like you've made plenty of rash decisions over the last couple of weeks."

He'd been quick enough to jump into bed with her. What was that if not rash? And *she'd* been rash enough to—

Oh, hell. No.

She was in *love* with him? No way. Not after what he'd just done.

But the tug in her heart remained, the tearing sensation inside of her going deep. And it hurt. God, it hurt so badly.

"You seriously want to stay? On the island?" he asked.

"Yes. I seriously do."

And she had seriously hoped that Deakin might want to stay on the island with her. Well, that hope was shot to hell now. If he was staying, she was going.

Hadn't she sworn off baggage-carrying men? Well, it looked like she had just picked out another one. But this time she was going to send him spinning away before things got out of hand.

Good grief, Lea. They're already way out of hand.

But she couldn't deal with this. Not right now.

Looking back, she should have seen the signs. If someone had stood outside the *taverna* and held up a neon sign they couldn't have made the message any more plain: He despised his scars. He'd installed the biggest, baddest fire alarms known to man and freaked out whenever one of them made a peep. Like at burned eggs. He flipped out over fake candles. Instead of really looking at them—trusting her not to make a stupid decision—he'd just reacted. Like he'd done over every other thing since she'd known him.

And the *pièce de resistance* was his knee jerk reaction now, to the clinic hiring her.

Well, that was the last decision he would ever make regarding her.

"We've had a lot of fun over the last couple of weeks. And if any of it meant anything I'm going to ask you to do one thing for me." She leaned forward. "I'm going to ask you to change your vote."

"And if I say no?"

"Then I'll leave. But it won't be without a fight."

"Why do you want to stay so much, Lea?"

She could see the confusion on his face, hear it in his voice. She didn't know how to make him understand how she felt about the island and wasn't sure she should even try. But she had to.

"Just because this island doesn't mean anything to you, it doesn't mean it can't to someone else. I love it here. I want to stay."

This time her voice didn't shake. It was calm and clear and filled with all the sincerity she could muster.

A muscle worked in his jaw. "You're absolutely sure?"

"Never more sure of anything in my life."

He stood to his feet and stared down at her, something hard and decisive appearing in his gaze before he blinked it away. "You have my vote, then. I'll tell Theo."

He didn't try to get her to change her mind. Didn't explain his reasoning or ask to talk things through. A wave of uncertainty went through her, but it was too late to take back the words, so she simply said, "Thank you. You won't regret this."

No other hint of emotion flickered through his eyes. "That's where you're wrong, Lea. Because I already do."

Then he turned on his heel and walked away.

When he was out of sight she sagged in her seat and laid her head on her desk as bitter tears splashed onto the wooden surface.

She had a feeling that in winning the battle she'd just lost the most important war ever.

CHAPTER ELEVEN

THE FIRST WEEK off the island had been the worst.

Deakin had sat in a bar in Athens and drunk himself into a stupor the first two nights. He'd spent the rest of his days trying to pull himself up by his bootstraps.

It was over. Lea had made her decision and he'd made his.

Right—like boozing it up with strangers who don't give a damn about you?

Broken bits of the past three weeks ran through his head, brushing against the damaged parts of his being and making him look at things in a new way.

Mythelios held so many terrible memories for him, but was that really the island's fault? No. It was his.

His first day back he'd shaken hands with several locals who'd murmured how good it was that he'd come home—and they'd meant it. There were people he loved there—Theo, Cailey, Ares, Chris, Petra, his Aunt Cecilia, to name a few. And they loved him in return. They cared about him despite his stupidity as a kid. They looked past his scars and saw the same Deakin they'd always seen. Their friend. Relative. Partner.

Even Stavros had apologized for his outburst about his dad the night he'd gone in to binge on ouzo—before Lea had come waltzing in and made him want her all over again.

He never had got to talk to her about leaving the island with him. Because she'd been dead set on staying, and so very angry about what he'd done. And rightly so. He'd had no right to take that decision out of her hands, no matter what his reasons.

In the end it had changed nothing. She'd stayed. And he'd left.

Her final words to him had haunted him: *"You won't regret it."*

How the hell would he *not* regret it? The woman he loved had chosen an island over him.

But had she? Had she really? he wondered. Or had he forced her into a decision she hadn't wanted to make?

No, he'd tried to force her into the decision *he* wanted her to make. And in doing so he'd sealed his own fate.

They couldn't have carried on a relationship from different areas of the globe even if she felt something for him. Had he imagined all of that? The way her hands had massaged his fear away when he'd discovered those candles on the boat. The way she'd kissed his scars. The way she had quietly asked what had happened to him. And all the time her eyes had been soft with understanding. Caring…?

Was that why he'd been able to see the devastation on her face when she'd realized he was the one who'd voted against her? He could understand her anger. But there'd also been a deep hurt behind those green eyes. A pain that rivaled his own.

So what should he do now? Fly off and move on to his next assignment? Or go back to the island and see if he could face down the demons of his own making and banish them? For good, this time.

Then he could sit down and talk to Lea. Get everything he'd wanted to say earlier off his chest. Even if she rejected him outright he would know once and for all.

As it was, the doubts were eating at his soul one glass of ouzo at a time. Soon there'd be nothing left.

Unless he did something about it.

Today.

And maybe that something should begin with a phone call to someone from his past. Someone he'd never quite made his peace with. Maybe then he could finally slam that door on all the painful memories and lock it tight. Once and for all.

They had a gardener who weeded the Serenity Gardens. But right now it was the only thing Lea wanted to do. It was her day off, but the thought of going back to that cottage, knowing the house next door was empty, probably for good, was just too depressing.

She'd gone to talk to Deakin the day after their confrontation in her office, hoping to understand why he'd done what he had, but it had been too late. He was gone.

He hadn't thought she'd want to stay? Why? Hadn't she shown how much she loved everything about Mythelios?

Including Deakin?

Except Deakin didn't love the island. She realized that the day they went to Delos. The change in him had been dramatic.

Her grief over Mark had made her wary of trusting her judgment again. So she'd painted Deakin with

Mark's brush and decided he was just too damaged to take a chance on.

But the whole idea of her job was that there was hope for everyone. As long as they were willing to work to improve their situation.

Was she willing to improve hers?

She'd thought she was doing just that, but now she wondered.

The heat beat down on her and she pushed her hat a little further forward on her head, another pang going through her. This was the same hat she'd worn on their Delos excursion. The first time she'd thought he might be as attracted to her as she was to him.

So why had he voted against her?

"I didn't think you wanted to stay."

So where did he think she wanted to go?

There was no answer to that question. She yanked another weed out and placed it on the growing pile beside her. She wasn't absolutely positive they were all weeds, but each tug released a little bit of the destructive anger and frustration she'd allowed to build inside her.

Where did he think she wanted to go?

That last night on his boat had been a magical experience. He'd made love to her like no man ever had. Not even Mark. A mixture of sexy urgency melded with slow, thorough loving. Different and yet the same.

So what was she supposed to do now? He'd left and she had no idea where he'd gone.

She could call his NGO. Except she wasn't really sure of the name of the organization.

Wasn't that just beating around the bush, though? She had his cellphone number. Why not just call him?

And have to listen to his voice as he told her he didn't love her?

Yes. Why not? At least then she'd know one way or the other and could move forward with her life.

Sliding her gloves off her hands, she reached into her pocket and pulled out her cellphone. She scrolled through the numbers until she came across one that was all too familiar. The question was, did she have the courage to call him?

If he didn't want to talk to her he would probably just let it go to voicemail. And then she'd still have her answer.

Just do it, Lea.

Before she could talk herself out of it she pushed the button. Her heart pounded in her chest, her mouth suddenly going dry. She wasn't sure she'd be able to talk even if he did answer.

There. It was ringing.

In the garden another person's phone began to ring. She glanced around, not wanting to have a conversation like this when someone else was in the area.

A shadow appeared on the ground next to her. The ringing phone was linked with whoever it was.

"Hello?"

Oh, God. That voice. He could be right here in the room with her it was so clear.

"Deakin?"

Someone crouched next to her and suddenly the voice on the phone was right in her ear.

"I'm right here."

She dropped the phone, turning in a rush to find herself face to face with the very man she'd been thinking about.

"You're *here*!"

He smiled. "Yes." He picked up the trowel beside her. "Is this one of your duties as the new staff member? Theo told me they hired you. Congratulations."

"Thank you."

She swallowed, searching for words that wouldn't be meaningless. He might only be here between flights or something. In fact this might be the last time she would ever see him, so she needed to make every second count.

He stood to his feet and reached down a hand. She let him pull her up, memorizing the feel of her palm in his. A slash of pain went through her. She didn't want him to go.

"Why did you vote the way you did?"

"It's complicated."

"We're *all* complicated, Deakin, and sometimes we need to break things down into simpler parts. You said you didn't think I wanted to stay here. Why?"

He blew out a breath. "I phrased that badly. What I should have said was that I was *hoping* you didn't want to stay."

"Why?"

She realized he hadn't let go of her hand. And she hadn't let go of his.

"I wanted you to come with me instead. To see if we could make what we had work."

A tiny seed of hope rolled around inside her. "And what *did* we have?"

"A chance for a future together." He lifted her hand to his lips and kissed it. "You want simple? Okay. Here it is. I love you."

"What?"

"A complicated compound broken down into its simplest form: Three words. I. Love. You."

"But you voted against me getting a permanent job here. You can't imagine how crushed I was when Theo told me that."

"I know—and I'm sorry. At the time I thought I was voting for *us*. Things in the meeting happened so fast, and I didn't think through the ramifications. Kind of like the night I lit that cigarette and blew my world apart."

"But you never told me any of this."

He smiled. "I never had the chance. Because Theo sideswiped me into doing something incredibly stupid. And then, when I came to see you to try and figure things out, you already knew about the meeting. I know how much you love Mythelios. I've done some serious soul-searching over the last week, and I think if I look at it through your eyes I might come to love it again too. But I'm only willing to do that if you think we have a future together."

A single leaf sprang out of that seed inside of her. "Simplest form?"

"Simplest form."

She swallowed her fear and gave it to him straight. "I love you too."

He tipped back her hat and looked into her face. "I never thought I'd hear those words from you—I thought I'd ruined everything."

Lea traced one of the scars on his neck. "You just fixed it. Thank you for coming back."

"I couldn't leave things the way they were between us."

"Neither could I. I was just trying to call you."

He smiled and planted a kiss on the tip of her nose. "What were you going to say?"

"I don't know. I only know I couldn't bear the thought of you never knowing how I truly feel about you." She went into his embrace, leaning her head against his chest. "And now here you are."

"I couldn't stay away. The *where* doesn't matter as long as I have the right *who*."

"I agree. We don't have to decide everything right now. I just want to sit here beside you and hear you say you love me again and again."

"I'll say it as often as you want. Every day. Every hour. Every minute."

"Oh, wait!"

His brows came together. "What is it?"

"Does this mean I have to bid on you at the auction?"

"No. And do you know why?"

She let him draw her close, not caring who might or might not walk in on them. "Why?"

"Because you won me—" he kissed her "—on that very first day, when you swatted my hand off that patient sign-in list. And now you're stuck with me. Here on this island. Or wherever we might choose to go."

"Shall we get a map and pick a location?"

His hands splayed across the small of her back, the heat of his touch setting off a tingle that was impossible to ignore.

"I don't think a map will be necessary for the place I want to take you." He traced a path up the middle of her spine. "All we need is you and me to make any place in this world perfect."

EPILOGUE

THE BOTTLE OF champagne struck the side of the vessel with a solid *thunk*, spraying golden bubbles and laughter in all directions.

"Isn't it bad luck to rechristen a boat?"

Lea gripped Deakin's hand, as if she were afraid the past month had been a dream. It hadn't. It was very real. And his fingers tightened around hers, trying to reassure her of that fact.

"No. It's a metamorphosis. A rebirth."

Kind of like Deakin's new lease on life.

"Well, I certainly like *Mythelios Rescue* better than its old name."

After his talk with Ville last month Deakin had made his peace with the past. Donating his father's boat to the clinic had been the final piece in that puzzle.

He and Lea had decided to stay on Mythelios—but it was an open-ended arrangement. Lea was willing to move. And Deakin was willing to stay. He'd opened his heart and suddenly the possibilities were endless.

They were in the process of redecorating his parents' house—another metamorphosis that was long overdue—and his aunt was helping them to turn the place into an actual home. For now they were shacked up in the little cottage. Where Lea cooked eggs with care. And where they loved long into the night.

He'd been right about life being perfect as long as he and Lea were together.

Theo got up and addressed the gathered crowd, starting by thanking Deakin for his generous donation.

"Now, take a good look around, ladies. We have a bachelor auction coming up. Unfortunately our single men seem to be dropping like flies around here."

Laughter rippled across the crowd, before Theo motioned that he wasn't done.

"Our very own Dr. Deakin Patera is now off the market and on his way to wedded bliss. So let's wish them well."

Clapping erupted in the Serenity Gardens, and the *Mythelios Rescue* nodded its approval from its new boat slip.

Deakin wrapped his arms around his fiancée's waist and smiled. "I love you."

"Love you too."

Then he kissed her, and everything else faded away.

Because it was Deakin and Lea in the most perfect place on earth.

* * * * *

COMING SOON!

We really hope you enjoyed reading this book. If you're looking for more romance, be sure to head to the shops when new books are available on

Thursday
28th June

To see which titles are coming soon, please visit
millsandboon.co.uk

MILLS & BOON

MILLS & BOON

Coming next month

LOCKED DOWN WITH THE ARMY DOC
Scarlet Wilson

Amber gulped. For infectious diseases she was fine. But she wasn't quite as confident as Jack at being thrown in at the deep end. It wasn't that she didn't feel capable. She would always help out in an emergency. She wasn't sure how qualified or equipped she'd be to deal with things. She'd never really worked in an ER setting.

It was almost as if Jack sensed something from her. He leaned over and whispered in her ear. "Don't worry. I've got your back."

Then he did something completely unexpected. He turned her toward him and lowered his forehead onto hers. It was a gesture of security. Of solidarity. Of reassurance.

Warmth spread through her. She looked up and met his gaze. His dark brown eyes were fixed on hers. They were genuine and steady.

She pressed her lips together and took a deep breath, so many thoughts flooding into her mind. Her brain was such a mess. All she could concentrate on was the feel of his hands on the tops of her arms and the gentle way his forehead pressed against hers. His warm breath danced across her skin. Her gaze was naturally lowered and she could see the rise and fall of his chest.

He was a doctor. The type of guy she'd spent most of her life trying to avoid any romantic entanglements with. And this was crazy. She'd already seen a flash of something in him that reminded him of the focused way her father used to be.

So, if she already had alarm bells flashing in her head, why wasn't she running for the hills? She could pretend it was the hurricane. That the only reason she wasn't moving was because she was stuck here.

But that wasn't what was anchoring her feet firmly to the ground.

That wasn't what was letting the heat from the palms of his hands slowly permeate through her jacket and trickle its way through her body. Her last few boyfriends had been as far removed from medicine as possible—a landscape gardener, then a chef. But somehow she hadn't felt this. This connection.

And she couldn't understand it. She'd only met Jack last night. And yes, they'd clicked. There was no doubt the man was attractive. There was no doubt her mind was imagining so many other places they could go.

Continue reading
LOCKED DOWN WITH THE ARMY DOC
Scarlet Wilson

Available next month
www.millsandboon.co.uk

LET'S TALK

Romance

For exclusive extracts, competitions
and special offers, find us online:

Or get in touch on 0844 844 1351*

For all the latest titles coming soon, visit
millsandboon.co.uk/nextmonth

*Calls cost 7p per minute plus your phone company's price per minute access charge

Want even more
ROMANCE?

Join our bookclub today!

'Mills & Boon books, the perfect way to escape for an hour or so.'

Miss W. Dyer

'Excellent service, promptly delivered and very good subscription choices.'

Miss A. Pearson

'You get fantastic special offers and the chance to get books before they hit the shops'

Mrs V. Hall

**Visit millsandbook.co.uk/Bookclub
and save on brand new books.**

MILLS & BOON